Prophecy of Ravens

KEN BLAKEMORE

Iponymous Edition
First edition published in 2015
By Iponymous publishing Limited
Swansea United Kingdom SA6 6BP

A CIP record for this book
Is available from the British Library

(EBook) ISBN 978-1-908773-98-2
(Physical Book) ISBN 978-1-908773-99-9

The publisher acknowledges the financial support of the Welsh Books Council.

KEN BLAKEMORE

Ken Blakemore grew up in northern England and now lives in Swansea. He first worked as a teacher in West Africa, where at one point he got mixed up in a military coup and had to escape across the border from Ghana to Burkina Faso.

He has travelled extensively around Europe, Africa, India, the USA and Australia.

After spells of casual work as a hotel night porter and in a slaughterhouse, a steam laundry and as a funeral director's assistant (his favourite), he finished a PhD on African education and obtained a job as a university lecturer.

He has worked in universities in the English Midlands and in Los Angeles, London and South Wales and has written a wide range of academic texts and articles, including a book on African-Caribbean and Asian migrants to the UK which won the Seebohm Book of the Year Trophy in 1995.

In 2006 he obtained an MA in Creative Writing with Distinction from Swansea University and has been a full-time writer since 2007. His performed plays include Half Marx, Love Bytes and Human Studies (the latter a BBC Radio 4 production).

He has also published poetry and a popular childhood memoir, Sunnyside Down.

Prophecy of Ravens is his first novel.

[DAILY MAIL Tues 16th February 2019]

KILLER BUG ESCAPES LAB

Authorities in the US have confirmed that the deadly virus now sweeping through California escaped from a laboratory.

The lethal bug got out when a science lab at a university in Los Angeles was severely damaged in last week's devastating earthquake.

So far an estimated 300 people with the virus have been hospitalised and a further 28, including five children, have died.

Kizuki Nishimura, 47, a boffin at the University of California Los Angeles had already been much criticised for developing new strains of bird and swine flu. The laboratory superbugs are highly lethal because the human body has no antibodies to fight them.

Nishimura's research was intended to throw light on why some strains of flu are particularly deadly – but now the virus has escaped it looks like the whole world is

(SEE OVER)

* Restrictions of flights to and from the US – see page 9
* How to spot early signs of 'flu – see page 11

[THE SUN Friday March 15th 2019]

LOCKED IN WITH THE PLAGUE

They locked themselves in with their patients – to await certain death. We can only bow our heads in humility and thank them from the bottom of our hearts.

Five brave doctors, sixteen courageous nurses, ten plucky health workers are sacrificing their lives at the Princess Diana Hospital, Leeds, for us.

By the time you read this, they may already have been taken by the Superflu plague sweeping through our country.

They could have chosen to run – but like the people of Eyam, a plague village in Derbyshire back in 1666, they stayed put.

They didn't take the coward's way out

They didn't risk spreading the deadly disease to their families, loved ones – and us

They did choose to stay to care for their patients until the very end.

We salute them.

*Will other health staff be as brave? A nurse speaks NEXT PAGE
* Stay at home with your fave flu buddie – curvaceous Sam PAGE 3
* What to do if flu strikes your family – PAGE 5
* David Beckham – my flu buddie is Vick   PAGE 8

MISSING – PAIGE HANLEY

I AM SEARCHING FOR MY DARLING WIFE PAIGE HANLEY. SHE DID NOT RETURN HOME FROM ORPINGTON ON EVENING OF 8 JANUARY. SHE WENT TO EMERGENCY CENTRE 1 ORPINGTON FOR FOOD

AGE: 36   D.O.B. 6/7/1983

HEIGHT: 5' 5"

HAIR COLOUR: BRUNETTE

LAST SEEN AT HOME: 8/1/20

DISTINGUISHING MARK: MOLE ON LEFT SHOULDER

I HAVE NO SPARE COPIES OF PHOTO AS WE WERE EVACUATED WITHOUT TIME TO COLLECT ANYTHING.

OUR HOME ADDRESS WAS: 56 LENHAM GARDENS, ORPINGTON, KENT

IF YOU HAVE SEEN PAIGE OR KNOW WHERE SHE IS, PLEASE PLEASE LEAVE INFORMATION AT THE NEAREST EMERGENCY CENTRE OR GET A MESSAGE TO ME AT EVACUATION CAMP B TUNBRIDGE WELLS

IF THEY RESTORE PHONE SIGNAL PLEASE CALL OR TEXT ME –

0770 679 8769

I MAY NOT BE ABLE TO RESPOND WITH PHONE BUT BELIEVE ME I AM DESPERATE TO FIND PAIGE PLEASE PLEASE HELP – I AM DISABLED.

PAIGE DEAREST LOVE IF YOU SEE THIS NOTICE DON'T GIVE UP I AM STILL HERE. I AM MISSING YOU SO MUCH AND I LOVE YOU SO MUCH

DARREN HANLEY

PS / PM 369-02

TOP SECRET

FOR THE EYES OF THE PRIME MINISTER AND COBRA
COMMITTEE ONLY

12 September, 2020   06.00

AGENDA

- Population movement restrictions – military options
- Compulsory hospital closures
- Mass graves
- Food and fuel rationing options
- International co-operation possibilities:
- Medical
- Biohazard protection equipment for essential personnel
- Sustaining central government – last resort option

KEN BLAKEMORE

Tuesday, 12th July 2022

THE ORDER OF SERVICE
for the Burial of
His Majesty King George VII

The Archbishops of Canterbury and York and the Bishops of
Llandaff and Swansea & Brecon, accompanied by the Moderator
of the Free Church Federal Council shall meet the Funeral
Procession at the entrance of Brecon Cathedral.
Then shall be sung:

I AM the resurrection and the life, saith the Lord:
he that believeth in me, though he were dead, yet shall he live:
and whosoever liveth and believeth in me shall never die.
St John xi. 25, 26

I KNOW that my Redeemer liveth, and that he shall stand at
the latter day upon the earth. And though after my skin
worms destroy this body, yet in my flesh shall I see God:
whom I shall see for myself, and mine eyes shall behold,
and not another.
Job xix. 25, 26, 27

WE brought nothing into this world,
and it is certain we can carry nothing out.
The Lord gave, and the Lord hath taken away;
blessed be the Name of the Lord.
I Tim. vi. 7. Job i. 21

KEN BLAKEMORE

[The NEW ZEALAND HERALD, Friday 13th February 2032]

LONDON GOES UNDER

CAPITAL EVACUATED, HOUSES OF PARLIAMENT UNDER WATER, BIG BEN STOPS, BBC CLOSES DOWN, GOVT MOVES TO OXFORD

TWO MILLENNIA – AND NOW IT'S THE END

We knew it would happen. Great Britain's population has dwindled to a few million, as has almost every other country's. We knew there was no health service there and that all telecommunications, food supplies, the currency and the transport system had broken down. But we clung to hopes – hopes that one day the Old Country would rise again.

That prospect now looks very remote indeed. Even if it is achievable, it will surely take generations – perhaps hundreds of years before the country that founded ours can be re-united with us again.

Reports from amateur radio enthusiasts in Britain and other parts of Europe have confirmed it: London, the last functioning European capital was completely evacuated in the middle of January following devastating floods that submerged the Houses of Parliament and much of central London under thirty feet of water. The flooding occurred after exceptionally heavy rainfall and high tides. Our radio contacts believe the Thames Barrage, meant to protect London from such extreme conditions is no longer operational owing to the breakdown of the UK's power grid.

They also informed us that the evacuation of London's remaining population was permitted to allow the dwindling numbers of immune survivors of the Second Pandemic to escape. The King and Prince George have been moved to safety in a biohazard refuge in Oxford,

SEE NEXT PAGE
– Are we next? The Third Pandemic Threat – see page 4
– End of the global Internet – but can NZ sustain its own? – see page 10
– More on the UK: Wills may abdicate – page 3
– Return to barter economy – page 4

1

They hadn't gone far beyond the English border.

'We sometimes get a bit of trouble here,' Gwynfor's father said. 'Nothing much, like.'

Gwynfor was puzzled. What kind of trouble? He wouldn't ask. This was his first run; he didn't want to look stupid.

'Look after these, will you?' Sylvan, the father, held up a pair of leather saddlebags. They were worn and scratched; soft to touch. Gwynfor was surprised by their lightness. Was there anything in them?

The father glanced at the chestnut mare. 'We'll fasten them on Bronwen,' he said. 'Make sure she's saddled up good and tight now.'

'OK, Da. I'll keep her at the back with me.'

A trace of worry crossed Sylvan's face, but he quickly cancelled it with a reassuring smile. 'Like I say, son, nothing much should happen. But just in case it does, walk the horse into the trees and stay with her, all right? Keep quiet and hide for an hour or two, then catch us up later.'

A hawk hovered above them in the cloudless blue sky: a male kestrel, pointed wings almost two feet across.

It was scanning the pitted sandy surface of the road beneath, minutely checking every stone and pebble for movement. Mice and voles occasionally scurried from one side to the other. The kestrel was always ready.

A thermal from the heath below suddenly lifted the bird twenty feet. It was a hot summer breeze. Sharp, acrid scents of human beings and horse sweat were carried on it. They mixed with the creamy coconut smell of gorse.

The hawk turned in the rising air now, scanning again. There was the sound of moving wheels coming up: hollow rumbling on stones and gravel.

Six wagons were moving slowly below: six wagons; twenty-six horses; a sheepdog running silently hither and thither; a large mastiff loping alongside the front wagon.

The hovering bird turned to face north now, spying the line of sandstone hills that reared up from the wooded plain ten miles away. Something glinted over there, a sudden reflection.

The kestrel concentrated on the road again. A minute later it plunged down, snatching something small that darted from the wheels of the leading wagon.

The previous night they'd camped on the Welsh side of the River Dee, Afon Dyfrdwy. This is no hardship, Gwynfor had thought, with the summer nights so warm and still. He'd taken a quilt from his box in the wagon. It was a patchwork quilt, a family one. His mother had folded it carefully and pressed it into his arms when they'd left two days before.

Wanting quiet, he'd walked some distance away from the wagons and the men. He'd spread the quilt beside a high, thick hedge. It was a recently harvested hayfield. He'd lain down under the stars, listening to the wide river flowing gently by. Stubble had gently needled his back through the quilt. He'd stared up, looking for patterns in the stars.

He wasn't able to get to sleep despite being so physically tired – all that running to and fro, not knowing the routine yet; the hundred and one things you had to do for the horses at the end of the day.

A mixture of excitement and fear was keeping him awake. I'll be twenty this year, almost a grown man, he thought. Senior college was over now. I'll be a trader like my da.

He let his mind drift over memories of graduation: that sunny day; the smiling faces of his teachers; his classmates yelling and whooping; those heady feelings of success. He still couldn't believe he'd got the highest mark in his year.

I've got to leave all that behind now, he told himself. Put it behind you, boy. It's good you've learned and can speak English and can write well and know all kinds of things, but it's time to put it to use now.

That was his father's voice in his head. He knew that. He accepted it. But one day, perhaps, he would get a chance to study at a university.

He dreamed of this, staring up at the stars, trying to picture how he could make it happen. Within minutes he felt himself falling, falling upwards towards the stars in the inky sky above.

The next afternoon, in the deeper woods, the six wagons came to a fork in the road. To the left was a new track, unmade and deeply rutted. Tomas, the driver on Gwynfor's wagon, explained that this was a short cut to another old road that led eventually to Chester, or New Deva as it was called now. He grinned at Gwynfor. 'There are tigers roaming about in that section, believe it or not.'

'No!' Gwynfor smiled and shook his head.

'Oh yes, huge things, massive teeth they've got on them. Have your head off in one bite. There was a place in Chester in the old time, see, where they kept strange animals from all over the world. The tigers got out – or somebody let them out. Duw, they've been breeding over there ever since, they have!'

Gwynfor looked at Tomas. This could be another of his stories. But it didn't matter whether it was true or not because they were taking the right fork, away from the tiger forest.

They were following a Good Time road, now. You could tell that from the occasional patches of worn tarmac showing through the tall grasses and weeds in the middle.

'We're heading for a safe bridge,' Tomas explained. He urged on the horses; their wagon had fallen behind the others.

About a mile further on was where it happened.

Gwynfor and Tomas's wagon was still about two hundred yards behind the others. They came to a steep slope downhill where the road twisted sharply to the right. Tomas heaved hard on the brake lever. The heavy wheels of their wagon scrunched and slipped on the sandy gravel of the road. They rounded the bend. The other five wagons were up ahead, standing still in a line.

At first it was quiet. It was difficult to make out why there was a hold-up.

'Why don't you take the wagon up to the others?' Gwynfor asked.

'Wait a minute,' Tomas said. He held the reins firmly. The horses champed and blew air from their nostrils.

The sun was dazzling here; they were in a spot where the trees had thinned. Gwynfor half-rose from his seat at the front of the wagon, shielding his eyes and trying to make out the knot of figures that were standing around his father and some of the drivers. They could just about hear the raised voices.

'It's the police, I think, Tomas.'

'Have they put a barrier up?'

'I can't see . . .'

'How many are there?'

'A dozen at least; maybe more.'

Suddenly there was shouting; a commotion. Three of the policemen were trying to restrain his father. He was pulling away from them, shouting something. Now the mastiff, Caleb, was going for one of the policemen, baying loudly. Gwynfor's father broke free. There was a bang.

Caleb went down.

The huge hound was lying on the ground, squirming, legs out sideways. Everyone in the tangled group stood still, looking at the stricken dog.

Gwynfor felt sick. 'I'd better go up there,' he muttered, climbing down.

'Wait!' said Tomas. He'd seen Gwynfor's father running towards them as fast as he could. Policemen were after him. He was waving frantically in their direction and shouting something.
Gwynfor remembered. He ran to the rear of the wagon and unhitched the mare. His fingers were trembling. The horse reared up, whinnying, nervous of the approaching men shouting. They were close now. It took a second for Gwynfor to grab her bridle. 'Now, Bronwen girl!' he called, trying to stop his voice sounding panicky. 'There, easy now!'

He was half-astride the mare when someone pulled him off. It was a red-faced Englishman: sweating, angry, hard blue eyes. He was wearing a navy blue police tunic. Gwynfor was bewildered as well as angry. Who was this man, to do this?

'Where d'you think you're going, you cheeky young bastard!'

the policeman shouted.

Gwynfor looked to his father, who was standing nearby, silent and white faced, held firmly now by three other policemen. Yet other bluecoats were running up.

There was a blinding flash of light. Gwynfor felt a piercing pain on the side of his head. He was on the ground, face down. There was a tiny, bright green fern right in front of his nose.

'There's no need for that now, come on,' his father said in a quiet voice. He was using English.

'Tell us where it is!' the red-faced policeman shouted. 'Or we're impounding all these wagons!'

Gwynfor sat up. The panting group of policemen around him made the air hot; he was finding it hard to breathe. His right thigh was wet. He wasn't sure whether it was blood or urine, and felt shame. He scrambled to his feet. Another policeman tripped him, laughing; then hit him hard on the back. Gwynfor heard the thud resounding right through. There was another blow, and another. His breath was being knocked out.

His father's voice was a long way off now. 'Stop, I'll tell you, I'll tell you!' he was shouting.

Gwynfor managed to turn his head to the side. There was a dark shadow, someone standing over him. Was he going to be hit again?

No, it was Tomas the driver.

There was a loud crack; a cry of pain. A horsewhip: Tomas had used the whip.

The policeman had both hands over his eyes. Before the others could stop Tomas he'd jumped sideways, holding the whip ready. It cracked again, this time across the chestnut mare's hindquarters. The horse screamed and took off full tilt towards the woods. Tomas ran in the opposite direction.

The policemen seemed to be transfixed, staring open-mouthed at the horse, not sure what to do. And in that moment the three men holding Gwynfor's father lost him. Each one must have thought the other two had a firm grip.

'You stupid fuckers – get him!' the red-faced officer shouted. But Sylvan was away. He was running like a mad hare back towards the leading wagons and their drivers, policemen in pursuit.

Gwynfor watched this through a mist. Everything seemed to be happening in slow motion. Seren, the farm collie they'd brought from home, came up to him. He felt the dog's cool, wet tongue licking his cheeks and his eyes. The shouting was further away now.

'Run Gwynfor, run boy!' a voice whispered. Gwynfor looked across to the wagon. Somebody was hiding underneath: Tomas!

Gwynfor nodded, sat up and retched. Tomas was right; he could get up and run. He turned his head to the side and vomited on the road. When he stood, the hot afternoon scene spun around. He walked towards the edge of the clearing, his legs so shaky that he wondered if he could make it as far as the deep shade of the trees.

2

Late July afternoon sun angled through the open windows of the Appeals Court. There was a lull in proceedings. Justice Lara Johnson could hear children playing hopscotch in the dusty square outside. The jingle of a harness. That would be Matt bringing the trap round into the shade of the porch. Court could be dismissed soon.

She felt a pang of hunger. They'd sat right through from nine this Friday morning without a break. A complicated land dispute case had taken them to midday. Then a long, hot afternoon's proceedings. It was an appeal against a sentence for domestic violence meted out by a community court out in the sticks. The low-ceilinged courtroom had been filled with glaring, sweaty relatives. Now they'd all gone. The courtroom was almost empty.

Lara had visions of her mother's home-made strawberry ice cream.

Gilpin – the court clerk – asked the secretary to call for the last two appellants. 'What's this last case? Lara asked.

'The two Welshmen,' Gilpin replied. 'They lodged an appeal, if you can call it that, yesterday. The father and son,' he added.

Gilpin was fussed and flustered in the heat. As usual by this time of day he was emitting a sour, penetrating odour from beneath his fusty black jacket.

'I'm not sure we can proceed with this case, Justice. I don't think this court has jurisdiction.' Gilpin looked across at a teetering pile of leather-bound law tomes. 'But I'll check…'

Lara's eyes flashed. She had green, feline eyes flecked with brown and gold: the eyes of a lioness. 'I'd like to hear what they want, Gilpin,' she said, raising her voice.

The courtroom fell silent. Jenny Smith, the secretary, scratched her pen across a new page of the Court Record.

The two appellants were ushered in through a side door and stood at the witnesses' rail.

Father and son looked around. Clearly the courtroom wasn't quite as awe-inspiring as they'd expected. After all, this was one of the most powerful courts in the English Midlands, or so they'd been told.

What they took in was a low-ceilinged and not very impressive room. What had this building been in Good Time – a school for young children maybe? The hall they were standing in had a worn parquet floor. Lunchtime apple cores and corncobs lay between the wooden benches, discarded by the furious farmers and their relatives. The windows were open wide. There was a slow, creaking ceiling fan. The acidic tang of human sweat still hung around, mixed up with the sweet cloying smell of talcum powder.

A single police officer stood behind them – a bored-looking, overweight blonde woman. Her blue shirt had blotched and darkened with sweat in several places, and she was leaning back as far as she could to catch a little breeze from an open window.

Then there was Gilpin seated below them at one table, Jenny Smith at another, and on the public benches at the front, facing Lara and the judge's platform, were several others: Star Edkin, the reporter from the New Warwick Beacon, notebook on her lap; a farmer who'd come to listen to the morning's proceedings, decided to stay on for the afternoon's entertainment and had fallen asleep, his head lolling; old Willow Sonji, a half-white, half-Asian woman with bright, black, mad eyes who attended every single one of Lara's court sessions; and finally a middle-aged woman with sagging jowls and sagging breasts who was knitting – incongruously in the courtroom heat – a pink woollen shawl.

Only Justice Lara Johnson herself fitted the part. It wasn't just her proud lioness gaze. Nor was it simply the theatrical props of the courtroom – the black gown, the raised judge's seat, the gavel on its little stand. It was because Lara radiated authority from every pore of her glowing golden skin. She had an imposing head of hair, reddish-brown in wide curls. She wasn't tall – only average height, in fact – but somehow everyone knew you didn't mess with Justice Lara Johnson.

At the unbelievable age of thirty-two she'd become the youngest judge ever appointed to the New Warwick circuit. She was already being talked about as a candidate for political office in the city's Legislative Council.

All this success, sighed the envious and the admiring alike – despite what's happened to her. Or more to the point, despite what's happened to her husband.

The older Welshman now looked at Lara, deference and hope mingling in his eyes.

'Case five six-three,' intoned Gilpin, not looking up from his papers, 'investigative hearing of an appeal by, um, Mr Sile-van Roberts?' Gilpin squinted at the names on the piece of paper in front of him and added, with a shake of his head, 'and his son who is also here present, er, Gw-eye? Gweye-n Four Roberts.'

'Begging your pardon,' said the son, blushing. His accent was strange to the New Warwick courtroom. The sentences rose and fell slowly like sheep trailing up and down mountain paths. 'Yes, sir, my father's first name. Actually 'Sylvan' it is. We say it like "Sill". And Gwynfor is my first name. We say that like "Gwin-vorr", begging your pardon again, of course.'

'Thank you,' said Lara, giving him an encouraging smile.

'And can you confirm,' asked Gilpin, 'that you are both residents of Lann-golern?'

'Llangollen', cut in the young man, pronouncing both double L's.

Jenny the secretary sat, pen poised, bewildered by the Welsh names. She'd never strayed far beyond the boundaries of New Warwick.

'Don't the appellants have a lawyer?' Lara asked Gilpin.

The court clerk gave her a sickly smile. 'It appears the appellants wish to represent themselves, ma'am.'

The two Welshmen exchanged puzzled glances. The father, Sylvan Roberts, was short and stocky and had incredibly narrow shoulders. Above the tiny, child-like shoulders he had a large head topped with tight grey curls. There was a crafty twinkle in his eyes. This didn't necessarily mean he was a rogue, Lara thought, but to be a rogue you have to have that intelligent look.

Gwynfor, unlike his father, was broad-shouldered and stood a clear foot above him. My God, he's a handsome one, Lara thought, but does he know it yet? He looks barely twenty. His long black curly hair fell in soft lustrous curls to his neck. As he stooped to confer shyly with his father, Lara noticed that he had perfectly regular white teeth, unusual in this day and age, and deep blue eyes with black flecks in them. His face was well-defined but still more boyish than full-grown man.

Get a grip, she told herself: stop gazing at this handsome young man.

She concentrated on Sylvan Roberts. 'Tell me,' she said, 'why you have come to this court rather than one in Wales?'

There was a brief, tense exchange in Welsh.

The father nodded and spoke. 'What happened to us – the attack, like – it happened to us in England. We couldn't get back to Wales; the way was blocked. We had to come south, to here.'

'North Mercia,' added the son, 'it happened in North Mercia.'

"This wrong that you spoke of,' said Lara, 'was it a wrongful judgement by another court? Are you seeking to lodge an appeal against the judgement of another court?'

They were puzzled at this: another exchange in Welsh.

Educated people knew about Wales and its mysterious language, but Lara had never heard it spoken before. She was fascinated by the rolling r's and occasional noises like escaping steam that came from the Welshmen's mouths.

Now they were looking even more confused.

Lara tried another tack. 'Or have you been sentenced by another court somewhere and want to appeal?'

'Oh no, we never did anything wrong!' the young one burst in. 'It's not another court we are complaining about. A crime against us it is.'

'A crime against you?'

'A crime against us no one will do anything about.'

'Ah, I see,' Lara said. 'But there's a problem here...'

'Public prosecutor's office on Thursday perhaps,' Gilpin interrupted, his head still bowed over his papers.

Lara thought a moment. 'This court,' she explained to the men, 'is an Appeals Court. If you think another judge or another court is wrong, you come here to ask to put it right.'

Father and son nodded.

'But there's another office in New Warwick that you could go to,' she went on. 'It's the office of the public prosecutor. If a crime's been committed and the police or no one else has done anything about it, you go to see her. She has a public hearing every Thursday.'

Sylvan's face fell. 'So you can't help us?'

The son leant forward and muttered something in his father's ear.

Sylvan shook his head, despondent. 'I don't know…' he said.

Lara breathed in the stifling air. 'Look,' she said. 'All right. Perhaps I can at least hear what you have to say. Tell me what has happened to you–'

'–Ma'am!' Gilpin had raised one hand. He was giving her a very disapproving look.

'–Yes, tell me what has happened to you,' Lara continued, glowering back at Gilpin, 'and I might be able to arrange a private hearing for you with the public prosecutor – with me present, if you wish – though I must stress, we might not be able to take any action if it's a North Mercian matter.'

'Theft, it was,' said the young man, his voice rising in indignation. 'In broad daylight. We have lost all our wagons – all six! And most of the horses were taken, everything.'

'And beaten black and blue, he was,' added Gwynfor's father. He grabbed his son by the shoulder and turned Gwynfor round. Then with care he lifted his son's loose brown tunic up to the shoulder blades. There were three red, wide weals across the young man's back, and purple-black bruising around the edges. The pattern reminded Lara of the marks left on a griddled steak.

Jenny the secretary said 'Ooh!' and raised her hand to her mouth. Gilpin glanced up, then took off his small round glasses and polished them.

'Did the same happen to you?' asked Lara, looking at Sylvan. At this question the father paused, looking uncertain. His son continued:

'No, my father got away. Lucky really: I broke free as well. I run – ran. Hiding in the forest, I was. But Da found me later. The dog helped. She's clever: a working dog, see.'

'Duw, we were glad to get out of that place!' said Sylvan. 'But I have no living now, nothing, see?' His voice faltered and he looked down.

There was a pause. Gwynfor said 'we don't know what happened to any of the drivers. Three of them helped my da get away, distracted them like, but we haven't heard from any of them yet.'

'Where were you going? And what was stolen?' Lara asked.

'Ox-ford,' replied the young man. 'Wool my da carries, mainly.'

'Wool?'

'Wool bales and blankets,' explained Gwynfor.

'And paper,' added his father. 'For printing. One wagon had paper bales. A new paper mill, there is, near the border.'

'So just wool...and paper?' Lara was incredulous.

'Yes,' said father and son in unison.

Alarm bells were ringing in Lara's mind. 'You must tell the truth,' she said. 'The penalties for buying and selling illegal drugs anywhere in or near New Warwick are very severe.'

'No, madam,' the father said straightaway. 'No drugs at all.'

'Nothing else?'

'No,' repeated the older man.

Lara was even more mystified when the son looked at his father, as if to check something, and then said 'but you haven't heard the half of it yet.'

'Go on,' said Lara levelly, 'because I've been asking myself some questions too. Why didn't you report this crime to the police when you were in the area?'

Gwynfor reddened. 'Because it was the police who attacked us!' he shouted.

His father was nodding furiously, muttering under his breath in Welsh.

Lara stared at them. 'Are you saying the police stopped you – assaulted you – all for wagons full of wool and paper?'

She noticed that Star Edkin was sitting up and scribbling furiously in her notebook. God knows what would appear in the Beacon tomorrow, Lara thought. This was all getting out of hand. There'd be lurid tales of drug running and rampant corruption in the police forces up-country, all safely quoted in inverted commas as 'proceedings in court'.

Gilpin came to the rescue. 'Justice, I beg to interrupt, but we can't proceed with any of this.' He was jabbing the page of a law book.

Lara sighed. 'Gilpin, come forward please.'

The sour smell of his body increased as he came close. Lara poured out a glass of water to distract herself. 'Well?' she said, trying not to breathe in.

'I've been checking the court ordinances,' he whispered, 'and it is spelt out very clearly. As I thought, such a serious accusation involving the police must be dealt with in the appropriate region – in this case North Mercia, as we know. They will have to go back to Chester. There's no point consulting the public prosecutor here.'

Lara was forced to stomach the smell of his mouth, as well as his body odour, as she bent her head closer to his.

'Yes, but this troubles me. They sound genuine.'

'The accusations they're making are dynamite, Justice. For that reason I advise caution. This court, if I'm permitted to say, can't just pick up a case like this in a casual way.'

Lara sighed with frustration.

'I'm sorry,' she said to the two Welshmen, 'but you've come to the wrong court. You have a serious case to be heard if what you say is true. But any case against your attackers must be heard in North Mercia first. They have jurisdiction over this, not us.'

The two Welshmen were open-mouthed, trying to piece together her English words. Sylvan, the father, shook his head. Surely this kind woman who had listened so carefully could not be washing her hands of them?

Lara picked up the gavel and banged it noisily on the desk.

'Before this court is dismissed,' she declared, 'let it be recorded that I have applied a temporary censorship order on this hearing – that is, case five six-three.' With a tight smile she added, 'Sorry Miss Edkin. Your editor can appeal to publish this hearing in three months' time.'

Star Edkin grimaced and snapped her notebook shut. Lara banged the gavel again.

'Will the court please rise!' Gilpin's voice rasped in the hot air. The few people sitting in the courtroom shuffled, standing slowly.

As Lara walked towards the rear door reserved for the judge, Gwynfor's young voice rang out.

'My father knows where your husband is!'

The trickle of sweat on Lara Johnson's back turned cold. She stopped and turned to look at him. There was dead silence in the room. Everyone's eyes were upon her.

3

As Lara was staring at the two Welshmen wondering what to do, her mother Rae was turning out a strawberry jelly. It was an experiment, this jelly, because she was using gelatine – something that was usually hard to get hold of even in a large settlement like New Warwick. Usually she had to use calf's foot jelly.

It seems to have done the trick, she had to admit, cautiously prodding the pink jelly with her forefinger and meeting a pleasant, firm resistance.

'Mmm, let's see what it's like shall we?' said Rae, lifting the glass jelly mould out of the cool ice box.

Pirate the house cat wove himself around her legs, expecting cream. 'Now you watch out, you tinker. If this lands on your head you'll be sorry!'

Arrow, Rae's granddaughter, giggled. 'He wants some. He wants to put his paw in it.'

'I'll give him jelly! Get out of the way, shoo.'

Arrow giggled again. She was all eyes now, watching as her grandma put the shiny glass mould top-down on the table and covered the quivering jelly with a large dish. 'Now watch, this is the tricky bit.'

'Can I do it?'

'Next time. I'm not sure this is going to work.' Rae held the dish over the glass mould bottom and quickly turned over both mould and dish, setting them down right way up. Then, under the gaze of her granddaughter, Rae gently eased the glass mould up and off the jelly. There was a sucking noise. Both Rae and Arrow held their breaths.

'It's a palace,' breathed Arrow, looking in wonder at the magnificent pink turrets and towers of the perfectly set jelly. The five o'clock sun, angling through a high window, seemed to light it up from the inside.

'Not bad,' said Rae proudly, 'not bad at all. They usually go splop all over the dish.'

'Splop! Splop!' The six-year-old girl ran, grinning, around the kitchen table.

Rae decided to join in. 'Wibble-wobble, wibble-wobble, jelly on the plate!' she sang, fuelling her granddaughter's excitement. She laughed as she caught the child by the middle.

'Grandma, stop tickling!' shrieked Arrow. 'Stop!'

'All right then. As long as you tell me what else you're going to eat as well as the jelly.'

'I love cake.'

'Well there's a surprise! What kind of cake?'

'Honey and nut cake.'

'Oh, honey cake, eh?' Rae gave her a knowing smile. 'Mm, well, I'm not sure there's any left.'

'There is! There is honey cake, there is honey cake, I know where it is!'

'So do I. Most of it's in your tummy isn't it! What about fish cake instead?'

'Urgh!'

'Liver and onion cake, then?'

'Urghh!' the girl giggled, knowing there was no such thing.

Rae fanned herself, feeling a hot flush coming. 'Phew, little Arrow. Let me sit down a minute.' She pulled out a kitchen chair and sat down. I'm getting a bit overweight now; I must do something about it, she thought.

Arrow sidled up, half-raising herself on to her grandmother's lap.

'Grandma, tell me about the time when you were little and you didn't have any food.'

As it happened, Rae didn't have time to go over that old story again. Jagger was barking excitedly in the yard. That meant he'd seen Lara approaching. Arrow ran for the door. She loved to see

her mother's trap coming round the broad sweep of the drive that
led up to Wellbrook House.

Rae felt a pang of disappointment when Arrow had leapt from
her lap. Never mind, she told herself, standing up stiffly and
stretching, I can tell her that story again soon enough.

She went out into the kitchen yard, blinking in the sunshine.
Her daughter had got down from the trap and was sweeping Arrow
into a big hug.

Lara looked up. 'Hello, Mum.'

'Hello, Lara.' Rae noticed her red-rimmed eyes.

Arrow had noticed too. 'Have you been crying, Mummy?'

'I have.' Lara put a hand up to her eyes. 'Oh, you two! I'll be
OK now.'

Lara pulled herself together. She took her daughter by the
hand and led her into the house. 'C'mon,' she said, 'tell me what
you've been doing with Grandma.'

Lara went upstairs for a deliciously cold shower. Her skin was so
hot it seemed to warm the cold water running down her back. She
looked up at the shower head, letting the fresh water and lavender
soap wash away the saltiness from her eyes.

Five minutes later, sitting alone and naked on her bed, drying
her hair with a towel, a few tears came back. She was holding
David's photo to her chest – a black-and-white portrait he'd agreed
to have taken in town.

The photographer had captured his personality perfectly: the
boyish enthusiastic smile, his curly hair, the nose that he (but not
she) thought was too big; those bright blue eyes; that restless look.
She'd promised Arrow a ten-minute swim before they ate and she'd
better hurry. Never mind my hair, she thought, it's going to get wet
again.

She wasn't feeling hungry any more after that heart-stopping
moment at the end of the afternoon. She took out a swimsuit and a
fresh towel, turning over in her mind whether she'd been right to
walk away from the two Welshmen and not talk to them.

It was so tempting to chase every lead. But I've had my
fingers burned so many times, she reflected. In the first few
months dozens of strangers had come to her with reports of
sightings of David. Later on there'd been stories brought to her by
travellers from the north and south, west and east – and from

France, even.

They all said, yes, they knew someone else who knew someone who could swear they'd seen him. Even these third-hand reports had set off flares of hope. She had followed up each and every one, almost wrecking herself with worry and exhaustion.

After two years of waiting there were still only two certainties. One was that David had definitely reached North Mercia – a part of the region known in Good Time as the county of Cheshire. They'd found his name in the guest book of a tavern near a place called Old Sandbach.

The second certainty was that he'd never reached the last-century nuclear power station at Sellafield, in the far north-west, which had been urgently demanding his help. She knew that because she'd been there herself, twice. She was certain they were telling the truth.

There had never been a body or – thank God – a gruesome severed finger. Nor had there been a ransom demand or a claim of abduction by any group. Nothing. She would like to have told everybody that she firmly believed he was still alive. That telepathically she knew his heart was still beating. But in all honesty she couldn't. She'd had fears for his life after the first three months. That sense of foreboding had only got stronger.

More recently, Lara had reluctantly started to picture how life might have to be. And with this change, her grief had started to come – not in a rush but more like blobs of condensation on a solid rock – a few tears at a time surprising her at any time of day or night. Anything could trigger them. Often it was the silliest of things like the fragment of a dream. When this happened she'd find herself standing and staring at nothing in particular. Once a shaft of sunlight on a tablecloth prompted a memory of the colour of the shirt he'd worn that last morning at home.

Curious, she thought: the young Welshman didn't shout we know where your husband is. He said my father knows. But his dad was standing next to him. Why didn't he say anything?

It's another false trail. The lad was just trying to get her to help – a desperate last shot. The father doesn't know anything except rumour. She couldn't go on letting herself be swept down these terrifying rapids of hope, only to find herself back in the stagnant marshes of uncertainty a few weeks later.

All the same, Lara couldn't get the memory of Gwynfor's face out of her mind. 'We thought you would listen!' he'd shouted. 'If you can help us, we can help you.'

The father, by contrast, had been pale and tense, looking straight ahead without expression.

Her impulse had been to run down the steps outside the courtroom, clasp the father by the arm and pump him for any scrap of information he had. When? Where? What was David doing and did he look seriously ill? Was he in danger? Imprisoned?

No, I did the right thing, she sighed, shuffling into loose sandals and picking up the towel. They're not going anywhere for a day or two. I'll get them checked over first. Lara made a mental note to contact Kieran Tyler, who in her opinion was about the only really effective inspector of police in New Warwick. Yes, I'll get Kieran to see if he can find out what really happened to those Welshmen, who they really are. Then I'll talk to them.

I've got to remember I'm Justice Lara Johnson, she told herself. Be impartial at all times, not petitioned or bribed or swayed in any way. To keep her resolve, she recited to herself the solemn oaths she had made when she became the youngest ever woman Justice in New Warwick.

A few minutes later, Lara was standing at the open kitchen door, bath towels in hand, while Arrow hopped around excitedly on the step in her swimming costume.

'Didn't you remember, Lara?' her mother said.

'What?'

'Ben's coming round this evening. He said you two were going to the new Moreton Morrell dam. It's the grand opening tonight!'

Lara clutched the side of her head. 'Oh God, I forgot. . .'

'I think he's really looking forward to it. I asked him to come round to eat with us first.'

'Oh, Mum!'

Rae frowned. 'Lara, it's not as though he's here every day!'

'Not every day, no.'

Rae smiled at her granddaughter. 'And I know somebody who'd like to see Ben at teatime, wouldn't you, love?'

Arrow sensed the tension in the air. 'Swim, swim, swim! C'mon, mummy!' she shouted, yanking Lara's arm.

'Yes, yes!' Lara said. She looked at her mother. 'I'll have to think about going to that thing with Ben later.'

The swimming pool at Wellbrook had been David's brainchild. David had left plans and had talked a lot about it with Ben, their friend and farming neighbour.

Six months after his disappearance, when Lara was feeling at a particularly low point one wintry Sunday afternoon, poring over some law books, Ben had appeared at their back door. He was holding the swimming pool plans David had given him.

Lara remembered how her mother's eyes had lit up when she'd seen Ben. She'd bustled around putting honey and spices in a warming pan to make mulled cider.

As the February wind blew and hailstones clattered against the kitchen windows, Ben told them both how he thought it could be done.

'It'll be great if we can make a start soon. A real treat for David to see it all sparkling ready when he comes back, eh?'

Lara had given way to Ben's enthusiasm. She'd agreed to go ahead with the project, though eddies of doubt stirred inside her. Thinking positively was one thing but it was tempting fate, surely, to make all these preparations for David's return? The situation was looking increasingly hopeless even then.

Also, she'd suspected from the start that Ben's interest in her was about more than friendship and neighbourly help. There was genuine kindness in him, no doubt. Ben was only twenty-seven now, but to Lara he often seemed younger, uninformed about the world beyond New Warwick. He was only a young farmer after all: heavy-footed, a stranger to books and ideas, his clothes and boots smelling of cow and horse dung if you came across him in the working day. Yet in other ways he was deep and serious, at least as seasoned by troubles and tragedies as she was. Both his parents had died in the Third Pandemic, leaving Ben as a lone fifteen-year-old with only the foreman and three farm hands to help him run a farm of nearly three hundred acres. God knows how he'd done it, but he had.

He'd got married four years ago. Tam, his bride, had been only nineteen – a wiry, boyish, tough-looking girl with short, curly red hair, snub nose and an infectious laugh. She was already over four months pregnant when they married – a hugely positive thing in today's world. Evidence of a pregnancy of three months or more was increasingly demanded by the parents on both sides before a couple got their families' approval to tie the knot.

Lara's memory of the wedding reception was still as sharp as day: the gentle bulge of Tam's belly under her cream linen wedding dress; the smile on her face as she stood to cut the wedding cake; the way Tam and Ben smiled at each other, clasping the big cake knife.

Four months later Tam had come to see her, her wiry frame now weighed down by her hugely pregnant belly. She'd joked about how jolting along the rough farm road in the pony and trap was the only way to get her baby started.

Within two days she was dead. Medicine and midwifery were improving in New Warwick, but not enough for poor Tam and her unborn son. She died in childbirth in Our Lady Diana hospital. David had rushed off in the middle of the night to see if he could help. And it was David who had put his arm around Ben's shoulders when it was all over.

Lara couldn't get past the dreadful symmetry of what had happened to each of them. Ben had lost a wife, while her husband had disappeared without a trace. But nor could she get past the asymmetry, the unfairness: he had lost a son as well, whereas Arrow was alive and well.

A few days after he'd first come round with the plans that grey February afternoon, the penny dropped with Lara. Busy farmer though he was, Ben needed the swimming pool project. She'd called him back. He'd come round straightaway, beaming with enthusiasm.

He spread out another, much bigger piece of paper on the kitchen table, animatedly outlining his own detailed plans. Lara felt her spirits lifting. This could be for Arrow as much as it is for me or David, she thought as she stood behind him, watching his big farmer hands holding a pencil over the plan.

Ben had talked about how he'd dam the little brook that ran through the field just to the north of their estate. A feeder pipe was to be run through to the back of their orchard, leading to a reservoir tank to supply the pool. The water itself would pass over several gravel beds and then through a replaceable tray filled with charcoal so that it would always be sweet and clean. The pool was going to be big – why not? – maybe forty feet long by fifteen or twenty feet wide, with a gently shelving bottom going down to a depth of six feet. Fresh water would run in constantly, the flow controlled by a little sluice fitted to the inlet pipe. It would run out through an outlet near the bottom of the pool at the deep end.

Could she get some men on probation, he asked, to dig it out? That would be the main effort, he explained; too much for his farm workers to take on, even in the slack winter time before the spring harrowing and all the other work picked up.

More than a few eyebrows were raised that March when Lara's boss, the Chief Justice, agreed to put six offenders on the job. She certainly couldn't ask for that kind of favour now. As a judge, she had to appear to be above any kind of corruption or tax-free backhanders.

The pool project had acquired magical properties, soothing her aching desire for David's return. And somehow, building it wasn't tempting fate any more. It was going to bring him back.

It took much longer than Ben or anyone else had expected, of course. The six, then eight guys on probation sweated and wheelbarrowed earth and mud all through the endless spring rains, then the baking heat of summer. By the end of August the pool was taking shape, but then it had to be lined and the channels and pipe-work installed. Lara paid a fortune for original Good Time tiles for the pool's sides and bottom, imported from a specialist warehouse near Oxford, beautiful dark blue and light blue ones with swirly mosaic patterns. She was also able to get original paving slabs for the pool surround. She paid for all the materials out of her own pocket, of course.

By the time the pool was ready to be filled it was getting towards winter again. They decided to cover it over and leave it till the following May and Arrow's sixth birthday for the grand opening party.

It was a great success, that party – an excited Arrow running everywhere, a load of kids from friends' houses running in a trail behind her. She was wearing a princess dress her grandma had made, Lara recalled. Blue satin: definitely Good Time stuff. Of course most of the kids wanted to try out the pool. Some of them had even brought special little swimming outfits made out of linen by doting mothers and grandmothers.

All had been open-mouthed when they got their first look. The pool was shimmering blue under cold May sunshine. Clean water chuckled continuously out of the hardwood spout at the shallow end. No one, including the adults, had ever seen anything like it before. It was so big! Not many adults or kids could swim. A rope tied with ribbons had to be drawn across the pool where the shallow part began to dip away towards the deeper end.

Grandma Rae had a childhood memory of being taken to a large indoor pool in the last year of Good Time when she was – what – three, four? Standing by this new pool had brought back a distant memory. The smooth, tanned skin of an adult woman. An impression of a deep pink swimming costume. A blurred blob of a face beneath a white bathing cap.

There was a distinct memory of another woman being there. Rae couldn't remember her proper name or what she looked like. She was simply Flu Buddie. Everyone had a flu buddie and simultaneously was a flu buddie to someone else. Was Flu Buddie the woman with the smiling face who'd bent down to lift little Rae out of the echoing water? Perhaps she was. But no, Rae had decided years ago, that was my mother. It's all I've got of her: deep pink swimming costume; cool flesh; solid arms encircling her.

The water in the new pool was freezing despite all the sun they'd been getting over the previous week. Some of the kids had sat on the poolside and touched the water with their toes, yelping and giggling. Then two or three of the older ones stood in the shallow end, the water just above their knees, turning blue and laughing, teeth chattering.

Ben ran out of the house bare-chested, wearing canvas trousers cut off at the knee. To cheers, clapping and laughter, he'd run through the party crowd and jumped straight into the deep end with a splash.

Ice-cold water scattered all over Arrow and the little girls on the edge of the pool. They'd shrieked even louder. Then, entranced, they'd watched Ben's form, a dark shadow, swimming expertly under water.

He'd swum under the rope to burst out of the water at the shallow end, grinning and blowing spray loudly out of his mouth and nostrils. To Lara he'd looked like an eager Labrador. Ben's long, straight black hair had been pressed down by the water. His enthusiastic brown eyes had searched for hers.

Looking down at him then, seeing his smiling, grateful eyes,

Lara had thought, no. No. It should be David down there in the water.

Do I still feel the same way about David? Lara asked herself again and again. Three months had passed since the swimming pool party, two years since David had gone. Two years! She could hardly believe it. So much had happened. She'd made a conscious decision to throw herself into work.

It was endless, distracting, and if she just kept going she wouldn't fall apart. Now she was getting to be a leading light in New Warwick society in her own right, not just as the poor deserted wife of Dr David Johnson. Apart from the occasional snide remark, New Warwick's small community of lawyers had to agree that her outstanding abilities were beyond question.

The water in the pool was warm now – nothing like that chilly experience in May. It was August and the summer recess was coming and Lara was feeling a mixture of relief and unsteadiness. She took her eyes off Arrow for a moment and floated gently on her back. Her submerged ears picked up the sounds of her daughter's legs paddling; and the steady chortling water from the inlet pipe.

When it was just herself and Arrow, she liked to swim naked. For children's safety, but also modesty, she'd had a high wicker fence erected around the pool. It meant that she could enjoy privacy, a rare commodity in New Warwick, and bask in the early evening sun. She felt every inch of her body relaxing after being cooped up in the hot, fusty courtroom. Still floating, she closed her eyes and felt the lap-lap of the pool against her sides. She allowed the sun's rays, still warm in the early evening, to penetrate deep inside her eyeballs.

'Mummy!' Arrow splashed around, showing off her new trick – cartwheels underwater. She's a good little swimmer now, thought Lara. In the two years since David had gone Arrow had lost her early childhood chubbiness and was on the way to being a lanky girl. She had a halo of blonde curls that clung to her head in the water. David's hair.

God, should I have talked to those Welshmen straight away? Lara pushed the thought away. She grabbed her daughter. 'Seal kiss?' she asked, grinning. Pictures of seals were in one of the creased Good Time children's storybooks she'd managed to get hold of.

'No way!' cried her daughter. The seal game always made her giggle, Lara swimming behind Arrow to catch her and give her a slobbery kiss. In the excitement neither of them noticed Ben.

Ben closed the creaking wicker gate as quietly as he could and tiptoed away from the pool through the little orchard. His heart was thudding. Had she seen him? That's torn it, he thought to himself, if she had. Before, hearing their voices and the splashing from the pool, he'd felt a punch of enthusiasm in his belly. He'd dive in and make a splash, surprise them.

I didn't know she'd be naked, he asked himself. Did I? The answer his conscience gave him was uncomfortable.

He walked slowly back through the apple and pear trees towards the lawn at the back of Lara's house. He was making for the table, shaded by a white awning, which had been set out for the evening meal. But he couldn't stop the vision of Lara's body flooding his mind's eye. It would return to him tonight in his lonely bed. She'd been standing waist deep in the pool, in profile, and he'd seen her honey skin, her beautiful arched back, the dip of her ample breasts just visible from the side.

He tried to press his sexual stirrings under the surface. But it was no good. He just felt hot and angry, the sexual frustration mingling with guilty feelings about David.

As he strolled across the lawn in the warm evening sun he saw Esther, the house help, walking from the house with a tray.

'Not going for a swim then?' she smiled.

Ben, flushing, sat down quickly. Esther turned with a mischievous grin to put dishes and a large jug of cream on the table.

What Esther didn't know was that she'd tempted Ben, one day at the market in New Warwick. He'd been sitting at a beer stall when she'd passed by. He'd waved to her, curious because she was carrying some old books. In fact she was a mystery to him: a good-looking woman in her late twenties, perhaps a year or two older, but no husband or boyfriend. Esther had been married, Lara's mother had told him, but her husband had run away because Esther couldn't get pregnant.

'What are you reading?' he'd asked her that day in the market after they'd said hello. 'Are you studying or something?'

'No,' she'd smiled, 'I just can't stop reading!'

She'd shown him one of her books, which she'd brought from the central library.

He'd squinted at the spine of the worn book cover, struggling to read the words. 'Pride and...'

'Prejudice' she'd said, smiling again.

'Oh...' he'd said, puzzled and embarrassed, not sure what to say.

And she must have been embarrassed too, in some way. She dropped the three books she was holding and he'd got off his bar stool to help her pick them up. She'd knelt down too, and as he got close to her he noticed how good she smelt: a mixture of meadow flowers and sun-hot grass.

He accidentally touched her arm, handing her a book, and felt skin that was incredibly smooth and silky. Black skin; a strong, firm body; an, open, heart-shaped face – she looked good. Oh yes, he'd weighed it all up in that moment. She'd be good with him, good as a companion on the farm, good in bed. It didn't matter if she couldn't have children. People said such negative things about barren women. Let them talk. After losing Tam, the risks of childbirth frightened him.

But despite all these attractions, she wasn't the right one. He'd handed her the book, and wished her well, and she'd promised to tell him what Pride and Prejudice was all about.

Rae swayed towards him now, a broad smile on her face. She called out as she walked across the lawn. 'Ben, you're here! Look, I've got some chilled cider for you.'

Esther had spent a long time arranging slices of ham on a wooden board. Now she straightened, wary eyes on Rae.

'Why don't you cut some extra ham for yourself, Esther? There's more in the kitchen,' said Rae. 'Then that's all, I think.'

Esther had been brushing against Ben as she moved around the table, pressing her nipples against his back for that extra half-second. 'Thanks Mrs Johnson,' she said in a flat voice, walking off. 'Just give me a shout when you want the jelly.'

And on the word 'jelly' they heard the wicker gate burst open and saw Arrow running towards them in a faded green towel, her wet hair slicked against her back and shoulders. She squealed with delight when she saw Ben. Behind Arrow came Lara, swathed in a big white towel and looking glorious, strolling towards them through the apple trees, smiling. No sign yet that she saw me by the pool, Ben breathed in relief.

A blink of a shadow crossed the lawn and Rae looked up, startled. With a cry of alarm she rushed across towards Arrow, arms outstretched, wanting to cover her.

Both Lara and Ben looked up, shading their eyes against the evening sun.

In the sky above them a black bird crossed – a crow, Ben thought. It dipped towards the house and lawn but then thought better of it, rising and flapping lazily into the distance.

4

That same crow flapped slowly on from its position above Lara's mansion, wheeling north towards the centre of New Warwick. It sensed possibilities in the warm updrafts of the hot summer evening, all the trace smells given off by a human settlement of close on ninety thousand people – spoiled food on rotting dumps and in compost heaps, the scent of wood smoke from open grills and ovens, the smells of roasting meat and of human and animal manure.

The crow banked over bronze fields of wheat and green-brown fields of ripening maize surrounding the city, then swooped lower over a patchwork quilt of kitchen gardens and straw-roof allotment huts leading up to the first lines of houses and roads.

The bird saw the human creatures running this way and that, their faces upturned like small round flower heads, mostly white discs but some brown and brown-black ones too. It could hear shouts and cries of alarm. The people were waving and pointing upwards.

There was a loud, eerie, disturbing sound now – a long, wailing sound that started low but developed into a prolonged, wavering howl. It was coming from a tall wooden tower topped with a rusting corrugated metal roof. The long wail was interrupted by a sharp bang from below.

A split-second before it heard the noise, the crow felt a sudden lacing of whispers in the warm air around it, a high-pitched buzzing like hornets that flew by in a millisecond. Sensing great danger, the crow turned and flew quickly due west, away from the puzzling noisy sprawl below.

The black bird passed over the Forest of Arden, once little more than an isolated patch of woodland surrounded by fields and hedges, noisy roads and housing estates two human generations back. Now it was the frontier of a new and growing wild forest.

Hushed in the evening stillness this forest, interspersed with stretches of scrub and heath as well as flooded land, stretched westwards for a hundred miles and more, as the crow might fly – as far as the Welsh mountains, way beyond the Mercian border.

Few human beings lived in the forest. All but a few roads and tracks had been taken over by dense brambles and undergrowth, saplings, and now by full-grown trees. So when the crow spotted two dark shapes moving quietly beneath the canopy of leaves it was curious. It banked and wheeled, turning to get a better look.

Two large horses, a chestnut and a grey, emerged into a small green clearing on the edge of the woods. Their flanks were streaked with dried, hardened yellow saliva. They stopped, their riders dismounting: two armed men, tired, unshaven, clad in leather tunics, one with a metal crossbow strapped to his back.

The horses were being tethered and bags were being lifted off them. The men were looking around them now. They were leaving their horses and walking the short distance to a ridge that gave them a view of the city in the distance. One looked back to check the horses, shielding his eyes with his hand from the setting sun. Now both men looked east towards the roofs and towers of New Warwick as they reflected the gently sloping rays of the evening sun.

5

Sitting at a pavement table at Woczinsky's in the central square, Star Edkin heard the siren and the gun going off. Only one shot, though. It would have flown away. In fact, she mused, even if a whole flock of birds flew over there wouldn't be any danger. But try telling that to the older generation; anybody over thirty. Star hadn't even bothered to glance up at the calm evening sky the way she'd been taught to at school when the siren sounded. In fact hardly any of the young clientele at Woczinsky's Café bothered. It wasn't cool to get worked up about stupid birds.

Star sipped vodka over crushed raspberry ice, stretched herself against the cane back of her café chair and spared a little smile for the knots of superstitious people in the crowded square who were still anxiously pointing at the sky. You could understand it, though, she thought. Children's stories and the plays they got you to do at school were full of images of Good Time and how the birds had spoiled it.

She smiled at her own fear, a slight shudder passing down her spine, when she remembered one particular story the teacher had read to them when she was seven. It was a simple enough story about a cute little smiling sparrow that hopped from one page of the book to the next. But each time it hopped it got bigger, until in the last few pictures it had grown to an enormous size and almost filled the page. By then it had a huge serrated beak and frightening shiny-black eyes. Its cute smile had turned into a terrifying grin, and its dainty feet into ugly dragon-sized talons.

In the end the two children in the story, a brother and a sister, managed – just – to fool the bird into eating some poison in a bowl of raw meat. They saved their parents from being eaten and they saved their community. Star sucked some vodka-raspberry ice. Oh well, another thing they got wrong, she thought.

Star tilted her tall glass – her drink had nearly all gone. It was still so warm, and she needed another drink after that long day in the courtroom. Still, she'd have to make it last: the pavement outside Woczinsky's was an expensive place to drink.

As a trainee journalist she didn't have much money to spare. It was a great place to hang out, though. You saw the whole world going by. This was where you made your contacts. She stared into the strolling groups in the square. Everyone looked more relaxed now. Shopkeepers stood outside their premises enjoying the evening sun, couples strolled by holding hands; a crowd of kids were eating ice creams across the square at Joe's; two young guys, street musicians, were picking at their guitars again and floating gentle lyrics into the warm evening air.

Where the hell was he, then? She was getting annoyed now. Star had barely had time to rush back to her lodgings on the East Side to have a bucket splash and get a change of clothes before whizzing back to the square. No time to eat anything. Did they have clocks in Wales? I definitely said half-past seven, she thought.

Then Star saw him. She smiled. He's so fit-looking, but God he looks clueless tonight. He obviously hasn't worked out where Woczinsky's is, or what it is. Star didn't get up or wave. She'd let Gwynfor walk around for a minute or two, looking this way and that, bumping into the passing couples and nearly tripping up an old lady.

He's seen me. She returned his relieved smile with a little grin. She was sitting exactly where she'd told him she'd be sitting and wearing exactly what she'd said she'd be wearing – the Good-style cut-off denim trousers, the red top. She was wearing original Good Time shades (they'd cost her more than two weeks' wages): maybe those threw him.

'Sorry,' Gwynfor said. 'The place where we are . . .'

'Hostel?'

'Yes, the traders' lodging place – it's a long walk.' He waved in the general direction of the north of the city.

He wasn't sweaty, she noticed. He'd changed into a loose

white smock, open at the front. The memory of those angry red-black weals on his back flashed through her mind.

'Maybe I should've ridden out to you,' she said.

'Oh, no, it's OK.'

'Would you like a drink?'

He looked embarrassed. 'Oh – ah, maybe some water?'

'I'm going to have something a bit stronger than that! And some hot pepper chips. I'm starving.'

'I'm very sorry,' said Gwynfor. 'I don't have money.'

Oh great, thought Star, this had better be worth it.

The Beacon wouldn't allow her expenses yet. Even if she got the scoop of the year she was still a trainee – and trainees didn't get exes. As a matter of fact, she said to herself with a stab of excitement in her chest, a trainee shouldn't be doing this at all. They'd want me to hand this story over.

'The journalist's supposed to buy the drinks,' she said. 'What'll you have?'

She'd already spotted Stefan the waiter in his grimy white jacket, and now she waved him over.

'Beer?' Stefan asked, glaring at Gwynfor.

Gwynfor looked across at Star. 'Do they have wine here?' he said quietly. 'I've never tried wine.' He looked up at Stefan's bulky figure. 'If it's not too expensive.'

Come on, thought Star, you can't be real. 'Stefan,' she asked, 'could we have two chilled whites?'

Stefan rotated his metal tray impatiently. 'All chilled wine gone.'

'Oh,' Star said. 'How about two whites, don't worry if they're warm, but with some ice?'

'We gotta Kentish sparkle, very nice. I put ice around the bottle.'

'Not a whole bottle,' said Star quickly. 'Two long glasses with ice?'

Stefan emitted a low growl and shook his head. 'I gotta open a whole bottle though isn' it?' He sighed. 'For you, OK. But pay in German Euros.'

'OK. Do we get two bowls of pepper chips with that?' Star said quickly. She flashed him a cheeky smile. Stefan stomped off like a bear troubled by hornets, shaking his head and muttering.

'Diolch,' said Gwynfor.

'What?' she said. She'd been distracted by his eyelashes, which were genuinely beautiful: black, soft and thick, like a horse's lashes.

'I said thank you – in Welsh.'

'Oh! Oh, cool,' she replied, 'no problem! Especially as this is your first time. With wine, I mean,' she added, grinning.

It had just struck her that maybe he was fancying her.

'Your English is very good,' she went on – realising as soon as she'd said it that she probably sounded condescending.

But he took it as a compliment, explaining how good the education system in Gwynedd was.

'Where?' asked Star. She had heard of Wales but not this 'Gwynedd'.

As he was explaining his homeland, Stefan reappeared carrying a metal tray. He glanced disapprovingly at Gwynfor and set down the two tall fluted glasses on the table. Ice cubes clinked and bobbed. There was only one bowl of sizzling hot potato chips but as they were free she couldn't complain. She felt ravenous, smelling their saltiness and the hot vinegar evaporating.

Gwynfor picked up his glass with both hands as if the wine was a sacred liquid and leant back in his chair. He swallowed about a third of it. No pleasure showed in his face.

'Like it?' she asked.

He shook his head slowly, negatively, from side to side. 'Aw, Duw, it's wonderful.'

She burst out laughing, popping the first chip into her mouth. 'Would your father have let you have wine if he'd come as well?'

'Definitely not,' he said with a smile.

'Why wouldn't he come? I really needed to talk to both of you.'

'After, outside the courtroom, we were both upset, couldn't think straight, you know? Why didn't the judge talk to us?'

'Mm. She might yet, you know. Don't give up.'

It is a shame his father didn't want to come, Star reflected. Tell the story in his own words – God, it would make such a good front page! That accusation about the constabulary up there. They'd get round the censorship order somehow. And the Johnson mystery was icing on the cake.

I doubt they really know where he is, though, she thought. They're the latest in a long line of David Johnson spotters.

Gwynfor twisted his tall body in the cane chair, making it

creak. He was pretending to look interested in the sights of the square, but she detected some emotion in his deep blue eyes.

'Is your father frightened of something – someone – in this city?'

Gwynfor stayed silent, looking down quickly before she could judge his reaction.

'Only if he is,' she continued, 'it seems strange that he allowed you to come alone, that you didn't stick together.'

'He said I'd be all right if I keep in the crowds, plenty of people round, like this.'

'New Warwick is a well safe place, you know, Gwynfor. You don't need to worry too much.'

'Things can happen anywhere, Da says. You can't be too careful.'

'Do you know where David Johnson is?'

'Honest to God, Star,' Gwynfor replied, 'I don't know where that man is. Da won't tell me. He says it's for my own good...'

He broke off, weighing something up. 'What it is . . . we're leaving tomorrow morning, early. Da says we don't have much time here. The thing is...' He paused again.

'The thing is, he went to meet someone who might be able to help us. You see, when we were coming into New Warwick a few days ago he thought he saw Morgan Williams in the street near North Gate.'

'Morgan Williams?'

'We were not the only transport on the road that day when the police ambushed us. Usually we like to go two or three transports together, you know, for safety. Morgan Williams was half a mile behind us.'

'Ah.'

'Da thinks because Morgan wasn't too far away, on a hill looking down like, he might have seen enough.'

'To be a witness.'

'To be a witness.' He sighed. 'But whether Morgan Williams did see me being knocked down and whether he will help us I don't know. Da was looking for him tonight.'

This is it, Star thought. This is what they mean by a lead. She could feel her blood pumping round faster.

But am I getting out of my depth? She could picture Alex the editor's scowling face and hear his screeching voice: 'what the hell did you think you were playing at? What have I always told you?'

'Listen, Gwynfor,' she said, leaning forward. Star took her precious notebook from a small leather bag under the table. 'How about if we finish these drinks? Then I'm going to give you a lift back to Northgate. Maybe we'll catch your dad and I can have a word with him.'

Gwynfor looked confused. 'Lift?' he said eventually. 'Sorry, I . . .'

'What I mean is I can take you back. To save you walking.'

He still looked puzzled.

'On my motorbike!' Star said proudly.

Half an hour later Star Edkin led Gwynfor round the side of Woczinsky's to where she'd left the bike. The evening shadows were lengthening now – it was nearly nine. Gwynfor noticed the sliver of a new moon and wondered how his mother was. Would the same moon be rising over the mountain for her to see?

Half a dozen small boys were playing around the bike, all barefoot and in dusty shorts. Star flipped one of them a fifty-penny. 'There you go, Splinter!' she said. The boy shooed the others away. They all stood in an expectant line, waiting for Star and the gawky foreigner to mount the bike.

Gwynfor was embarrassed. In the world he'd grown up in, young women didn't behave like Star did. If they rode anything at all they rode it side-saddle. And as for a motorbike, well, he'd only ever seen two or three in his whole life – and all of them had been only good for scrap.

'Is this a genuine Good Time bike?' he asked. If it was, it could be over sixty years old.

Star motioned to the faded red paint on the fuel tank. He was able to make out the letters S-U-Z-U-K-I. It looked genuine enough. She was putting on a little leather jerkin that she'd left wound around the handlebars. 'It gets cold,' she explained, 'even on a warm night like this.' Then she opened a large box on the back of the bike, putting in her leather bag and lifting out two small helmets. They were made of thick leather, with flaps, and they were topped with rounded metal skullcaps. 'Here, put this on,' she said, handing him one.

'What does it drink, what makes it go?' asked Gwynfor. She was lifting her body up and jumping on a pedal to get the engine going. It fired and stopped.

'Petrol. Good old-time petrol. It won't run on bio.'

'Petrol!' Gwynfor was amazed. She'd got the engine going now and an intoxicating smell filled the air.

'It's the only perk of my job' shouted Star. 'The Beacon pays for it! Ready?'

The boys cheered and ran after them as Star drove the smoking, throaty-voiced bike across the dusty yard to the gate. As they picked up a little speed on the road Gwynfor put his arms around her leather jerkin. She felt incredibly slim and small, yet firm and compact.

They were weaving through crowds of people on the street. He gripped her more firmly, feeling that he could almost encircle her narrow waist with his big hands. She turned her head at one point and shouted something about holding on to the side-grips, but he shook his head and continued to hold onto her. She turned once more and gave him a smile.

Now they were clear of the crowded roads around the square. Star steered the bike on to Boulevard Thesby. This was a wide, dusty road bordered on each side by young trees and a track for pedestrians and cyclists. Gwynfor remembered walking into the city this way, wondering who Thesby was.

They were going north: he could see a blood-red sunset on their left. Long strips of purple cloud lay motionless in a turquoise sky. Set back from the road there were lines of single-storey houses with corrugated iron roofs painted red. The wooden houses were painted yellow, blue and green in a recurring sequence.

With the long straight road in front of them Star was able to open the throttle. There was a rush of cool wind on his face, and again that intoxicating smell of petrol. He swallowed a gnat before remembering to close his mouth. Then they sped across a short bridge, the bike wheels humming over wooden slats. He picked up a momentary pong from an open sewer.

In no time the bike was decelerating, the engine pop-popping as Star steered them off the boulevard into one of the eight or nine little squares and compounds that made up the Northgate area. She turned her head. 'Which way?' she shouted.

Gwynfor signalled for her to go straight on. Earlier on, he hadn't come this way but he was pretty sure his lodgings were nearer the North Gate itself.

Star slowed almost to walking speed as they crossed the first small square. Lanterns had been lit outside two pubs. In the middle of the square there were people sitting on benches at rough wooden tables. Several men turned their heads to look at the motorbike as they passed, setting down their tankards in surprise. Star and Gwynfor were able to quickly scan their faces. Gwynfor's father wasn't there.

Then, coming into the next square, Star saw out of the corner of her eye a huddle of people in another alley leading off to the left. She didn't know why, but something told her it was worth investigating.

Gwynfor shouted 'No, keep straight on!' but she turned the bike in a big circle to the left. She cut the engine and let the bike freewheel up the narrow alleyway towards the group. As they approached, the bike's headlight picked out four men and a woman. They were looking this way and that with worried expressions. At their feet was what looked like a coat, ruffled up into a mound.

Star felt Gwynfor jumping off the bike before she managed to stop – he almost tipped the bike over. But then, despite his haste to get off, he just stood, frozen. The five people stared at them. Then Star heard Gwynfor shouting.

He ran forward. One of the men made a half-hearted attempt to restrain him. Another was pointing up the alleyway saying 'two of them! We tried to stop them!'

Gwynfor was already pulling a dark blue cape off the body beneath. A long, howling wail came from deep inside his chest.

Star ran up, knelt to the ground and put her arm around his shoulders. At the same time, for the sake of her little notebook, she committed to memory the sight of what lay in front of them. From the position of the puddle of dark blood, she guessed Gwynfor's father had been knifed through the ribs.

6

Ben had persuaded Lara to stay for the fireworks. They stood side by side on the concrete parapet of the dam, leaning on the safety rail and looking out across the new reservoir. A crowd of New Warwick bigwigs – the lady mayor, council officials in suits, women in summer frocks and hats, even Alexander Laczko the Regional Commissioner – milled around chatting to each other under a striped awning at the far end.

He felt out of his depth mixing with the so-called cream of New Warwick society. But here was a chance to be close to her.

The sun was setting now, its rays casting giant caricatures of each of them across the shimmering golden water. Lara shivered. Ben took this as a cue and placed his left hand gently on the small of her back. He didn't care a toss if the high and mighty saw him with his arm round her. They'd gossip whatever you did.

They could see their two giants' hips touching briefly on the surface of the water. Lara gave him a tense smile and edged her back away from his hand. She turned her head, squinting into the sun, and raised one arm to protect her eyes. Ben knew every little angle, crevice and shadow of her beautiful face by heart.

'What's on your mind?' he asked. 'You seem a bit far away.'

'Sorry. Something's been on my mind all evening. In the courtroom today…'

She had to break off. The portly figure of Alex Blennerhassett, editor of the New Warwick Beacon, had detached itself from the nearby crowd and was rolling towards them. Of all the people in this crowd I didn't want to talk to right now, Lara said to herself, it's Blennerhassett.

'It's the fireworks any second,' Blennerhassett said. 'Not coming to join us?' He smiled and winked heavily at Ben.

God, thought Lara, look at the fat on him. Blennerhassett was wearing his off-white cotton suit; Lara had seen it many times before. It was creased and stained but it must have cost a fortune originally, cut as it was in a genuine Good Time style – and in genuine cotton too.

'Mr Blennerhassett,' Ben nodded, looking at the fat man steadily. 'All right?'

Lara decided not to say anything.

Alex exaggerated his operatic, mock hurt smile. 'Lara! You're avoiding me – why?'

Ben frowned. 'She's got a lot on her mind at the moment. If you'll excuse us, Mr Blennerhassett.'

Lara groaned inwardly. That was exactly the wrong thing to say.

The fat man's eyes widened in mock surprise. 'Oh, really?? What could possibly be disturbing the serenity of dear Mrs Johnson?'

Lara was tempted to say fuck off.

'Okay, she said instead, 'let's get it over with, Alex.'

Blennerhassett gave her a mischievous grin. 'Now what could you mean by that?'

'You haven't seen Miss Edkin since she left my court this afternoon?'

There was a twitch of annoyance on Blennerhassett's large round face.

'No. As a matter of fact Lara dear, I haven't. She should have phoned the office at six o'clock. 'Why? What has the young lady has been up to?'

He glanced down at his wristwatch, a priceless Good Time heirloom that gleamed silver-grey in the evening light. It was a mechanical action Tissot that had belonged to his great-grandfather. This man had passed the watch to Alex's grandfather who, Alex told everyone proudly, had been a leading reporter for The Sun, an important national daily in the days before the Pandemics.

'You might as well know now,' Lara said. 'I had to put a

44

censorship order on the final case in court today. Not because it was anything of importance but because I know how imaginative that young lady of yours can be.'

Blennerhassett's eyebrows lifted. 'Oh…?'

Before he could say any more, Lara said 'let's see the fireworks, eh, Alex?'

She linked her arm in Ben's and pulled him towards the crowd of New Warwick bigwigs. Looking back, she noticed the newspaper editor was following them with a cautious, thoughtful look on his face.

When they joined the group the sun had almost gone down. The slight figure of the grey-haired Lady Eleanor Pascal, Mayor of New Warwick, was stepping on to a wooden dais in front of the parapet railing.

'Ladies and gentlemen, it gives me grite pleasure…' (the Lady Mayor spoke with an old-fashioned West Midlands accent) '…and fills me with grite proyde in the achievements of ower community, to declare this dam owpen – on behalf of the citizens of New Warwick, South Mercia and the whole of Griter Ingerland.'

Eleanor Pascal reached down, holding her weighty mayoral chain to one side, as Ruth Brown, the chief city engineer, handed her a beribboned bottle of Best Hereford Champagne Perry. The bottle was attached to a length of white cord tied to the safety rail. The lady mayor balanced herself on the platform. She leant forward and then – with a nervous whoop – flung the bottle out and over the edge of the dam. It fell, swung and hit the light grey wall with a satisfactory smash. Fizzy wine spumed down.

Ben grabbed Lara's arm and pulled her across the parapet to the downstream side where they would be able to see the first surge coming from the turbine spillway. Within seconds a trickle of brown water was followed by a gushing creamy torrent.

Everyone else had rushed across to look as well. There were smiles and cheers as the crowd gazed down. Suddenly a line of multi-coloured lights sprang up on the south-east bank of the reservoir. They dimmed, then reached full power and glowed fully. Everyone cheered again. In the fading evening light Lara and Ben could just make out a line of spectators standing on a ridge beyond the reservoir perimeter. It looked as if the whole of the nearby village of Moreton Morrell had turned out to watch: mums, dads and children holding hands. A spectacle like this didn't happen often.

The fireworks started with a big ground-shuddering bang. The shock caught Lara unawares and she gave a little scream, grabbing Ben's arm before she could stop herself. She laughed, relaxing, and he squeezed her arm, grinning back at her. Then they stood straight, heads back, taking in the show.

For a few moments Lara forgot the courtroom, the fact that she was a judge and an adviser to important city government committees. She forgot David for a second.

And then she realised that she hadn't let go of Ben's arm. Nor had he let go of hers. She turned to look at his face. 'Isn't it terrific?' she said. 'I feel like I'm a kid again!'

'Yes.' Ben's throat felt constricted. It was terrible. David was in his mind, but he couldn't help it. He leant towards her and kissed her full on the mouth.

What surprised Lara was the delicateness and tentativeness of his lips as much as the kiss itself. Her immediate response was to kiss him back. Her body seemed to know very well what it was doing. She could feel herself melting, letting her tongue seek his.

'Oh, God!' she said, pulling her head back, shocked. What was she doing?! Had anyone seen?

She looked around to check – and that was when she saw the commotion – a stirring of loud voices around Blennerhassett.

People weren't looking at the fireworks any more. Something else must have happened when Ben was kissing her. It was getting dark now but she could just about make out a small wiry figure talking animatedly to the New Beacon editor.

Star Edkin was waving and pointing towards the city with one hand, holding her crash helmet with the other.

7

Star bumped and swerved her motorbike up the dusty contractor's road that led away from the Moreton Morrell dam. It was almost dark now. The bike's engine strained as she opened up the throttle after skirting each pot-hole. This is too much, she thought. The day isn't over yet and more's happened than in a whole year. And now I've got Lara Johnson – the Justice Lara Johnson – on the back of my bike! Unbelievable . . . yet there was the weight of the other woman's body as Star wove the bike this way and that.

She glanced over her shoulder and gave her passenger a reassuring smile. Lara nodded back but didn't return the smile. She was hanging on, her arms down by her sides, her hands tight around the side-grips. With her glittering posh dress and dignified expression she retained an oddly statuesque look as she sat bolt upright on the pillion. Star remembered a tattered history book from schooldays with pictures of ancient Egypt in it. It's like having a Sphinx on the back of my bike.

By the dam, when they'd started to move off, someone in the small crowd had thought to grab a fancy shawl and tie it hastily around Lara's shoulders as he jogged alongside the moving bike.

What was his name? Ben – that was it. She remembered Lara shouting that name, and asking him to follow them to the hospital as quickly as he could. There were whispers among those in the know about possible new loves in the life of the famous Lara Johnson – maybe he's one of them, thought Star.

She smiled to herself as she remembered how the high and

mighty judge had slapped a censorship order on her that afternoon. And now here she is, commandeering Star's motor bike and telling her to get them to the hospital!

The disbelief among that crowd of bigwigs had been something else – the women in their evening gowns and finery, the lady mayor with her gold chain, the men in their formal suits all staring at her, mouths dropping open. And that Ben sweating in his check shirt: he'd said wait, he could fetch the pony and trap.

Others had come forward – the lady mayor had offered her lumbering limousine and several others had cars, but valuable minutes would have been wasted. There was no doubt Star would get them there in the shortest possible time.

Alex Blennerhassett had waddled off as quickly as his fat legs could carry him, shouting to Star 'for God's sake girl, phone me when you get something! He was using the Beacon's only car to get down to the office and hold the front page.

They'd reached the main road now, which thankfully had been resurfaced. The bike's tyres hummed on the inky smooth tarmac. Star guessed that Lara Johnson, in her flimsy dress, low cut with shoulder straps, would be shivering despite the shawl. They were going really fast now. Star felt the pressure of Lara's body leaning in a little, pressing against her back.

Her heart skipped a beat as she remembered her other passenger that evening; how he'd pressed much more firmly against her. Poor Gwynfor! He shouldn't have to be going through this.

The mystery of having parents at all, real people that you knew and loved – and yes, sometimes argued with – crossed her mind yet again, just as it had a million times during her orphanage childhood. And what a terrible mystery, she thought, to be faced with losing a father like Gwynfor's so suddenly. What must it be like?

But there was this slender thread of hope. Hang on, she whispered to herself, hang on, Gwynfor's dad. They'd reached the last long straight stretch now. She opened the throttle as far as it would go. Needles and pins prickled inside her stomach. This could be a big story and she'd get there first.

In the daytime this road would be clogged with slow-moving carts from the countryside. They'd be carrying loads to market, long-distance wagons hauled by oxen or big carthorses. And there'd be gaggles of pedestrians, donkeys, wandering goats and sheep as well. Now it was empty, a black strip beckoning them into the darkness ahead.

Next to the Moreton Morrell hydro-electric scheme and Radio New Warwick, the Hospital of New Hope was the third pride and joy of the City State of New Warwick. Built brand-new and opened three years ago, New Hope consisted of a cluster of single- and two-storey brick buildings. This layout was designed to minimise the ever-present risks of cross-infection and contamination. Medical scientists in Oxford were leading the way in the recovery of antibiotics research and manufacture, but it was proving to be a long hard battle. This hospital was also the only place in New Warwick – in the whole of the Midlands, in fact – that could deal effectively with serious accidents and emergencies.

Star drove her bike right up to the front entrance. A large electric light covered with night insects cast a yellow glow over the turning area. She hurriedly lifted the bike on to its stand as Lara sprinted inside to find out where Gwynfor's father was.

Star caught up with Lara as she strode along a path beyond the reception building.

'He's in that one,' Lara said breathlessly, pointing to a long low building about fifty yards away, 'Ward C.'

They cut across a lawn and flowerbed and in through the main door, looking to left and right to check their way. Luckily a medic in a white coat, wearing a stethoscope, was already half-way down one of the long corridors. Turning round, he seemed to guess immediately who they were looking for. He squinted at them through heavy black-framed spectacles and waved.

'Dr Gupta,' the doctor introduced himself as they strode along the shiny linoleum.

'How is he?' asked Lara.

'He's clinging on. A miracle really. There was only one incision, as if his attackers ran away before finishing the job. But it is very serious. Normally a wound like this results in the lung cavity filling with blood. Then the lungs too. The patient drowns. He's struggling, but this hasn't happened yet. He's lost a lot of blood. A clot formed, but when he was moved…'

Dr Gupta pushed open a swing door and led them into the intensive care room. There was a strong smell of antiseptic. Electric

49

side lamps on the walls were glowing dimly. Two nurses were standing by a bed. There was a metal stand with two tubes dangling down towards the patient, one blood-red and the other with clear liquid in it.

Sitting close up to the bed, bent over and with his back towards them, was Gwynfor Roberts. As they approached, he looked up at them, his eyes red-rimmed and bewildered. He croaked something that neither Lara nor Star could make out.

Star put her hand on his shoulder. 'Is he still breathing?'

The young man nodded and blinked back tears.

His father looks very small now, Star thought. He looks even smaller than in real life. And then she caught herself: this was real life.

Sylvan's exposed chest had silver, grey and black hairs all over it. His tiny shoulders made him look even more child-like and vulnerable, but his large, out-of-proportion head with its grizzly grey hair gave him a noble appearance.

To Star it looked as if he was dead already: his complexion was grey-green, his cheeks sunken. Except, no, there was a faint movement in his chest. A tube carrying oxygen had been pushed into one of his nostrils.

Tears pricked her eyes and she couldn't fathom why. It wasn't as though Gwynfor's father was significant to her in any way. Her legs went weak and she felt dizzy. She dragged a spare chair to the bed and sat down beside Gwynfor.

Dr Gupta had taken the two nurses to one side and was talking to them in a low voice. They murmured a reply, and then the doctor turned to address the visitors. 'His pulse is very weak. It's very critical now that he's not strained in any way.'

Lara stepped away from the bed. 'Doctor, can I have a word with you a moment?' Gwynfor gave her an angry look. Star put her hand on his arm, pulling his attention back to his father.

'Listen, doctor,' Lara whispered, 'I know how important this is. I don't want to be responsible for this man's death if he's got any chance. But is there any way I could ask him just one question?'

Dr Gupta's face was expressionless. 'I know who you are. It's your missing husband, isn't it?'

Lara nodded. 'I had a chance to talk to him earlier today and missed it. Quite honestly, I don't know whether he knows anything significant, but in court today they were both vehement about it. I believe that if I could ask just one question…'

'It's too dangerous. And that young woman – is she a reporter? I don't want this man's life to be endangered for the sake of a newspaper. I've already had to ask someone else to wait outside.'

Lara studied his face. 'Oh?'

'Security police. A detective of some sort.'

'Look, don't you think the son should be talking to him at least? Keep his father going, keep him conscious?'

'He can hear us, it's true,' admitted Gupta. 'A moment ago he squeezed the nurse's fingers in response to her voice.' He thought for a moment. 'All right. It might be good. Let the son try a few words.'

A moment later Gwynfor was bending over his father again. Star could hear the Welsh words soothing, coaxing, swishing back and forth like small waves on a beach of smooth pebbles.

Sylvan opened one eye, then the other. It seemed to cost him a huge effort. His blue eyes no longer twinkled and they were unfocused at first. But then they fixed on the foot of the bed where Lara stood. She looked back at him, leaning forwards.

Sylvan's pupils dilated and his chest heaved a little. One of the nurses came forward to feel his pulse, saying in a loud voice, 'Easy now, Mr Roberts! Don't talk if it's too difficult.'

But Lara couldn't help coming round to stand right next to Sylvan's head, opposite Gwynfor. Her olive skin glowed in the semi-lit room. It seemed to breathe delicate perfume of roses over the deeply wounded man.

Sylvan had closed his eyes after the nurse had spoken but, sensing Lara's perfume, he opened them again. His eyes were smiling vessels of pity, love, regret all stirred up together. This beautiful woman had the burden of carrying on! He would be blessedly excused.

Lara had heard the son use a term of endearment, a Welsh word. She had no idea what it meant. But something told her to use it now, and to use his first name instead of Mr Roberts.

'Sylvan, cariad,' she said into the Welshman's ear. 'I'm looking for David. David Johnson.'

The father looked at Lara tenderly. He had been turning to go, climbing the mountain behind Llandynan towards the Horseshoe

Pass, faithful Seren at his heels, a wooden staff in his right hand, clear cold air of autumn in his lungs. You could breathe up here. Duw duw, what a difference! And look at that view. Llantysilia Mountain against a still, blue sky.

But now this woman with the golden voice had called him cariad; she had brought him roses from her garden to take with him. Gratefulness welled up in his heart. He had to stop a moment to thank her. It feels so good to be alive, he thought.

He decided to wait a moment where the path levelled out for a few yards and widened into a patch of grass surrounded by bracken. He noticed how diamonds from last night's storm had been strewn carelessly upon cobwebs in the bracken. They flashed and blinked in his eyes, like the diamond raindrops glittering on the dress of this kind angel standing over him.

'Da?'

Now that's Gwynfor, he thought. Sounded like he was at the bottom of a well or somewhere. He needs help. Sylvan managed, with a huge effort, to swivel his eyes to the left. Ah, there he was. He was all right. Words for his son were queuing in his mouth to come out, but he hadn't the strength to say any of them. He managed to drag the corners of his mouth into a smile and saw his son's eyes filling with tears. Don't cry, Gwynfor, bach.

Then Sylvan remembered that the angel woman was still there. He felt sorry for her too. She was still searching, whereas he'd already found his wife and home. And she was English, he recalled, though she didn't look English, more like those traders from countries beyond Spain...North Africa. He would need to use the English, though.

'Bronwen,' he said, quite clearly and distinctly, and then added something in a faint whisper that Lara, Star and Gwynfor failed to catch.

The three visitors stared at each other. Gwynfor was about to speak, bending over his father again, but one of the nurses put a restraining hand on his shoulder.

I'm glad I was able to do that, thought Sylvan, before I'm on my way. He'd come to a point where the path went through a narrow cleft in a huge grey rock. A spring of icy water trickled into a reddish-brown pool at the base of the rock. He decided to cup his hands and take a sip before carrying on. The water chilled his insides. It tasted of earth and roots. So cold now, despite the sunshine. High up now, see? He stamped his feet. Better get going, he thought, in case the weather turns. He whistled to Seren and took one last look at the sunlit valley below, before turning on his heel and striking out for the pass.

8

Afterwards, Dr Gupta took Gwynfor by the arm and led him into a side room. Star had made a move to go with him but an emphatic frown from the doctor made her fall back.

Gupta kept his voice low and allowed Gwynfor to sob quietly for a minute or two. He said how sorry he was that they hadn't been able to save his father. Then, in the detached way doctors have, Gupta told Gwynfor that he was to come back tomorrow with the name of an undertaker. There would be a delay before his father's body could be released; perhaps a few days. The authorities would want a full report. There would have to be an inquest. And he mustn't forget to register his father's death in the morning.

Gwynfor could follow only a few of these words. He felt terribly alone in this foreign land. And now his father, his guide, the one who told him what to do, had gone. There was a huge screaming void in his head; he couldn't think at all.

'How will I get my father back home?' was all he could think of to say. His voice croaked and was sore with the effort of saying just those few words.

Dr Gupta patted his hand. 'One thing at a time,' he said.

Gwynfor stumbled out of the doctor's office and found a door that led into warm, enveloping dark night.

There was no sign of Star outside, but that judge woman was waiting. He felt her hand on his arm. He stood not knowing what to say or do next. He wished she would take her hand off his arm.

Someone else was running into the area in front of the hospital now – a man in a check shirt. He was looking around, his eyes glinting in the faint light from the electric lamps.

'Ben!' Lara Johnson shouted. 'Over here!'

Gwynfor felt the English lady take her hand away. He stared at the man, who was walking quickly towards them. He was sweating and looked hot.

'You got here quickly,' Lara said.

'I brought the four-wheeler, both horses,' Ben panted.

Lara looked at Ben. 'It's bad news, I'm afraid.'

Gwynfor felt the man's hand – a big, heavy hand – fall on his shoulder. Why did they have to keep doing this, touching him? It was making it all too real. If only they'd stop looking at him this way and touching him, everything would be a dream and his father would still be alive!

'I'm so sorry,' Gwynfor heard the man say.

All Gwynfor could do was nod and fight back the tears. At that moment Star came rushing up.

'Ooh, sorry!' she shouted. 'I had to race across to that reception building. Beg the use of a phone.' Her eyes were wide with excitement. 'I caught the front page!'

What a crazy girl, Gwynfor thought. He felt his heart warming to her though.

She was looking down at the ground now. 'Sorry Gwynfor' she repeated. 'I got carried away.'

'It's all right,' he said, glad she wasn't making any attempt to touch or hug him.

Lara Johnson gave Star a disapproving look. 'We were about to sort out where this young man could stay,' she said. 'He can't be on his own–'

'–No, no, it's okay–' Gwynfor tried to interrupt, thinking of the hostel he'd go back to.

But Lara Johnson was ploughing on. 'Ben here can look after you,' she said. 'Can't you Ben?'

The man in the check shirt nodded. 'That's fine – er, Gwynfor is it? Yes if you want you can come back with me. Stay at the farm. I've got the four-wheeler here so no problem.'

'And you can bring him back in the morning, can't you Ben?' Lara said, giving Gwynfor a sympathetic look. 'You'll have to sort out an undertaker, but we can help you with that. Then they'll do the rest. You really shouldn't be on your own tonight,' she added.

Gwynfor wanted to say no, he'd be all right. Better to be in the hostel and be near his countrymen. He could talk in his own language and explain everything to them and they'd help him. But he couldn't get the English words out to tell her this. His throat had got paralyzed somehow.

There was an awkward silence with everyone looking at him.

'Is that what you want, Gwynfor?' Star asked. Or do you want to come back to my flat? It's not very big, but you can have the bed.'

Lara Johnson was shaking her head firmly. 'I don't think that's a very good idea.'

'What d'you want to do, Gwynfor? I promise I won't bombard you with questions. You can just crash out at my place.'

The formidable lady was fixing him with her eyes again.

'Gwynfor, Ben here has the four-wheeler ready and waiting. We'll leave now, go round to wherever you and your father were staying and pick up your things. And Ben will take care of you at the farm. It's peaceful and quiet out there.'

Gwynfor was summoning the will to say no, he'd rather go with Star, but before he could speak he was interrupted by someone coming up behind him.

There was a rasping cough. They all turned round to see a hard-bitten man in a worn-out leather jerkin standing near them in the darkness. He was smoking a foul-smelling cigarette. When he inhaled, as he was doing now, the tip of the cigarette glowed. Gwynfor could hear the crude tobacco crackling like a bonfire.

The smoker threw his cigarette end to the ground and stepped on it. Looking at Ben, he said, 'How far out is your farm?'

'It's about five miles south-east of the city boundary. Why?'

Lara Johnson was glaring at the man, clearly very angry. 'Yes! Who the hell are you?'

The man shrugged his shoulders, reached inside his jerkin and produced a large, heavy badge in a leather holder. He waved it at them all.

'Chief Inspector Mick File. Inter-Regional Security.'

'What?' asked Lara, glaring, 'Inter-Regional Security?! I've never heard of it!'

File gave her a pitying look. 'Not many people have.'

Lara Johnson raised her voice. 'You simply can't walk in here and start asking questions! What authority do you have? You have to get clearance from the city police!'

He stared at her in a tired way, like a teacher dealing with a slow-witted child.

'I'm working out of Oxford,' he said, producing another cigarette. 'And I don't have to get clearance from anybody.'

Lara looked like she wanted to carry on arguing but Ben put a restraining hand on her arm.

'Why did you want to know where my farm is?' Ben asked.

File ignored him, pulling a battered metal lighter from his pocket. The lighter clinked and he lit his cigarette. Inhaling, he looked at Star. 'And where's your place?'

'It's on the East Side, off Old Leamington Boulevard. Shakespeare Street, number forty-three.'

'Is there a landlady or a street warden or something?'

Star nodded.

'But otherwise quite anonymous? You could slip in and out?'

Star nodded again. 'Yes. If he wants to come with me, he'll be OK.'

'Number forty-three,' File murmured. He'd pulled out a little stained notepad and was writing the number down with a pencil.

'Look!' said Lara angrily, 'Are we sure any of this is right? This young man could stay here in this hospital, come to that.'

File grimaced. There was an awkward pause.

'And what did you mean, anyway?' demanded Ben. 'What's wrong with him staying at my place?'

File shrugged his shoulders. 'Probably be OK. I wouldn't risk it. It's more what might happen on the way.'

Ben stared at him.

Then Gwynfor spoke. 'I'll go with Star . . .' He bowed his head slightly towards her. 'On the motorbike.'

'What about your things?' said Lara. 'You won't be able to carry much.'

'We can leave them till tomorrow,' said Star. 'It doesn't matter.'

'You can forget his things for the time being,' File informed them, 'because the lad's kit and his dad's aren't in the hostel now. They're down at the central police station.'

'What!' Lara stared wide-eyed.

'No point going back to those lodgings,' File said simply,

putting another poorly made cigarette into his mouth. 'Scene of crime, all taped off.'

Now File was talking fast, seeming not to care whether Gwynfor or anyone else took in what he was saying. 'I'll get a proper look over your lodgings tomorrow, laddie. Fairly important as there's been a break-in at your lodging house – you didn't know about that did you? The local plods will do the fingerprints, get the woofers out to sniff your belongings, all the usual malarkey – mind you, fat lot of good that'll do! – and I'll see you in a day or two, eh, young man?'

When Star got Gwynfor back to her flat it was nearly two in the morning. Luckily the landlady had gone to bed. A small oil lamp glowed in the hall, sitting in a tray of sand. Star blew it out as they tiptoed past, as she was expected to do. Mrs James had got used to Star coming and going at all hours.

Once they were up the bare wooden stairs she fumbled in her jacket for the door key. As she did so she thought back to what that strange detective guy had been saying. What if someone was in there, waiting behind the door?

They came into the familiar stuffy atmosphere. It had been another hot day – she should've left the top window open. She saw Gwynfor sinking immediately onto the bed, sitting up but rubbing his eyes, trying to take in where he was.

The desk in the corner was cluttered with papers and files. The stained Good Time dressing table with its blotched mirror had two drawers half-pulled out: one drawer had a cotton shift and some underclothes dangling out of it. The narrow bed with its cheerful striped coverlet and single pillow was unmade.

Star slipped off her flat leather shoes and pulled back the torn and patched curtain that divided off the main room from the kitchenette. She took care to tread softly on the bare wooden floor.

'I'm getting something for you to drink,' she whispered.

She turned on the tap from the water filter and filled a small kettle, which she set on the metal tripod over the biogas.

By the time she brushed through the curtain again, holding two mugs of camomile tea, he was asleep where he sat. His body was tilting to one side over the pillow. Fetching two large cushions from the deckchair sofa on the other side of the room, Star propped herself up on the bed beside him.

She stroked his black curls and gently, gently, eased him down so that his head was resting on her lap. She carried on stroking his hair until she too dozed off, sliding down sideways to his level, cradling his heavy head with her small, slim body.

Neither of them noticed the gradual lightening of the sky two hours later, but by seven o'clock – another two hours – Star had woken again. Her neck was stiff. Her arms and back hurt from sleeping at such an odd angle.

She had a strong urge to sink down and try to sleep again in the lee of that wide, sheltering back of his. But no, she must get up.

Gwynfor was still dead to the world. She reached over for the pillow and eased it under his head. Then she got up, pausing for a moment to look down at him. She noticed a small brown mole on his left side. Then she picked up her towel from the rail on the back of the door and, snatching a fresh shirt and knickers, tiptoed out to the bathroom on the floor below.

As she rinsed her hair in the cold water of the washing bucket, Star pictured how the front page of the Beacon might look that morning. She squeezed excess water from her short hair. What mattered was her status in the office. She was starting to prove she really was going to be an ace reporter.

Star heaved the heavy bucket over to the sluice, tipped it and watched the grey used water gurgling away.

Her landlady didn't read the Beacon – she was Church of Diana and they thought the whole idea of newspapers and the work of journalists was evil. After all, Mrs James had explained to Star one day, it was 'the Damned Paparazzi' and 'the Devilish Tabloids' that'd been involved in the plot to end the life of Our Lady in this world.

But whether Mrs James read newspapers or knew what the historic terms 'paparazzi' and 'tabloid' actually meant was irrelevant now. It wouldn't take her long to find out who this shy, grief-stricken young stranger in her house was. As soon as she went out to the shops she'd hear the gossip and put two and two together.

Couldn't I take a chance? Star thought. Just smuggle him out of doors mid-morning, when her other five co-tenants would be out? That might work. Except she wanted to give Gwynfor the chance to stay more than one night.

Since she'd been in the house Star had twice let boyfriends

stay over. Each time there had been an embarrassing moment when Mrs James had walked into the hall as they were coming or going. She had an uncanny, almost telepathic ability to sense everyone's movements around this large, creaking wooden house. She wasn't that strict, and she didn't mind the occasional boyfriend staying over but she was incredibly nosey. If she did discover Gwynfor as the secret hideaway in the attic flat it would be all over the neighbourhood. Just what they didn't need. Star shivered. She'd have to tell Mrs James, hope she'd let him stay – and keep her trap shut.

She dressed quickly, brushing her fingers through her wet hair as she tripped down the wooden stairs.

When Mrs James opened her door to Star's gentle knock she saw her young tenant standing there with damp hair and a towel round her shoulders. To Mrs James she looked even more slight and elfin than usual. The landlady's heart warmed. She had a soft spot for Star, even though the silly waif wanted to be a journalist.

She often caught a glimpse of her when she was rushing to work in the mornings, and she'd shout 'Cheerio dear!' or 'See you soon!' One day, Mrs James said to herself, she'll see the error of her ways.

'Can I come in for a minute, Mrs James?'

'Come in, love, come in,' smiled the landlady.

Mrs James was a tall forty-something. She had long hair the colour of fading straw. This morning it was pinned up at the back with a big wooden spring clip. When she inclined her head she reminded Star of a picture of a giraffe she'd seen once. Not only because of her long, elegant neck, but also because of her liquid, trusting brown eyes.

Mrs James hadn't been up and about for long, yet already the heavy application of mascara had been made. It accentuated the naïve giraffe look.

'I feel completely undressed without the mascara,' she'd told Star one day. 'Why don't you try some, eh, love?' she asked gently. 'I can show you how to put it on.'

Mrs James saw Star as the poor deprived orphan girl who'd never had the chance to learn the womanly things of life. 'You'll have to excuse me,' she was saying now, 'afraid I'm not dressed yet.'

'Don't worry, Mrs James, please.' Star smiled at the shocking pink dressing gown. It was mock Good Time, quilted and made of the kind of rare artificial fibre that you couldn't find anywhere these days.

Thirty minutes later Star and Gwynfor were sitting at the dining table in Mrs James's sunny back room. Star's landlady had insisted. A large breakfast was absolutely compulsory.

'Oh no, Mrs James, really, please don't worry,' Star had protested. 'I don't know whether Gwynfor would be able to face any.'

Mrs James had stared at the thin girl. 'Ten minutes. Be down here, the both of you, and don't talk such rubbish.'

The day was going to be hot again. The two young people looked out through the open French windows at the landlady's small garden, which was overcrowded with lush beds of summer flowers.

Mrs James came rushing in with a large tray. She beamed at Gwynfor as she set down on the table small plates, cups, bowls, knives and forks, a large jug of creamy milk, a dish of white butter, a large earthenware jar of marmalade and a small basket with a dark brown loaf in it. The warm yeasty smell of recently baked bread wafted over them.

Then the long neck bent over Gwynfor. 'Now, Gwyn-Four,' she breathed.

'It's Gwyn-vorr, Mrs James,' Star interrupted.

'Oh, sorry, Gwynfor. Do you eat bacon?'

Gwynfor smiled back, absentminded. 'Er, yes. Thank you.'

'I thought you weren't allowed to have bacon in the house,' Star said to Mrs James, glancing across at the gaudy picture of Our Lady on the wall. It was well known that the Church of Diana had blended some Islamic beliefs and religious prohibitions into its theology, including a ban on eating pork.

'Oh well,' said Mrs James indulgently. 'Just now and again . . . most of my friends do, you know. We call it shush. Like, "would you like a shush sandwich?"' She laughed and went back into the kitchen.

'Diolch, thank you,' Gwynfor said to her retreating back. 'Did you tell her everything?' he asked Star.

'Not what happened before you got to New Warwick. But I had to tell her about...' she paused to find the right words '...what happened to your father. She'd have found out soon enough anyway. I told her why she's got to keep quiet about you being here.'

Star remembered the look of open-mouthed horror on Mrs James's face when she'd told her about the knifing and what had happened at the hospital. But as she'd hoped, the landlady's shock hadn't turned into a demand to get Gwynfor out of the house as soon as possible. Star knew that Mrs James loved dramas because, despite herself, she always wanted to hear the gory details about stories in the Beacon that she'd heard about. Now a drama was unfolding in her very own house! It was like a parable from the life of Our Lady Herself, a parable in which Mrs James could star as a minor saint.

Gwynfor was looking around the room now. He seemed too dazed to take much in.

Star leaned her head towards him. 'Has the Diana cult spread to Wales?' she whispered.

'No,' he said distractedly.

'They want to ban newspapers. And most books. There's a whole list. Mrs James is OK, though.'

Gwynfor pointed to a small marble altar in the corner of the room. 'What is that, Mrs James?'

Mrs James was coming in at that moment, carrying another tray.

'My Altar of Eternal Vigil,' she said proudly, putting the breakfast tray on the white tablecloth. 'Do you like it, Gwynfor?'

He had a nonplussed look on his face. 'It's very nice, Mrs James.'

She rubbed her hands and looked pleased. 'I thought you would! You look like a very spiritual young man to me!' She stood still a moment, and then said 'we await the great day when Her Spirit returns – and her flesh and blood – in a living body. She could return as a Prince or a Princess, man or woman!'

Then she gave a self-conscious laugh and touched her hair to check that it was still in place. 'Now, I hope you two are hungry!'

It turned out that Gwynfor really was. He was ravenous with that deep, keening hunger that comes when someone close has died.

As a very special treat Mrs James had gone to her larder and unsealed the airtight can of Arab coffee beans that lay on a cool, dark shelf at the back. Soon there was a bewitching smell that Star and Gwynfor had rarely encountered – the aroma of simmering coffee from freshly ground beans.

It was only when they were sipping from cups of the fragrant, bitter drink that Gwynfor said he'd suddenly remembered something.

'What is it?' asked Star.

'How could I forget her?' Gwynfor replied. 'She won't eat until I go there! She's trained that way, see.'

'Who? What are you talking about?' said Star.

Gwynfor looked at both of them. 'Seren!' Seren, our dog. 'You remember? I told the court how she found me in the forests – after we had to run away?'

Mrs James's eyes were wide. 'A special dog! Gwynfor, does it have miraculous powers?'

Gwynfor smiled. 'You could say that. Seren in Welsh means the same as Star, it does.'

Star grinned back. 'Where is she? I need to see my namesake.'

'She's at the stables, near where we were staying. We can't keep dogs at the lodgings, see. Da left her with the stableman looking after our horse, you know? The mare that Da and me escaped on.' There was a sudden catch in his voice. 'The only horse we've got now.'

'Has she got a name too?' Mrs James asked, intrigued.

'Of course,' said Gwynfor. 'It's Bronwen.'

As Star swung the bike left on to the Old Leamington Road at the bottom of Shakespeare Street she glanced to the right before twisting open the throttle and speeding towards the centre of town. They were heading as quickly as they could for the Northgate area where the traders' quarter was.

Mrs James had looked a little crestfallen as Star had insisted that she and Gwynfor had to hurry now, gulped down the last of the landlady's precious coffee and made for the door. But at least she'd managed to push a small package into Gwynfor's hand. It contained bacon and other meat scraps, a few bread crusts and some broken biscuits.

'For Seren,' she'd whispered, 'your wonderful dog.'

As they were getting on the bike, Gwynfor muttered 'Duw!' and said to Star, 'the trouble is the bloody dog won't eat this. But I didn't like to say anything.'

As they neared the market area near the city centre she had to slow the bike to walking pace. The road was congested with pedestrians, cyclists, horse-drawn vehicles of all kinds.

'I'll cut up there,' Star shouted to him, pointing to a narrow side street a little further on.

'OK. But could you stop at that butcher's? I need to get something else for the dog.'

Star was impatient to get to the stables. She'd been puzzling over his father's last audible word, Bronwen, and she couldn't wait to find out why the horse was significant. But she suppressed her urge to ignore him and coasted the bike to a standstill outside the butcher's shop.

Inside there were some translation difficulties. Gwynfor explained that he wanted a particular kind of meat for a dog. He didn't know the English word for lungs. The cheerful grey-haired butcher frowned, holding a hand up to his ear, puzzled by Gwynfor's accent.

Gwynfor, blushing, pointed to his chest, panting in and out. The butcher chuckled. 'Oh, you mean lights!' he beamed.

Star couldn't help breaking into a laugh, fishing out a fifty-penny piece to pay for the scrap meat. By that time the other customers were talking in more hushed tones, pointing to Gwynfor.

'What did he say?' the toothless old man was asking.

Of course, Star realised, they've all seen the front page of the Beacon.

'Are you the young Welshman? Whose father was murdered?' whispered a stout middle-aged woman.

It would have been polite to answer their questions but Star was in a hurry. She pushed Gwynfor into the sunlit, noisy street. As she revved the engine and the bike started to move off, she glanced behind to check for other vehicles and bicycles.

She noticed a dusty, dark blue Toyota in the line of vehicles behind them. Cars were unusual these days but not so remarkable in the streets of New Warwick, so she didn't think any more of it. It was only when they'd raced up the whole length of Boulevard Thesby and she'd checked in her side mirror that she noticed the car again, way behind, motoring along at a discreet distance, its windscreen glinting in the sun. Her heart skipped a few beats but she decided not to say anything to Gwynfor.

Five minutes later they were in the travellers' stable yard, a cobbled square surrounded by a high brick wall and, beyond that, by three-storey lodging houses. A small, taciturn man with leathery skin had appeared when Gwynfor jangled the bell at the gate. He nodded briefly, seeming to recognise the young man. He led them across the cobbled yard, strewn with straw, to a small shed behind the main stable block. He pointed at the door and left them. They could hear at least five dogs barking.

But Gwynfor's black-and-white collie was quiet, waiting patiently. Star was amazed. Seren's bright eyes were glinting with joy, but her tail was only wagging cautiously – as if to say, I know I'm not normally allowed to wag this. She must be starving, thought Star.

Gwynfor didn't show any emotion or stroke the dog. He let her out of the pen, talking a quiet stream of Welsh. Then he carefully opened the messy parcel of sliced-up cow's lung.
Star bent down. She couldn't resist stroking the dog's neck. Gwynfor shook his head. 'Sorry', he said, 'Don't fuss her. She might not eat then. You're a stranger to her, see.'

He set the parcels of food on the ground, outside, both the raw meat from the butcher and the leftovers from Mrs James. He nodded to the dog. Seren looked up at her master for a moment, an enquiring look in her eye, and then she began to eat hungrily. Star noticed that the wary dog ate only the raw meat; she left Mrs James's scraps alone.

The stableman was in the doorway holding a small, crudely made wooden bowl.

'Goat's milk for the dog – she wouldn't eat anything I left her.'

'Thank you very much, Mr Rogers,' said Gwynfor.

'Your father, he was a good customer here. Ten years at least.'

'Yes,' said Gwynfor.

'A very bad thing.' The stableman shook his head. 'You can't believe it.'

They stood for a moment and then walked around the corner back into the stables to look at Bronwen.

'There's no need for payment,' said the stableman impassively as the three of them inspected the mare. She was a grey with a full mane; she looked in good condition.

'Oh no, da would have wanted me to pay.'

'No, no,' the stableman replied, lifting up his hand. 'No, I won't hear of it. Only thing is, I'll need to know when you're taking her.'

'All right. I have to see about my father's funeral, and then I can tell you.'

As the two men talked, Star peered into the stall in which Bronwen stood. She's a fair size, thought Star, though she had to confess she knew next to nothing about horses – unlike her contemporaries, none of whom could afford the exotic luxury of a motorbike. The mare was snorting, lifting her head to reach some hay that was held in a wide fodder box fixed to the wall.

Star went into the stall and patted Bronwen's flank. It's just a horse, she thought; there's nothing else here. She sighed, looking intently into the stall's corners. There was yellow straw, horse dung, a warm sweetish smell. Nothing hidden, no clues at all.

Gwynfor was in the stall now with her. While he hadn't demonstrated any affection to the dog, he was completely different with the horse. Star stood watching him as he nuzzled the mare's neck with the side of his head, talked softly into her ear and stroked her. When he looked up, his long black eyelashes were tipped with tears.

She felt sorry for him but decided to ask the question anyway: 'Gwyn, why do you think your dad mentioned Bronwen at the end…?'

He shook his head. 'I don't know.'

She was wondering whether to ask him more questions when the stableman came up to them carrying two large leather pouches joined by a wide strap. They were standing in the yard now, just outside the stable door.

He held the saddlebags up to Gwynfor. 'D'you want these now?'

Gwynfor looked puzzled and didn't answer.

'Only your father left them with me for safekeeping with the saddle and the other tackle.' He shook his head. 'Feels like there's nothing much in 'em, but you could leave 'em here if you want, they'll be safe enough.'

Star was on tenterhooks but held her tongue.

'I'd better look inside them,' said Gwynfor.

The stableman handed the worn, tan-coloured saddlebags to Gwynfor without a word. 'Just give me a shout. I'm round the back at the smithy.'

Gwynfor unnotched the strap of one of the bags and lifted the flap. They both stared inside.

'Looks like computer stuff,' breathed Star, wide-eyed. She took out a plastic box. It was square and shallow with a transparent lid. Inside it there was a black plastic tray. And inset in that was a small shiny metal disc no bigger than Star's thumbnail.

'What's that, d'you think?' Gwynfor asked, mystified.

'It's a memory tab. For a computer.'

'And what's this?' He was holding up a tiny, black, oblong object.

'A memory stick. We've got one in the office. This is all Good Time stuff.'

'What are they for?' asked Gwynfor. 'Why did Da have these?'

'They're very precious. Didn't you know that you're supposed to have a special permit to carry these?'

Gwynfor shook his head. 'Da didn't talk about these things. But I think I know when he got them. It was a few days before we started out. A man, a stranger from England came to see him and Da wouldn't tell me why this man came.'

'Look at this!' Star had been unable to resist opening the other saddlebag. There was a large folded piece of paper inside; a chart of some sort.

This was why a saddlebag had been used, thought Star. The memory tab and the stick could have been carried unobtrusively in a leather purse, but not this sizeable chart. She opened the chart. It was large enough to make her stretch her arms wide.

'What's that?' Gwynfor squinted at it. It was incomprehensible to him.

'The top half is just lists of numbers. They've been printed by a computer. And the bottom half, see? It's a map.'

'You're right,' Gwynfor said. 'I recognise England and Wales but Scotland has been missed off. What are those rings on the map for? Big black rings.'

Before she answered, Star turned to get the sun behind them: it was dazzling them. She was facing the stable wall now, holding up the large chart. Suddenly it was pulled sharply. 'Gwynfor!' she scolded.

But Gwynfor hadn't touched the map. Star realised that he was staring, open-mouthed, at a small neat tear in the chart. She jerked the paper down quickly. There in the stable doorpost was a stubby crossbow bolt.

Star thought how peculiar it was that she had time to stare at the brightly coloured feather fletches on the end of the bolt. Gwynfor was also transfixed. Then he jerked into action, leaping for the open stable door. He made a grab for her arm, aiming to pull her inside.

'No!' she screamed, pushing him violently, using all her strength to knock him away from the door – though she also succeeded in knocking herself to the ground in the process.

She'd realised instinctively what would happen next. And sure enough, right there in the top section of the stable door was the second bolt – an evil little flower sprouting. It would have gone right into Gwynfor's back if she hadn't knocked him sideways. The noise of it hitting the door – a hollow thud like a big nail being hammered in – seemed to come as an afterthought. It was a sound that echoed in every cell in Star's body.

She scrambled to her feet. There were three simultaneous thoughts in her brain: he's going to die with the next arrow; I'm going to die; the bowman can't miss three times. It was like a nightmare in which you have to move or jump to save your life but you can't because every muscle's paralyzed.

It was Gwynfor's turn to act quickly. He yanked her arm with terrific force and they virtually flew to the corner of the stable block.

As they leapt around the corner, they collided with something bulky, leathery and immovable. Star had all the breath knocked out of her and staggered, fighting for breath. She found herself on the ground again, this time on her bottom her back to the shaded wall.

They'd run into a giant – a red-faced Viking with a blond-reddish bushy beard and moustache. His bulk was protected by a thick brown leather jacket covered with metal studs; he wore a leather skull cap topped with metal – like a giant version of the safety helmet Star wore on the bike.

The Viking grunted, squinting at them, a puzzled look on his face. He held a rifle loosely in his right hand, the long black barrel pointing upwards at about forty-five degrees. He motioned to them to stay quiet and to keep close to the wall.

Now he was stepping sideways a little, leaning cautiously outwards from the protecting shadow of the wall, his eyes focused on a high building opposite. It was from this direction that the bolts seemed to have come.

His rifle cracked twice. Loud but not as deafening as you'd think, Star told herself, though in truth she'd almost screamed when he'd fired it.

'Bagger,' the giant said quietly, looking down at his chest.

Star recognised the accent. A southerner. Then she noticed what he was staring at. It was the third bolt, sticking out from the top of his chest where the collar bone is.

The portly giant shook his head and looked at them with puzzled, pale blue eyes.

'Bagger me,' he said.

Star felt a hysterical urge to giggle. A crossbow bolt was sticking out of his chest and this mountain of a man was moving around in circles, talking in a quiet voice as if he'd stubbed his toe or something.

She heard another noise – a persistent cracking from the stable yard as if fire crackers were being let off. Once, in between the bangs, there was a tinkle of breaking glass from high up somewhere.

The giant was leaning against the wall at the corner again now, putting his head forward very carefully to the edge, his rifle cradled in his left arm this time. Star instinctively put her hands to her ears.

Another deafening bang and there was more tinkling of breaking glass.

'Hold it, Jeff,' a voice said from the yard. 'They've scarpered.'

'Bloody hell,' breathed the giant.

Chief Inspector File walked round the corner, shaking his head as he took in the sight of the bolt protruding from the giant's chest. There was a cigarette between his lips and he was holding a chubby black revolver.

'Jeff, Jeff, good God, this is the third time! You're just too big a sodding target.'

The giant propped his rifle against the wall. 'Fack off,' he said under his breath.

'Is it far in?' asked File, coming up closer, squinting and drawing on his cigarette.

'Nah,' said the giant, managing a weak smile. 'Had my

protection on, didn' I?'

File smirked at Star and Gwynfor. 'You two lovebirds okay?'

Lovebirds? thought Star. What?

'Were you following us?' she said to him. Was yours that dark blue Toyota?'

File nodded. There was respect in his eyes this time. 'That was us. Not the clowns with the bows and arrows.'

The Viking giant had undone the front of his leather jacket. He was lifting the right side of it, wincing. 'Ow! Lucky it was the collarbone, not an inch above or below, boss. It's bleedin' agony, actually.'

File sighed. 'They'll have to cut the jacket off around it. That's another one you'll be claiming for I s'pose. Just don't catch one in the dick next time. Expenses aren't a bottomless pit.'

Jeff grinned. 'They'd have to be a bottomless pit if my dick was involved.'

File stuck his revolver into a holster on his belt and took something else from inside his jacket – a black, chunky, oblong object. He tugged a thin metal wand out of it, flicking a switch as he did so.

Star was fascinated. She'd never seen one of these things before. Another new gadget to come out of Oxford.

The air around them was suddenly filled with a loud crackling noise. 'Blue One, Blue One,' File was saying repeatedly, 'Come in Blue Two.' After a few moments there was the distorted metallic sound of another man's voice.

Star couldn't make out much but it sounded as though their attackers had got away. File was talking to someone else now, calling in medical help to attend to giant Jeff's injury. Then, when he was talking to a third person – someone who Star felt was more senior – the radio went dead. File was saying 'We've got something interesting, boss' when he stopped mid-sentence, staring at the little black box, shaking it from side to side.

'They can't get the sodding batteries right' he said, fuming.

For a moment Star thought he was going to fling it to the ground, but instead he turned his attention to the stableman, who'd just come out to see what all the fuss was about.

'We're taking those with us' File said to the stableman, pointing to the saddlebags Gwynfor was still clutching.

Gwynfor didn't say anything, but lifted them to his chest. He didn't want to let them go.

'His father wanted him to have those,' the stableman said defiantly to File. 'And he left them in my safekeeping to make sure he did get them.'

'Well that's all right then,' File said, lighting a cigarette, 'the young lad doesn't have to leave them behind does he?' He had an amused look in his eye. 'Because we're taking him as well.'

It was only after Gwynfor had been taken away in the dark blue car that Star noticed something glinting in a patch of dandelions near the stable door.

The stableman had asked her if she was all right now – if she'd be alright on her motorbike. She said she would be, though she still felt shaken up and angry about Gwynfor being bundled into the car and her not being able to stop them.

She fetched her bike and wheeled it over to the spot where she'd seen the glinting. Looking quickly to left and right, she stooped down to feel around in the yellow flowers and dark green leaves.

Yes, there it was. It was the plastic box with the tiny metal memory tab fixed inside it. Somehow it had dropped out of the saddlebag when they ran round the corner. Star took out a red handkerchief and wrapped it round the plastic container. Then she placed the package in the box on the back of her bike, together with the spare crash helmet. She wheeled the bike back to the gate, gave it a vigorous kick start and roared off towards the Beacon office.

9

Rae liked Saturday mornings. Usually they were a time when she could put her feet up and have a good natter with Lara. Another supply of coffee beans had arrived in town last Wednesday. Esther had managed to buy two pounds of them in the market. Cost a fortune! But it was so nice sitting and having a coffee with Lara. She usually did her nails on Saturday mornings. They'd sit together on the big sofa and they'd put some Good Time music on the sound system, hits from the musicals were her favourite, and Arrow would be chattering, running to and fro fetching drawings for her mum to look at. Goodness knows, Rae told herself, the child sees precious little of her mother during the week!

On Sundays Lara would be in her study all day, likely as not, her nose in paperwork. Getting ready for Monday and the following week: all that work she had to do! Not just the court stuff but the umpteen committees she was involved with. Committees for this and committees for that! So Saturday mornings were a treat; a pleasant little island of relaxation.

But not this Saturday morning. Lara was like a cat on hot bricks.

'Come and sit down!' Rae said, patting the seat next to her on the sofa. 'The coffee's getting cold.'

Lara frowned. 'Okay.'

'What's up with you this morning?'

'What d'you mean?'

'You're dressed. You usually stay in your dressing gown on

Saturday mornings.'

'I've been trying to phone Kieran Tyler.'

Rae gave an exasperated sigh. 'Come and sit down for goodness sake!'

Lara sat next to her mother. 'I can try again in ten minutes.'

'Relax! This is your Saturday morning down time.'

Lara laughed. 'Down time! – what ancient phrase is that?'

Rae gave her daughter a rueful smile. 'You know what I mean. Don't give me cheek.'

Arrow bounced into the room carrying a black riding hat. She had a tentative smile on her face.

'Mummy, are we going to fetch Trixie this morning?'

Lara couldn't disguise her lack of enthusiasm. 'Oh. Well…'

Arrow was hopping from one foot to the other. 'Pleeez, Mummy!'

Rae looked at Lara. 'She's been waiting all week for this you know.'

'All right, all right!' Lara sighed. 'Yes, we will go–'

'–Yes-s-s-!' Arrow jumped up and down, grinning at her grandmother. 'We are going to Ben's this morning! We are going to fetch Trixie!'

'We're going to look at Trixie, Arrow,' Lara corrected. 'You can ride her round Ben's yard and the little field. We haven't decided yet when you can bring her here.'

'I'm going to get ready!' Arrow shouted.

'Can you wait until Mum makes one or two phone calls?'

'And then can we go and see Trixie?'

'Yes. Then we can go and see Trixie', Lara said – though these latter words were lost as the girl ran out of the room.

Rae pursed her lips. She was about say it's not as though you spend every hour of the day with your daughter, is it? Why don't you show a bit more enthusiasm? But she thought better of it. Instead, she poured some coffee into Lara's cup.

'What's the urgency about ringing Kieran Tyler on a Saturday morning?'

Lara gulped some coffee. Rae noticed she was avoiding her gaze.

'Well, something happened yesterday,' Lara said. 'Quite a lot happened actually.'

'Oh?'

'And Kieran Tyler's about the only one I trust to find out something.'

'I wish you wouldn't talk in riddles, Lara.'

Lara ran her fingers through her hair. 'It's just...I don't want to build up any hopes. In you or me.'

Rae studied her daughter's face and took a sip of coffee. 'Another sighting of David,' she said quietly, feeling a faint sinking in her heart.

Lara met her mother's eyes now. 'Possibly – I've got to talk to someone. Today if I can.'

'I see. And you've got to talk to Kieran Tyler.'

'Well, it's a long story, Mum. But Kieran might know where the person I've got to talk to is.'

Rae shook her head. 'Don't tell me any more. But Lara, you said it yourself. Be careful. Don't build up too many hopes.'

When Lara left the room, Rae felt guilty. She should've been excited when Lara told her there might be another lead opening up. Grabbed her by the hands and said don't build your hopes up too much, Lara, but I do, do hope this time they might find him! But no, she couldn't do it. Couldn't deny that sinking feeling; keep that sad look out of her eyes.

She'd always been able to see why Lara loved him. David was a fit-looking man, he had that boyish enthusiasm and he laughed a lot. Those sparkling blue eyes and that daredevil attitude – she could see why she'd been excited by him in the first place because she was a go-getter herself.

But she'd never been able to dispel that uneasy feeling when she was around him. Nothing you could put your finger on, exactly. He was always considerate towards her, made a fuss of her on her birthdays, never gave the impression directly that he wished she wasn't living under the same roof as them...but then again, she'd sometimes caught a rather cold look in his eye; a preoccupied look. Sometimes he'd seemed to look right through her.

Perhaps it was because he was Dr David Johnson, the great nuclear scientist. One Christmas-time, she recalled, they'd had a lot of their posh friends to dinner – people from the university, doctors and lawyers – that type.

There'd been a lot of loose, carefree talking and laughing. David's face had been flushed with a few too many mulled wines.

You couldn't hold it against him having a good time, fair play – all that hard work he did the rest of the year.

She'd been getting two pork joints from the pantry (she was doing a supper for twelve that night) and she had to make sure everything was ready. David and the other men didn't know she was within earshot and could hear them laughing and joking about her 'odd ideas'. At least she was pretty sure they were saying things like that. Making out she was an ignoramus.

Her face had gone red with anger. She could remember Lara asking her if she was all right. She'd been able to bottle it up, not say anything. But a moment's thought would surely have told him she could never have had an education as good as his; never had even the remotest chance of getting on like he had, with his posh parents and his lucky family who'd escaped every single Pandemic. What did he know about the hardships and difficulties she'd had to go through? There were things she'd had to endure that he could never imagine – things she'd never told Lara about. And it was all so recent! It felt like yesterday: the times when you were so hungry you had to give your body to a man for a scrap of food. The times when you thought you'd met a friend at last, just getting to know them and within a week they were dead – just another corpse to be thrown into the lime pit or onto cremation pile. And yet here was this young generation forgetting already.

And yes, David could put on a show of affection but had he really made Lara happy? Never convinced he was the right person for her. And now he's been gone two years, Lara's starting to make it to the top. That tells a story, doesn't it? He was holding her back.

Not that David would have tried to stop her in an outright way, no. But he wouldn't have wanted to play second fiddle. Too competitive. More than once I saw that look in his eye when he'd come home and she wasn't there – still in town in her office or sitting on some committee, probably – and he could be really bad-tempered. What he wanted was to be off on the next adventure, the next mission, so he could come back and impress everybody and be more in the limelight than her.

Rae put the coffee things on a tray and took them through to the kitchen. Stop thinking like this, she told herself. Get behind your daughter and hope they do find him this time.

Thinking about Lara put Rae in mind of her own mother. The swimming pool and the memory of the pink swimsuit. The touch of wet silky skin. The arms enfolding her, picking her up. The face a white oval, a blur, the trace of a smile…what she'd give now to have that blurred image focused and sharpened so she could see every detail! Did she have a nose, ears, eyes like mine?

Both her mother and father had died in the First Pandemic when she was a little girl. Then there'd been a succession of poorly staffed emergency orphanages and children's institutions until she'd reached the age of fourteen; after that a dispiriting string of boyfriends and mean-hearted men.

Until Hamid, Lara's father, came along. Rae was nearly thirty then, she believed, though she'd never known her exact age. She'd become a nurse. She was unqualified and little more than a domestic skivvy if truth be told, but it was a regular job at a time when getting any employment was like finding gold under your bed.

Hamid had been the first man Rae had ever felt she could trust. He was a trader with some kind of North African background, Morocco or somewhere he said, though he wasn't sure himself – he'd been orphaned by the First Pandemic too. He had no family that he knew of.

All he'd been left was a small stringed instrument, like a banjo but with a deeper more liquid tone. It had strings made of old Good Time nylon fishing line, and nearly always one was broken. He used to pluck it and play silly tunes. Generous, cheerful, warm and kind: those had been Hamid's trademarks. But then, out of the blue, he left.

There was no explanation – just a scrawled note 'Goodbye Rae, love Hamid' left on the kitchen table with five creased, greasy hundred-pound notes. It was hardly enough to pay for a week's food. She was eight months pregnant with Lara at the time.

So when David had disappeared without trace Rae had expressed suitable shock and surprise, but truth to tell she hadn't been surprised or shocked at all. In the back of her mind she'd been expecting it all along. Didn't men do this? Who's to know, she thought to herself, that this fine David hasn't found another woman somewhere?

And now two years had passed and she was ashamed to admit she was beginning to feel this guilty relief he probably wasn't coming back. She could run this big house for Lara, with Matt and Susan and Esther. And she could look after that little darling

Arrow while Lara kept on rising to bigger and better things.

While Rae was washing the coffee cups and saucers downstairs, Lara got to the phone upstairs. She was just about to dial the exchange to try Kieran Tyler's number again when it rang out.

'Mrs Johnson, it's Star Edkin.' The young reporter's voice was tight and edgy. 'I hope you don't mind me bothering you? Only something's happened.'

Lara tried to keep the frostiness out of her voice, still annoyed about what had happened with Gwynfor Roberts the night before. 'You're not bothering me – go on. But remember we're on the phone.'

New Warwick's recently installed phone system had no direct dialling. All calls had to be routed through an operator at the central exchange; the city's telephone operators were notorious eavesdroppers and gossips.

'Gwyn– sorry, the person we were at the hospital with last night has been taken away.'

'What! Taken away? Who's taken him away?'

'That man…you know, the one who was in the special police – File. They said it was for his own protection.'

'The young man we're talking about – is he in the central police station?'

'I don't know.'

'I thought he was safe staying with you.' Lara couldn't help an accusatory note creeping in.

'I was there, with him. Something . . . happened, Mrs Johnson, just an hour ago. Someone tried to kill us.'

'My God! Who? How? What happened?'

Star told her the whole story in a rush, not stopping for breath.

'Phew! And you – are you all right?'

Star's voiced cracked a little. 'I'm all right Mrs Johnson, thank you. Listen, I was wondering if I could come out to see you. There are other things you need to know.'

'Where are you now?'

'The Beacon office.'

'Aren't the senior staff handling this story? Is Alex Blennerhassett in the picture?'

'One of the staff will be phoning you, Mrs Johnson. We will

be running a big story on this. But it's important for me to see you, honest.'

'All right. But everything'll be off the record. OK?'

'Cool! When can I come?'

Lara twisted a coil of her hair, remembering Arrow and Trixie. 'I can't do the next few hours. How about later, about four? And Star?'

'Yes, Mrs Johnson?'

'Thank you.'

When the young reporter was off the line Lara picked up the receiver again. She jiggled the cradle to get the operator.

'Hullo caller, what number?' asked a drowsy female voice. Lara glanced across at the grandfather clock on the landing: it was getting on for eleven o'clock already.

'Inspector Kieran Tyler's home number, please.'

There was a pause. 'Hang on please, Mrs Johnson.'

Lara heard a click, a ringing tone and then, very distantly, the operator speaking. There was a pause, followed by another click. Lara suddenly felt a tug on her leg. It was Arrow jumping up and down, complete with riding hat.

'Mummy, are we going?'

'Yes, be quiet a minute,' whispered Lara.

'Mummy, when?'

'In a minute. Wait! Hello?' She'd heard Kieran Tyler's voice.

'Hello, Mrs Johnson. Sounds like you've got your hands full there.'

'Ah, Kieran, I'm so sorry to trouble you at home – Arrow, stop it!'

Tyler chuckled. 'I know what it's like. We're in the middle of getting a barbecue ready. Got my wife's family over.'

'Oh I shouldn't have bothered you.'

'It's OK. What is it?'

'I think I've got a new lead on where David is.'

'Go on.'

'You know that killing yesterday, the knifing?'

'I wasn't on duty but I heard about it. The Welshman.'

'The murdered man – he knew where David is, I think.'

There was another pause. 'I see.'

'And Kieran, there's been an attempt on the life of that man's son. Just now. I've had Star Edkin, that young reporter on the

Beacon, on the phone.'

'I know her.'

'She and the young Welsh guy both nearly got hit. Crossbow attack. They were at a stable in the traders' quarter somewhere.'

'Where's the Welsh lad now?'

'That's the thing, Kieran. That's why I've phoned you. Some police unit I've never heard of, Regional Security or something, have taken him somewhere. Who are those people?'

Lara heard Kieran sigh. 'New outfit, England-wide. They can pull rank anywhere.'

'Somebody called File seems to be in charge.'

'I see. So File's got him.'

'I know this is a lot to ask but I really need to talk to that young Welshman. His name's Roberts. Is there any way you could help? Find out where he's being held?'

Inspector Tyler laughed. 'I needed that perfect excuse to escape the in-laws.'

'Kieran, I didn't mean straightaway–'

'–No worries, I'm on my way!' he laughed. 'But Lara,' he said, his voice turning serious, 'take care won't you? Only the usual precautions. Just keep an eye out, you know? Do all the sensible things.'

10

When Lara and Arrow strolled into Ben's farmyard, hand in hand, they found it deserted. So were all the stables, the big barn and the other buildings. They clanged the bell outside the front door of Ben's house. No one came. Arrow looked up at her.

'I'm really sorry, chicken. Mummy forgot. It must be the harvest.'

Ben had been harping on about it for weeks – how it was always tricky to work out when it was just the right time to get the wheat in, how you had to hire the horse-drawn reaper-binders and co-ordinate with the neighbouring farms who'd be hiring the machinery next – she'd forgotten all this.

Arrow had already run across the yard to look in the paddock beyond for her beloved pony. Lara followed her. Someone else was over there in the field, a dark figure approaching. Her chest tightened. She tensed herself, ready to grab Arrow and run. But it was just Old Dom, one of Ben's farmhands, a whiskery stooping figure in old woollen trousers, tied at the leg bottoms with string. He'd come on his ancient pushbike, which she could see propped up against the hedge. He looked up and waved stiffly to her, smiling.

It was mid-afternoon by the time Lara and Arrow started to walk home. They had to get back in time to meet Star Edkin. Lara had had to drag Arrow away from playing with the other kids on the edges of the wheat fields, excited by watching the plodding horses

81

and the clanking reaper-binders.

Now, as they walked home in the afternoon heat, Arrow kept stopping to pick wild flowers from the hedgerows beside the dusty track. They each had sizeable handfuls: buttercups, poppies, wild pansies, reddish-purple vetch. Arrow had some pink corncockle from along the edge of the field where they'd watched the harvesting.

The girl was dragging her feet. Lara tried to hurry her along, but stopping to pick flowers was the payback for missing the pony ride that morning. Every time they stopped she looked anxiously through gaps in the hedge, scanning the fields beyond, pretending to Arrow that she was looking for another flower.

We should have left earlier, she thought. No one had a watch, of course. They'd sat picnicking in the shade of a wide hawthorn hedge until Ben and the six or so farm workers all suddenly stood up as one, without any signal or warning, brushing crumbs from their rough farm trousers. It was time to work on the wheat again.

Out of respect for Ben and Lara, the farmhands had sat in a group a little way off while they ate their sandwiches and swigged rough cider from large brown bottles. They'd chattered politely, sounding like the low hum of bees, no swearwords or expletives audible.

She'd had to get used to this since becoming a justice: the way ordinary people tended to stop talking to each other when she appeared, then smiled at her in a polite, slightly awkward way.

Since she was seventeen Lara had got used to the way men's heads turned as she walked past them. In fact she remembered smiling to herself about this one hot summer's day in Oxford when she was in her final year. She'd gone to sunbathe with some of her friends down by the river. Lying on the cool, damp grass, she'd thought: it's too easy. I don't even have to make an effort in any way; the men's eyes still track me. There was a silly randomness to it – who was attractive to men and who wasn't.

Ben knew he didn't easily fit into what he called 'the top circle' that Lara moved in – the barristers and lawyers, the deputies and officials who ran the legislative council. He'd liked it sitting with Lara and Arrow in the field, a cloth with food spread out between them, a little apart from the boys with their cider and grinning faces.

And I do have a lot to be proud of, he thought, scanning the unbroken line of tall golden wheat still to be harvested. I was orphaned and I've managed it all on my own. Okay I don't have the education and I don't read books but I'm a farmer with this tidy lot of land and that's something vital today.

Every summer the Beacon listed the size of the wheat harvest in each of the districts around the city, with individual farms mentioned if they were especially productive. Ben was hoping for a three-star mention this year, he'd told Lara.

Earlier on, seeing her entering the field with the little girl he'd had butterflies in his stomach just thinking about last night by the reservoir. That kiss: she'd definitely responded to him. She would again soon, he felt sure. The trouble was, with Arrow running around and the men nearby they hadn't had much chance to talk. When it was time for them to go he'd managed to squeeze her hand briefly and ask her if he could call on her later in the evening. She hadn't squeezed his hand back but she had said yes, okay that'd be fine, so that was great.

Now, as they unharnessed the horses and led them to the deep shade of the drinking troughs by the hawthorn hedge, Ben wondered if the men had noticed how he was looking at Lara. So what if they had? He didn't care.

When Lara and Arrow got home Star Edkin had already arrived.

'You've got a visitor,' Rae shouted from the kitchen.

Arrow ran into the cool kitchen ahead of Lara, then stopped, holding one hand shyly against her mouth and staring at the young woman who was sitting at the big kitchen table, her elbows on the pale scrubbed surface. Rae, squeezing lemons over a shallow bowl, smiled and looked at her granddaughter. 'I'm doing lemonade,' she explained. 'Say hello to this young lady, won't you? She's called Star.'

Star smiled at Arrow, who stood still, maintaining her silence, hand still in mouth. 'Lemonade's very special, isn't it?' Star said. 'I haven't seen lemons for a long time. They come from France and Spain.'

Arrow nodded. 'I've seen rabbits today,' she said solemnly. 'At Ben's farm they were running away from the machines. In case they got killed.'

'Oh, I see.' Star smiled again.

Her big, dark eyes, lean wiry body and short, spiky hair seemed out of place in this calm, cool kitchen. To the child it seemed as if a fascinating wild animal, a fox or a female wolf had come inside and was sitting at the table. Her front teeth very big and white, and she was emitting a strange musky odour; not unpleasant, definitely strange.

Lara came in. She'd had time to wash the perspiration from her face and to brush her hair.

'Hello, Star.' Her voice echoed in the large kitchen. 'Is my mother looking after you all right?'

'You might've said, Lara,' scolded Rae. 'I didn't know we were going to have a visitor. I haven't made a cake or anything.'

'I thought we'd be back a bit earlier, Mum.' Turning to Star she said 'but I bet my mother's already tried to force-feed you, cake or no cake.'

Star smiled. The thought of actually going into the home of the famous Lara Johnson had been intimidating at first. Now it seemed a lot more ordinary.

'She won't touch a thing,' Rae said, looking at Star's skinny frame.

'Would you like to see my room?' asked Arrow. She was excited now, standing on tiptoe.

'In a few minutes, Arrow,' Lara said. 'Star's a special visitor, and she's going to talk to me for a little while first. Why don't you help your grandma with the lemonade and then you can bring us two glasses on a tray.'

Lara led Star from the kitchen to the library, which was on the ground floor on the east-facing side of the house.

Star took in the quiet luxury of it all. Wellbrook was an old house, early Victorian by the look and feel of it: high ceilings, well-polished oak floors strewn with richly patterned rugs, a chandelier in the hallway, a huge mirror in its gilt frame, a Good Time 'modern' vase on a special stand, landscape paintings on the walls retrieved by the New Warwick authorities from the abandoned art galleries of big cities like Birmingham and Wolverhampton.

In the library Lara closed the door behind them and motioned for Star to sit in one of two small armchairs beside a window. Star noticed the impressive lines of red leather-bound scholarly books on the shelves that lined two of the walls.

'So what have you come to tell me?'

Star told her that Gwynfor had explained 'Bronwen' was the name of his father's horse. That they'd gone to the stables. And how that had led to the stableman giving Gwynfor the saddlebags.

'What was in them? Did you get a chance to look?' Lara's green-gold eyes darkened. The big cat getting ready to pounce.

'We only got a moment,' Star explained, and then she told Lara about how the crossbow bolts had started whizzing past their heads. 'One saddlebag seemed to be empty, but then we found a memory stick and a case with a memory tab in it. In the other saddlebag there was a big chart.'

'You mean, you went through all this just this morning?' Lara looked shocked.

Star nodded, surprised to find a single tear pricking one eye. She sniffed and took a deep breath.

'And where are those things?'

'The special police took everything when they took Gwynfor away.'

'Damn! You didn't get any idea of what the memory tab might have had on it? There was no label on the case?'

The little gleaming metal wafer that Star had picked out of the dandelions by the stable door was burning a hole in her pocket – or more precisely in the red kerchief that it was wrapped in. She'd decided not to mention anything about that tab. She wanted to see for herself what it contained.

'There was no label. And I was only able to hold up that chart for a minute.'

There was a pause. Lara frowned, looking through the window at the neatly mown lawn and the white dust and gravel on the driveway.

'But what I did see – or I think I saw,' continued Star, 'is that the chart was something to do with radiation. Nuclear stuff. And I remembered that that was what your husband was working on when he disappeared. Also, I did notice there were some Welsh names or words in the printed notes along the bottom.'

'Can you remember any of them?'

'I'm sorry, I honestly can't. It looks so strange, that language. But Gwynfor might have recognised something.'

Lara nodded. She had to see that lad.

Half an hour later Star Edkin was on her motorbike again, heading back towards New Warwick.

She'd been with Lara Johnson another five minutes before there was a hesitant tap on the study door and Arrow had come in, walking slowly, serious-faced, shakily carrying a tray with two tumblers of home-made lemonade on it. Star had gulped down the drink, intending to leave right away. But there'd been no way she was allowed to go without eating something – Lara's mother had forced her to eat two shortbread biscuits.

As she took off on the motorbike, accelerating down the gritty driveway, Star glanced back at the three generations of Johnson females standing on the front steps of their grand house – Lara the tallest; then the dumpy figure of Lara's mother in the middle; the little girl Arrow next to her.

The sun was lower in the sky now; it had gone five o'clock. Strong rays blinked and flickered through the trees, which is why she was dazzled for a moment and had to look down. And which is why, as she sped past, she didn't see the two shadowy figures crouched in a spinney to her right.

Instead of taking the main road back into the city, Star turned left on to another unmade road two miles further on. She was going due west now, directly into the early evening sun. People working in the fields looked up as she passed, waving to her noisy bike and its following plume of dust. The wheat harvest was going full tilt.

In another mile Star had come to the Old Warwick Road – a paved road, much patched and mended – which she'd been told had been called A429 in Good Time. She turned right onto this road and headed north. It skirted the western edge of New Warwick: she could already see and smell, to her right, the familiar untidy jumble of out-of-town sheds, workshops, greenhouses and rubbish dumps.

Star had always liked this road. Here, on the western fringe of the growing urban settlement, it always seemed so busy and full of life. In winter the roadsides were brightly lit with cheap and cheerful burger stalls and takeaway tandoori joints.

And yet a few miles out of the city, either to the north or the south, this road soon became deserted. Unlike the trunk road to Oxford, which was busy with horse-drawn carts and lumbering loads the whole of its length, the old A429 always conjured up in Star's mind the lure of escaping to empty and forbidden areas.

Now, as she headed in the opposite direction, due north, Star came to the end of the free section of the A429. Up ahead were the toll gates that barred the entrances to the old great motorway road that in Good Time had been the M40. It ran south-east to north-west at this point. Beyond the M40, continuing north, there was another old-time road. It was in very good condition, but it soon petered out in the ruins of what had been, decades before, a large industrial city called Coventry. It was this latter road that Star was heading for.

There was a scowling old man in the box at the toll gate. He demanded seventy-five pence. Star threw him a fifty-penny and roared the bike around the barrier before he could do anything.

As the bridges over the old motorway were blocked off, Star took her bike down a short-cut – a steep, narrow, unmade track. This led in half a mile to the excellent road north that was unusually well maintained, straight and fast. Only one carriageway had been kept open, of course – the other, its lost partner, had been abandoned many years before. The abandoned side was now completely obscured by brambles and thickets of buddleia, willow and alder.

There was no other traffic. Star was able to push the bike up to eighty. At this speed it didn't take her long to reach the turning for the university; it was just a few miles. On the university road it was back to much slower speeds. In places the road had become little more than an overgrown track. Trees arched right over it, their branches coming down dangerously low. Tall drifts of dried-up brown grass filled the middle of the road, and Star had to cross through these from time to time, scattering clouds of seed behind her as she did.

In another twenty minutes she reached the gatehouse of the university. She stopped the bike at the barrier, showing the large pink-faced porter her press card and passport and explaining to him where she was going. He nodded, handing her a visitor's form to fill in. As she did this he lifted the barrier and explained where the mathematics and computing building was – though she knew already.

Most of the original Good Time university buildings had been abandoned many years ago, their large plate glass windows removed for safety and replaced with boarding – though much of this, too, had since rotted and fallen away, leaving large black rectangles where futuristic tinted glass had once reflected the sun. The sound of the bike's engine echoed emptily off these buildings, now mere shells of what had once been busy places for academic gossip, endless meetings, students sitting for hours in front of screens and computer monitors, lecturers receiving and sending thousands of emails every day.

Star swung her bike around a bend and passed the shanty town of small, clapboard houses that had been erected for the six hundred or so students, and came up to the mathematics building. It was fronted by neatly cut swathes of lawn dotted with small groups of birch trees.

She switched off the engine and coasted the bike round the back of the building, where she'd arranged to meet Butcher. She wheeled the bike round a corner, hiding it behind a large bush, and quickly opened the box on the back. She put her helmet inside and took out the small plastic case in the red handkerchief.

Butcher had seen her – she'd seen him wave from a ground-floor window. Then she heard a lock turning in the door. It swung open, Butcher's head poking round. He was her age – they'd been close buddies ever since orphanage days, more or less like sister and brother – though he was much taller than Star. Butcher had a shock of greased black hair that stood in a vertical brush above his forehead and there were permanent shadows around his eyes. He looked like a startled raccoon.

'Come on then,' he said, motioning with his hand. He gave her an anxious look. 'You took your time.'

'Sorry,' Star said, going in.

Butcher was wearing a white coat. He had a spare one under his arm, which he handed to her. 'Put this on. Be a technician like me, eh?'

Star struggled into the long white coat. It looked ridiculous – so long it almost reached her ankles. She tried to suppress a laugh. Butcher giggled too. 'Keep it on, though,' he said, his face straightening, 'in case anybody comes. Wait here a minute. I'll put the generator on.'

Butcher disappeared down some stairs that led to the basement level, skipping two or three steps at a time. He was back within three minutes.

'We can't be too long,' he panted. 'There's no one else in the building, not usually at this time on a Saturday. If anyone hears the generator they might be suspicious. And then I'll be in deep shit.'

Star could hear the distant throb of a bio-diesel engine. 'I really appreciate this, Butch.'

He led the way up three flights of stairs to a corridor on the west side of the building. It was flooded with evening sun, hot and airless. He opened a door into a large darkened room full of desks and computer screens. As they went in Star noticed that the air was cooler.

'Air conditioning comes on with the power,' Butcher explained, leading her to one of the nearest desks. 'OK. Where's that tab?' He pressed something on an oval box at his feet. The screen in front of them lit up, went black, then lit up again, bathing them in blue light. Star undid the red kerchief, opened the case and took out the shiny coin-sized memory tab. 'Mm,' he said, taking it from her carefully. He pressed a button on the front of a computer and a tiny tray emerged. He pressed the tab on to the tray and pushed it back in.

Star had seen this procedure twice before, but at the Beacon she hadn't yet graduated to the status of computer user. Only the privileged few were permitted to go into the room with the sacred machine in it. Star had occasionally been allowed to watch but she'd never so much as touched a computer or a keyboard.

Year by year computers were becoming ever more temperamental, scarce and valuable. Apart from the stock of machines at the university, only some government offices and a few businesses, including the Beacon, had one or two each. Getting rebuilt computers from Oxford was virtually impossible these days, so starting a computer research and rebuilding facility had become a top aim of the university.

Butcher was tapping the keyboard rapidly now. Star found it hard to decipher what was on the flickering screen. In this respect she was typical of her age and generation. Hardly anyone, except for lucky or talented individuals like her companion, had ever been exposed to visual images on TV screens or computer monitors.

Star could just about follow the stories in the ancient Good Time films and cartoons that were replayed from time to time. But the content – that strange lost world of big buildings and streams of cars and glossy people talking too fast – was alien and hard to understand. And the visual tricks they used were confusing, the way the images jumped about and scenes shifted without warning.

By leaning forward and concentrating, Star could make out what was on the screen now. It was a simple message in a box:

The contents of this tab are encrypted
Enter password:

*****

'What does that mean?'

'I can't open it unless you know the password.'

'Password?' Star couldn't hide her disappointment. 'I didn't realise . . .'

'You haven't got the first idea, have you?'

'This tab was being carried by that man who was murdered yesterday.'

Butcher's eyes widened. 'Fuck me! Not that guy who was stabbed?'

'Don't breathe a word to anybody for Diana's sake.'

He shook his head. 'No. Course not.'

'I'm trusting you, Butcher.'

'Yeah, yeah, OK . . . but that's kinda irrelevant if we can't see what's on it.'

Star sighed.

'It's got to be five letters. Look at the number of asterisks.'

Star bent down again, peering at the screen. She thought about Lara's missing husband. 'Try "David".'

Without comment Butcher turned to the keyboard and tapped in D-A-V-I-D.

'Nope.' The words 'Invalid Password' showed on the screen. 'What about the Welsh guy's first name?'

'Yes! "Sylv" something.'

'Sylv? That's only four letters.'

'Sylvan!'

'That's six, stupid.'

Star pulled a face.

'Never mind,' said Butcher, 'something might come.'

They tried all sorts of words; abbreviations of names such as 'J-O-H-N-S' and 'D-J-O-H-N', to no avail. The 'Invalid Password' message kept coming up.

'D'you know any names of nuclear power stations?' Star asked at one point.

Butcher raised his eyebrows. 'What?' He glanced anxiously at a large clock on the wall.

'We'll have to give up,' Star sighed again. She turned away and went to a window, parting the wooden slats of a Venetian blind to look out at the shimmering leaves on the birch trees below. The evening shadows were getting longer. She shivered; the air conditioning was making the room quite cold now. Butcher was tapping the keyboard, trying random letters.

Star turned back to look at the screen, her eyes readjusting to the darkness of the computer room. A sequence of images from the previous twenty-four hours reeled through her mind. The most vivid one, the most terrifying, was the image of that short metal shaft; the deadly crossbow arrow that had suddenly sprung out of the stable doorpost.

'I think I'd better shut down,' Butcher said, glancing up at the clock again.

'No, wait!' Star lifted an arm up high. 'Try Arrow.'

Butcher shrugged his shoulders. 'OK, one more go, then. He hurriedly tapped out A-R-R-O-W. The screen suddenly blossomed.

'Mint!' he shouted.

'Wow!' screamed Star. 'I knew it. It's his daughter.' She jumped over to the monitor, getting up close and trying to read every word beneath each of the icons that had appeared on the screen.

'Whoa, sister,' Butcher said, smiling, pulling her back a little. 'I can't see. Wait, look, I'd better open this one first.'

'Whoa, brother,' Star grinned, digging him in the ribs.

'Stop it!'

'What're you doing now?'

His fingers were racing over the keyboard. The computer whirred and groaned a little. She looked at the clock. It was almost seven – they'd been there nearly an hour.

'Here we go. I can open the documents now. There are six files, Star. Whoa! They're big, man, two of them anyway. You won't have enough time to read 'em.'

'What are they?' Needles were pricking inside Star's stomach.

'Which one should I open first? What about this one?' He pointed to an icon in the top left-hand corner of the screen. Star squinted at it.

'Bullion supplies?' she said, puzzled.

'There's this one, 'Currency, the new..."

Star frowned. The words underneath each icon didn't make any sense at all. There was nothing about nuclear power and nothing obviously linked to David Johnson.

'Um, let's try that one first.' She pointed to another icon at the bottom of the screen. The word 'Message' was written beneath it.

'Yup, good choice. Not much in it, so you can read it quickly,' Butcher said, double-clicking the mouse.

A page of text – only a paragraph – came onto the screen. Star stood back. Her eyes were swimming.

'Shall I print it? It's only one page.'

She nodded. The printer began to whine and she heard paper sliding in. She felt her heart thumping as she read:

TO: *Section 1, Office of the Prime Minister*
FROM: *Arrow*
FOR THE EYES OF THE PRIME MINISTER AND SECTION 1 STAFF ONLY

Butcher whistled through his teeth.

Star said 'leave this to me. Don't breathe a word to anybody. You haven't seen this, OK? In fact, don't look – it'll only get you into trouble.'

But despite her warning they both found themselves staring at the screen. Star couldn't make sense of the message, but particular words and phrases seemed to jump out:

Risk assessments...containment...offensive possibility still v. real... plans for a new currency...I'm in W now...

'Can you save this somehow?' she asked him, 'this and the other files? I mean, if the tab gets lost . . .'

He shook his head. 'It's too risky. Someone would find the file. If it's this hot...'

Star nodded. 'Is there any way you could print them?'

By now Butcher had clicked on another icon and had opened the 'Currency' file.

'What, each document? It'll take ages, man. I mean, look at this one – over a hundred pages. Did you bring any paper?'

She shook her head. 'I didn't know to bring any...'

He grimaced. 'When the office release paper it's like they're giving you their own blood or something. Oh well, they won't miss twenty pages or so I s'pose. I could print the first few pages of each document.'

'Yeah, good idea. Let me look at this one.'

As Butcher activated the printer Star focused on the screen again, reading through the text. The printer began to whirr and the first page of the second document started to shush into the tray.

It was then that they heard the sudden bang of double doors on a floor below.

11

Ben couldn't hurry the men away. They'd worked hard enough and been willing to stay on late. It was a Saturday night and their wives had appeared with more food and cider. They'd be expecting a bit of a sing-song and a harvest party, of course. He shook his head. Should've thought of that. He'd had to break it to them: he hadn't got a keg in yet. He could read the words 'you stingy bastard!' in Jack the foreman's eyes when he told him.

But Ben had been relying on having one big harvest do on Thursday or Friday when they'd definitely have finished the last field. Oh well, it couldn't be helped now. Let's hope I can get them to work on a Sunday, tomorrow, Ben thought. The summer rains could come any day now.

He didn't want to be too obvious about wanting to get away but he was aching to see Lara. He'd been thinking about her all day, his mind's eye lingering over every part of her: the taste of her mouth and tongue the evening before, the smell of her thick, lustrous hair as he'd held her close, the sight of her breasts and the tempting curves when he'd glimpsed her in the swimming pool.

Once or twice it had been quite dangerous: he'd been daydreaming and nearly got his hand trapped in a chain on the side of the reaper. It was Jack who'd saved him. He'd shouted 'Hey!' over the clanking noise of the machinery and then smiled at him, shaking his head.

When the foreman had suggested the men and their wives and the kids might all gather round outside the barn till it got cool at about ten or so, just to have a little get-together, he'd said yes. By that point – it must've been getting on for half-eight – Old Dom had appeared clutching the battered Good Time acoustic guitar he always played at get-togethers.

Ben had taken his cue and apologised for not joining them, getting a few knowing looks and laughs in return.

He ran over to the house to get a shave and a quick bath. The sun was beginning to set. As he crossed the yard he heard a shout. 'Ben!'

He stopped, turned and tried to make out who it was. She was standing at the entrance to the yard: dark brown skin glowing in the evening light. She was wearing a short, strapless red summer dress. She had her hair up, tied with a matching red ribbon, and somehow this had the effect of drawing the eye to her long, graceful neck.

She was grinning at him. 'How goes it, Ben?' Her voice echoed in the empty farmyard. 'I came to see if I could give you a hand.'

'Hi, Esther!' He hesitated a moment but stood where he was. 'They're all in the field outside the big barn.'

She took a step towards him. 'You having a harvest party? I came to see if I could help. See you later?'

He smiled. 'You go over. I'll be back later.'

That wasn't exactly a lie, Ben said to himself a few minutes later as he sat in the shallow metal bath scrubbing the dust of the fields and the sweat from his body. I will be back later – but exactly when depends.

It wasn't far to Lara's house – only a quarter of an hour if you walked fast – so Ben decided not to take the trap. Despite his strong urge to see Lara, he wanted to spin out the anticipation and excitement a little longer. As he strode along the narrow track he hummed a tune and lifted his nose, sniffing the still-warm, almost liquid air. He smelled the summer night coming: grasses and the dry scent of the newly mown wheat in his fields, the leathery smell of cow manure from the bottom pasture he was just passing.

At a sharp right-hand bend in the cart track Ben took a short cut – a narrow footpath, almost completely grown over – that went more steeply up Spring Hill before coming down to the valley where Lara's house was. Ben pushed through heavily scented clutches of cow parsley as he walked briskly on, within a few minutes reaching the more open ground at the top of the hill. There, panting a little next to some patches of bracken, he paused a moment to cool down: he didn't want to get too sweaty now.

He took a deep breath and plunged down the steeply descending path, coming quickly to the place where the reservoir pond for Lara's swimming pool was. He skirted that and entered a small spinney of young ash and sycamore. Lara's big house was close but disappeared from view at this point. It was almost dark now. Ben had to pause again for a moment to check which way the path went through the tangle of moist ferns and undergrowth ahead.

It was then that he saw someone move in the thicket a hundred yards away to his right. A large man: a crouching bulky figure one second, now a shadow standing. Ben felt the back of his neck prickling. He had an urge to shout to this stranger. What the hell was he doing, lurking in the woods outside Lara's house? He took a deep breath, but then checked himself. What if there was more than one of them?

Since yesterday evening he'd pushed aside all thought of that murdered Welshman. And that strange, arrogant policeman in the leather coat and his oblique references to how it might be dangerous out here. It seemed then like he was talking rubbish but...

Lara's safety was the most important thing. Be sensible, get to the house first. You don't know what you're up against. Or even whether this is anything suspicious at all – it might be nothing.

'Where the hell's farmer boy got to?' grumbled Lara.

Her mother smiled. 'He'll be here soon enough. They pretty well have to work till sunset at harvest time, don't they?'

'Mm.' Lara and her mother were still outside, having whiled away the early evening watching Arrow practising cartwheels on the lawn. Eventually Rae had brought out some snacks and taken Arrow off for a bath. The girl was in bed now, protesting that it was too early because she could still see some light.

Lara would have been glad of a low-key, tranquil evening without Ben coming round yet again. Some time to think things through. To work out what had been going on with those attacks on the Welshmen. Why was this Inter-Regional Security outfit so interested?

Usually Saturday evenings meant a charity dinner and dance; or if not some social function, a play or a concert at the New Shakespeare Theatre or a Good Time film at the open air cinema in town.

She heard something in the distance. The background hum of the generator in one of the outbuildings masked it. Was it a shout? Probably nothing, she thought. Still, I'll lock all the doors and windows tonight.

If you're coming round, Ben Frobisher, she thought to herself, I wish you'd hurry up.

Keeping his eye on the dark figure to his right, Ben walked quickly on.

He heard the man bellow 'hey, you! Stop right there!' and felt his stomach clench.

He looked back. The man was starting after him. Don't worry. I know this little stretch like the back of my hand. He felt adrenalin pumping into his bloodstream. Checking the trees and the path ahead, he ran as fast as he could. He plunged on and down, air searing his lungs. Men shouting behind him. Two at least. The sound seemed distant, as if he was dreaming this but he knew they were close.

Now he heard a gurgling throaty growl behind him and knew what was coming. A searing pain in his left leg. He fell headlong into a hawthorn bush, thorns scraping the left side of his head.

He was on his back, looking up at the bared white teeth and yellow eyes of something half-Alsatian, half-wolf. The dog's jaw hovered over his face and neck. Another dog, equally big, now had its teeth clamped on his left arm, near the top. They were both growling deeply, rhythmically to each other, as if building up to a fight over a bone. Ben knew that if he moved just a quarter of an inch those teeth would sink further into his arm. And that the first dog could have his throat out in two seconds.

There was a faint tinkling sound from inside the house.

'It's the phone,' her mother called.

'Lara Johnson speaking.'

'Hi Lara. Kieran.'

'Kieran! You're not still on duty?'

'Don't worry, I'm going home now. Sorry but I've hit a brick wall. All I know is the Welsh kid's being held somewhere in New Warwick but I can't find out where.'

'You're sure they haven't taken him off to Oxford?'

'Doubt it. Not for a few days anyway. There's the inquest for one thing.'

'Did you get to see File?'

'That's what took the time.'

'And?'

'He wasn't giving anything away but he did seem pleased with himself.'

Lara proceeded to tell Tyler about Star Edkin's story about the saddlebags and their contents.

'Okay Lara. I'll try to see our Chief on Monday and see if I can persuade him to find out what's going on. This Inter-Regional mob poking around...I don't know, we're being kept too much in the dark—'

There was a loud pounding on the front door.

Lara gave a start, nearly dropping the receiver. '—Just a minute, Keith.'

'There was something I wanted to tell you—'

Thumping bangs again.

'—I'll ring you back – or can you ring me in a few minutes?'

Lara put the phone down and ran downstairs. Rae had come into the hallway. She was looking up at Lara with a scared expression. The banging on the door was even more insistent the third time.

Lara fastened the chain across the inside of the doorway before she opened the heavy front door. Peeking through the gap, she saw a policeman on the step, standing in the gloom. He was dressed in a short protective jacket, navy blue, and a peaked cap.

'Mrs Lara Johnson,' he said flatly. It was a statement rather than a question. 'Sorry to disturb you, Mrs Johnson. NWPD. We were detailed to watch your perimeter area. Apprehended this gentleman. Could you please confirm you know him?'

The policeman moved sideways so that Lara could see Ben through the narrow crack in the doorway. He was standing a few paces away, white-faced, staring at her. His face was badly scratched down one side and there was a large tear in one of the legs of his trousers. Immediately behind him was the stern red face of another policeman, a very big man, who'd twisted Ben's arm up his back and was holding him very firmly.

'Look out Lara!' Ben shouted, both anger and fear in his voice. 'I don't trust these men!'

Lara's mind raced. Were these policemen?

Star Edkin and Butcher stared at each other for a full two seconds after they'd heard the doors bang.

Then without a word Star lunged towards the button on the computer that released the tray holding the tab. The tray emerged, she edged out the fingernail-size disk and thrust it into the plastic case. She stood up, conscious of the stupid lab coat flapping round her ankles.

Butcher's hands were twitching back and forth over the keyboard. He tapped furiously, glancing first at the screen and then at the closed door behind them.

As she wrestled herself out of the long white coat they heard another door bang – much closer this time. Footsteps – two people, it sounded like – were getting louder. And there were voices.

Butcher was looking at Star, open-mouthed. 'What the fuck are you doing?! Keep the coat on!'

'I'm going!' she hissed back.

'No! It'll be much worse if you run for it. I'll cover for us–'

'–Butcher, listen! This is the story, okay? I came here to meet you for sex. Got it?'

He stared at her, open-mouthed. 'What?'

'I came here to meet you, you were showing off all you know about computers,' she whispered fiercely, 'and we're boyfriend and girlfriend and we were going to have sex. That's the story! Stick to it!'

They froze. A door some way down the corridor was being opened. There was a pause. The door closed. The footsteps started again, getting even closer. Butcher knelt, flicked a switch in the wall. The computer died.

Star was already on the opposite side of the room, jamming the plastic case into the back pocket of her trousers.

But now she'd stopped dead.

'Ohh!' she cried, remembering the printed notes. She turned

and ran back to the computer. Her face had the grim, concentrated look of a hundred-metre sprinter battling for first place.

Butcher's face was completely white. 'Ground floor window. Gents!' he croaked.

Star gave him one last look as she snatched the two sheets of paper from the printer tray and ran, head down, back to the door on the far side of the room. She opened it as quietly as she could and slipped through, closing it gently behind her. As she tiptoed away she heard loud voices in the computer room shouting at Butcher.

Now she was in a large, dark, square room with yet more desks and computers. She sprinted across it to another door in the corner. There were no voices now, no one shouting after her to stop. Panting, she found herself running down some back stairs. Down one, two, three levels. She ran along a corridor on the ground floor. There was the gents' toilet.

She burst in. A strong smell from an unflushed urinal. Her eyes swept across to a window of opaque glass. The sill was only at waist height. The window opened with a simple catch at the bottom.

Star eased herself out, struggling backwards bottom-first into the grassy summer evening air. She couldn't help thinking, what crazy thing am I doing?

Dropping softly on to the grass, she looked left and right: no one coming. No sounds either, except the sweet dangerous songs of birds. She held her breath, pushing back the fear, telling herself you've got to expect this out here. The university's next to the outback: of course there are birds everywhere. It's all superstition; it's all superstition.

Finding out how to get off the campus without being caught – that was the important thing. She felt her back pockets to check the little plastic case and the two printed pages were still there and then walked cautiously around the maths building, keeping to the shadows.

She saw the bush where her bike was, helped it off its stand and wheeled it away, pushing it between deserted buildings towards the perimeter road, looking carefully this way and that. Only when she'd found a gaping hole in the rusting wire fence, with a well-worn footpath leading down a dusty track to the university workers' settlement did she dare start the engine. Even then, Star kept the bike's headlamp off until she found the winding university sidetrack that led back through the twilight to the main road, and then on to the softly glowing streetlamps of New Warwick.

'Let him go and back away, please!' Lara said, keeping the door chain fastened.

The policeman squinted at her. 'You must confirm you know this man.'

'I do – he's my neighbour, Mr Frobisher.'

In the fading light Lara could see the other policeman slackening his grip on Ben.

The first officer nodded. 'You sure? You sure you'll be all right?'

'Yes I'm sure. Now please let him go. Can you confirm your identity?'

The policeman on the doorstep shrugged and waved his arm around: didn't his uniform speak for itself?

'I'm DC Hopkins,' he said. 'And that,' he said, pointing at the other one, 'is DC Smith.'

'Okay, and which station are you working out of?'

A curt nod. 'Central, ma'am. You could check with Inspector Tyler – he's detailed us to be here.'

Lara supported a limping Ben into the hall.

Her mother was standing facing them. 'Ben! Lara, what's going on?!'

'It's okay, Mum. Ben ran into two policemen. And a dog.'

'Oh!!'

Ben winced. 'Two dogs actually. Bloody massive buggers.'

Rae took Ben's other arm and mother and daughter led him into the kitchen. Rae was clucking with sympathy each step of the way.

Lara heard the phone ringing. 'I think I know who that is. Mum. You look after Ben while I go and answer it.'

When Lara re-entered the kitchen five minutes later, Ben was having the dog bite on his shin washed and fussed over. He was sitting on a towel on the kitchen table, both feet resting on a chair. One leg of his trousers was rolled up. Rae was bending over his wound, swabbing it gently with a white cloth. A metal bowl with bloodstained water in it stood on the table.

'Your mother's looking after me' Ben said with a stoical smile.

'Ben, I'm so sorry. I had no idea Kieran Tyler had put two of his men out there. I've just spoken to him and told him what happened. Sometimes that fellow's just too damn efficient! But he did tell me to say he's very sorry about what happened.'

Ben's looked sad rather than angry. 'I shouldn't have run for it. I just wanted to get to the house, make sure you and your mother were all right.'

Rae straightened up. 'I don't know! What were those men doing unleashing wild dogs like that? Without any warning!'

Ben nodded. 'It's true. They didn't shout 'police!' or anything. They certainly didn't act like policemen creeping around in the woods like that.'

'What I want to know is,' Rae said, 'why is the house being guarded anyway? What's going on, Lara?'

'It's only a precaution, Mum. No need to worry.'

'–You say that, but–'

'–No honestly Mum, don't worry.' Lara turned to Ben. 'And I will have another word with Kieran. He ought to tell those men to be more careful with the dogs.'

His gentle brown eyes were upon her. She felt her body soften and quelled a sudden urge to put her arm around his shoulder.

Her mother was applying some surgical spirit to his wound now. Lara bent down to look at it. Fortunately it didn't look too bad: a nasty gash, true enough, but it didn't look as if it needed stitches. Still, they didn't know how deeply the dog's teeth had gone in. It was certainly worse than the neat row of teeth marks on his arm.

'Dear, dear,' Rae said. 'Shouldn't we call the doctor?'

'You should get it looked at,' said Lara, though there was less conviction in her voice. There was nothing much more a doctor could do than her mother was doing already – cleaning the wound and hoping for the best.

'I'll see a doctor if it turns nasty.'

'Don't roll your trouser leg back down,' Rae said. 'Get them off and Lara can fetch you some shorts of David's to put on.'

Lara eyes widened. Then she and Ben looked at each other and burst out laughing.

Upstairs, she went to the big chest-of-drawers in her bedroom and pulled out the bottom drawer. Earlier that year she'd reluctantly taken all David's clothes out of his wardrobe. They were now in boxes in the loft, each one labelled. But some items she'd kept in their bedroom, including this drawer full of socks and underclothes and the T-shirts she sometimes liked to wear herself at bedtime.

At the back, yes, there they were – a pair of cut-off shorts that went down to the knee – well, down to David's knees, she mused. She'd never compared her husband's height, weight, shape, with Ben's.

She turned to go back downstairs but paused for a moment, holding the shorts in her left hand. She went over to the dressing table where David's portrait stood in its silver frame and kissed it lightly. Then she went out onto the landing and headed towards Arrow's room.

She stood for a whole minute looking at her daughter sleeping in the weak golden light. It's amazing what they can sleep through, Lara reflected, remembering the awful banging on the front door. Thank God the child didn't wake. There would have been all sorts of fears to settle and explanations to give.

Arrow had a father she still sorely missed, but Lara was sure David was beginning to dissolve in her everyday consciousness. She'd been told over and over again that her father had disappeared, not died; that one day he might reappear, but these concepts of future and of continuing to exist without proof were difficult for her to grasp and integrate into her world.

Lara kissed her daughter lightly on her forehead, blew out the candle, closed the bedroom door and went downstairs.

An hour later Rae announced she was going to bed. As she left them she smiled conspiratorially at Lara.

Lara grimaced, hoping Ben hadn't seen that conspiratorial glance. Rae could be really embarrassing sometimes. Against her better judgement Lara suggested a nightcap and led Ben into the big living room.

She opened wide the French windows. Sweet, heavy perfumes from the flowers outside, mainly night-scented stocks, began to fill the room. While she was pouring out two large glasses of Canterbury cognac Ben pulled a soft rug over to the French windows and suggested they sit on it half-in, half-out of the doorway.

'We can look at the night sky' he said. 'Beautiful night – look at that moon!'

For a moment she wanted to resist his idea but then gave way thinking what the hell, it is a beautiful night and he deserves this after being set upon by dogs.

There was no sound except the rhythmic chirrup-chirrup of cicadas. The swathes of stars above were silent but their very brightness seemed to lend them sound, as if the galaxies were crackling and fizzing with electricity.

They sipped their fiery cognac, not saying anything, staring up at the stars. Time passed: ten, twenty, thirty minutes? She wasn't sure.

She shivered a little. A moment later she felt his arm tentatively encircling her back. The heaviness and solidity of it surprised her. She didn't pull away: it felt warm and comforting. Still neither of them said anything.

The shorts she'd given Ben to wear were David's old blue denim ones. They go back a long way, she reflected, and began to try to work out when David had acquired shorts made of such valuable Good Time material. A memory of she and him making love in the shade of an apple tree, in an orchard somewhere, drifted into her mind. He was wearing them that summer, then. Was that when they were students? Surely those shorts couldn't go back that far!

Ben was leaning back against one of the doors, sighing.

Lara put a finger in her glass of cognac. He gave her a questioning look, the moonlight silvering his dark brown eyes. Wondering to herself why she was doing this, she traced her finger, wet with spirit, over the dog bite on his upper arm, going from red bump to bump, tooth mark to tooth mark. He recoiled a little, wincing but still smiling.

'It's an antiseptic,' she said, dipping her finger in again.

'And a waste putting it there,' he said, holding her wrist and guiding her wet finger to his lips. She let him suck her finger tip, enjoying both that sensation and the playful smile in his eyes. This was so funny! The cognac had given her a pleasant woozy feeling. It was so nice to be warm and close to someone again, just for a moment.

She returned the smile, intending to tell him this was fun but now it was time to stand up and say their goodbyes.

But she didn't get the chance. Before she could say anything he'd taken her in both arms and was kissing her on the lips, much harder and much hungrier than the last time. His tongue was in her mouth, almost down her throat. She felt the power and bulk of him. She tried to pull her head back but his strong farmer's hand was holding her firmly at the back of her neck, forcing her face and lips into his.

Now he was pushing her back onto the rug. His thighs were against hers, pushing. She could feel his erection pressing through the thick denim of the shorts.

For a second or two her body said, why not? Just as it had with that first kiss at the dam. The shorts were David's: she visualized unbuttoning them as she had with him in that orchard, taking out his cock and teasing, sucking him. Seeing David's cock rigid with desire, with lust for her; guiding it into her, feeling him fill her...

Why not?

'No!' she said, managing to push his head back.

He uttered a groaning noise, his eyes pleading. 'I know this is wrong' he whispered. 'But I love you, Lara! I love you! I can't help it!'

That did it. She twisted herself out from under him and sat up, rubbing her eyes.

'You can't love me.'

He was sitting up now. His voice was more normal. 'But I do.'

It's tragic, she thought. If he'd wanted just sex there's a chance I would have done it – just once. But now he's told me he loves me.

'I'm sorry, Ben. I can't – you can't.'

He nodded. He looked utterly miserable.

She stood up, smoothed down her skirt, pulled the rug inside and closed the French windows.

12

Before she went to the Beacon office with her story, Star needed to decide what to do with the red-hot memory tab and printed notes in her pocket.

She stopped the bike outside Dev's, an Indian food stall she often called at. Dev's place was in a little backwater, a quiet alley off Market Street. Dev, an amiable, rotund Gujerati guy, had rigged up festoons of lights which cast an unearthly multicoloured glow over the mixed collection of metal chairs outside.

Saturday night in New Warwick was getting into gear. When she switched off the bike's engine Star could hear shrieks, laughter and thumping music from the open air dance zone in the city centre. Noisy gaggles of people strolled by the end of the alley. Star sat on a stool at the bar, surreptitiously checking over the customers sitting on the metal chairs: there's no one who knows me. Then she remembered. Scan all the surrounding buildings and windows. Think crossbow.

She felt bad about leaving Butcher in the lurch. Would he be able to stick with the story? Would he remember what she'd told him to say?

I should take the tab and these printed pages to the office now, she thought. Combined with what she'd witnessed over the past twenty-four hours it would make a fantastic lead on Monday morning. She smiled, picturing Alex Blennerhassett's fat face yet again. Wait till he sees what I've got. And Miff and Stu, the two senior reporters, they'll be amazed too.

But then, will it really be like that? A quiet voice inside her head said no, it won't be like that at all. Yes, they'd be only too happy to grab her story. But would she get to write it; get the credit?

There was another, even more worrying, possibility. Alex, fat toad that he was, might just sit on the story because of security and worries about getting into trouble with the authorities. She'd only been at the Beacon for a year but she'd already begun to pick up just how restricted things could be. Nothing was said openly: Miff and Stu grumbled to each other about censorship and Blennerhassett's caution. But they never seemed to get really angry when stories were spiked or when leads deemed 'too sensitive' weren't followed up.

New Warwick stood for liberty, sure; they were all told that at school. Everyone was proud of the constitution. You had to swear allegiance to it when you graduated from high school. There were elections every five years; different cultures and religions had to respect each other and live peacefully side by side; and there was the equality drive ('A Fair Go for Every Citizen' – it had helped Star get her training place at the newspaper).

'A beacon of democracy' was the city republic's motto. That's why the Beacon was called the Beacon, after all. But it was New Warwick's only newspaper. There was the recently launched Radio New Warwick but only a small minority could afford, or even find, a working radio. In any case most of the local radio news stories and discussions were lifted from the Beacon; they didn't have any journalists themselves.

Star had gradually come to realise New Warwick might have ninety thousand and more inhabitants but it was a tight-run ship dominated by a relatively small group. They were almost all senior officials and elected representatives who came from the same network of interrelated families, the City Founders. These were the people who ran things – people like Blennerhassett, in fact. They all knew each other, did things for each other – and covered up for each other.

Lara Johnson was the exception. It was the reason Star admired her. She seemed to be genuinely independent, willing to speak her own mind.

She nibbled an onion bhaji. And what about Gwynfor? Her heart softened as she thought about him: his sad, serious face that morning; the shock and bewilderment in his eyes when he was pushed into File's car. I must get to see him, she thought. I can't hand this tab over to anybody until I have.

'Dev,' Star said, leaning forward over the counter.

The food stall owner was frying koftas; a look of concentration was on his face as he wielded a large slotted spoon over a pan bubbling with hot smoking oil.

'Call it two-fifty for the bhajis!' he said, his wide, rubbery face grinning.

'OK,' she said, putting some coins on the counter. 'Dev, can I ask you something?'

He stepped back, wiping his hands on his grubby white apron. 'What?'

'Can you do me a favour? I need you to look after something small for me. Just for a few days. Nobody must know it's here.'

Star should have remembered that aroma of tobacco as soon as she opened the front door. By the time she realised, it was too late.

Mrs James appeared in the hall looking flustered and apologetic. 'Sorry, dear, I had to let them in, you see.'

She glanced up the stairs with a worried look.

'Come on up, love!' a distant voice shouted. 'We're wait-ing!'

File. She could still turn and run. But something told her it would be useless. Anyway, she was tired, it was late; maybe it was time to bluff it out.

When she reached the landing she found the door to her flat ajar. File's tobacco smoke had drifted out, blue strata hanging motionless in the air. She went in to find him sitting sideways in the creaky cane armchair, one leg flung up and over the side. Another man, a tall, good-looking black guy in a well-cut, Good Time-style jacket, stood at the far end of the room. He glanced at Star only briefly before continuing to poke around her belongings in an absent-minded way. Star noticed that he had small perfectly formed ears that sat tightly against the sides of his head, but that one of them – his right one – had been mutilated. The bottom half was missing, as if some sharp-toothed animal had neatly bitten it off.

'Hey, it's my lucky Star,' File grinned.

'What do you want?!'

'Not very much at all. Just you. Which isn't much, when you think about it.'

The black man gave out a quiet laugh – almost a cough.

File turned to him 'Wouldn't you say, Orpheus? That I'm always content with just a little?'

'Yeah but why not reach for the stars, man?' the black man said, and giggled.

'What are you doing in my flat? Have you got a search warrant?' Star realised her voice sounded too frightened and high-pitched.

File laughed as if search warrants were the funniest things in the world.

'OK love, before any warrants or anything, how about you tell me a story? About what were you doing at the university. Any story will do. For starters anyway.' He chuckled, amused at himself again. 'You were just there, with your little friend – or should I say, big friend...?'

Star's insides froze. How could they know so quickly?

'Who says I was at the university?'

File burst out laughing. 'Oh no, no, no,' he said, drawing on the last of his cigarette.

'Search my flat then. You won't find anything.'

'We already have, darlin',' the black man said. The sound of his voice was as smooth as cream. He smiled at her; a lightning flash of pure white teeth, a smile so quick that she thought she'd probably imagined it. 'But we haven't searched you yet. Have we, boss, eh? Nooks and crannies, eh?'

File chuckled and rubbed his hands. 'Nooks and crannies' he repeated, nodding. 'Yes indeed. I'm looking forward to this.'

'I'm not, boss,' replied the other. 'Bitch be like scrawny chicken. Way too lean, man.'

They both laughed. 'I must apologise on behalf of my colleague, Miss Edkin,' File said. 'I'm afraid he does actually eat birds now and again, would you believe.'

'They sacrifices, man.'

'They're not! You eat them afterwards!' File laughed again and looked at Star. 'Honestly: chickens, wild turkeys, pigeons. He does, yes. I think he'd even eat a crow if he had a chance. Disgusting, isn't it?'

Instinctively, Star wrapped her arms around herself. They can't do this to you. They won't. They're just trying to frighten you. She backed away, almost reaching the open door. She jerked her head round and shouted downstairs. 'Mrs James!'

The two men laughed at her.

Before Star could take in what was happening File was at her side. One second he was sprawling in the cane chair looking as if he was going to take out another cigarette and the next he was gripping her arm.

The black man was at her other side, holding her right arm at the top and at the elbow. Chuckling, they lifted Star up between them as if she were a child and carried her downstairs to the front door.

13

On Monday morning Lara got Matt to drive her to her office at the Legislative Council. Lara wanted to get in early to organise a phone call to the Regional Commissioner, Alexander Laczko.

At ten she had a meeting with the reform group – a small group of like-minded progressive reps, all women. They were going to discuss their strategy for the run-up to the council elections in October.

While Lara waited for the switchboard to call her back she sat in her office reading through a draft of a new law about the adoption and fostering of orphaned children. But she couldn't concentrate: her eye kept wandering back to the telephone that was on the far side of her desk.

That morning's edition of the New Warwick Beacon was also lying on the desk, left there by her conscientious secretary. Lara picked up the paper with interest. She remembered the Edkin girl saying the paper would be running a big story today on the murder of Sylvan Roberts and subsequent events. She'd also suggested that one of the senior reporters would be phoning Lara. But no one from the Beacon had been in touch.

She was surprised to find that the paper led with a report on troubles with the money supply and inflation. This was hardly front page news. Problems of inflation had been going on for years. So where was the big story, the latest development in the hunt for the murderers of the Welsh trader? What about the attack on his son and Star Edkin at the stables on Saturday morning? They'd had crossbow arrows shot at them, hadn't they? Had Star been making it all up?

She turned the pages carefully. On page four she saw a short, blandly worded article – little more than two paragraphs – with the headline 'Hunt for Trader's Killer Goes On'. It simply described a 'continuing police search' over the weekend, but there was no mention of the special police unit from Oxford. She put the paper down and tried to carry on with her work. But her mind wouldn't settle; the more she thought about it, the odder it seemed – this curious lack of coverage of the biggest news story in New Warwick for months.

Fifteen minutes later the phone on her desk rang. She was excited: the call to the Commissioner had come through sooner than she'd dared hope.

'Yes?'

'Lara?' It was Blennerhassett's wheezy voice.

She frowned. 'Alex, I'm expecting an important call any minute…'

There was a cough. 'I'll be quick. I was wondering if you might be able to help with something.'

'Go on.'

'Our little Star.'

'What do you mean?'

'Did you know she's in police custody?'

'No! Why? Where's she being held?'

'"Helping us with our enquiries" is all I can get out of them. I can't find out where she is or who detained her. And they've slapped a security order on me so I can't see her or get a solicitor in.'

'That doesn't sound right at all.'

'Lara, can you do anything?' He sounded plaintive.

'I'll see what I can do.' She made a mental note to call Kieran Tyler again. 'Did the police tell you she'd had several crossbow arrows fired at her on Saturday morning?'

'God, no, they didn't.'

'She was with that boy – the trader's son. Someone tried to kill them. This was all supposed to be in your newspaper this morning – what happened? And did you know some secret police unit from Oxford is operating in the city? I've never heard of them, but according to Miss Edkin they're the ones holding the Welsh lad.'

And then it dawned on her. They were holding Star Edkin too, she was certain of it.

'Honestly Alex,' she continued, 'New Warwick needs to know all this!'

'Lara, talk to me about it!' he wailed.

'Mrs Johnson,' a woman's voice interrupted, 'I have the regional commissioner on another line.'

'OK, thank you,' Lara replied. 'Alex, I'll have to go.'

'I'll call you back in–'

She heard a click as Blennerhassett was cut off.

'Lara?' It was Alexander Laczko: a friendly, measured voice.

'Commissioner!'

'Oh, Alexander, please.' A pleasant, light chuckle. 'You wanted to meet?'

'Yes please, if it's possible later this week?'

'I can do better than that, Lara. How about this afternoon, two o'clock? I'll send a car.'

There was another click. As the most powerful do, he'd hung up without waiting for a reply.

Lara put down the receiver. She wandered slowly back to her chair, surprised at how quick and easy it had turned out to be, getting an appointment with Alexander Laczko. It's probably just chance, she mused, tidying up the papers on her desk.

Lara decided to give her apologies and leave the reform group meeting just before midday. She felt bad about it because there were still some important items to be discussed before lunch, but she wanted to go home before the commissioner appointment at two o'clock.

Lara had phoned home to arrange for Matt to come to pick her up. As the trap rattled home along the dusty country road, the midday sun blazing down, Lara thought about clothes. Good Time style was back in, especially among the elite, so she decided on the cream linen suit.

It was only when she was in the shower that Lara remembered about the car the commissioner had promised: it would be going to her office in town. She dashed on to the landing. Rae was bustling around upstairs and laughed to see her daughter there, clutching a towel around her middle, dripping water on the rug as she talked anxiously into the phone.

Half an hour later Rae was watching Lara again as she got into the huge black limo. She stood on the front step. Some sense of occasion had prompted her to take off her apron, though she still held it, loosely folded, in one hand. Rae had no idea why Lara was going to see the regional commissioner but surely this was a sign of how well she was doing now. A perfect moment she'd always treasure: the glorious sunshine; the official car on the drive; Lara looking so beautiful; this great house her daughter had won with her success.

She turned to go back inside. Then she smiled to herself, remembering what she'd seen on Saturday night. Before turning in she'd come back downstairs for a glass of water. Tiptoeing past the big living room she'd heard something like a low moaning noise. Half-frightened, half-curious, she'd put her head round the door.

It was too dark to see properly – the generator was off and they hadn't lit a candle – but the moonlight coming through the open French windows had been enough to see Ben with his arms around Lara. They were kissing passionately!

Had it led to anything else, she wondered. Cross fingers it had. That night she'd lain awake as long as she could, listening out for any creaking or muffled cries of sex. But in the end she hadn't been able to fight off sleep. But surely they'd been to bed together? It's showing in her face now, Rae thought; you couldn't miss it.

Ben hadn't been round to see them since Saturday night – so busy with the harvest. She hoped he was all right after that horrible dog bite. She was looking forward to seeing him. If he's bedded Lara he'll be as happy as the cat that got the cream – and so will I!

Lara had forgotten how silent it was in these old-time limousines. The driver, an anonymous figure in a blue cap, was separated from her by a thick glass screen. She was feeling nervous. Would the commissioner agree to her plan?

She sank back into the soft red leather seat, breathed in the beeswax smell from the limo's polished woodwork and watched the hedges and fields slide quietly by.

When the car stopped outside the gatehouse two soldiers in khaki uniform and maroon berets sprang to open the high wrought-iron gates. The car passed them, scrunching on to gravel, a soldier on each side. This is another world, Lara reminded herself. She smiled, feeling faintly embarrassed when the soldiers saluted smartly as the car whispered past.

Lara looked over the chauffeur's shoulder to the great house that lay ahead. Coughton Court never failed to impress. Lara had been to various receptions and meetings here in the past few years, but this was the first time she'd ever been invited on her own account. She noticed small groups of red deer grazing the wide swathes of grassland either side of the drive. The warm yellow stucco of the house glowed in the afternoon sunshine. Two flags flew above the turrets: the cross of St George and a Union Jack – the latter a quaint reference to olden days, when there was a UK.

This was a Tudor mansion, Lara had been told on one of her previous visits. Literature left behind in the house spoke of it belonging to the Throckmorton family, dissident Catholics; apparently it dated back to the 1530s.

In the late twentieth century and early decades of the twenty-first, Coughton Court had been open to the general public and had become a popular place to visit. Its beautiful gardens and grounds were still being well maintained, by the look of it.

The driver was opening the car door for her. As Lara stepped out she noticed manicured, cone-shaped evergreen bushes standing in an orderly line along the front of the house. Two peacocks were walking in stately fashion across the perfectly trimmed lawn. The gravel beneath her shoes had been raked clean.

Nowadays Coughton Court was rarely, if ever, visited by ordinary citizens. For the past five years it had been an exclusive centre of central government power in South Mercia and the official residence of the Regional Commissioner, Alexander Laczko. Only those with a degree of power and influence could make the journey up the long gravel drive – visiting ministers and administrators from the English government in Oxford, local civil servants from the various South Mercia offices; high-ranking military officers; and representatives of the thrusting new urban councils and city states such as New Warwick and New Worcester. People of substance like me, Lara told herself, taking a deep breath. She walked quickly up the steps towards a young, smiling army officer who was standing to welcome her.

It was a significant honour, Lara realised, for the commissioner to have already emerged from his rooms. She was just taking in the scale of the entrance hall, the sweep of the grand staircase, when she saw him coming down.

Alexander Laczko was smaller and slighter than Lara remembered. Maybe it was just that this wasn't one of those weighty public occasions when he was surrounded by officials and security men. He was wearing a Good Time-style suit, a subtle blue-green that looked light and summery, and an open-necked white shirt. As he gripped her hand and smiled warmly at her, Lara was reminded of that aura of power and authority that went with the people at the top – an ease of manner, almost casualness; a lot of eye contact.

Laczko's eyes were the palest, eeriest shade of blue that you could imagine. Despite this disconcerting paleness they didn't lack expression. They twinkled and laughed, raking up and down as he took Lara in. 'Lara, my, how well you're looking,' he said.

'Thank you,' she smiled.

'And how good of you to come at such short notice,' he continued, as if the appointment had been his idea all along. He turned, putting a hand on her arm. 'Do come up.'

They climbed the wide staircase and walked along creaking, highly polished floors to a reception room. Lara wondered how old Laczko was. How long would he be continuing as their regional commissioner? Early sixties, was he? It was hard to tell. He had almost no hair – just a white-grey down covering his pate – but his slight body was taut and muscular, his face was smooth, his skin unwrinkled and light brown.

There was something reptilian about him, she thought, but not in a particularly alien or frightening way. As a child she'd once been invited to touch a snake – a harmless one that had been brought into the classroom by one of the teachers. It lay coiled in a wooden box in some straw, a warm electric lamp shining over it. She was the first in her small class brave enough to dare to touch. The snake's skin was surprisingly dry and warm. With the firmness and decisiveness of an eight year old she'd decided snakes were okay; they were friendly.

Laczko led her to a comfortable wing-back armchair. They sat facing each other, their chairs close to a large Elizabethan window. Lara looked through the tiny diamond-shaped panes. The formal garden below had symmetrical beds of roses and espaliered apple trees, but the view was distorted and fragmented by the ancient, thick glass. One window was open to allow in the summer breeze. She could hear a push-mower on a distant lawn.

Laczko was exchanging pleasantries with her, asking her about her work as a judge, when a young man in a crisp white tunic knocked politely at the door and brought in a silver tray with coffee and biscuits.

'Will you take some of this?' Laczko asked her, smiling again. And turning to look at the waiting young man he said, 'It's all right, I'll do this.'

'Mm, it's lovely,' said Lara, sipping the high-status aromatic black liquid.

'It was a present, a taster, from our Saudi friends. Trade mission.'

'Really? I didn't know we'd got links that far.'

'Yes – we are a little off the beaten track aren't we?' he smiled warmly. 'But it's only a matter of time…'

'Mm.'

'Now, Lara,' he said, settling back in his chair and looking up at the ceiling. 'Talk to me.'

'I've decided that I must have one more try,' she said.

'To find your husband.'

'Something tells me that this might be the last real chance I'll get.'

'Something tells you?'

Almost without pause, and punctuated only by the sound of the lawnmower, Lara talked for several minutes about the case of the Welsh trader and his son. How they seemed to be on the verge of telling her something vital. She told him about the murder and the subsequent attack on the son. How some unseen enemy or power seemed to want to stop a secret getting out. Couldn't that secret involve David's whereabouts? She felt in her bones that it did.

'I still need to talk to the son,' Lara said, 'but he's been whisked away by some new police unit from outside.'

'Inter-Regional Security.' Laczko was sitting up now and looking at her. Then he put his hands over his face and rubbed his eyes for a moment. 'We know about them.'

Yes of course, Lara realised, he would know about them. But did he know about Gwynfor being taken into custody?

She cleared her throat. 'Whether or not I get to see the young lad, I have a feeling I've got to act quickly.'

'Of course, seize the day!' smiled Laczko. 'Your internal passport's in order, I presume?'

'Yes. But I've gone four times before and look where it's got me, Commissioner. The police up north seem even more hopeless than they are down here – oh, sorry!'

Lara stopped herself, worried she'd said something out of order.

Laczko didn't say anything. He simply waved his hand, encouraging her to go on.

'It's just, you know, no one ever seemed to get their backs into looking systematically for David. It was always all down to me in the end. And now, if that Welsh trader's to be believed, the police seem to have got out of hand completely – in North Mercia, anyway.'

'So...?' Laczko smiled, folding his fingers together in a steeple.

'I need more backing this time, Commissioner. That's why I've come to see you.'

'You want this to be a region to region kind of thing, for me to apply some pressure?'

'Yes.'

'And which region are we talking about?'

'I'm not absolutely sure.'

'But not Cumbria or the north-west any more.'

'Perhaps not. As I say, I'm not sure. So far I've drawn a blank up there, even though some of the earliest reports said he'd reached Sellafield. No, I think North Mercia is where I should look more. There's a close connection to Wales, and North Wales is where the trader was from. And North Mercia's where he was attacked by that irregular police unit.' Lara regarded him carefully. 'Is there something going on in North Mercia?'

Laczko ignored her question. 'Anywhere in Wales I can't deal with, so that's out.'

She nodded. 'They're independent now, aren't they?'

'The correct term is "autonomous",' Laczko smiled. 'But yes .'

'I'm stuck, then, if David's being held there.'

'Not necessarily.'

'Oh?'

'The Welsh are a law unto themselves, yes. But just like

England – Greater England, should I say – the Welsh nation has fractured and regionalised, to an extent anyway. The northerners hate the southerners and the southerners hate the northerners. Gwynedd – that's the northern province you're thinking about – has more ties economically with North Mercia, with Chester and the other settlements round there, than it does with anywhere south of the mountains. Do you want some more? Do help yourself.' He gestured at the coffee pot.

'No thanks.'

Laczko suddenly stood and began walking up and down. 'I'd like to make a proposal.'

Lara tensed. 'What do you mean?'

'I'm so glad you came to see me. North Mercia is the key for both of us, wouldn't you agree?'

Lara nodded cautiously.

'Even if David is in Gwynedd somewhere, North Mercia is the key' he repeated. 'And my opposite number in Chester – Marek Stettin – he'd be the best person to start with. Assuming your husband is somewhere in that corner, Marek's the man to winkle him out for you if anyone can.'

He sat down. Lara leant forward, her eyes eager. 'Would you be willing to contact him?'

'Of course.' He gave her a serious look. 'But my proposal is this. Go directly to Marek. Make your appeal for help in person.' There was a twinkle in his eye. 'He'll be much more likely to pull out the stops when he sees you.'

'What do you want me to do for you?'

'Simply keep an open mind. Look for your husband, Lara, but keep an open mind as you search.'

This was puzzling. 'Is that all?'

'Yes. Apart from coming to tell me what you've observed, seen and heard up there, of course.' He smiled broadly and helped her to more coffee.

'I suggest two vehicles,' he continued. 'We'll organise them, and drivers and bodyguards of course. Would three to four weeks away be sufficient, d'you think?'

Lara nodded, mentally picturing Arrow in the summer holidays running to the swimming pool every day without her. But then in late September her court duties would resume and in October there were the legislative council elections to think about.

'Is there any chance of going in a few days' time?'

'I was hoping you'd say that. What about a week today?'

'Phew! Yes, but…there's another problem I'm afraid. Funding it all.'

Laczko nodded. 'We'll take care of all that. I've been thinking about this for some time. Something's been holding you back in your search for David.'

'You mean…?'

'A lack of reward money. I'd like to send a substantial sum up with you. Who you give it to is at your discretion – as long as they will beyond any doubt lead you to David.'

This was better than she'd dared hope for. 'Of course – thank you!'

Laczko stood up again – a cue for her to go.

'We will, of course, keep as close an eye on things as we can. Above all, your health and welfare are our primary concern, you know,' he smiled.

When they shook hands at the door, she noticed how light and dry his fingers were.

14

They pushed Star Edkin out of the house and slammed the front door. She blinked in the strong sunshine, dazed for a moment.

She walked to the front gate and looked back at the house. It was a typical, anonymous-looking New Warwick two-storey wooden house – a red corrugated-iron roof, blue and white painted clapboard at the front, and a big hydrangea bush spreading over the low fence. It could be anywhere.

Star opened the gate and stepped onto the pavement – and that was when she saw him. He was standing on the opposite side of the road in the deep shade of a horse chestnut tree. He gave a little wave and walked across the road to her.

'Hey, Star.'

'Gwynfor! What are you doing here?!'

He was wearing a shirt that looked new; she certainly hadn't seen it on him before. It was made of some coarse blue material – too heavy for this hot summer weather. All the same, he didn't look hot. He looked thinner and paler than she remembered.

'Where the hell is this?' she said, looking around. It was a quiet, dusty suburban road.

'It's called Laburnum Road, and down there is Republic Avenue,' said Gwynfor, pointing to the south.

He smiled. 'I've come all the way from Wales and now I'm telling this girl where she is in her own city!'

Star stared at him. 'How did you know I was here?'

'Because they kept me here as well,' he said. 'They let me out yesterday, and told me they'd be letting you out this morning.'

'It's so weird. We were both there and neither of us knew!' she said half an hour later.

They were sitting on metal chairs in the shaded alleyway outside Dev's snack bar. Gwynfor had insisted on ordering food even though she wasn't hungry and she still felt dizzy: the effects of spending the past two days and three nights in that house.

'Look!' said Gwynfor with a bitter laugh. He was holding up a fistful of euro notes. 'I'm the one with the money this time. And you've got to eat, Star.'

'Where did you get that?'

He shook his head. 'Bloody mad, they are. They kept punching me in the stomach–'

She reached over and touched his hand. '–Oh Gwyn!'

He shook his head again. 'Kept me awake night and day; no food…and then when they let me go they gave me this money!'

'Really weird! Maybe to keep you quiet…'

Dev appeared and she asked him for parathas with scrambled egg for both of them.

'They let you keep your notebook,' Gwynfor said. He'd noticed her taking it out of her back pocket.

'It's got a bit squashed. I usually carry it in my leather bag. But yes, they gave it back to me. They kept it all the time I was in there – went through it with a fine toothcomb I s'pose – but there was nothing in it they didn't know. So I got it back. Can't tell you how relieved I was!'

He smiled at her. 'Ever the reporter.'

'You bet.' She smiled back.

'Did they hurt you?'

She took a deep breath, deciding not to tell him how File and his companion had made her strip in front of them. How File had stuck his fingers into her anus and vagina and the black guy had sat there laughing.

'Not really. It was more frightening than anything. Like you, no food. Kept awake a long time. They wanted to know who gave your dad those saddlebags. When I told them I didn't know – and you didn't know – they started playing this horrible classical music really loud. Plinkety-plonk, plinkety-plonk, screechy- screechy over and over again! That was fucking torture, I tell you.'

He laughed. 'They did that to you too! I didn't mind, actually – it was Bach.'

'Bach?' She smiled at him, puzzled, and decided to carry on.

'Anyway, like I say there was nothing I knew that they didn't. So I couldn't tell them anything they were interested in, right? So they wouldn't turn that music off. It nearly did my head in.'

She didn't want to tell Gwynfor how she'd gone to the university with the memory tab and got Butcher to use the computer. That was why File had taken her to the house, after all. That was why they'd piled on the pressure and burned her with a cigarette. They knew she'd been up to something with Butcher. She'd had to hope and against hope they'd believe the story about her going up there just to fool around with him.

Butcher must have convinced them somehow. She'd been very, very lucky – she knew that. File had only burned her four times, twice on each breast. She'd been shaking with fear because the other guy had a knife and was threatening all kinds of things.

But she'd held out. She hadn't given them the pleasure of hearing her scream. She'd won! The ordeal had stretched her nerves to breaking point and she right now was ready to jump at the slightest noise. But she was tougher after all that. I can do anything now, she told herself.

Dev appeared behind the counter. The food stall juddered with his weight. He nodded, put two plates on the counter in front of them, then banged down some cutlery and backed away, giving Star a meaningful glance.

'And you,' she asked Gwynfor, making her voice soft, 'are you okay? They didn't do anything else…too bad?'

He looked at her with his deep blue eyes and blinked with his impossibly long lashes. She wanted to put her arm around his neck and kiss him, and ask him if they'd burned him too.

He sighed. 'It wasn't too bad, like.'

'Did they give you back those saddlebags with the memory stick and that chart?'

'No.' He shook his head. 'They had to be sent to Oxford. Further investigations, they said.'

The memory tab and the two pages of printed notes were just a few feet away from where they were sitting, in Dev's safekeeping. Shouldn't she tell Gwynfor about them? They were his property, after all. No, her survival instinct told her, hang on to them a little longer.

'What will you do now?' she asked.

'I want to go home.' He looked away for a moment. 'But there's this inquest, see? It's tomorrow.'

'I s'pose you've got to think about the funeral too.'

He nodded. 'I know. They told me about that as well. Next Monday. They've arranged it all for me.'

'They've made all the arrangements without consulting you?!'

There was a desperate look in his eye. 'Star, I can't have my father being buried here! Can I? They said it's going to be impossible to take my father back home but that can't be right can it?'

'No' she said, putting her hand over his. 'No. That isn't right.'

'I was at the traders' lodgings last night, you know, in Northgate. Quite a few of the lads are there, drivers and that from Wales. They said they'd come; sing some of the old hymns. There's one consolation at least.'

Star thought hard for a moment. 'What if your dad's body was cremated?'

Three days later Gwynfor was stepping up to his father's funeral pyre in a small field bounded by tall willow trees and a stream, a mile outside the edge of the city. Star was standing right at the front of the group of mourners: a crowd of over fifty people in the hot afternoon sun. A priest dressed in white robes was handing something to Gwynfor now: a burning stick.

Gwynfor took it in his right hand but turned round for a second, hesitating while he looked for Star's face in the crowd. A tall, lanky figure with his black locks falling down to his shoulders, he was dressed in white too: a plain smock and loose trousers which Dev's family had given him. The sun disappeared for a few moments behind a large gun-metal grey cloud.

The last three days they'd held hands a lot and talked – about how they'd survived the bolts from the crossbow; about his dad; about how she'd never known her own father or mother.

He was stooping now to apply the flame to a huge pile of wood under the coffin. The priest was showing him where.

On one side there were about ten men from New Warwick's small Hindu community, including Dev, also dressed in white. Dev's wife Sunnita and a small group of Indian women were nearby too, standing in a separate group, chanting. They were all in saris, muted colours. Someone – Star couldn't see where – was playing a portable harmonium, a threading, wheezing tune to accompany the chanting and the jingling bells.

Star glanced back at the people behind her. She'd glimpsed Lara Johnson with that farmer guy, Ben whatshisname.

Lara looked stunning in black. She was wearing a small, elegant, black pillbox hat, a neat black veil coming down to her eyes. Her farmer friend looked uncomfortable in a borrowed suit. It was a Good Time-style one, too small for his big chest and wide shoulders.

Behind Lara and her companion was the contingent of traders, drivers and stablemen from Northgate. A lot of people, it seemed, had liked Gwynfor's father.

Two days ago Gwynfor had told Star that Lara Johnson had come to see him to tell him not to worry about funeral expenses: the city would be paying. A cremation was permissible, but only the Hindus could do it.

'I told her I was very grateful,' Gwynfor had said.

'I'm glad it's worked out,' she said. 'Now you can take your father's ashes home and scatter them on the mountain.'

'You know,' Gwynfor said, 'I think Lara Johnson still believes I know where her husband might be. So I told her again, honest to God Mrs Johnson, if I had known anything at all I would really have told you.'

'I know you would've.'

And then he'd told her that Lara Johnson had smiled in that determined way she had and said she was leaving on Monday, come what may, to go up-country to look one more time for her husband.

A gust of hot wind from the funeral pyre blew over her. Perhaps she was standing too close? She wanted to be near Gwynfor, though. She bit her lip; she felt tears coming. No one from the Beacon office had come. She felt very alone standing at the front of this crowd.

The priest was saying prayers, standing back from the rising flames; now he turned to face them all. He switched to English, intoning in a loud voice. 'Oh Supreme Light, lead us from untruth to truth...'

Flames burst out all around the sides of the pyre. The priest had to raise his voice even more.

'...From darkness to light, and from death to immortality.'

Then she saw that Gwynfor too had stepped away from the pyre, moving from the intense heat. He was looking directly at her. His mouth was moving: he was singing!

She couldn't make out any of the words through the roar of the burning pyre, the women chanting, the harmonium humming and the little bells jingling.

She leant forward, smiling at him through her tears. She lifted her hand to her ear to show he should sing louder. The pyre crackled and whooshed. Smoke was everywhere now; for a moment she couldn't see him in the billowing white.

Then, from behind, Star heard the men from Gwynfor's homeland. They'd soon latched on to what he was singing. Gradually the male Welsh voices – sweet, with a melancholy note cutting through – swelled over the Indian women's chanting:

Nefol Dad, mae eto'n nosi . . . Gwrando lef ein hwyrol weddi...

Star found herself stepping forward, walking up to join Gwynfor by the blazing pyre. The air above it was a dancing distortion – now too hot to bear.

Hand in hand, they turned to look into the crowd, their eyes smarting, as the men's singing and the women's Gujerati chants wove through the smoke.

15

That weekend the weather broke. Fork lightning struck the mast and studio-shed of Radio New Warwick; an employee was seriously injured. On the Saturday flash floods swept through the city and a small boy, aged four, fell into a storm drain. He was swirled away in an instant and his body was never recovered: people talked about it being washed into the River Avon. Acres of maize were bludgeoned to the ground by the torrential rain; sorrowful cattle stood on muddy islands in flooded fields.

Lara Johnson fretted: would she be able to get away tomorrow? Would the expedition have to be called off? Some years the summer rains lasted well into September.

Lara detected a quiet relief building in her mother. She, Lara, might not be going – not soon anyway. It was really annoying: her mother kept looking out of the window, shaking her head and giving Lara meaningful glances.

But she couldn't start arguing with her mother again – not in front of Arrow, who'd been so clingy the past few days.

She suppressed a sigh and went upstairs to find out if the phone was working yet. She picked up the receiver: nothing. It could be days before they fixed the lines. There was a lightning flash. And another. Twenty seconds later the thunder came. Arrow came squealing out of her bedroom, excited, running into Lara's arms. Her mother, laughing, held her tight and picked her up, whirling her around.

'Ooh, you're getting too heavy for this!' But her words were drowned out by another round of thunder.

Arrow took Lara's hand and led her mother into her parents' bedroom. The storm was nearly overhead now. They sat on the bed to watch the lightning. David's face in the photo on the dresser smiled and flickered at them.

'Mummy, Grandma says the thunder's huge barrels rolling down in the sky.'

'Silly nonsense. She used to tell me that.'

'Look, Mummy!' Arrow pointed to a dark figure running towards the house from the direction of the orchard, stooping as he ran through the rain. There was a dull green cape over his head and shoulders. For a moment Lara thought it might be one of the two policemen who were still on guard duty.

A few minutes later Ben was drying off in the kitchen, a steaming mug of sweet apple tea in his big red hands, a glum expression on his face. He'd come to tell them the wooden bridge at Wasperton had collapsed and the road to Newbold Pacey had washed away completely in some places.

'And half my maize crop's been knocked flat!' he added, shaking his head.

Rae was bustling to and fro, tut-tutting. 'Oh dear Ben, that's terrible!'

He looked at Lara, who was standing uneasily by the door. 'I'll be surprised if you can make a start tomorrow.'

She didn't reply.

Arrow was standing on one leg by the kitchen oven, wide-eyed and quiet she stared at Ben. She was sucking a thumb, a battered misshapen teddy bear hanging from her other hand.

'I mean,' Ben continued, 'from what I've heard it's really bad. Up-country it could be even worse.'

Rae put on a cheerful smile. 'Look, Arrow! Help me get these scones out of the oven, they're done,' she said.

Lara walked out.

Ben gave Rae a worried glance.

Lara's mother was bending at the open oven door, removing the tray of hot scones. Arrow was at her side, hopping from one foot to the other.

'Now careful, Arrow, the tray is really hot!'

'Did I say something?' Ben asked Rae quietly.

Rae put the tray of scones on top of the range and fanned her hot face with a tea towel.

'Fetch us three plates, Arrow, there's a good girl.'

While her granddaughter was distracted, she turned to Ben and said 'I don't know, she's really on edge about this trip.' In a loud whisper, she added 'I wish she'd forget going, I really do. I think you need to go and talk to her, Ben.'

He found her in the study, sitting at her desk. He knocked softly on the door even though it was half-open and they could see each other.

'Are you all right?'

'Yes. Why shouldn't I be?'

'You got up and went out without saying anything.'

'I wanted to write a letter.'

There was a single sheet of paper on the desk in front of her. He noticed that she'd written just two lines in her neat handwriting.

'I see,' he said, feeling awkward, not sure what to say next – though his heart was brimming over and he wanted to take her in his arms and kiss her and try to make up for what had happened on that Saturday night.

'It's just…' she said, her voice controlled, 'it's just that I could've done with you not worrying Arrow like that. About the weather and the roads. Or Mum, come to that.'

'Sorry.'

'Even if the trip has to be postponed tomorrow I'm going soon.'

'Yes. OK. I should've thought.'

She sighed 'It's no big deal I suppose.'

'All right, but I am worried you'll be all right. This trip…I mean, are you sure–'

'–Am I sure it's worth it?!' Lara's eyes flashed. Her voice was angry and low. 'Is that what you mean? Is it worth it, trying to find my husband?'

'No, no! No of course I don't mean that, Lara. Stop…'

He was flummoxed; what should he say?

'Stop what,' she said coolly.

He took a deep breath. 'What I mean is, I'll never stop worrying about you, Lara. I love you too much for that. All right,

131

it's wrong and I'm sorry about what happened that night. Like I told you before, I realise it shouldn't have happened. I got it wrong, I…you know! But honestly, I know you've got to find David. I know you've got to go.'

There was a pause. She looked at him, her expression softening.

'And, well…' he was twisting his hands together, trying not to say the wrong thing.

'…And well, I'll miss you so much, Lara Johnson!'

He was so glad when she leant forward in her chair, reached over and took his hand. There was no kiss, but that touch of her hand meant a lot.

The next day the rain eased and Lara did go.

She, Arrow and Rae were sitting in the kitchen finishing breakfast. Arrow ran to the window and peered through the raindrops on the glass. 'Mum! They've come!'

Lara's eyes met her mother's.

'You'd better go and get your bags,' Rae said quietly.

Lara glanced up at the antique clock on the wall: eight-thirty and they were here – just as the commissioner had promised.

Lara walked quickly to the front door. 'Give me a few minutes,' she said.

The driver, a clean-shaven Asian man in his early forties, nodded. His face was expressionless. 'I'm Saleem, your driver.'

'Won't you come in a minute, Saleem? I'll need help with the bags.'

Saleem nodded. 'Wave to me when you're ready to go, madam. Then I'll drive to the door and get your bags.'

He turned to walk back to a Land-Rover parked a little way off. There were two vehicles on the drive, both battered and a faded green colour. Lara could make out another man sitting in the front of the first vehicle. In the second vehicle there were two men sitting in the front.

Lara rushed upstairs to a bathroom and did what she needed to do. Then she scouted round her bedroom to make sure she hadn't left anything important. Finally there were some papers and a bag to collect from the study – and the letter to leave for Ben.

In the hallway, her mother and Arrow were standing close together, silent and white-faced.

Lara knelt down to put her arms around her daughter. 'Brave girl, don't worry about me. Okay?'

Arrow nodded, holding back the tears.

Lara had to brush a tear away from her own eye. 'And look after Grandma,' she smiled.

Straightening up, she said to them 'I'm only going to be away a few weeks aren't I?'

'Take care, Lara,' her mother said, as Lara hugged her. 'Let's hope this time…you know…'

Lara nodded. 'Love you, Mum. Love you Arrow, bye!'

She opened the front door, heaved her two bags into the porch and gave the driver a wave. He came running up, nodded gravely to the three of them and seized the bags without saying anything.

'Ben – what about Ben?' Rae looked shocked.

Ben had gone clean out of Lara's mind. 'Mum, I have to go now.'

'Can't you wait a few minutes? I'm sure he'll be here any second. He really wanted to say goodbye.'

'I'll be back soon. I'm sorry, Mum – but he did know the time I might be going. Oh – there's a letter for him on the table in the hall, okay?'

She turned to go, blowing a kiss to Arrow. Her daughter buried her head in her grandmother's skirt.

''Bye, love you!' Lara said one more time, then half-ran, half-walked to the waiting Land Rover.

As they drove down the drive Lara looked back just once. Through the misted rear window she could make out the figures of her mother and daughter receding rapidly into the distance. Both were still waving.

Then, running across the lawn to join them, was Ben. The Land Rover was nearly at the end of the long drive now, so he was a matchstick man. He was waving his arms frantically. They rounded a bend; he was gone.

When they got to the central square ten minutes later, the rain had completely stopped. Dark sheets of water covered large areas. The delicate mauve and green leaves of the maples around the square hung down in a bedraggled fashion.

Lara noticed most of the shops and traders' stalls around the square were still closed. There was a big notice over the market hall saying 'Cancelled Today'. The bank would be open in a minute, though. The city clock over the legislative council building clanged once for the half hour: it was coming up to nine-thirty.

Lara had a few moments to meet the rest of her retinue: Anwar, Saleem's brother and driver of the other Land-Rover, and the two soldiers from the South Midlands Regiment who'd be accompanying them, one in each Land-Rover. Tall and muscular, the soldiers nodded in her direction and gave her taut, polite smiles.

Lara was glad not many people were about. Having armed soldiers trailing round with you was embarrassing. She made her way quickly towards the bank. As she was about to go up the steps she heard her name. Lara stopped and turned round. A slight figure was walking quickly towards her.

'Mrs Johnson?'

'Star! How are you?'

'You going then?'

Lara nodded in the direction of the two Land-Rovers. 'As far as we can get, anyway. You could put me in tomorrow's paper: 'Lara Johnson leaves on expedition to the wilds of the north.''

'I've been sacked.'

'What?'

'Mr Blennerhassett told me to pack up straightaway and not come back. Just after the funeral.'

'Oh Star, I'm sorry!' Lara looked angry. 'I'll have a word with him – he can't do that!'

'I didn't have a contract. I'm only a trainee. Anyway, it's my own stupid fault.'

'He's made enough mistakes in his time believe me, Miss Edkin.'

Star bit her lip. 'I'd better be going. I've got to return the bike.'

'And how's Gwynfor?'

'He's gone.'

'Gone! Already?'

'Yesterday morning.'

'The storms were bad in the afternoon.'

Star shook her head. 'He's mad. I tried to stop him. But he went to the stables, got the horse – Bronwen, you know, his dad's horse? And the dog.'

'I hope he'll be all right.'

'He's mad.' Star rubbed one eye. 'He did come round to see me, say goodbye though.'

'We'll look out for him on the road' Lara smiled.

Star looked sad. 'Okay. You never know. Thanks, Mrs Johnson.'

After an hour's delay Lara had signed for and collected the two locked cases of money that had been left for her at the bank. The Land-Rovers were now bowling along Boulevard Thesby. Within a few minutes they'd passed through North Gate. As they turned left to head for the main road north, the first shaft of sunlight hit the sodden fields ahead of them.

Just before they reached the junction for the A429, where there was an untidy collection of Chinese food stalls, bars and massage parlours, Lara glanced up from the papers she was looking at. There, about two hundred yards ahead was someone dancing around in the middle of the narrow road, arms waving.

Saleem didn't slacken the pace of the Land-Rover one bit. 'Tsk, tsk, now what is this?' he said in a low voice.

'Stop, Saleem!' Lara shouted.

The vehicle slowed a little. 'You sure?'

'Saleem, for God's sake!'

He hit the brakes. The other vehicle skidded to a halt behind them, slewing to avoid a shunt.

As Lara opened her door, the soldier in the back jumped out and began sweeping his submachine gun to and fro. This is getting ridiculous, she thought.

She turned her attention to the figure who'd brought them to a halt.

'Star! What the hell…? You nearly caused an accident!'

'I'm really sorry, Mrs Johnson.'

'How did you get here?'

Star inclined her head to one side. About twenty yards away, standing behind one of the food stalls was a young man with sticky-up hair and thick eyebrows. He had a bruised face and a black eye. Star's motorbike was next to him.

'Mrs Johnson, I should've asked you before. But the idea just came to me after you went into the bank. So I dashed back to the

135

flat to get a few things.'

Lara frowned. 'Get a few things?'

Star touched the small bag she was carrying.

'Er, just a few clothes...and stuff. Will you take me with you, Mrs Johnson? Please?'

16

They were hurtling down a fast road towards the South Mercian border. Glancing at the countryside whizzing past, Lara noticed that open fields and fenced meadows were already giving way to longer and longer stretches of woodland. She could still change her mind and ask Star to go back.

Lara had been expecting to make this journey on her own – a time to think, to prepare herself for what might lie ahead.

But now she had to adjust to that faint musky smell Star brought with her – not completely overpowering but feral, unsettling somehow.

'Want some, Mrs Johnson?' A creased paper cone full of roasted nuts was held in her face.

'Thanks, no.' Lara managed not to gag at the aromas of hazelnut, sickly honey and vegetable oil.

She looked at Star, who was munching and staring out at the passing scenery. What made this young lady tick? Why exactly had she been so intent on coming? She was a clever one and no mistake. Polite and deferential one minute, confident and self-possessed the next.

When I hesitated back there, she knew how to play her cards. She'd been quite firm: let me get in the car first, then I'll tell you about this information I've got about your husband.

'Honest, Mrs Johnson, no one else has seen it. Really, it'll help you.'

'Why not give it to me now, then?' Lara had asked.

'It's too complicated. I saw some stuff on a computer as well. Take me with you and I'll explain it later, as we go.'

Lara felt angry. She didn't like being bargained with. But in the end she'd given way. She could always chuck this wretched Edkin girl out if the so-called 'information' she claimed to have was worthless.

They were at the border now. Lara could see the high, newly painted white fencing coming up. Saleem slowed the Land-Rover, saying he'd take their passports through the control area if they wanted.

'No, it's OK, Saleem,' Lara said. 'We'll get out and stretch our legs – long journey ahead.' Lara was secretly hoping the border police might for some reason stop Star going through.

When Lara jumped down from the car she noticed a new signboard on a gantry overhead. 'BYE BYE SOUTH MERCIA' it said, in letters two feet high, alternating red and pink.

Star was looking at it too. She turned to face Lara. 'You can't believe those stupid colours can you?'

Lara couldn't stop herself smiling.

Getting through the border control took only a few minutes. When she was filling in the exit traffic card, Lara wrote 'personal and work reasons' under the heading 'Reason For Leaving South Mercia'.

On the way out of the building, Star said with a solemn expression 'I wrote 'Holiday' in that section' and gave Lara a wink. They both laughed.

Once they'd crossed into West Mercia and entered the deeper forest the road became a lot worse. They were heading west on the one usable lane of an old Good Time motorway which had once had four lanes each way. Now the one old motorway lane had become a narrow, pot-holed, two-way strip.

In some places the road surface had crumbled away altogether, exposing the red Warwickshire mud and stones underneath. There were deep ruts in the road. Sometimes they had to reverse and pull into the side to let horse-drawn carts and wagons get past. Usually there was a long train of them – as many as fifteen wagons at a time.

Even when there was no traffic they could rarely get above twenty miles an hour. Sometimes potholes and deep ruts were replaced by wide pits and hollows full of cloudy red floodwater. It was hard to judge how deep they were, and sometimes the Land-Rover slewed and sank alarmingly into them.

By late afternoon, after four hours or so of strenuous travelling they were ready for a break. They'd been following another old-time motorway track which Lara knew from previous journeys had been called M5 in Good Time. Every so often they'd come to a place where a bridge had collapsed or was too unsafe to cross. This had entailed detours of up to five miles in some places, trailing up hill and down dale until they could cross a new bridge – usually a sketchy structure made of wood that would vibrate alarmingly as they went over.

Now they'd come to the end of the M5. There was a barrier in front of them. In the old days the motorway had entered a long, raised section at this point. All of it had become severely weakened over the years and some sections had collapsed completely.

Lara remembered from her school geography that this part of the world had once been called the Black Country.

'Why black?' Star asked. She'd asked Lara a hundred and one questions that day.

'The Industrial Revolution – didn't they teach you about that in history? All the fires and furnaces they had, the metal bashing and factories belching out fumes – the air must've been thick with black smoke.'

'Wow,' said Star, looking down over the rolling forests below.

They'd parked in a large, grassy clearing near the top of a steeply sloping hill. A creek – much enlarged with floodwater – was rushing over a weir, a loud soothing roar. A dozen goats, tethered by long ropes, were nibbling the grass. On the other side of the clearing, a hundred yards away, were some wooden buildings and a sign advertising fruit teas, beer and snacks.

The other Land-Rover, now throaty and loud because of a damaged exhaust pipe, clattered into the clearing. The two drivers talked quietly to each other and the soldiers got out and went towards the café, with Lara and Star walking slowly behind them.

As they sipped chilled goat's milk mixed with crushed summer raspberries, looking out over the clearing, Star had yet more questions to ask Lara. They were sitting on the café's rickety veranda. In the far distance, perhaps ten miles away, a single very high tower could be seen above the swathes of forest and undulating dark green hills. Something metallic on the top of it glinted in the sunshine.

'Mrs Johnson…'

'You might as well call me Lara.'

'Oh! Okay…um, Lara…' Star smiled tentatively. 'Have you ever been to any of the old towns and cities? Ever been taken round?'

Lara shook her head. 'Those school trips were before my time. I can remember when I was in junior school some of the older high school kids went, but soon after that they decided it was too dangerous. What about you?'

'No, but I've always wanted to see one of the old cities. What was that one called, over there?'

'That was Birmingham.'

A faraway look came into the younger woman's eyes. She told Lara about a secret expedition she'd made once on the motorbike to the Cotswolds, a hilly area of lost villages and towns thirty miles south of New Warwick.

Lara smiled, sipping more milkshake. 'You were taking a risk.'

The two soldiers burst out of the café behind them. They ran, whooping and shouting, back across the clearing towards the river a hundred yards away.

Lara and Star watched, amused, as they stripped off their uniforms: a brief glimpse of white buttocks and tanned legs and backs, and then they'd splashed feet-first into a deep pool below the weir.

Saleem the driver came to stand next to them. He looked faintly embarrassed, as if it was his duty to distract the women from the naked, whooping men in the water.

Lara leant back in her chair. 'Saleem, where've you been?'

'Prayers, madam.'

'Ah, I see.'

'My brother's inside getting something to eat now.'

'I was just saying, that was Birmingham over there, wasn't it? Where that high tower is?'

Saleem nodded. 'My family was there. My great-grandfather came from Pakistan in the last century – the year 1956, we were always told.'

'Pakistan!' Star said, wonder in her voice.

'I've been in that old city,' Saleem continued, 'when I was a young man, about twenty. You were still allowed then.'

'You went back to find where your family had lived?' Star asked.

'No, no. My grandfather knew those houses had fallen down. The whole street had gone. He went back and found the road had been replaced by a river. It must've been underground, you know, in the old days. No, we went to try to get a very holy, very special copy of the Koran from a big mosque that had been in the centre of the city.'

'Wow. Did you find it?' The younger woman's eyes were wide.

'Tsk, no.' Saleem's eyes were sad. 'Roof collapsed, you know? Everything inside the mosque had been spoiled.'

'Oh, no.'

There was a trace of amusement in Saleem's eyes. 'Actually I don't think such a Koran existed. It would never have been left there, you know, when the city was closed down. Stories and fables get around, you know . . . and sometimes the old people forget. Then they make things up. No doubt it seemed very important at the time.'

There was a pause as Saleem and the two women stared across the sunny clearing. The soldiers were still enjoying themselves in the water, throwing a leather ball back and forth.

Then Saleem, whom Lara had put down as a reserved man, told them all about the wonders he'd seen on that expedition twenty years before into the old, abandoned city. How trees – sycamores, oaks, elms, limes, you name it – how all these trees, some more than thirty feet high, had forced their way through cracks in roads and pavements. Already, two decades ago, they were marching up the widest roads and streets and branching out through windows from the insides of buildings.

'My grandparents, you know, they grew up in that city. They used to tell us there were already a million trees there. In the parks, gardens, along the streets. Even before all the troubles and plagues. Imagine how overgrown it is now!'

'Were there lots of birds flying round?' Lara shivered.

'Of course. Haven't you seen them around here too?'

It was true. Neither Lara nor Star had wanted to say anything but they'd noticed small birds flitting around the clearing as soon as they'd arrived, and the roar of the creek couldn't drown out the birdsong.

'It's a losing battle everywhere,' Lara said. 'My neighbour's got a farm. He's put a bird scarer in nearly every field. They bang away, get on our nerves, and there are regular nest eradications, but...'

Star sighed. 'It's all rubbish, isn't it?'

'You're probably right,' said Lara. 'The last pandemic was Super-TB, nothing to do with the earlier viruses like SARS and bird flu. Or so David used to say. And that's what we really need – more science, more scientists.'

It had now gone five. Lara and Star climbed into the back of the Land-Rover. The sun glimmered through hot, humid banks of cloud. They were heading for a government rest house situated two hours' away to the north-west. But their progress, Saleem informed them, would very much depend on the state of the roads. After leaving the old motorway track they were following a winding switchback road that led through the ruins of one of the old Black Country towns.

On the hillier stretches between sudden drops into steep-sided valleys, thick forest gave way to more open country. In one place they passed a lone tower block. It looked as if it had housed people in the old days.

'Wow, it's huge,' said Star, her mouth wide open. The height of the building was accentuated by dangling galleries of Virginia creeper and other trailing vegetation. The whole structure had become a massive column of greenery which, as the vehicles laboured past, seemed to reach right up into the sky. After they'd passed the tower block the track ran through a wide expanse of open land. Grey-white stones, chunks of concrete, peeped through ground-level weeds and flowers.

Lara was relieved to see open spaces after the endless winding gloom of the forest tracks. Where the towers had fallen, smaller plants and bushes had bloomed – goldenrod, thick with insects, the purple and pink flowers of tree mallow, ox-eye daisies, buddleia, broom, brambles, and, an astonishing sight, a dazzling swathe of blue, red and purple lupins hundreds of yards across.

A bit further on Saleem looked up, scanning the sky, and shouted 'Eagle! Over there, to the right. See?'

And there, sure enough, very high up: fierce, graceful wings.

'Awesome,' Star breathed. 'Were they, like, a royal bird?'

No sooner had she asked this question than Saleem pointed out something quite different. 'Over there, to the left!'

A sudden flickering of silver through the trees: a stretch of open water. And just beyond the trees a magnificent sight: a swan, wings outstretched, swooping slowly down towards the lake. A line of spray suddenly lit up behind its outstretched feet. On the lake, which they could now see was extensive, black moorhens and tufted ducks bobbed.

But of all the surprising sights they saw that day the most startling were the grey animals with long tails and large hind legs that bounced and sprang across their path.

'What the hell are those!' Star shouted, laughing.

'Bloody things,' Saleem grimaced. 'Wallabies. Lost a windscreen once with one of those bloody things jumping in front!' Lara saw Star grinning at her, making a face at the grumbling Saleem, and found herself smiling again.

KEN BLAKEMORE

17

That evening, after they'd eaten together, Lara demanded to see the information Star had promised to give her. They were sitting facing each other across the highly polished surface of a fine antique dining table. There was still plenty of evening light but inside the dining room it was already dark enough for the steward to have lit candles - which now glimmered softly between them. This was Boscobel House – a large timber-framed farmhouse built in the seventeenth century, now converted into a government rest house.

A few miles to the east – they'd passed it on the way – was Chillington Hall, a much bigger and grander Georgian mansion with an impressive portico of Greek columns. Chillington had become the residence of the West Mercian Regional Commissioner.

As a small military detachment was quartered at Chillington Hall, the two soldiers had been dropped off there to spend the night.

Once the two women had been shown their rooms – Lara's spacious bedroom with its four-poster far grander than Star's servant quarters, of course – the two Asian brothers had disappeared. They were going to spend the night a few miles further on, in a small Muslim township on the main road north.

Many small settlements of Muslims, like the one Saleem and his brother were now heading for, dotted the land. Most could trace their roots back to the dispersals following the closure of big cities like Birmingham, Coventry and Wolverhampton decades before.

These cities had been where, in Good Time, some of the Asian communities – particularly the Muslims and the Sikhs – had played an important role in the old engineering and components industries. They'd also run many subsidiary enterprises like taxi services, garages and spare parts businesses.

So it wasn't surprising that it was the Muslims and Sikhs who'd gradually taken over as the two main guilds responsible for maintaining and nursing Good Time vehicles and engines. These two groups, fiercely competitive with each other, drove, cannibalised, de-computered and rebuilt nearly every ageing, decades-old car, truck and tractor in the country. And on top of that, the same family businesses were becoming the blacksmiths and farriers, the wheelwrights and coachbuilders of the new horse-drawn age.

Lara lifted the almost-empty carafe. 'Go on. This stuff isn't very strong.'

She poured the remaining thin red wine into Star's glass and called for another half-carafe.

'You seem very quiet, Miss Edkin.'

Star looked up. It was very daunting, this grand place. When she'd seen the other guests arriving in their fine clothes, loud confident voices booming, she'd asked Lara whether it wouldn't be better if she ate alone in the servants' quarters.

'I haven't brought anything to wear – like posh' she'd whispered.

In truth she'd brought almost no clothes at all – just one country linen shirt, a couple of pairs of baggy knickers; that was it. When she'd rushed back to her lodgings to grab the secret papers she'd barely had time to stuff even these into her bag.

'Come up to my room for a minute,' Lara had said.

When Star had got there she'd found that it wasn't one room but three. There was a bedroom, a dressing room and a bathroom. A manservant and a maid were just leaving: they'd been refilling a hip bath with hot water. The maid had winked at Star as she left, smiling broadly. The soapy bath water gave off a beautiful smell: was it lavender?

'You hop in that bath,' Lara had said to her, holding out a large, fluffy bath towel. There had been no choice. 'I'll sort something out for you,' she'd added. 'Don't be long.'

When Star had emerged from the bathroom, her short hair wet and the towel wound tightly around her, she'd found three long dresses draped over a divan in the dressing room. Lara had called out, 'Try the dark red one. It's a bit tight on me so it'll be more your size.'

When Star had put the dress on she'd found the length OK but the high neckline too loose, sagging down. Lara was over thirty and had a full, curvy figure; Star was a lean, wiry young woman.

But when Lara had come into the dressing room she'd nodded, then frowned, saying 'It's a waisted dress, see?' Then she'd stood behind Star and pulled on some laces that Star hadn't noticed at all, so neat and tidily tailored was the dress. The bodice had fitted more snugly then.

Lara had stepped back, looking at Star and still frowning. Her face had broken into a smile and she'd said, 'Have a look at yourself.'

There was a full-length mirror. Star saw someone she didn't recognise: a slim young woman in a long dress made of soft dark red material.

'It's the New Medieval look,' Lara had said. 'It'll take over from Good Time soon, you'll see.'

But the strangest, most striking thing about the woman in the long mirror was her eyes – dark, luminous, brown eyes that were almost black. They were radiating flashes of excitement and trepidation. When she saw herself, Star breathed in with surprise.

Lara had stood next to her and said, 'it's a tad too big but you do really look good in it.' Then she'd taken another towel and rubbed Star's short spiky hair until it was nearly dry.

'Try this gold brooch thing. It'll keep your hair up on that side.'

Star looked in the mirror again. The broad golden hairclip gleamed, and was indeed holding up her hair in the way Lara had suggested. Then a strange want had struck: suddenly, just as she'd wanted to kiss Gwynfor a week before, she wanted to plant kisses on Lara Johnson's cheeks, eyes; her whole face.

When they walked into the dining room, heads turned. Three loud-mouthed tax inspectors, their faces already ruddy with wine and beer, were seated at the next table. They stood awkwardly, one knocking his chair over, grinning and mumbling respects as Lara and Star had taken their seats. During the meal Star couldn't help whispering to Lara how she'd seen all three men sneaking glances at them.

Now, everyone else had finished eating and left their tables.

Lara refilled their glasses and looked expectantly at Star. The younger woman reached down for a leather purse she'd brought from her room. She untied the tight lacing along the top of the bag and took out a single folded piece of paper, which she placed on the table.

At the same time, sitting alone at his kitchen table, Ben was opening Lara's letter.

Since he'd watched the Land-Rover disappearing at the end of the drive, he'd had a depressing day foot-slogging through mud, shit and ankle-deep water. The rain had stopped at last, that was one blessing, but the biofuel tractor wouldn't start.

He'd had to work with the horses, getting them to pull a cartload of hay bales round, fetching fodder to the cows stranded in the lower fields. But that hadn't been easy for the horses, with the ground so sticky and heavy going.

All the while, trudging through the mud, he'd thought about this letter.

The realistic side of me knows very well what'll be in it, he'd told himself. So why get so excited? Because the other side of me, the mad side of me that can't stop thinking about her, still hopes.

More fool you.

He ripped open the envelope and read. He was never a quick one at reading.

Dearest Ben,

By the time you read this I should be well on my way. I suppose it would've been better to talk to you before I went, explain what I feel, rather than leave you a letter. But I'm afraid I couldn't bring myself to sit down and talk to you properly the last few days. I was too worked up, preoccupied planning this trip and worrying about work. I'm sorry – I hope you understand.

What I wanted to tell you is that you're a fine man, Ben. To me you've been one of the best and truest friends I've ever had. I don't want what happened that Saturday evening to spoil that. As far as I'm concerned it didn't happen – and I hope it doesn't hurt you for me to say that. I know you were hoping for so much more. But if you can possibly allow it, what I want is to carry on seeing you as I've always seen you – as a great friend and neighbour – and that's why I want to set that Saturday evening aside.

I would hate it if you stopped coming to see us, share meals with us and all that. Arrow thinks the world of you and my mother's always had a soft spot for you! Above all, I'd miss you if you weren't that trusty friend next door who I can call on, who tells funny stories about the farm and the animals and who helps keep my feet on the ground.

As long as there's a possibility David's alive, it could never be more than friends and neighbours between us, could it? – I know you've always realised that, deep-down, because David meant a lot to you didn't he?

But I also wanted to say (and I'm sorry if this is really hard for you) that if the saddest thing comes true and we discover David's never coming back I would still see you as a close friend rather than someone I'd fall in love with and start again with.

Please believe me, it's nothing to do with you as a man or your qualities. You're a very attractive man, Ben, good-looking, gentle and kind.

It won't be easy for you if what you said about your feelings for me is true, but don't take it too hard. Put me out of your mind as a future lover, partner, wife, whatever, as soon as you can. Give yourself a chance with someone else.

I'm very, very sorry Ben if this letter has left you feeling as if you hate me for writing these things. Please believe that I honestly want the best for you and I want us to remain best friends.

With love,

Lara

Lara picked up the note Star had laid on the polished dining table and unfolded the creased page:

Written in haste, might be interrupted. Here, temp containment seems to be working but materials for perm security still req. [see other document]. NB V important, offensive possibility still v real, though of course I don't know the pol. sit.

I've detailed what I know of their economic strategy but it's not my field. All the info I've copied Mar 12 comes from usual Mid-North source. Date of origin n.k. Advise minimum time frame, could be within 6-9 mo of March?

One source ['see Bullion' & 'Production Ops'] suggests plans for a new currency! Something no one's considered? Poss. production site / mint in Eng

somewhere [York?].
    I'm in W now, urg request rescue, try Deva again for

Lara read down the page quickly. Then she went back to the top and scanned down again.

'Is this all there is – just this one page?'

'Yes. I think he must have been interrupted by somebody.'

'It's David, I'm sure of it.' She was staring into the middle distance now, deep in thought.

'He says something about March in there, doesn't he? So not so long ago…'

'Five months! Anything could have happened in that time.'

'I'm sorry, Mrs Johnson. I know I should've given you that note as soon as I got it.'

Lara jerked her chair back and stood. She picked up her glass of wine and started to pace up and down the stone-flagged floor, firing questions at Star.

'Has anybody else seen this note?'

'No. Um, well . . .'

'Well what?'

'Butcher. He's my friend, the one you saw with the motorbike this morning. He saw the message when it was on the computer. But honestly he's good, he won't…'

'On a computer??'

'Yes. That's how we got the note. We printed it from a memory tab in Gwyn's father's saddlebag. It fell out, you see…'
Star faltered, seeing Lara's reaction, and then carried on: '…I found it and took it to the university. To get Butcher to use the computer.'

'You found a memory tab! Star, why the hell didn't you tell me?'

Star plucked at the sleeve of her dress and looked down.

'Honestly!' Lara said, staring hard at the younger woman, 'I can see why Blennerhassett …never mind. Where's that tab now? You have brought it with you?'

Star shook her head.

'You haven't!' stormed Lara. 'Why not?'

'Because of what it says…it does say 'possibility very real' or something doesn't it?'

Lara nodded. 'So?'

'What is that possibility? I guessed it might be some huge danger – I don't know what. So I gave the tab to Butcher and made him promise to take it to the legislative council in Warwick – the First Minister's office. I put it in an envelope with a note to explain. Butcher will have done that, Mrs Johnson, honestly he will...'

Lara stopped pacing up and down.

'Okay. At least you didn't give the tab to Blennerhassett. And you haven't given him a copy of this note?'

'No.'

'I suppose you did the right thing with the tab, thinking about it.'

Star felt a weight lifting off her chest and took a fortifying sip of wine.

'It's just that I won't be able to look at the rest of the stuff on it now' Lara continued. She sighed. 'Not that it would have been easy finding a working computer in these parts.'

Star picked the note up from the table and looked at it.

'When I read this, Mrs John– er, Lara, it seems like it's talking about a military threat – like war? Did you know anything about this?'

'I'm amazed by it,' Lara said. 'Absolutely amazed. Nobody in New Warwick I know has been talking about any kind of military threat or civil war or anything like that.'

She put her glass down and gave Star a worried look.

'Should I go back to Chillington House right now? I could get a radio message sent back from Chillington to Oxford, maybe?'

Star felt flattered now. A moment ago she was being shouted at; now she was being consulted.

'Lara, there was a memory stick in the saddlebag as well as the memory tab I found. And a map, chart thing. File took them off Gwynfor and sent them to Oxford. So the Oxford government will know what's in them won't they?'

'You're right.' Lara walked over to the table, refilled their glasses and sat down. 'Let's hope File's passed them on to the right people at the top. I'll send a letter to our commissioner tomorrow – Alexander will check with Oxford.'

'Mrs Johnson, I know you were angry with me for not telling you about that memory tab before. But honest, I don't think there was anything on it that would've told you where your husband is. The other documents were all about some economic stuff as far as

I could see. Nothing to do with nuclear power stations or your husband.'

Lara nodded. 'I see.'

'And Lara...?' Star was opening her leather purse again. With a smile on her face she took out another piece of paper and held it up. 'Butcher managed to print the first page of one of the other documents. The security men were coming so we didn't have time to print anything else. But I did grab this – here you are.'

Ben folded Lara's letter in two and sat at the table, unable to move for more than an hour. When the light began to fade he got up, walked stiffly to the back room and unlocked the door to a wall cupboard.

He took out a dusty cardboard box, very old, which had been covered many years ago with rose-patterned wallpaper. Someone in his family must have glued it on. The rose pattern was very faded now, almost colourless in places. The wallpaper covering had been ripped and come off the box in places.

Placing the fragile box on a table, he opened it and looked inside. Then, one by one, he took out the things that had mattered to him most in his life.

He laid them out on the table:

The portrait photos of his mother and father, one of each of them when they were young, in their early twenties he supposed, and one of them together on their wedding day. They were pictures he still couldn't bear to display anywhere in the house;

The heart-shaped box containing a lock of his mother's hair – glossy, black and immortal;

The photo of his favourite dog, a cocker spaniel called Sprite;

The last will and testament of his father, Jack Frobisher;

Love letters from Tam, tied together with a red ribbon in a bundle also containing his love letters to her;

His and Tam's marriage certificate;

Tam's death certificate.

He spent nearly an hour looking at each of these things, touching them, reading them, until the tears rolled down his cheeks like a river. He didn't sob; he didn't break down completely. He was proud of being strong like that.

Then he put each item back in the box in order, one by one, finishing with Lara's letter on the top of the pile.

There was one item he hadn't taken out. It was at the bottom of the box underneath everything else, wrapped in a white cloth.

It could stay there for now. He'd carry on. He refused to believe she could be so certain about him, or about herself.

As it was getting late, and was almost completely dark, she decided to save the second paper until she went to bed. The two women said goodnight to the steward, who gave them candle lanterns to light the way to their rooms.

Star's room was in an annex above the stables so Lara, instead of going straight upstairs to her own rooms, walked outside with the younger woman to get some air. It was a humid, hot night. In the far distance the horizon flickered with occasional purple flashes and they could hear faint rumbles of thunder.

Lara was thinking about the note Star had shown her. She was even surer now that it must have been written by David. But the contents had caused her pangs of disappointment. There was nothing personal in it, no request that whoever received the message get in touch with her as soon as possible.

Her mind drifted back to the ominous warning in the note: 'offensive possibility still v real'. She thought about Arrow, tucked up in bed back home. Her maternal instincts were kicking in. Should she turn round and go back?

No, she told herself, you must go on. You must, because there are never certainties in this world. She might rush back to New Warwick like a frightened chicken and in a month's time find all hell breaking loose and the city crumbling around them. No, she had to go on and play her part in trying to stop this.

Alexander Laczko's words floated into her mind: keep an open mind…tell me what you've observed, seen and heard up there.

It was clear where her duty lay.

Twenty minutes later, Lara got into bed. The oil lamp on her bedside table radiated a lot of heat. Two moths were fluttering around it, battering their wings on the opaque glass. She turned the lamp down to a dull glow and unfolded the note to read:

ECONOMIC STRATEGY – FIRST STEPS

INTRODUCTION

Having a bold, well-thought-out economic strategy will be the key to establishing authority in the new realm. Its importance cannot be over-emphasised.

Seizing the reins of the economy could be even more important than military might or coercion using paramilitary forces. And in the early stages of takeover, economic control will certainly be more important than 'soft' power – i.e. persuasion and winning over opinion formers; patronage and redistribution of property to those who collaborate with the new order.

The common people need not be aware of our economic strategy. In many ways it would be better if they were kept in the dark. If they can be given a sense of a higher authority at work, expertly husbanding the resources of the realm, competently resolving persistent economic problems, so their trust in, and admiration of, the new order will grow.

In all fields of public life, efficient control from the centre will be of key importance. Every opportunity must be taken to convince the common people that their new government is trustworthy; that it will look after them, and that they will not need to bother themselves overmuch with its mechanisms and workings.

It will be in the field of economics – money, taxation, trade and commerce – that this strategy will be particularly important. If the new realm can guarantee economic stability, then year by year the majority will be increasingly reluctant to envisage going back to the days before the new realm.

Today's economic problems signpost the way to what must be done.

The first and most important task facing the new realm will be to tackle inflation.

Presently, fluctuations in money supply and simple confusion about which of the several circulating currencies to trust means that everyone hoards the currencies thought to be more valuable – for instance German Euros. Everyone tries to spend only the weaker currencies. As a result, the weaker currencies such as the old UK pound progressively lose value and become ever weaker.

Those who save money naturally want to save it in the sound currencies.

Thus much of this wealth is locked into unproductive savings; it is not being invested to stimulate production or the development of infrastructure. The chronic shortage of capital for investment means barter has become commonplace in many rural territories (and even in some of the urban settlements); ever more local currencies (LETS) are launched. As LETS are trusted only in limited local areas, the size and scope of trading zones and markets are stunted.

In sum, the unfortunate citizen of Greater England (and of the autonomous regions of Wales, Scotland and Northern Ireland for that matter) does not know from month to month the value of the notes and coins in his pocket or the value of the crops in his fields. Similarly, his wife has no reliable way of calculating the price of goods she takes to market or buys from there; nor does she know the value of the clothes in her wardrobe or the bed linen in her blanket box.

History provides a valuable lesson. In the sixteenth century an economic adviser to the first Queen Elizabeth, Sir Thomas Gresham, elucidated the principle that 'bad money drives out good'. 'Gresham's Law', as it came to be known,

Lara turned the sheet of paper over, willing the writing to go on even though she knew the reverse side was blank. She sprang out of bed, pulled on a nightshirt and started pacing up and down.

The contents of that single page were astonishing. Unless it was a fake or a hoax of some kind, an unknown group or groups were planning a coup or takeover of some kind. From the sound of it, a very ambitious takeover involving the whole of Greater England! What were their motivations? Was some foreign power behind it?

Lara was desperate to tell someone. Am I the only responsible official in England, she wondered, who knows about this?

She picked up the paper again and held it close to the oil lamp, inspecting it closely. If she roused the stableman she could get a horse to carry her to Chillington Hall right now.

But what would that achieve? She knew there'd be no night duty staff in a place like Chillington Hall. She could hammer on the door of the officer in charge of the garrison or disturb the commissioner but neither would look very favourably on her if she woke them at this late hour, crying that someone was plotting to take over the economy. And even if they took her seriously, what could they themselves do before morning?

If only the wretched Edkin girl had shown her these notes last week! What if an invasion or something starts tomorrow?

Feeling hot, she went over to the cabinet in the corner of the bedroom, unlocked it and checked that the cases containing the money were still safely stowed away. Then she opened the window and pushed it wide open to get some air.

She rested her elbows on the windowsill and stared out into the velvety darkness. All was silent except for the continuous see-saw sound of the cicadas. The rest of the big house was slumbering peacefully.

The purple flickers of sheet lightning seemed to be getting nearer, brighter; the rumbles of thunder a little louder. No stars tonight.

She thought about the night she'd sat on the floor with Ben, the French windows wide open and them sitting half-in, half-out of the doorway. Plenty of stars that night!

Had she been wrong to write that letter to him?

The things she'd learned tonight, the ominous nature of the note she'd just read, had made the world seem that bit more unpredictable. She wanted to feel Ben's arm around her again; feel his warmth and be with someone uncomplicated and unaware of all this. Like when they were simply sitting on the step like two children marvelling at the intricate lacework of stars.

Had it been wise to be so definite with him about the future? To close it all off like that? She knew they weren't suited at this stage of their lives. Probably they never would be. But who knows? she asked herself. Who knows?

As she lay down and closed her eyes, Ben was doing the same. She soon drifted into sleep, but he didn't. He lay awake thinking, keeping his eyes shut so that he could picture her face in every detail.

She would come back one day. He would see her again. But how was he going to bear waiting – and did he have to bear it?

18

The next morning, as she woke, it took Star a full minute to realise where she was. Sunlight was streaming into the small timber-framed room. From below she could hear the low murmur of voices; the sound of a horse clip-clopping into the yard.

She lay in bed for another minute, playing back the memory of how she'd looked last night and smiling to herself. Then she got up, pulled out the chamber pot from under the bed and squatted. When she'd done she went over to the window and yanked it open. She was careful to make sure the man and woman standing in the yard below could see only her head and shoulders – she was still naked. Outside it smelled as if there had been heavy rain in the night; puddles in the yard were reflecting the morning sun.

Star called out, 'Piss gully?'

'Ah, don't worry, love, I'll see to it,' the woman replied. 'There's a place on the landing. Just leave the pot there.'

She was the chambermaid who'd prepared the hip bath yesterday evening. She smiled up at Star and shouted, 'Your lady's up and gone already.'

'What!'

'She said to wait here. Come down to the kitchen, why don't you, for some breakfast?'

They'd laid out a bowl of warm creamy milk laced with honey. Next to it was a pile of toast nicely arranged on a red check cloth. Star was glad of it, and – as Lara wasn't there – also glad to be sitting in the kitchen rather than the formal dining room with all the fat middle-aged guests.

'D'you know where Mrs Johnson went?' Star asked, dropping half a piece of toast into the bowl.

The groom from the yard, an old red-cheeked man with bushy eyebrows, had wandered in to sit down and pass the time of day. His country cloth trousers and his boots smelled of horse manure. To him, this thin city girl with striking brown eyes was a curiosity; he loved talking to travellers.

'Your lady? Her wen' up main road to catch the mail.'

It took a moment for Star to unscramble the accent. She nodded and slurped some milk into her mouth with a silver spoon.

'We did tell 'er,' the man continued, 'the mail goes early, like.'

Star gave him a wry smile.

'These parts be well interestin'' the groom said after a silence.

'Oh yes?'

'Oh yes. Well interestin' they are. Did oo see Chillin'ton?'

'The Hall? Yup. We dropped the soldiers off there.'

'Your lady's got soldiers with her, has her?' The man's eyes lit up – gossip potential.

'Only two,' she said, wondering if she should have told him.

'Ar, well, when you gone from Chillin'ton a few mile you come to the Royal Oak: did oo see that?

'No. A pub?'

'Right, a pub from the very, very old days. Oo must 'ave passed it. There was a King Charles, see? A king of the whole of England once 'pon a time. But there was a civil war: Round'eads and Cavaliers!'

'We never learned about that at school.'

'School?!' The red-faced man thought this was very funny. 'School don't come into it. Everybody round here knows the story behind that pub. We get told it on our mother's knee don't we?' He cleared his throat. 'What happened was, like, the king's side lost, oh dearie me. He had to run frit hiding all the way like. And guess what, one o' the places he hid was right there. That's why it'n the Royal Oak, see? He hid in that ol' oak tree when soldiers from the other side came looking. They was as near to him as to spit.'

'Is the tree still there?' Star asked.

She didn't get an answer. A pony and trap was rattling into the yard: Lara was back. The groom gave her a brief glance, stood up stiffly and walked out as quickly as he could.

'All around up north seems to be going its own way now,' said Saleem.

They were in the Land-Rover bumping along the winding road that led in thirty miles to the border with North Mercia and in less than sixty to Chester, its capital, now renamed New Deva.

After the thunder and heavy rain in the night the woods looked fresh and green. Raindrops sparkled on ferns and bracken along the roadside. The forest was thinner here. There were islands of brightness where locals had burned away patches of undergrowth and trees for cultivation.

Lara knew what Saleem meant. Each time she'd made the journey north she'd noticed the gradual change too. A slackening of the capital's grip on things once you got beyond the Midlands proper. Nothing you could put your finger on, exactly. It was more an accumulation of tiny, subtle changes – the suspicious looks, the way people spoke to you; the way they sometimes refused to fill in forms and blatantly disregarded the laws and regulations passed by central government in Oxford.

'Put it this way,' answered Saleem, 'I wasn't surprised when I heard about that gang, the ones that held up the Welsh guys up here, you know?'

'Did you know the gang had police uniforms on?' Star asked him.

Saleem kept his eyes on the road and shouted over the noise of the engine. 'That's what I mean about these parts up here. Perhaps they were police. They're all getting to be a law to themselves, bloody bastards excuse me speaking that way.'

'This young lady,' Lara said, pointing at Star who was sitting in front with them, 'this young lady knows the son of that poor man who was murdered afterwards in Warwick – you heard about that too?'

'Yeah, yeah – I knew about that,' Saleem said. He gave Star a sympathetic glance.

'So we're on the lookout for two men now,' said Lara.

'What d'you mean, Mrs Johnson?' the driver said.

'My husband…and young Gwynfor, the Welshman's son,' she said. She looked at Star, smiled and added 'who I believe Star here has a soft spot for!'

A look of annoyance crossed the young woman's face.

'Oh, he's headed this way as well, then?' asked Saleem.

Star sounded grumpy. 'He's going home. It's somewhere in North Wales. He's taking his father's ashes back, if you must know.'

'Well, depending where, he's probably come this way,' Saleem said.

He was concentrating on getting the Land-Rover past two stationary wagons laden with piles of maize cobs.

'If you try to cut through the forest from anywhere round here to Wales,' he continued, it's bloody difficult. So, yes, he is probably on this road.'

'This is really why Star wanted to come with us' Lara teased.

'Oh, so he is your boyfriend!' Saleem laughed. 'Why didn't you get on that motorbike of yours and come looking for him yourself?'

'He's not my boyfriend actually.' Star tried to sound annoyed. But despite herself there was a hint of a smile on her lips.

'Come on then, what was it? Why did you come?' Lara said.

'Got chucked off the Beacon, didn't I? But I thought, well, why should that stop me? This is a story, isn't it?'

Lara looked at Star carefully. 'What do you mean?'

'I'm writing it all down – well, not everything! I'm keeping a journal.'

Lara looked impressed.

'Oh, I'll check everything with you first – for factual accuracy' Star said quickly. 'I just want to write the story, Mrs Johnson. And be in the story.'

At that moment they came to the first significant settlement. It was the confusingly named Newport – confusing because it was, in fact, an old town. The triumphant sign on the roadside said 'Newport – Another Rescued Settlement!' This meant that it had been abandoned during the Pandemics but had subsequently been resettled and reclaimed.

'So even this place was new once,' Saleem said glumly as he edged the Land-Rover through a smelly market on the high street. Goats, sheep, horses and cattle strayed across their path. A grinning rustic drover with no teeth shouted something incomprehensible at them. The road was a sticky mess of flies, dung and mud. Crumbling centuries-old houses and shops lined the main street. Everything looked dirty and faded.

But on the far side of town there was a great contrast. Shimmering in the bright sunlight and rising majestically from a surrounding circle of tall eucalyptus trees, a massive white temple topped by a large blue dome came into view. It was situated on a small hill about a quarter of a mile to the left. A great flight of white marble steps came flowing down from the temple's front entrance, meeting a paved square at the bottom which was lined with young plane trees.

'Wow,' said Star, 'can we stop and look at this?'
Saleem was reluctant. 'I thought you might not be able to resist this' he sighed. 'Mrs Johnson, you want me to stop?'

'I think it's worth a quick look,' Lara said.

'I don't want to get too far behind Anwar,' Saleem said. 'May I suggest you look only at the outside of the temple? Ten minutes?'

He slowed the Land-Rover and steered left up a narrow lane into the tree-lined square.

Once they'd climbed out they realised how breathtakingly big the temple on the hill was. Lara and Star stood side by side, looking up at the huge dome. Small white fleecy clouds were drifting past in the wide blue sky, disappearing behind the dome and reappearing moments later on the other side, somehow seeming to magnify the grandeur of the place.

Private Roycroft, the soldier who'd ridden with them today, laid down his submachine, lit a cigarette and sat on a low wall.

Star walked over to a twice life-size sculpture in the centre of the square. It was on a plinth of gleaming black marble. She stared up at it. They'd caught a glimpse of it on their approach. Now she could see what it was – a fine sculpture in smooth, clean white stone: a fleeing hind, neck outstretched, leg muscles shining in the strong midday sun.

There was a simple inscription in gold lettering on the side of the black plinth:

DIANA 1997–?

'I really want to go up those steps,' Star shouted across to Lara Johnson and Saleem. She looked up towards the huge building at the top. 'Come on!'

Saleem was shaking his head. Lara was standing still, looking uncertain.

Without waiting for a reply, Star began to climb the steps. But then she stopped. The tall black wooden doors at the front entrance to the temple, way above, were opening outwards slowly and simultaneously. People were coming out – women in hats, men in formal coats and suits.

'It's a wedding!' Star shouted down. 'Let's go and look.'

But Lara was waving and shaking her head. 'No, Star! It's a funeral, I think. Come back!'

'Did you get married in a church or anything like that?' Star asked Lara twenty minutes later.

They were back in the Land-Rover and Saleem was driving as fast as he dared, pushing forty miles an hour here and there on the less rutted stretches. They hadn't yet caught up with the other Land-Rover.

Since their stop to look at the Church of Diana there'd been a lot more roadside shrines. Every half-mile or so there seemed to be another one. Some were life-size statues of Diana, Queen of Hearts. Others were small figurines or statuettes placed in neat little grottos. Each one had a glass case beneath it containing offerings: a scattering of coins, a vase of wilting flowers and little bags of sweets.

They'd just passed one made of pink-brown marble. Diana was kneeling as if in prayer, her hands piously together, her eyes lifted heavenwards, imploring. A wrought-metal crown of thorns and roses had been screwed on to her head. As they passed it Star glimpsed rust-stained tears pouring down her face – clever plumbing to awe the faithful. She made a mental note to record the sight in her journal.

'No, we didn't want anything like a religious ceremony,' Lara said. 'We were both brought up secular. David was actively against all religion, actually. Said there's a real danger it'll create a medieval society again.'

'Did you agree with him?'

'No, not altogether, but we didn't argue about it.'

They'd come to a fork in the road.

'Hope Anwar remembered to take this road!' Saleem shouted,

choosing the left fork. 'I told him that this way goes to a place called Whitchurch. It's quicker to Chester this way.'

'D'you mind me asking, Lara, where you got married?'

Lara blinked, surprised. 'Oh! No, I don't mind. We got married in Oxford. If you'd been to Oxford University it got to be a custom to go back to your old college to get married there. Eight years ago now! Hard to believe. They put up a marquee on the lawn – they still have lawns in Oxford, all neatly mown! And you invite your old professors and tutors as well as friends and relatives. If you want, there's a humanist celebrant to do the ceremony – which is what we had.'

Lara's mind drifted back. Mum had looked nice in that blue and white dress and she had a nice hat too. She'd been overawed, though, by the professors in their gowns and by some of David's loud relatives, specially his Uncle Tim and Aunt Sophie.

Only two of Mum's friends came. She didn't really know anybody at my wedding. David was unusual in having a large family. They were lucky. Tons of people, me and Mum included, have no family to speak of: no grandparents, uncles, aunts, nieces, nephews, cousins...

As Lara was bumping along in the Land-Rover thinking about family, her mother was standing in the kitchen garden at the back of Wellbrook House. The weather had cleared up: it was a sunny day.

'What d'you think, Matt?' she asked the driver, gardener and general handyman. 'Fruit pie or summer pudding?'

Matt was digging a shallow trench to sow a late crop of peas. He straightened up, gasping as a twinge of arthritis got him. He squinted at her.

'What?'

'Fruit pie or summer pudding? I want to make something for Ben Frobisher. He looked proper miserable yesterday when Lara left. And he's had all that bad luck with the floods and the rain beating his crops down and everything. He needs cheering up.'

'If you don't mind me arskin', what's a summer pudding when it's at home, Misses?'

'It's very nice. You need redcurrants, blackcurrants, raspberries, strawberries – any summer fruit really – and you press the fruit down in a bowl in between slices of white bread.'

Matt looked unimpressed. 'Bread? Oo, I see. Well the redcurrants and blackcurrants have nearly finished. You might get enough…and the raspberries haven't come on that much yet.'

'Sounds like a pie then. I can see some nice rhubarb over there.'

'You can't go wrong with a pie, Misses. Pie and custard – fills a man up.'

19

At the border there was no sign of the other Land-Rover. They'd come to a halt in the wagon park on the West Mercian side – an empty, dusty red patch of ground in the middle of miles and miles of open heath land covered by gorse and bracken and dotted with small stands of silver birch trees. The early afternoon sun beat down.

Saleem switched off the engine. A single bird was singing – a lonely, bewitching trilling that rose and fell, rose and fell. Lara couldn't help thinking how beautiful the sound was, for all the frightening associations between birds and death.

Saleem sighed and looked even gloomier than usual. 'What shall we do, madam?'

Lara put on her sunglasses. 'Let's drive up and ask at the barrier if they've already gone through.'

Saleem muttered something inaudible about his stupid brother and then said 'thing is, it's not like him to go on so far ahead. He wouldn't cross the border without waiting for us.'

'They couldn't have got behind us somehow?' Star asked from the back seat. 'Perhaps they took the other fork in the road back there, then he realised he'd taken the wrong road, turned round and came back – which means they might be here any minute?'

Saleem shook his head. 'I don't know. Silly bugger probably carried on the other road and now he's waiting for us at another border crossing. Bloody idiot.'

Lara was impatient to get on. 'I don't think we should waste time waiting. Go to the barrier, Saleem.'

Saleem sighed. 'Yes madam.' He started the engine and drove up to the control post.

A large woman in a grey uniform and a peaked cap looked down at them. She was sitting in a raised wooden shelter beside the horizontal pole.

'Will you all please get out of the vehicle?' she said.

At the side of the crossing point two men, also in grey uniforms and peaked caps and wearing sunglasses, regarded the Land-Rover carefully.

She came out of the shelter and bustled round. There were endless questions about where they'd come from, where they were going and why. She was particularly interested in why a soldier should be accompanying them.

Saleem grew tetchy. 'Has another vehicle like this one crossed through just now?' he asked.

The big woman didn't give anything away. 'Is it carrying soldiers as well?' she asked.

'Yes: one.'

'Oh,' she smiled. 'Then for security reasons I'm afraid I can't say. Now, have you got your transit cards? I need to stamp them.'

Lara had begun to fear the border official would demand to see inside their bags and cases. Alexander Laczko had signed an official form authorizing her to carry the two cases of money to North Mercia, but there was every reason to believe any form would fail to satisfy such a nit-picker even if it had been signed by God Almighty.

Eventually she let them go. Lara got in the front, as before, and Star sat with Private Roycroft in the back. Before starting the engine Saleem took one look behind him to see if the other Land-Rover had turned up. Still no sign of it.

They crossed no-man's land on a bumpy, pitted track and drove up to the North Mercian border post.

This was more impressive than the simple wooden structure on the West Mercian side. North Mercia had obviously been able to lash out on a proper, brick-built border post, a single storey building with walls freshly painted in cream and the window frames picked out in light blue. A flag with the North Mercian crest on it – a shield, a golden lion and three wheatsheaves – fluttered from a high pole, and next to the flagpole was an equally tall radio mast.

Saleem stopped the Land-Rover under a canopy. He grabbed everyone's passport and transit card and was starting to get out when a young woman at a side window motioned with her hand to tell him to stay where he was.

A moment later the young border official came up to the Land-Rover on Saleem's side. To Lara she looked no older than twenty – a pretty young blonde with an easy, confident manner wearing shorts and a blue sleeveless top.

'Welcome to North Mercia!' she said, leaning into Saleem's window. She gave them all a big smile. 'Lovely weather you've brought!'

She barely glanced at their transit cards, simply initialling each one with a pencil.

'Here are our passports' Saleem said, holding them out of the window.

'Not necessary,' the young woman said. 'You may go through now.'

Saleem looked a little stunned. 'Oh! Thank you. Just a question, young lady: has a vehicle like this one gone through here in the past hour or so?'

She gave him a concerned look. 'Oh, I'm not sure, sir. I've only just come on duty. I'll ask.'

She went back inside the building and came out a minute later. This time she was accompanied by a relaxed middle-aged man, grey-haired and wearing white shorts and a short-sleeved military-style blue shirt.

The man looked in through Saleem's window. 'Good afternoon,' he said, taking a quick glance at each one of them in turn. 'We've heard that you're a party visiting the Regional Commissioner in Chester – is that right?'

'That's correct,' Lara said.

'Fine,' he said. 'Just follow the road straight on to Chester. There's a right fork in a few miles but stay on this road. Oh and yes,' he said, looking directly at Lara Johnson, 'a Land-Rover similar to yours passed through border control half an hour ago.'

'With four men in it' Lara said.

The man gave an imperceptible nod.

Saleem opened his mouth to say something but Lara jabbed him with her elbow.

'–Thank you very much, that's very helpful' Lara said quickly.

The border official lifted his hand in acknowledgement, stepped back and motioned for Saleem to drive forward to the barrier.

As they moved off, the official turned and ran back into the building. Star thought this was odd. He'd strolled out in a leisurely way to talk to them but he'd run back inside like a scalded cat.

As they approached the barrier the young woman who'd ticked their transit cards was at the side of it turning a handle. The horizontal pole lifted up and they were through. As they passed through she gave them a cheery wave.

Saleem whistled through his teeth. 'That was all bloody strange!'

'You nearly blew it by interrupting me, Saleem!' Lara told him, patting him on the shoulder.

'I nearly said two people as well!' Star laughed.

'I am right though, aren't I?' Lara said. 'He definitely agreed when I said four people in the other Land-Rover.'

'Excuse me ma'am' Private Roycroft said, 'but he didn't seem to confirm or deny it really – he just gave a little nod. It could be he didn't notice or remember there's only two in it.'

Saleem gave a heavy sigh. 'Maybe...but I don't know. This feels wrong. Not like Anwar to charge on ahead like this. I think the whole thing bloody suspicious.'

'I noticed something else' Star said from the back seat. 'The man said a Land-Rover passed through border control half an hour ago. That doesn't necessarily mean the border post we've just been through, does it? It could be another one – like if they've taken that other road?'

'How would he have known, though, Star?' Lara said.

'Didn't you see that ginormous radio mast, Mrs Johnson?'

Saleem shook his head. 'I still don't get it. Anwar wouldn't go through any border without waiting for me.'

'There's no point going back now,' Lara said. 'We'll just have to get to Chester and find out what's happened when we get there.'

The road leading north-west out of Whitchurch was surprisingly good. It was an old A road of Good Time origin that had been completely renovated and resurfaced with recycled tarmac. No more winding and rutted tracks. The Land-Rover's tyres sang on the smooth black surface. They reached the dizzying speed of sixty miles per hour. The road was even wide enough for large vehicles going in opposite directions – something they hadn't seen since leaving New Warwick.

A listing bio-diesel truck limped past heading back towards Whitchurch. It had a large painted sign over the driver's cab: 'REVERE DIANA'.

They reached the crest of a hill. Suddenly a completely different landscape came into view – a landscape that stretched to the horizon, unhindered by the all-enclosing forests.

'Wow!' Star gasped, 'look at that!'

To her surprise she felt a lump in her throat: she wanted to cry. This was a magical landscape. A landscape she'd only been told about or seen in pictures in school history books. To her it was the lost world she'd read about in novels like Mansfield Park and Pride and Prejudice.

And now it had all suddenly opened up in front of her – in reality! A landscape of orderly green fields and neat hedges; the landscape of an England that had been lost.

'They managed to keep this area clear of trees,' Saleem was explaining, 'even in bad time. It's always been famous for dairy – cheese, yogurt, butter, all that.'

And sure enough they could soon see groups of cows, some black and white and some light brown, grazing in the fields.

As the Land-Rover went round a bend, Saleem had to slow right down to pass a two-wheeled donkey cart going the same way. It was laden with four large milk churns. An old woman wearing a red headscarf was sitting in the back. She stared at them with hostile curiosity. But the cart's driver – a girl of about fourteen with a face as brown as a berry – smiled and waved her donkey switch cheerily at them as they edged past.

'Did you notice?' said Lara. 'Both of them were wearing red headscarves.'

'It all looks so orderly,' said Star, gazing out of the window at a long, low building set back from the road. It looked recently constructed. There was a large white signboard in the field. In bold green letters it said 'COUNTY DAIRY No. 26'.

Saleem was putting his foot down, anxious to get to Chester and to find his brother. They were doing over seventy now – a bewildering speed. Only Star had ever travelled this fast before, on her motorbike.

Saleem slowed for a sharp bend, but not quite enough. As they screeched around it, they almost ran head-on into a large truck.

It was looming up in the middle of the road, headlights blazing – a huge, ancient, dark-green army lorry. It was an astonishing sight; it must have been pulled out of mothballs after decades in storage somewhere.

They were lucky: Saleem had dropped down a gear. Otherwise they'd have skidded out of control when he hit the brakes. He flung the Land-Rover hard over to the left. The truck swept past with inches to spare, horn blaring.

Then there was another one roaring towards them. And another. A few seconds more and then yet another...and another...

Saleem pulled the Land-Rover into the side. The trucks kept coming. Some looked so battered and rusty that it was a marvel they could move at such speed. Star counted out loud, getting to a total of twenty three. The road shuddered as each one rolled past. They were all army trucks: some were open, carrying shrouded humps that looked like weaponry or bio-diesel fuel drums, but most were covered, with soldiers looking out of the back.

When they'd all passed it seemed unnaturally quiet. A cloying smell like cooking oil hung in the air. Bio-diesel.

Saleem looked at Lara Johnson and shook his head. 'My God,' he said.

The miles clicked by quickly on the smooth black road. In another twenty minutes or so Saleem announced that they were almost half-way there.

Then, just when they'd got used to the luxury of the smooth tarmac, it stopped abruptly. They'd reached the top of a low rise. About half a mile ahead they could see the edge of the forest coming to meet them again – a black belt of shadow topped with an undulating layer of green.

The tarmac road continued into it like the shaft of a spear, but their way was blocked. A large wooden signboard had been pulled across:

'DIVERSION FOREST CLEARANCE'

A line of crudely painted red arrows instructed them to turn sharp right on to a sandy, pot-holed single track road.

Saleem groaned. 'Here we go.'

The Land-Rover heaved and waddled along the bumpy track.

'It's funny,' said Star, leaning forward to speak to Lara, 'but I don't think those army trucks came down here. I think they must've come straight down the good road.'

'Why d'you say that?'

'There would've been a lot of marks, tyre tracks on the good road coming our way, from where they left this dusty track and came onto the tarmac.'

'You're right! I don't remember seeing any tyre marks like that, either.'

'And there wasn't any dust or mud on their windscreens or round their wheels, was there?' Star added.

Smart kid, thought Lara. She could be a real asset on my staff.

If she was right it meant the convoy couldn't have been on this rough track. That meant the diversion sign had been pulled across in the last twenty minutes or so, after the convoy had passed. But there'd been no sign of any workmen. It had been suspiciously quiet where they'd turned off the good road.

'Saleem,' she said, 'I know this sounds crazy, but if we don't see another vehicle or anything coming the other way in, say, another ten minutes, I think we should turn back. I'm worried about that military convoy. Something's kicking off.'

Saleem gave her a serious look. 'Yes, Mrs Johnson. I think that is a wise move.'

A tense five minutes followed as they went deeper into the forest. They seemed to be climbing off the plain now. It was hillier, with steep turns in the track and sudden dips and gullies.

They smelled the smoke a minute or two before they came upon it. Star noticed it first. 'What's that smell?'

'I'll just go over this next little hill,' said Saleem. 'Then we can take a look, assess the situation.'

As they lurched over the crest they had a shock. Squealing and screaming, mad with panic, a group of black wild pigs was charging along the narrow track towards them. Behind them was a cloud of sandy red dust. And behind the red dust a dense wall of white smoke was drifting towards them.

Saleem slammed on the brakes.

The Land-Rover slid sideways, almost completely blocking the track: they were in a narrow rocky gulch. There were two loud metallic bangs against the Land-Rover; more pig squealing; Saleem cursing. The wild pigs kept coming. They rocked the vehicle this way and that as they squeezed past. Then they were gone.

Saleem flung open the driver's door and jumped out, running to look at the front of the vehicle.

'What's he doing!' hissed Lara.

The billowing smoke was almost upon them.

Saleem looked up, shaking his head. 'Bloody headlight gone!' they heard him shout.

Then he was back behind the wheel. The Land-Rover skidded backwards up through the narrow gulch.

'Bloody pigs!' he cursed under his breath. 'One bugger's tusks dented bloody wing as well as busting bloody headlight!'

'You can reverse into that clearing over there, on your left!' Private Roycroft called from the back.

'Okay I can see it!' Saleem replied. He edged the Land-Rover back. He couldn't see much in the fog of white smoke and he didn't want to hit any of the trees.

'Go on, go on…okay…stop!' said Private Roycroft. 'There's someone behind us!'

A figure materialised out of the haze – a tall, muscular man with close-cropped hair and a single gold earring. He was wearing leather breeches and a coarse sleeveless country smock, dark green or grey.

'Hey, wait!' they heard him shout. Star could just about see a Forest Ranger badge sewn on to the man's smock as he pushed past her window. He gave her a brief smile.

Now he was standing outside the driver's door. Saleem wound down the window.

A sawn-off shotgun barrel poked right into Saleem's neck.

'Switch the fuckin' engine off!' the man told Saleem, leering. 'All of you out now!'

Lara wanted to shout out, take control. But she was paralyzed. All she found she could do was focus on a small dark-blue tattoo of an eagle, wings outstretched, on the man's right forearm.

Suddenly the rear passenger door on Private Roycroft's side was wrenched open. Another shotgun barrel was poking in – this time right up against the side of the private's head. The soldier had reached for his sub-machine gun, but too late.

'Come on, move it please!' the man said again, chuckling as if this was a hell of a funny joke. 'Getting smoky, innit?'

The two women were made to stand about forty feet away from the Land-Rover. Even at this short distance the bulky vehicle had assumed a hazy outline. They coughed and sneezed in the thickening smoke.

Star couldn't stop trembling. Saleem and Private Roycroft had been forced to lie down, their faces buried in the yellow-brown carpet of pine needles.

The first man was watching over the two women, his gun crooked casually in his right arm. His eyes were dark brown, calm and unblinking. He looked them up and down lazily, then put two fingers in his mouth and blew a series of piercing whistles. Answering whistles echoed through the smoke. More and more of them came. Sketchy figures running.

They were setting about the Land-Rover with a will, now. Lara's trunk was open and her clothes were being strewn around. Someone made off with Private Roycroft's submachine gun. Five or six of them – including two women, Lara noticed – were going through the bags. Jabbering magpies. Two others were inside the vehicle, banging and clattering as they forced panels and fittings aside. Lara tried to make out faces, fix on distinguishing features or clothes but they were too far away and it was too smoky.

It didn't take them very long to find the two money cases.

Lara's heart fell with a bump. Oh no, she thought; oh no.

One, a runtish man of about thirty with a shaven head and very few teeth, held the cases up high and whooped. He ran towards them, brandishing the two slim cases and smirking. As he got closer Lara could see he was even uglier than she'd first thought. He was also wearing a sleeveless jerkin, but unlike the bigger man's it was made of leather, greasy and blackened with sweat.

'Get back you little sod!' the tall man with the tattoo shouted. Then he laughed, shaking his head at Lara as if to say 'you've got to sympathise with me…the servants these days!'

The runt looked puzzled, then angry.

'Take those cases over there' the tall man ordered. 'And bring me some rope. We've got to tie these cows up,' he leered at the women, 'before we take 'em for milking.'

'I wanta ride that one first, Captain.' Runt was pointing at Star.

Star started saying, 'No, no, no.'

The tall man pointed the barrel of his shotgun high over the runt-man's head and into the trees. There was a deafening bang. Lara and Star both cried out. The faces of the gang turned towards the tall man.

'Okay you lot – packing up time!' the man shouted, keeping his gun pointing towards the two women.

Star looked across at Lara, her big eyes even wider than usual. She wanted to say please, please, make all this go away.

'Put your hands behind your backs, cows!' runt-man shouted.

Lara and Star put their hands behind their backs.

Star felt a rough cord being slipped around her wrists, then the cord being tightened savagely. They were going to be led away!

But then a horn sounded – a high-pitched wailing sound. The horn sounded again, followed by a long crackle of gunfire. Twigs snapped overhead. Torn leaves drifted down through the smoke.

The tall man looked alarmed. 'Fuck it!' he said urgently to runt-man. 'Let's go! No, arsehole! – leave 'em!'

Star felt the cords loosen. She looked around cautiously. The hazy figures of the gang had all disappeared. The tall man in the Forest Ranger smock had gone too.

She felt her heart beating hard. She wanted to be sick.

Saleem and Private Roycroft were getting up, brushing leaves and twigs off their clothes. They looked unharmed. Lara was walking over to them. Star could hear her talking to them in a low voice. Relief spread through her veins, but for the moment she couldn't move. She was shaking all over.

The hunting horn blew again – so loud that it made them all jump.

Suddenly a dozen hunting dogs, brown and white patched, bounded into the clearing, panting, their noses close to the ground, swirling around them. Several brushed against Star's legs and she felt the lash of a tail against her knee.

Now she could hear men's shouts getting closer – and the low, drumming sound of horses' hooves moving at a fast canter.

Seven horses and their riders appeared out of the dense white smoke.

The first one almost collided with Saleem. It was a magnificent black steed of eighteen hands. As it reared up it whinnied – a piercing scream – and Saleem backed away in terror.

'Whoa!' the man on the black horse shouted. 'Whooah there!'

The rider was a tall man in his forties. He had shoulder-length black hair, a sallow complexion and what looked like three days' stubble on his face. He was wearing a red leather tunic and loose-fitting black trousers. A shotgun was crooked in his arm, pointing up to the forest canopy. The other huntsmen were carrying similar guns too, Star noticed.

The leading man walked his horse around them. His dark eyes weren't exactly welcoming.

Looking down at Lara, he said 'what has happened here? You are...?'

'I'm Justice Lara Johnson. We've come from New Warwick.'

The horseman shook his head and frowned. Then he leant forward in the saddle and reached down to shake her hand.

'My, my,' he said. 'I am Marek Stettin, Regional Commissioner of North Mercia.'

KEN BLAKEMORE

20

That afternoon Rae had made the rhubarb pie for Ben. At first she'd thought she'd walk over to the farm with it – the walk would do her good, get a bit of this weight off her. But then Matt brought Arrow back from school and the girl had wanted a fuss making of her, as usual. She wasn't showing much sign of missing her mother but Rae thought it best to stay at home rather than leave her with Esther.

'Esther,' she said at six o'clock, 'on your way home d'you think you could go to Ben's farm with this pie for him? I've made an egg custard to go with it.'

Esther was only too happy to oblige.

At half-past six she was knocking on Ben's door.

No answer. She set down the basket with the pie and the bowl of custard in it, and looked around. The farmyard was quiet apart from grunts coming from the pigsty in the far corner. All the farmhands must've gone home. She knocked again, more loudly, but again no reply.

Not wanting to give up, she strolled around the house looking in through the windows. I'll try the back door, she thought. Before she reached the door, however, there was another window to look in.

And that was when she saw him. It was too dark inside to see properly but she could make out that he was sitting at the kitchen table. His arms were stretched out on the table and his head was laid flat on it. He must have fallen asleep? But there was something about the awkward way he was sitting, something about the shape his body that unsettled her. She squinted, trying to see what was on the table. Just some pieces of paper and a black object...

Her heart jumped. A gun – it was a handgun. She ran to the back door.

Stettin had arranged for one of his men to ride with them in the Land-Rover to guide them to his official residence, Peckforton Castle, where he said her party could rest and recover from the ambush. It was only three miles away.

Lara had been both stunned and hugely relieved.

'This is amazing!' she said. 'I was on my way to Chester to see you!'

He'd nodded and given her a serious look. 'We were out hunting. It was extremely fortunate we happened to come across you. If that scum had taken you...it wouldn't have been easy to get you back.'

She'd told him about the stolen money.

He shook his head and gave her a regretful look.

'Tsk tsk! This gang of bandits has been operating round here for more than six months now. I've been threatening the local authorities and the police with fire and brimstone but they seem unable to do anything about it. But I'll see what I can do. I'll get some of my own men onto it.'

Star mentioned that the leader of the gang had been wearing a Forest Ranger badge. She asked Stettin 'does this gang ever put on police uniforms to fool people?'

He'd given her one glance and ignored her.

From that moment on, Star took a dislike to Stettin. His eyes were a dirty blue colour, as if black ink had been mixed in with the blue. Cold, arrogant eyes.

'What should I do?' Ben asked. He'd been crying; he looked altogether desperate.

Esther, sitting on a chair next to him, took his hand. She'd read Lara's letter and seen the devastation it had wreaked upon him. Her heart went out to him, but most of all she was feeling angry. Angry with that stuck-up Lara Johnson and angry with him.

'Ben, until they prove her husband is dead she's still a married woman! And now put that gun away. Or better, throw it in the river or the deepest pond you've got.'

He nodded, fetched a white cloth which was lying on a sideboard and carefully wrapped the handgun in the cloth. Then he went over to the corner of the room where an old cardboard box was sitting on the floor, and threw the gun into it.

She didn't know whether to stand up now and offer him a hug; offer him her body in whatever way he wanted.

She must sit where she is. She mustn't blow this.

He came and sat at the table opposite her and put his head in his hands.

'I can't live without her,' he said. His voice was muffled by his hands. 'I want to go after her!'

'Ben, that would be the worst thing you could do,' she said softly.

How ironic, she thought, I should be telling him to go after her and proclaim his undying love. She'd be sure to reject him completely, and then he could be mine.

Stettin offered them food and a bed for the night. Saleem, Private Roycroft and Star Edkin were offered separate accommodation from Lara below stairs in the servants' quarters.

'If you don't mind, Marek,' Lara said, 'I'd like Miss Edkin to have a room next to mine and to eat with us – she's my personal assistant.'

Star overheard this and felt buoyed up – especially as she saw Stettin's face fall when he heard Lara's request.

'All right, yes…' he'd said reluctantly, 'that should be possible.'

Now Star was standing with Lara and Stettin looking out over the battlements of Peckforton Castle's keep. He was giving the two women a guided tour of his domain.

A fresh early evening breeze had picked up. Star breathed in deeply. Below her was a wide vista of cultivated fields and pastures – geometric shapes of gold, brown and green interspersed with clumps of trees, ponds and glittering lakes. It was the landscape that had taken her breath away when she'd first seen it earlier that day, coming down the hill after Whitchurch.

Over to the west were the Welsh mountains where Gwynfor might be, a faint purple-blue line on the horizon.

'What's that castle over there?' Lara was asking Stettin. She was pointing in the opposite direction at a high, rocky crag, about a mile to the east. The massive rock, red sandstone streaked with black, was like a broken molar rising spectacularly from the surrounding plain. On top of the crag were the rounded walls of a medieval castle glowing white-grey in the sun.

'That's Beeston Castle. Finished in the thirteenth century, I think. Peregrine falcons nest there now. Looks rather romantic, doesn't it?'

Stettin's unsmiling eyes had fastened on Lara. 'But it didn't just fall into disrepair,' he continued, 'it was dismantled after the Civil War in the seventeenth century – to stop it ever again being a centre of resistance to central government.'

'Why wasn't this one pulled down as well?' Lara asked.

'Ah, but this castle isn't really old' he replied.

'It must be!' said Star. 'It's a medieval castle isn't it?'

Stettin addressed Lara as if it was she who'd made the remark. For the first time in their company he became quite loquacious:

'Peckforton Castle looks genuine because in design it is a medieval castle, although it was built in the industrial age, in the 1840s. An aristocratic landowner, Lord Tollemache, had it built. It was finished in 1851. It was quite the fashion in those days to build in the medieval style. Tollemache wanted the real thing, not a big country house disguised as a castle. This is a proper feudal fortress. It would have done the business in the days of Edward the First.'

Star gave him a dry look. 'And now you've got this castle to rule from.'

Lara laughed lightly. 'I think Mr Stettin would prefer the term 'govern' or 'administer' rather than 'rule', wouldn't you Marek?'

Stettin gave a nod. 'Every regional commissioner has to have a substantial residence. Your Alexander Laczko...I believe he has a pretty grand place hasn't he?'

'It's about a quarter the size of this!' Lara laughed.

Stettin allowed himself a thin smile.

'Actually, Mr Stettin, Alexander Laczko isn't really our commissioner,' said Star. 'Yes he's the representative of central government in South Mercia, like you're the government's representative here in the north. But New Warwick's a city state. We've got our own laws, our own democratic government separate from the region.'

Stettin looked at Lara. 'Should we go down now? Before we

eat I'll show you the communications room. I know you'll be anxious to get in touch with the rest of the world tomorrow, Lara?'

Star decided to give them the slip. Stettin was really getting to her – the way he'd looked at Lara just then. Damn it, she thought. I'm going to have a look around. What else was in this huge place?

She followed them down, their footsteps echoing on the spiral stone staircase. When they reached the level below, Lara and Stettin were deep in conversation. Star trailed behind them along a carpeted corridor. But instead of following them down the next flight of stairs she carried on along the same level. She was now in a narrower corridor, again carpeted and lit dimly with glimmering electric lights.

At the end of the narrow corridor she came to a doorway that opened onto a wide gallery. This stone-floored space had diamond-paned windows looking out on to a courtyard below. She'd reached a corner of the castle where the west and north walls of the main keep joined. She could carry on round or retrace her steps. But then she suddenly noticed something more intriguing – a low wooden door set into the corner of the gallery. Above the doorway a small wooden shield had been fixed to the wall. Star shivered when she saw the design on the shield: against a white background, three large black ravens arranged in a triangle.

She looked to check whether anyone was coming, and quickly lifted the latch on the door beneath the shield. It clinked and lifted easily. The door opened outwards.

In two seconds she found herself clambering up a very steep, narrow, winding stone staircase inside a turret. There was a mineral smell of damp stone. Natural light shone weakly from a small window high above. She reached the top step and pulled open a door that was set into the thick wall. After the gloom of the stairway the bright daylight was dazzling and she had to close her eyes for a moment.

When she opened them again, what she saw made her heart stop.

Stettin showed Lara into the communications room. It was a square, brightly lit room below ground level, way down in the depths of the castle. He'd mentioned how the castle was lit and powered by a hydro-electric turbine. As they'd entered this area it had struck Lara that Peckforton, not Chester, was surely Stettin's centre of operations. Administrative staff were hurrying from office to office carrying papers and files.

Stettin left her with an earnest young man who showed her to a seat in front of a panel of lights and dials. He explained that they could make radio contact from Peckforton to almost all the other regional commissioners in Greater England, including Alexander Laczko's residence at Coughton Court.

'We've even had radio communications with two centres in Scotland and one in northern France!' he said proudly.

Then – and this was the mind-boggling part – he went on to explain that some regional centres including New Warwick were able to make a further connection from their radio stations to local telephone systems.

'Are you saying,' she asked him, 'that you can actually connect me with phone numbers in New Warwick?'

'Well it's the Coughton Court radio station that plugs into the New Warwick phone system, but yes,' he smiled, 'though I should warn you that the sound can get distorted and sometimes we lose radio contact altogether – it can take hours to get it back, depending on what frequency the other radio station's using.'

She was excited. 'Could we try New Warwick now?'

'I already have,' he said. 'I tried radioing Coughton Court about fifteen minutes ago. But no response – I don't think there's anybody staffing the radio station there outside working hours.'

She'd badly wanted to hear her daughter's voice. 'Never mind,' she said, 'until a few minutes ago I had no idea anything like this was possible – it's fantastic! I'll be here first thing in the morning.'

Star lifted her hand nervously to receive the hawk. The man had given her a thick glove to wear. Now he was telling her to hold out her hand to make a perch. Star felt herself trembling inside. She couldn't believe she was doing this. It went against all the warnings that had been drummed into her as a child:

Don't stay anywhere near a bird.

If you're near one, run away and raise the alarm.

She took a deep breath as she felt the kestrel's yellow scaly talons gripping her forefinger. Then she breathed out as slowly and calmly as she could. The bird was terrifying to look at but incredibly light. Fragile as a paper lantern. She glanced at the smooth, blue-grey downy feathers on the kestrel's head and in awe at the chestnut brown feathers on its wings and back.

Her heart stopped again when the kestrel turned its head. It was fixing her with its coal-black, shining eyes.

'Am I holding it right?' she heard herself say.

'Of course – there's nothing to it' the man said, taking a small rectangular-shaped bottle out of his pocket. It was made of clear glass and Star could see it contained a clear liquid. The man unscrewed the top, put the bottle to his lips and swigged. He let out a sigh – almost a gasp – screwed the top back on the bottle and replaced it in his pocket.

This was the man whom she'd faced only fifteen minutes earlier when she'd opened the door that gave onto a flat roof. He'd been standing on the roof not five yards away. She'd stared at him, wondering what to say. He'd straightened up, hearing the turret door open, and stared back.

He was a short, stocky, red-faced man of about fifty. He was wearing a dark green smock, the Peckforton Estate uniform, and on his head there was one of those round Muslim caps made with soft brown material and decorated with a colourful band of geometric patterns in green, red and white.

What had rooted Star to the spot hadn't been fear of this man, unwelcoming though he'd seemed, but the huge, black, cawing birds flapping all around him. There'd been seven of them – all loose and free to hop anywhere; a cackling, raucous din.

The birds had come out of a wire mesh enclosure behind the man. He was reaching into a basket and throwing the ghastly birds scraps of bloody red meat. The ravens were squabbling as they snatched the meat pieces. They flicked the fur-edged morsels up into the air with their ugly black beaks and swallowed them down whole. It was totally disgusting and had made her want to retch.

Quite why she hadn't turned tail and scrambled in a panic back down that narrow spiral staircase she couldn't say. It was the shock more than anything – that and the thought that if she moved too quickly, the ravens would have seen her and flown at her. She'd been terrified at the thought of their beating wings all around her head.

Seeing her standing there, paralyzed with fear, the man had laughed. Then, moments later she'd watched as he tempted each of the ravens back into the pen and fastened the door.

After that, the raven-keeper had motioned for her to follow him.

This is crazy, she'd thought, but curiosity had got the better of her. She had to follow him; she had to put her journal before any feelings of fear no matter how strong they were.

He'd led her across the flat roof to a long wooden shed that had been built against a blank wall. Outside the shed door was a low wooden bench.

'Sit there' he'd told her – the first words he'd said to her. 'Don't run off and tell everybody you've been up here or I'll be for the high jump. And you will be, young miss,' he added, pointing a finger.

It was a moment after this that he'd returned with the hooded kestrel on his arm. She'd nearly jumped out of her skin.

But again her curiosity had got the better of her.

Now, she smiled to herself as she held the hawk on her right hand, thinking how incredible the experience was. She motioned for the man to take the bird back, which he did.

'Why didn't you want me to tell anybody I've been here?' she asked.

He frowned. 'Just don't,' he said.

'Why did you show me the hawk?'

'You ask too many questions.'

'Are they for hunting?'

He nodded and spat on the ground.

'That's illegal! It's illegal to keep birds!'

He laughed and took the bottle out of his pocket again.

She noticed that his fingernails were very dirty, and the backs of his hands were covered with dense black hairs. Perhaps he liked frightening people with these birds? Well, he had another think coming. She wasn't frightened.

'Can I come up here again?'

The scornful look on his face disappeared. He looked at her with some interest.

Before either of them could say anything, however, the door in the turret opened. A young man – eighteen or nineteen, rather gawky and with long, lank mousy hair – came out and looked across at them.

'My son Will,' the bird man said.

21

When Star came down from the roof where the ravens and hawks were kept she retraced her steps back to the carpeted corridor where she'd slipped away from Lara and Stettin. But she wasn't sure where to go from there. She decided to go down another flight of stairs.

She was walking along another corridor when a young woman servant wearing a red headscarf came towards her. The maid had an anxious look on her face.

'Are you Miss Edkin?' the servant said, breathless.

'That's me.'

The servant motioned with her arm. 'Excuse me miss but they've been looking for you everywhere. Will you come to the dining hall right now? It's this way; they've only just sat down, I believe.'

She led Star quickly to a large open hall with massive oil paintings of landscapes on it, up a short flight of steps, down another corridor and then into a huge dining hall.

Ornate tapestries hung on the walls – faded colours; medieval hunting scenes depicting men on horses with falcons on the arms; ladies wearing long gowns and strange headdresses – and on one wall there were hunting trophies: stags', boars' and one tiger's head mounted on shields.

Star was surprised by the number of people. She'd been expecting to eat with Lara, Stettin and perhaps a few others. But at least thirty men and women were sitting either side of a fifty-foot long table. They were making a real din, their voices echoing around the hall.

The maid led Star to a vacant space next to Lara, who was talking animatedly to Stettin, seated opposite. Star recognised a few of the men who'd been in Stettin's hunting party; one of them smiled and nodded to her as she sat down.

Lara turned to her. 'Where have you been? I was worried!'

Star glanced at Stettin, who was now busily talking to a dark-haired woman on his right.

'Tell you later' Star whispered. 'This is a strange place, I can tell you.'

Servants were reaching over their shoulders and putting large silver serving dishes of sliced roast wild boar in front of them. Star felt Stettin's cold eyes on her for a second; saw his sarcastic look.

He leaned forward. 'Ah, Lara, I see your personal assistant has at last managed to catch up with you.'

Lara frowned at him. 'My personal assistant has a name: Star Edkin.'

'A curious name,' the dark-haired woman sitting next to Stettin said, looking directly at Star.

Was this Stettin's wife; lover? Star wondered.

Stettin leant forwards. 'Lara, this is my twin sister, Sibila. Sibila, this is Lara Johnson, a high court judge from New Warwick.'

'So you were the victims of the unfortunate ambush?' Sibila smiled.

'That's right' Lara said, raising her voice to be heard above the din. 'We're very grateful indeed to have been rescued today!'

'Marek is very resourceful – sometimes a little too busy for his own good, perhaps?' Taking a sidelong glance at her brother, she smiled playfully and landed a little punch on his arm. Stettin ignored this; he was now busy talking to the man on his left.

Star, nibbling a piece of pork, took a good long look at Sibila. She had Stettin's long, straight black hair. They were obviously identical twins – the same sharp noses, tiny ears and high cheekbones. Their eyes were identical too: the same arrogant, steely dark blue hue. To Star, Sibila looked exactly like Malificent, the wicked witch in the Sleeping Beauty cartoon video they'd been allowed to watch every Christmas at the orphanage.

Lara was now in an involved conversation with Stettin about the political situation in North Mercia. Star noticed how Sibila kept shooting smouldering, jealous glances at Lara. She toyed with the food on her plate with a knife, looking as if she could stab Lara with it any minute.

When the meal had nearly finished a large space was cleared in front of the great table and a big canvas sheet drawn over the stone floor.

It was soon clear what this was for – the after-dinner entertainments.

There was a sequence of three ten-minute acts including a juggler, a troupe of five male tumblers, all sinewy and naked except for leather pouches to contain their genitalia (prompting a lot of ribald laughter from the women around the table) and two overweight, heavy-breasted women wrestlers – also naked except for thongs that disappeared completely between their flabby buttocks.

When the wrestling was over there was much shouting and applause. Stettin stood up and raised his arms. He spoke quietly, but his penetrating voice was heard by everyone. The hall fell silent.

'Please, please,' he said, 'the final one is something special.'

A pale-faced young woman with blonde hair that reached down to her waist walked into the centre of the performance area. She was wearing a long green dress.

She looked at Stettin, giving him a brief smile, and began to sing.

She had a haunting voice, pure and magical. She sang three songs unaccompanied, each song distinctly different in tempo but all three having the same wistful tone that spoke of a longing for home, for big open skies, glittering blue lakes and the leaves of silver birch trees rustling in a cold wind. She sang in a foreign language. To Star it sounded like Polish but it might have been Lithuanian or Latvian. She finished the last song and bowed to the audience, a shy smile on her face.

Star looked at Stettin. He was clapping vigorously, his eyes glistening with tears.

After dinner Lara and Star went up to confer in the room Lara had been given.

'I'm exhausted!' Lara said, collapsing into a small armchair by the window.

Star stifled a yawn. 'It's been quite a day' she said, sitting on the bed. 'And I haven't written in my journal yet.'

'You're very lucky you're able to! I dread to think what would've happened to us if Stettin and his men hadn't come along.'

'Mm.'

'You don't sound very appreciative.'

'I am, Lara. That was a horrible experience. I'm still in shock. It's just…'

'What?'

'I don't know. I can't put my finger on it. It's Stettin…the way he is. And this place – it's mad.'

'What d'you mean, mad?'

'Well, it's like he's created a whole feudal world for himself isn't it? I mean, those tacky cabaret acts after dinner – what were they like!'

Lara smiled.

'You know when you and Saleem were talking about the north going its own way, the authorities up here taking the law into their own hands? Well, Stettin's the prime example.'

'I don't know, I think he's genuine enough. He's letting me use this fantastic communications room they've got here. It'll link up with the phones in New Warwick!'

'Wow – I didn't know they could do that.'

'So I should be able to get through to home tomorrow – and let Alexander Laczko and people in the legislative council know what's going on.'

'Did you tell Stettin about all those army trucks? Does he know what's going on?'

'Mm, his reaction was rather surprising actually. He didn't seem all that concerned. Said he'd check with the North Mercian military attaché in Chester but he assumed it was just routine manoeuvres.'

'It looked like anything but routine.'

'I agree. He did admit there are some worrying signs of tension up here in the north.'

'But according to him no actual threats of civil war.'

'No. He does seem to be very well informed.'

'Does he know anything about your husband, Mrs Johnson?'

'I've mentioned David and he said we could talk about him tomorrow, before we go. There hasn't been much time yet.'

Star decided to tell Lara about her escapade and her discovery of the ravens and the hawks.

Lara shook her head. 'That's fascinating!'

'You see what I mean about Stettin being a law unto himself? No way is anyone permitted to keep birds or be in such close proximity to them.'

'But you actually held one, you say?'

'Well it's not as though there is any actual danger from them now, is there? It's just overcoming all that ingrained aversion we've been given. And I didn't exactly hold it – it just perched on my arm, like this.' She held up her right forearm and used her left hand to mimic a hawk standing on it.

Lara smiled at her. 'And you actually want to go back up there?'

'I met a guy up there called Will.'

'Oh yes?'

Star laughed. 'He's goofy! A real country bumpkin. He's the son of Pascoe, the bird man I told you about. Yeah, I think he does fancy me, so I might play along with it a little. He might be useful to us. He wants to leave this place but it turns out he can't.'

'Why not?'

'Because you've got to get permission. From the estate.'

Lara's eyebrows lifted. 'You mean from Stettin's office?'

'That's right. Stettin gives everyone who works for the estate a minimum wage and they look after you in bad times, apparently, but they want to tie everybody down to their little job and their little cottage.'

Lara shook her head. 'That means no free movement of labour. It's against the law.'

'Exactly, but Will said he's a tied worker. He helps his dad with the falconry, mainly–'

'–Falconry! What an archaic word!'

'Yeah, it tickled me when I heard Will say it.' She chuckled. 'Falconry! Anyway, he does the 'falconry' and he also does forestry work but he's fed up with both. He wants to get on in the world, go exploring, he told me. He couldn't get enough of me telling him about New Warwick!'

Lara gave her a wry smile.

Star winked. 'Like I said, I think he fancies me. I want to find out more about this place.'

'Okay, you do that. But I'm hoping to leave tomorrow

afternoon, if the Land-Rover's okay.

22

Next morning after breakfast Lara went down to the suite of offices below ground level looking for Marek Stettin. A secretary told her he'd left a message for her: he would be returning soon but she should go ahead with the radio link to New Warwick.

Pleased, she went to the radio communications room and found the same technician she'd seen the day before.

'Mrs Johnson, good morning!' he said, smiling. 'Come this way'.

He showed her to a desk which had a microphone and a pair of headphones lying on it. He asked her to sit down and showed her how to put on the headphones and how to use the microphone.

'Just speak into it in a normal voice, Mrs Johnson. Give me a wave if you don't get any sound or if it fades, I'll be over there.' He pointed to the desk with all the radio equipment in front of it.

'As I'll be talking to the phone operators,' he went on, 'I'll need the names of the people you want to reach, please. But remember, radio connection can be lost so it's a good idea to get the most important call in first.'

Lara thought for a moment. It was tempting to get a call put through to home first.

'I'd better speak to Alexander Laczko first, at Coughton Court' she said. 'Then my mother – just ask for my home number, Wellbrook House – and then could you ask for the office of the First Minister of the New Warwick Legislative Council?'

She put the headphones on and for a few minutes heard nothing but a whooshing sound. Then she heard an exchange between the radio operator sitting a few feet from her and a radio operator at Coughton Court.

Eventually, after more whooshing and a series of clicks, she heard the Coughton Court radio operator talking to the phone exchange in New Warwick.

And then she was through. She heard a female voice saying 'Regional Commissioner's secretary' and within a few seconds she was talking to Alexander Laczko.

Nervous that the radio signal might be lost, Lara quickly explained how the previous day they'd seen a large convoy of military vehicles heading south. Stettin had seemed surprisingly relaxed about it all, but the signs looked ominous to her.

'Thank you for telling me that, Lara' she heard Laczko say. He sounded far away. There was a background noise like thousands of small pebbles hitting a hard surface. 'I'll be sure to inform Oxford immediately. Where are you now?'

She told him – and about the ambush that led them to being at Peckforton Castle.

'Lara!' she heard him say through the drizzling pebbles, 'are you all right?'

'We're being well looked after, thank you. I'm hoping to move on today if possible.'

'I would advise against that, Lara.'

Lara frowned. 'Oh?'

'Consider staying at Peckforton for a few days at least.'

Star felt frustrated. She'd already tried without success to leave by the main gatehouse and drawbridge.

She wanted to walk around the perimeter of the castle, get the measure of the place and see it in its surroundings. But she'd been turned back by two guards, a man and a woman in dark green Peckforton uniforms who'd told her she needed an exit pass.

'It's for your own safety' the man had explained.

'It's the animals,' the woman guard added. 'Sometimes wild dog packs come right up. We've even had reports of a tiger in the area.'

'Where do I get an exit pass?' Star asked.

There was a second of silence until the male guard said, 'You get given one. You don't ask.'

For a crazy moment Star had thought of jumping past them and running full pelt down the road, the two of them straining to catch her. What had she got to lose? At worst they'd just drag her back. But then she thought better of it. Shrugging her shoulders, she turned back and walked slowly into the shadow of the gatehouse, thinking that she'd go in search of Saleem and Private Roycroft in the servants' quarters.

She drew a blank there too, so she went back outside. In a stable yard off the main courtyard she'd noticed three gleaming black SUVs standing in a line in front of a garage and workshop. Star had never seen such big, new-looking vehicles before.

The double doors of the workshop were wide open, so Star stepped inside. She saw two Asian mechanics working on the engine of a Land-Rover, but it wasn't Saleem's.

She asked the two men about Saleem and their vehicle.

One man straightened up, smiled, and shrugged his shoulders. His mate was muttering a few words in Punjabi, which Star couldn't catch because he still had his head in the engine.

The first one said 'we think him and the soldier have taken their wagon to Chester, getting damage repaired or somethin'.'

After the call to Alexander Laczko, the radio and phone exchange operators succeeded in getting her through to home.

Her mother answered. 'Lara! Is it really you? Where are you?'

'I'm in North Mercia, Mum – in a place called Peckforton Castle.'

'Oh – that sounds grand! Are you all right?'

Lara went on to reassure her she was only calling because she had the chance to do so – the fantastic radio-to-phone linkup. After they'd talked for a minute or two her mother put Arrow on the line.

'Hello Mummy!' Arrow sounded intrigued. 'Are you looking for Daddy? Have you found him yet?'

Her daughter's voice sounded so far away – so vulnerable, happy and innocent.

That was when it hit Lara. All the accumulated shocks and traumas of the previous day's journey, and particularly the ambush – those moments of pure terror – seemed to combine with a compelling feeling that she ought to be home. That she should never have started on this crazy venture. She had no real clues as to where David was. She had no idea there was going to be this danger of civil strife or war.

She started to crumble. She held it together while Arrow carried on about how Matt had found her three girl rabbits and how she was going to put them in a hutch he was making for her and would Mummy be back for the fun sports day at school. But when Rae came back on the line and asked her if she was really all right and why was she staying at this castle, Lara's voice cracked.

She avoided actually crying, and tried to quell her mother's anxieties.

'It's okay Mum, honestly. Don't worry. It's just that we ran into some trouble on the road yesterday. But luckily the Regional Commissioner happened to be close at the time – he got us out of trouble and now we're safe.'

Her mother sounded unconvinced. 'All right, Lara, but if you get any more setbacks come home, for God's sake.'

'I'll think about it, Mum. I wanted to move on today but it looks like I'll be here for another day or so.'

'Do you want a word with Ben?'

'Ben's there!'

'Yes he is – he's standing by the–'

The line went dead. Lara raised her arm to let the radio operator know they'd lost the link. The operator, who had headphones on, nodded and frowned. He was turning a knob this way and that and staring at the dials in front of him.

Lara heard a lot of whooshing and crackling through her headphones, but nothing else. After a few minutes they gave up. It meant that for now, Lara wouldn't be able to connect with the First Minister's office in New Warwick. But she had to admit to a certain feeling of relief at not having to talk to Ben.

Rae stood holding the phone receiver for five minutes hoping to hear Lara's voice again but eventually an operator came on the line to say they'd definitely lost the connection.

Arrow had already run off but Ben was still on tenterhooks standing next to her.

'No good,' Rae said to him. 'Maybe they'll try again soon.'

Ben nodded. His face, normally brown and healthy from the sun and outdoor work, looked pale and drawn. Such a hang-dog look about him, Rae had thought when he'd turned up at the back door half an hour before.

When the phone rang it seemed as though he was about to tell her something important, but he seemed to have forgotten that now.

As they walked into the kitchen, he pressed her to tell him more about Lara – what was the name of that place she was at and what had happened to her yesterday?

She made him sit down at the kitchen table and insisted he drank one of her herbal teas. She wanted to soothe and mother him a bit. Poor lad! He was even more smitten with her headstrong fool of a daughter than she'd realised. But never mind, chances were she was on another wild goose chase and he'd be seeing her soon.

Don't you worry, Ben,' she said, handing him the mug of tea.

He was staring into the middle distance, shaking his head.

'I don't know. I think I should go and find her. I just have this feeling something's not right. If there's nothing to worry about I can come back, can't I? But if there is a problem I can help her get out of it.'

Star was helping Will feed the ravens, tossing pieces of raw meat to the huge black birds. As they cawed and hopped around her feet she had to use every ounce of mental strength not to walk away.

'Doesn't your father usually do this?' she asked him.

The lad grimaced. 'He's the worse for wear with drink this morning.'

Star remembered the bottle of clear spirits Pascoe had pulled out of his pocket.

'He drinks a lot, does he?'

Will had a sad face. 'Blind drunk last night, the old bastard.' He sighed. 'So I have to do everythin' today.'

'I don't mind helping!' Star lied, forcing a smile.

He brightened up. He was intent on trying to impress her.

'These birds are canny, you know. They can understand every word you say. And this one, Midnight here, he can talk!'

'He can't! Birds can't talk!'

'You've heard of parrots haven't you? They can talk.'

'I don't know what you're talking about!' she laughed. 'Make this one talk, then.'

'Oh no, he won't talk now. Not unless Dad's here.'

'Mm. Why don't they fly away?' She looked up at the sky. 'They're out of the pen, there's nothing to stop them is there?'

He gave her a knowing smile. 'Ah, well, we clip their wings, see.'

She winced.

'No, it don't hurt 'em like. Oh and I shouldn't tell you this, but Dad don't clip Midnight's wings. He trusts that bird to stay, and he does! He don't wanna leave his mates I s'pose. But Dad says, if Midnight wants to go he's got a perfect right. My dad's a bit sick in the head, see. No wonder Mum couldn't stand 'im.'

'Will, do you know a way of getting out of this castle? Not through the main gate, I mean?'

He ignored her. 'These birds are really valuable. Really rare. That's why they'd never let 'em fly away. Did you know these ravens was in the Tower of London? Well, they're the chicks of the ones that was there anyway.'

Star looked blank. 'The Tower of London? What was that?'

The boy giggled, pushing back strands of lank hair that had fallen across his forehead.

'I dunno! What Dad said was in the old days before Good Time, ravens belonged to the king. And the king kept them in the Tower of London – well some, anyway! But if the ravens ever left the Tower or anything bad happened to them, the king and all his family would die and the kingdom would collapse.'

'That's true. London was closed down, wasn't it? So the ravens did leave and the kingdom did collapse.'

'But now fuckin' Stettin's got 'em. Fuck 'im.'

She stared at him. Wheels turned in her mind.

'Hey Star,' Will said. 'Let's put these boggers back in the pen and I'll open yon shed and show you the hawks. Would you like that? We've got an owl too! And carrier pigeons – not that we fly them now, they use that radio thing instead.'

As Ben was leaving Wellbrook House he heard what sounded like a car approaching. He turned back and walked around to the front of the house. An open jeep was speeding up the drive, a cloud of white dust behind it. As it drove up, Ben recognised Kieran Tyler behind the wheel.

The jeep skidded to a halt and Tyler jumped out – a

suntanned, lean man with close-cropped hair. He was wearing shorts and a light blue police shirt.

He came up to Ben and shook his hand – a strong grip. 'Ben Frobisher!' he grinned.

Ben nodded. 'Kieran.'

'I'm sorry they let those dogs at you. I gave those men a right rollicking.'

'I know – I heard. Thanks. No harm done – it's healing up nice.'

'Actually it's the guard on the house I've come about. Mrs Johnson's gone?'

'Yes.'

'Not sure we need a man standing around all the time now.'

Ben thought a moment. 'Have you checked with that whatshisname, File – that odd feller?'

'I have, as a matter of fact.'

'Did he say anything about how things are up north, where Lara's gone?'

Tyler stroked the side of his face. He looked as if he was about to say something, but didn't.

'Only I was just in the house with Lara's mum and Lara actually came through on the phone!'

'No way! Where from?'

'Don't ask me how they can do it but she was speaking from a place called Peckforton up in North Mercia. The thing is, Kieran, I'm worried. Something bad happened yesterday – she wouldn't tell her mum exactly what, but it sounded like they were forced to stop at this Peckforton place.'

Kieran Tyler nodded. 'Mm.' He turned to face the same way as Ben, so that they were both looking out over the grounds and the long drive leading down to the boundary.

'The thing is, Kieran, I'm thinking of going after her.'

Tyler narrowed his eyes. 'What – on your own? How will you get up there?'

'Horse? I could take two horses…or, I don't know, the mail truck leaves for the north every other day, maybe I could get a ride with them.'

Tyler shook his head. 'I don't think you should do that.'

'Why not?'

'You won't catch up with her, man. And on your own…'

Ben pulled a face. 'I'm still going.'

Tyler sighed and walked past Ben to the front door. Turning he said 'Ben, before you go let me find out some more from File. You might not realise what you're flying into.'

He pulled the front doorbell cord and they heard it jangle inside.

Ben looked up at Tyler.

'Kieran,' he said, 'how about you come too? In that jeep we could be up there in under a day.'

23

Later that morning Star found Lara in the entrance hall of the castle.

'Phew!' said Lara. 'Let's go outside – I need some fresh air.'

'Where have you been?'

'Well first I went down to the radio room – got through to Alexander Laczko and got through to home as well – and now I've just been with Stettin.'

'Oh right, I've got one or two things to tell you. We should find somewhere quiet.'

They walked out into bright sunshine. The main courtyard had no seats or shade, so they took some outside steps that led up to a viewing area on the castle walls. They stood side by side, their arms resting on the top of the parapet as they surveyed the pine woodland dropping away beneath them on the steep hillside.

Star went first. She told Lara about how she'd tried to go out through the main gate but had been turned back – and then how she'd gone looking for Saleem and Private Roycroft and been met with frustration there too.

'I know,' Lara broke in. 'Stettin told me they'd taken the Land-Rover to Chester to get some repairs done. But I find it very strange Saleem didn't come to tell us what he was doing.'

'That's what I thought. Also, I found this big vehicle workshop – it's in a yard off the main courtyard. I reckon they could've easily done any emergency repairs there.'

Lara looked worried. 'I wonder where Saleem and our soldier

are. And the other Land-Rover – they seem to have vanished into thin air.'

Star shrugged her shoulders and went on to tell her what she'd learned from her second visit to the roof where the birds were kept.

'I've got that Will eating out of my hand. He's sworn me to secrecy, but he's shown me a way out of the castle only he and his father know about.'

Lara looked amused. 'Don't tell me – the inevitable secret underground passage?'

Star smiled. 'No – they've got a rope ladder up there.'

'A rope ladder!' Lara, shocked, looked over the parapet at the considerable drop to the ground below.

'It's all right – it's quite safe: he showed me. They keep it hidden in a big wooden chest.'

'Rather you than me.'

Star looked at her for a moment. 'That's right.'

'What…?'

'Why not? I could slip away tonight, hopefully get to Chester – Will said it's only ten miles away so I could walk it if necessary! Find out what's going on. See if I can find Saleem and the other Land-Rover. Raise the alarm – 'cos I don't know about you, Lara, but I'm beginning to think we've been trapped here. What d'you think?'

'I can't let you take all those risks on your own. No, I can't let you do that.'

Star sighed. 'Well think about it, Mrs Johnson.'

'Let's give it a bit more time. I'm not sure we are trapped here. I haven't worked Stettin out yet.'

Star made a face. 'I have.'

'I wanted to get going again today but it looks like it might not be possible now. Let's hope Saleem turns up this afternoon.' She frowned. 'Alexander Laczko told me he wanted me to stay here a few days–'

'–What?!'

'He wouldn't say why, except I guessed it was something to do with our safety.'

Star pursed her lips. 'This place doesn't feel safe to me. It gives me the creeps.'

'Well, I'm not going to follow his advice. As soon as we can I want to get to Chester and see if we can get some more leads there on where David might be.'

Star raised a forefinger. 'Ah, I saw something on the roof that might be a clue.'

Lara's eyes widened. 'Really?'

'Yeah, when Will was showing me the hawks and that he also showed me the pigeon loft.'

'Go on' said Lara, puzzled.

'Carrier pigeons – they're amazing. Apparently they used to use them to carry messages in little containers attached to their legs. You take a pigeon from one place which it knows as home, put it in a basket and take it to another place. Then when you want to send a message to the first place you just attach it to the bird and it flies home with it! Hard to believe, isn't it?'

Lara nodded. 'Come to think, I have read about carrier pigeons in one or two old books. I thought they were mythical birds.'

'No, they were real enough. I saw all the nesting boxes where the pigeons were kept. The pigeons have gone now but the boxes are still there with the homes of each one written on them. The thing is, there were all the places you'd expect – Chester, New Stafford, New York and there was even one for New Warwick – but one place stood out because it was Welsh: 'Wylfa'.'

Lara shook her head. 'I've never heard of it.'

'I'm surprised, because there's an old nuclear power station there.'

'Really! David never mentioned it. Or he might have and I've forgotten. He always went up north or to Scotland, not Wales.'

'Well, I asked Will where Wylfa was and why they needed to send messages there and he said it's because of the nuclear power station. It's in a place called Anglesey.'

'Anglesey…' Lara said, thinking.

Star grabbed Lara's arm. 'This is the most important thing, Mrs Johnson: North Mercia controlled that old power station for a while! They took it off the Welsh, whether by force or agreement Will didn't know. But he did say they had two dozen carrier pigeons for Wylfa at one point. They were sending messages from here all the time.'

Lara looked at Star and nodded. This young woman really is on the ball. But don't praise her too much; it'll go to her head.

'It might not be significant, Lara.'

'It's the best lead we've had so far. Good work. You remember the message he sent? The one you printed? The words are imprinted on my brain. He said something like 'I'm still in 'W''. I thought 'W' might mean Windscale in Cumbria, which is an even older power station than Sellafield. And I did wonder if W might have meant Wales, rather than a specific place – one reason I thought we should head this way even though he'd never mentioned Wales. But perhaps it's W for Wylfa.'

'Something to probe Stettin about,' Star said. 'How did you get on with him this morning?'

Lara gave Star the gist of her meeting with Marek Stettin but was careful not to tell her about the effect he'd had on her.

He'd been offhand – not downright rude but preoccupied and impatient to get away. He hadn't been at all helpful when she'd asked him whether he knew anything about David or whether he could help her find people in Chester who might have information.

He'd shrugged his shoulders and given her a sour look. 'How should I know? I represent central government in this region don't I? I don't know every little detail of what goes on.'

Lara's eyes flashed angrily. 'My husband is a renowned nuclear scientist and engineer! Dealing with the nuclear power stations isn't a little detail – and it very much is a central government matter!'

He'd looked her up and down, his cold dark blue eyes raking over her body. She'd picked up his body odour – sweat and leather because he'd been riding that morning, overlain with a nutmeg-and-citrus perfume he must have rubbed on his skin. She'd hated herself for it, but in that precise moment of confrontation she'd felt the pull of animal magnetism towards him. For the first time she'd taken in his physical presence – his muscular physique and the way his limbs moved with casual strength.

'Okay, okay,' he'd said, fixing her with that insolent look. 'I've had a communication from Alexander Laczko asking me to assist you. And I will. I will make enquiries with the North Mercian authorities. And I will find out about your driver and vehicle.'

'And another Land-Rover was accompanying us' she reminded him.

He'd ignored that. Standing up, he said 'you will have to excuse me. I've got very urgent and important things to see to.'

'Oh well, I won't detain you with my unimportant things then! I hope we can be on the road this afternoon.'

He ran his fingers through his long, black hair.

'You will have to wait for your driver and your Land-Rover to return. I can't spare you any staff or vehicles right now.'

'Something happening?'

'Let me put it this way, Lara. It's in your interests to stay with us for a few days.'

He'd given her a crooked smile. 'You will see.'

That night, alone in a four-poster bed in her room in the castle, Lara went back over her meeting with Marek Stettin – not just the things he'd said but the way he'd looked at her and the way she'd felt, confronting him.

She was overcome with guilt and pushed the thoughts away, deliberately conjuring up memories of David instead.

She remembered the moment she'd fallen in love with him. They'd been close together, standing in a group with other students in a pub in Oxford. She'd found herself gazing intently at his big square hands, and noticing how the ends of his forefingers seemed to bend upwards slightly.

Later that spring, one day just before Finals, they'd walked miles along paths in the open countryside. He'd recited scientific and mathematical formulae over and over again to get them into his head; she'd tried to outdo him by expounding upon obscure points of law as they strolled along.

In the late afternoon, lying on their backs and looking up at the blue sky through apple tree branches, she confessed she couldn't live without him. He'd kissed her tenderly on the lips and told her he couldn't live without her either.

She'd quickly learned, after that, that such moments of romance with David were rare. He preferred to make light of things, crack a joke, play catch me if you can – but that was part of the attraction in those early days.

Had she ever succeeded in catching up with the real David, finding the wandering spirit behind those light-hearted eyes?

When Arrow was born, she thought she had. For a few short months he was home a lot, rushing back from the lab or the office whenever he could, taking turns to soothe their tiny baby to sleep in the middle of the night.

Before the year was out, however, he was planning another research trip. The first one, when Arrow was ten months old, was to France. He'd promised to be away for no more than three weeks. As it turned out it was nearly three months. He came back thin, haggard, highly excited by what he'd discovered from nuclear scientists over there – and was then mortified by missing Arrow's first word.

'And where, where are you now, my love?' Lara whispered for the millionth time.

24

The next morning, after he'd checked the cows had been called up and the girls were doing the milking and he'd seen Jack and checked through the day's work with the lads, Ben got on his horse and rode into New Warwick.

He hadn't got the luxury of a telephone at home so he didn't know whether Kieran Tyler would be there. No matter, he'd wait for as long as it took.

He tethered the horse to a rail outside the central police station and rushed in. It was another warm day: he had to mop his brow with a handkerchief.

'Is Inspector Tyler in yet?' he asked the policewoman at the desk.

He was told to wait, and in five minutes was shown up to Kieran Tyler's office.

'Have you thought it over?' he asked Tyler.

'I'd like to do it, Ben...'

'–But. There's a but.'

'I ran it past the chief and he thinks it's a mad idea. One, I can't go racing off with a police jeep just like that – it's the only one we've got! Two, he says he can't spare me. And three, he's worried about treading on the other forces' toes, especially up north.'

Ben gave him a sardonic look and began to get up. 'Okay, sorry to waste your time, Kieran. I'll go on my own.'

Tyler lifted his arm. 'Wait! Give me the rest of the day. I'm concerned about Lara's safety just like I've always been concerned about David Johnson going missing. But don't forget, Lara Johnson is a very resourceful lady. She won't take kindly to us chasing up there on her behalf if she's doing fine with the team she's got. So I need more information. How dangerous is the situation up there? We don't really know. I need to talk to File again and get him to use that radio of his.'

Ben had a reluctant look on his face. 'When can you let me know?'

'I'll come round to the farm tonight.'

Lara and Star breakfasted alone in the big dining hall. There was no sign of Stettin, his sister or the other house guests. Their whispered conversation echoed around in the huge space. The fierce eyes in the trophy heads of the boars, stags and the single tiger stared down at them.

When they'd finished, Star announced she was going up to her room to write up the last two days in her journal.

'You'll need a new book soon,' Lara said with a wry smile, 'with all the things that have been happening! I'll buy you one when we get to Chester.'

Star gave her a moody look. 'If we ever get there.'

Lara frowned. 'I know. I'm going down to that radio room right away. Then I'm going to find Stettin and pin him down – see if he can't lend us some transport if Saleem still hasn't shown up.'

When Lara got down to the lower ground floor she found frenetic activity. Most of the office doors were open – she could hear telephones ringing and urgent conversations going on. Preoccupied-looking secretaries and administrators pushed past her in the corridor, avoiding eye contact.

She knocked on the door of the radio communications room and there was a delay before it was abruptly opened by a woman in a white blouse and grey skirt.

'Yes?'

'I'm Lara Johnson – one of Mr Stettin's guests – and I've been given permission to use the radio. I need to contact New Warwick on important state business–'

'–I'm sorry but that's out of the question today.'

Lara fixed her with an angry glare. 'It's very important I make this call. Do you understand?'

The woman swallowed, but maintained her stance.

'All radio channels have to be kept open for incoming traffic today. I'm sorry.'

The woman was talking gibberish but it was obvious she wasn't going to give way.

'All right,' Lara said, 'I'll go and see Mr Stettin about this.'

The woman nodded and shut the door.

Lara marched up to the nearest office and put her head round the door. Inside, two men and a woman had their heads together round a large map on a table. They were talking urgently and quietly together. Lara was too wound up to catch what they were talking about.

She tapped on the door. 'Can any of you tell me where I can find Mr Stettin?'

They stared at her. After some hesitation one of the men said 'I think he's in the Operations Room.'

'And where's that?'

The woman spoke up now. 'It's probably best if you speak to his personal secretary first – three doors along.' She pointed.

Lara met another barrier in Stettin's secretary, a tall blonde woman in a smart grey suit and impersonal grey eyes to match. It took Lara a whole three minutes to persuade her to take a message in to Stettin. And then another half-hour before the man himself appeared, unshaven and distracted. He was wearing brown leather trousers and a loose open-necked white smock.

He stared at her. 'Come up to my office. I have something for you.'

Stettin bounded up the stairs. She hurried after him, a few steps behind, and followed him into a large wood-panelled room on the ground floor.

He fell into a seat behind a huge oak desk strewn with papers. 'Sit down, please.'

She sat.

Stettin looked at her, reached down and slammed a slim black case on the desk.

'You found the money! Have you caught the gang?'

He gave a half-smile. 'We found only one case. They must have divided the money. My men surprised three of the criminals in a village hideout.'

Lara felt confused. 'Well…thank you at least for that!'

Stettin picked up a wooden ruler from the desk and played it along his lips. 'We will continue searching – there is a chance we'll find the rest of the gang.'

'I wanted to ask you, Marek. If my driver and escort don't come back soon, could you kindly arrange transport for me and Miss Edkin to Chester this afternoon? I need to find out what's happened to them. I need to get moving.'

Stettin stared at the space above Lara's head. 'I'm sorry Lara, but every vehicle we have will be tied up this afternoon. And for the next day or so.'

Lara lost what little patience she had left. She jumped to her feet. 'You said that yesterday – this is ridiculous! What's going on, Stettin? I feel like we're prisoners here!'

He put down the ruler, steepled his fingers and gave her a long, hard look.

'It's time I was honest with you, Lara. Something very momentous is about to happen. Something that will change the whole country forever.'

He broke off and pointed to a whisky decanter and glasses on his desk.

'Would you like a scotch?'

'No thanks.'

He gave a brief nod, sloshed a hefty measure of whisky into a glass and downed a good half of it.

'I'm sorry you had to experience that traumatic hold-up, Lara. But in a strange way it's fortunate it brought you here. Because as a result you are going to witness a historic event: something unique. And that's why I'm going to insist you prolong your stay with us.'

Lara's cheeks reddened with anger.

'Alexander has asked you to stay put, hasn't he? He's got plans for you, hasn't he?'

'What? How do you know what Alexander said to me?'

'Because he told me himself – we were talking together just now.'

Stettin smirked and gulped down the rest of the whisky. 'And if you don't believe me, you can check with him yourself in three days' time. When he'll be here.'

Lara felt her world falling apart. Laczko was her ally; her support. He represented the solid, reassuring power of South Mercia and New Warwick; he was her back-up. But now, it seemed, he was Stettin's ally. He was also behind whatever was going on.

Her mouth dropped open. 'He didn't tell me he was planning to come here!'

Stettin laughed. 'I'm sorry to give you a shock, Lara! I told you I was going to be honest! Yes, Alexander Laczko and...some other very important people. But before they arrive, we're expecting an even more important visitor!'

She stared at him.

Stettin stood up. 'I have to go now – excuse me. There are still a thousand and one things to do.'

Lara got to her feet, feeling dizzy. Stettin was holding the door open for her.

'Relax for the rest of the day, Lara.' He waved his arm in a vague way. 'There is a swimming pool – the castle used to be a hotel in Good Time – and I have a good library here...By tomorrow morning the preparations will be completed. Then I can relax too, for a day. Tell you what! I'll take you hunting in the morning.'

'What?'

'Yes, we'll take the hawks. Why not? And while you're riding next to me I'll explain it all, I promise. You'll be very, very glad you stayed – especially as soon I will have definite news of your husband.'

Star had to let Will kiss her twice before he agreed to her plan. He tried to put his hand up her blouse too, but she drew the line there. The kissing was bad enough: his breath smelled of stale onions and his clothes stank of bird shit.

But he was grateful; in a strange way it was touching to see just how grateful he was, grinning at her – his gap teeth and his goofy expression.

'Tonight, then?' she said. 'Eleven o'clock?'

He looked worried. 'I honestly absolutely cannot do it tonight, Star. I know the old man will be up here till all hours drinkin'.'

'I'll suck you off if we can do it tonight.'

Amused, she watched surprise and sore temptation cross his face. This was beyond his wettest dreams.

But he shook his head. 'No – it's got to be tomorrow night.'

'All right – same time, eleven o'clock. They do strike the hour here, don't they? And be sure you're ready.'

His eyes were alight. 'And then will you suck me off?'

'I'll think about it. When I get back. You've got to be waiting to drop the ladder for me, same time the following night. And if I don't show, the night after that – ten o'clock. Got that?'

He nodded. 'Yep, got it, but what if Dad's up here?'

'You'll just have to distract him. Get him out of the way somehow…I don't know, tell him there's a fire started downstairs or something; knock him over the head with a mallet!'

Will giggled.

'You want to come with us don't you, when we get away? You want to come to New Warwick and get a life?'

'Yes, o' course I do, Star! O' course! Anyways, if I stay and they find out what I done, fuck knows what they'll do to me.'

At six o'clock, when the farmhands had already gone and Jack was taking his leave, Kieran Tyler drove the jeep into Ben's farmyard.

'Wait there please Jack,' Ben said, 'I might need to have a word with you in a minute.'

Tyler got out of the jeep and stood waiting for Ben to come up.

'Well?' Ben said.

'Pack your gear, Ben,' the police inspector said. 'Six in the morning, we're going.'

That evening Lara and Star sat through another lengthy banquet at the long table. They watched again as Sibila stroked Marek Stettin's arm and leaned up close to him to whisper into his ear. As before, Stettin seemed to ignore her completely – and as before, Sibila threw jealous glances at them. The hatred in her eyes grew in intensity when they excused themselves and Stettin, leaning across the table, smirking, took Lara's hand and kissed it.

They went upstairs. Earlier, Lara had told Star about her meeting with Stettin. Now they were able to discuss the full implications. They talked for over an hour.

'The biggest shock was discovering Laczko also seems to be involved,' Lara said. 'Perhaps that means other regional commissioners too?'

'Who d'you think this other important visitor is?'

Lara shook her head. 'It's a mystery. But I'll find out tomorrow morning – or so he said.'

'We could escape tomorrow night' Star said. 'I've got the bird-man's son to co-operate.'

Lara gave her a thoughtful look. 'No, Star, I still think we can't go. There are bound to be patrols out there, we don't have any transport...wild animals...we'd have to make our way in the dark and find the right road...No, it would be jumping from the frying pan into the fire. I shouldn't go and you shouldn't go.'

Star stayed silent.

'And there's another thing,' Lara continued. 'Stettin has told me that in a couple of days' time he'll know where David is.'

'And you trust him?'

'No, but there's a chance he's genuine about that. He's trying to win me over for some reason. I can tell. I can't afford to ignore this chance.'

KEN BLAKEMORE

25

Ben woke before dawn. He lay awake until first light thinking about Lara. Then he got up and went downstairs to heat up some water for shaving and to make himself a nettle tea.

He lit the biogas and, while he waited for the pan to heat up, got out the old cardboard box and took out the framed photos of his parents. He placed his mother and father carefully on the kitchen table and kissed each one before going back to the box.

He took out his father's pistol. It felt cold and heavy in his hands. This handgun was at least seventy years old, genuine Good Time. He studied the lettering on the side of the barrel: Wilson Commander. Made in the USA.

He knew it still worked – he'd loaded the magazine with eight rounds and fired it twice into the midnight sky just a few hours ago. It had set the yard dogs barking but no one had come running – the farm was far enough away from other houses for the noise not to have alarmed anyone.

He walked over to the kitchen table and picked up the picture of his father. 'Dad, I know you're worried about the farm,' he said out loud, 'but you needn't be. Because I'll be back, don't worry. And I'll be bringing a lady with me – a lady who one day will be here with me on this farm. She'll bring her daughter with her and we'll have more children together, I swear.'

The hunting party left an hour after breakfast. Star watched from a narrow window in the keep of Peckforton Castle overlooking the

main courtyard. She could see the grooms leading out the horses
one by one. Stettin was standing apart from the noisy talkative
group. Now Sibila was joining them. She was wearing long, shiny
brown boots and she'd put up her hair in order to wear a riding
hat. After exchanging a few words with her brother, Sibila mounted
a pale grey stallion. Taking their cue, the others in the hunting
group mounted their horses too, and at a signal from Sibila the
whole group except Stettin cantered out of the courtyard.

Now Lara was walking quickly into the courtyard. Stettin was
saying something to her. He led her to a docile-looking pony being
held by one of the grooms. With help from the groom, Lara
mounted the pony and a moment later she and Stettin were on
their way, pony and black horse trotting side by side.

They moved at a gentle trot. Ahead of them was a wide forest track
leading steeply downhill through woods of pine and spruce.

Like Star, she'd felt oppressed by the great castle. She was still
in a trap, she knew that. But all the same it was good to get out into
the fresh air even if it was going to be difficult or impossible to
escape.

It was a long time since she'd ridden a pony. She'd had her
share of getting used to horses when she was a kid but she'd
forgotten how pleasurable the sensations were: the jogging motion;
the sense of control; being so high up; the rush of fresh air; the
smells of bracken and trodden grass, horse and leather.

They'd fallen behind the other riders but Stettin seemed in no
hurry to talk. They were reaching a cluster of log cabins now. As
they approached, several young children ran out from behind the
houses. They were laughing and whooping, excited to see more
horses coming. But as Lara and Stettin came up to them they
became silent and shy, standing in a line. Lara noticed one in
particular – a girl of about Arrow's age. She had stringy brown hair
and was wearing a mud-stained red smock. She looked up at Lara,
wide-eyed, a thumb in her mouth.

The single-storey dwellings looked as if they'd been
constructed recently. The log walls had been painted a dull reddish
colour. The thatch on the roofs was new, pale gold. Every one of
the small windows had been glazed. Every cabin had identical
shutters painted bright green with red rose designs stencilled on
them.

As they passed between the cabins an old lady in a black dress and headscarf burst out of one of the wooden cabins, calling to Lara at the top of her voice. She was holding up a large red embroidered scarf.

'The grandmother wants you to take this scarf to put on your head,' Stettin explained. He pointed upwards. 'The sun. She says a lady mustn't go bare-headed in the sun.'

'Ah…thank you,' said Lara, smiling down at the old woman, uncertain what to do.

'Take it,' said Stettin. 'We can return it on the way back.'

Lara took the scarf and thanked her. She folded it into a large triangle and placed it over her hair, tying it loosely beneath her chin. The old lady crossed herself, looking at Lara, then clapped delightedly and burst into quavering song.

As they trotted on, Lara noticed a Diana figurine in one of the windows of the log cabins, a small light burning in front of it.

As their horses trotted on, Lara decided to tackle Stettin before they caught up with the rest of the hunting party.

'What exactly is going on, Stettin? You said you were going to explain everything.'

'Call me Marek, please.'

She gave him a hard look.

Unperturbed, he said 'we are about to do what must be done – if this country is ever going to amount to anything again.'

'You're the one who's supposed to be guaranteeing the rule of law. Making sure that there's political stability in this region.'

'Lara, England is fragmented beyond all recognition. It's time to reach beyond the laws of a weak and incompetent government.

'Reach beyond? What does that mean? And what do you think gives you the right?'

'The right? I'm glad you raised the question of legitimacy, Lara. I agree – the right to govern is the most important question there is.'

'Parliament has the right! We have elections, remember? And the city states have their own elections – we can govern ourselves!'

Hearing her raised voice and sensing her anger, the horses were starting to break into a fast canter.

Stettin reined in his horse. 'Whoa, stop for a moment!' he shouted to her.

She pulled hard on the reins, made the pony turn round and walk back to where Stettin was. He'd dismounted and was standing beneath an oak tree.

She got off the pony – or rather started to slip off until Stettin caught her foot and helped her down. Feeling him holding her hand for an instant, one arm around her waist to guide her down, she sensed that animal attraction again and cursed her instincts.

He seemed to know what she'd felt. He was giving her an insolent grin.

She stood under the tree, facing him.

'We do have legitimacy, Lara,' he said. 'We're not betraying the constitution. Not the original constitution.'

Lara looked away from his intense gaze; those cruel dark blue eyes mottled with black.

'The post-pandemic restoration of parliament was a fine thing in many ways,' Stettin continued, 'but in one very important respect it broke with the old constitution. You could even say that it betrayed the past. Cheated us of our inheritance.'

Lara shook her head. 'I don't get it.'

There was a sudden gleam in his eye. 'England, and the United Kingdom as was, was a constitutional monarchy.'

It took her a few seconds to realise. She stared at him. Her mouth dropped open. 'You're not serious!'

He was nodding his head. 'Yes we are, indeed we are.'

Lara burst out with incredulous laughter. 'A monarch? Who?'

Stettin looked at her without expression now. 'Didn't your study of the law include the history of the British constitution? The key role played by the king or queen?'

'A little, yes – the role of the Crown and the courts – but I've never really known much about the actual royal family.'

'Up to 2022 we had George the Seventh. He'd been known as Prince Charles, but when he was crowned he chose George, one of his other names. He had two sons, William and Harry; their mother was the Princess Diana, the first wife of Charles. You know all this?'

Lara nodded.

'There was always some suspicion, by the way, that Harry wasn't the natural son of Prince Charles but the result of some liaison between Diana and another man.'

'It caused a split in the Church of Diana, I know that.'

Stettin allowed himself a suppressed smile.

'The question mark hanging over Prince Harry's legitimacy,' he went on, 'became very important for the succession to the throne. There was an angry quarrel, a great falling out between the two brothers. This happened after William abdicated in favour of his son George in 2042.'

'Why did he do that?'

Stettin stroked his chin. 'Some historians say he'd always felt diffident about becoming king. But I think it was because he wanted to make sure that George was crowned. That the succession would definitely pass to his son and not be stolen by his brother and his descendants. This was when the Second Pandemic was sweeping the world. No one felt safe–'

'–I suppose he wanted to be certain his son had at least a few years on the throne' Lara interrupted.

Stettin nodded. 'Probably that was the reason for the abdication. I don't know. Whatever, William's son became George the Eighth – the last king to sit on the throne. He died in 2046, a few years after the coronation, at the beginning of the Third Pandemic.'

'Was his father still alive then?'

'He was – he'd survived, though his beloved wife Queen Kate hadn't.'

'Was there any attempt to bring him back to the throne?'

'The record isn't very clear. Everything was falling apart by then. There was an emergency government and the constitution had been suspended. William was an ageing, grieving man. But some accounts say that old Prince Harry made a bid for the crown in the middle of the crisis. He was an impulsive man, apparently, and had himself declared king in Oxford.'

'So he was the last king?'

Stettin shrugged. 'I doubt it. He was never recognised as such. In all the chaos and disruption of the time, so many deaths, the whole question of royal succession simply wasn't dealt with. It must have seemed irrelevant – though perhaps if the royal family itself had not been so divided, a clear succession would have been decided. But don't forget, many of the royals had died too. The survivors left Britain to live in various parts of Europe.'

There was a pause. She could hear rooks caw-cawing in the trees.

Lara had to admit that despite her distrust and deep dislike of Stettin, he'd held her attention with his story about the royal family.

'So – will your very important visitor be a descendant of Harry or William?'

'A descendant of William – of his son George. George had a daughter, you see. Princess Eleanor was six when he died, and she's in her mid-forties now. When everything was falling apart, when she was a child, she was taken to one of the western regions of France – what's now the Brittany Region.'

Lara put her hand to her mouth. 'This is crazy. Can she even speak English?'

Stettin cleared his throat. 'We're not expecting Eleanor to be the next queen of England. We're awaiting the arrival of her twenty-year-old son, Prince Charles. He'll be our next king. Charles the Third.'

Tyler's jeep made good progress that morning. By midday they'd reached the centre of the Midlands and the point at which the old M6 had crumbled away. They followed the narrow unmade road that replaced it and at one o'clock came across a road sign advertising fruit teas, beer and snacks. Tyler steered the jeep into a grassy clearing nibbled by goats, beyond which was a huddle of wooden buildings, including a café. There was a river to one side of the clearing: Ben could hear the constant rushing of water over a weir.

Sitting outside over a bottle of local beer and roast beef sandwiches, they discussed their plans again.

'The last you heard of Lara,' he said to Ben, 'is that she was in Peckforton Castle. But she might well have moved on from there today.'

'But we don't know where to, do we? I still think we should go straight to the castle. If she's gone from there they'll tell us where to find her.'

'It's not much out of our way to go to Chester first, though – it's only a few miles further north. I reckon she might well be there now. The thing is, Ben, I know one or two uniforms in Chester – old mates from police college days. Who knows, we might need a bit of help.'

Ben looked sceptical, but nodded all the same. 'Okay.'

'To tell you the truth,' Tyler added, 'our inter-regional man Mr

File was hinting about a lot of trouble brewing up north. He wouldn't give much away – that bastard never does – but given the way he kept laughing at me as if I was mad coming up here, I reckon we should proceed as quietly and cautiously as we can.'

Before Lara and Stettin could finish their conversation under the oak tree, Sibila came galloping toward them on her grey stallion. Her face, normally alabaster white, was red and angry. She wheeled her horse around them, glaring down at Stettin.

'Marek! What are you doing? We're all waiting!'

He gave Lara a brief apologetic smile. Again, just for one second Lara felt an illicit thrill of collusion with this man – and again she hated herself for it. But there was no denying that electricity had been there. He'd made Sibila wait even though he knew it would make her angry; he'd favoured Lara.

When they reached the hunting party, Lara saw that most of them had tethered their horses to young willow trees lining the far side of a wide track that went round some cabbage fields. But Sibila and two other women were still on horseback, scanning the horizon, their hands above their eyes.

In the shade beneath the willows there was a small four-wheel cart and a brown horse hanging its head as it munched from a nosebag. A man of about sixty wearing a flat, round cap with geometric designs on it was attending to a line of baskets on the cart. Lara guessed what was in those baskets.

Once she'd dismounted, a stable boy appeared to take charge of her pony. Stettin walked over and quickly took her arm. She had no time to pull it away.

'Now, Lara, come and meet our falconry expert, our bird man.'

The man in the flat, round cap turned to face them. Lara noticed that he had a flushed, unhealthy-looking complexion and a surly look in his eyes.

'This is Pascoe,' said Stettin. 'He's the best – probably the only – real expert on hawks and hunting birds in the whole of England.'

Lara thought of saying 'not surprising, as keeping birds has been banned throughout the land', but thought better of it. This must be the bird man Star had talked about. She took off the headscarf and shook Pascoe's hand. 'Hello, Mr Pascoe, pleased to meet you.'

Pascoe bowed his head slightly. 'Pleased to meet you, ma'am. Have you come very far?'

'This is Mrs Lara Johnson, Pascoe,' Stettin said, as if this explained everything.

When he heard her name, Lara noticed, there was a sudden flash of apprehension in the man's eyes.

'We'll get on, then,' Pascoe muttered. He opened one of the baskets, bringing out a hooded kestrel for them all to admire. Everyone except Sibila and her two companions gathered round in a semi-circle.

'When you've let it go, how d'you make sure it'll come back?' Lara asked. Pascoe didn't answer. He removed the hood from the bird's head and launched the kestrel into the air from his gloved hand.

Two minutes later he picked up a long string with a small piece of meat attached to the end of it, explaining to the assembled group that this was called a lure. He pointed to a large oak tree, about a hundred yards off, where the kestrel had settled. Then, swinging the string lazily around his head, the lure high, he stared across at the hawk. Immediately the bird launched itself into the air and flew back to him, snatching the meat morsel before settling on his outstretched arm.

'There, my beauty!' Pascoe said, smiling fondly down at it. He stroked its head before settling the kestrel and replacing its hood. Then, as the guests began to talk among themselves, he brought out a peregrine falcon.

Lara took in the sight of the falcon's aggressive beak. It was bigger than the kestrel. It had barred plumage on its underside, scaly yellow legs and fierce eyes. Lara felt butterflies in her belly. She knew that although she'd kept a calm expression, Pascoe could tell she wasn't. He was looking at her with interest.

'Over there!' Sibila was pointing to something in the sky. Pascoe quickly undid the peregrine's tether and launched it.

'There, go!' he shouted. 'Peregrines are very fast hunters,' he explained to Lara and the other guests. 'They fly high above their prey and then dive down fast like, take 'em by surprise, see?'

'I forgot the binoculars,' Stettin said. He'd come to stand close to Lara's side. She could smell his warm skin. They both had their hands to their foreheads, scanning the empty sky. Their elbows touched. Lara remembered standing on the dam, next to Ben.

'What did you see, ma'am?' Pascoe shouted to Sibila.

'Ducks over that mere,' Sibila replied. 'At least I think…'

They waited a few more minutes. Pascoe scanned the skies anxiously.

Then she was back, circling over the cabbage field. 'That's my beauty!' Pascoe shouted, a wide smile on his red face. He put a short, flat wooden tube in his mouth and blew. The hollow whistling sound brought the falcon circling back to him, the limp body of a collared dove in its talons.

KEN BLAKEMORE

26

By four that afternoon, Ben and Kieran Tyler had reached the border between West and North Mercia. Their journey had taken at least two hours longer than they'd expected. After passing through Newport and glimpsing the famous Diana Cathedral they'd had to keep stopping at army checkpoints – one every few miles. At each one, the reluctance of the soldiers to let them proceed had increased.

At the West Mercia border post, a perspiring, heavy-breasted woman in an ill-fitting blouse told them the border had been sealed on the North Mercian side.

'Traffic's still coming through from their side,' she explained. 'But I'm afraid they won't let you through – there's no point trying.'

Ben's heart sank.

Kieran drove them back to the crowded lorry park, where a huddle of drivers hoping to cross into North Mercia had gathered.

They talked to two local drivers at a tea stall who told them of a back road – little more than a narrow track – that they could get a jeep through. The route was complicated, so Tyler took out a pencil and wrote down the directions on a small piece of paper.

'Wait 'til it's dark and don't tell 'em I told yer!' their informant said. He was a big-bellied man in a much stained smock. 'And keep yer fockin' 'ead down,' he said to Ben, 'for fock's sake. There's fockin' soldiers everywhere.'

He grinned expectantly. It took a moment for Ben to realise:

he took a hundred-euro note out of his wallet and slipped it to the man.

After dinner in the great hall of Peckforton Castle that evening, Star complained of a headache and slipped away during the entertainments.

She'd worried Stettin might suspect something, but he didn't. She was of no consequence to him; he'd carried on talking to Lara without even turning his head when she mumbled her excuses and left. He was looking at Lara in a different way now, she noticed – a definite sexual interest combining with some political grooming process. It was horrible to watch.

She felt bad about leaving Lara without telling her, but Lara would stop her going if she knew. But they were both in danger, weren't they? It seemed to Star that the only option now was for her to get out and fetch help. Stettin was ruthless – he could do anything and get away with it – and his weird sister was even more of a worry. Sibila's jealousy and signs of mental instability were becoming more obvious by the hour – Star reckoned she really could do Lara serious harm.

She made her way upstairs to her room, collected her bag – putting inside two bread rolls she'd brought up from the dining room – and then she went to the door of Lara's room. She looked up and down the corridor to check no one was coming, and slipped inside. She took out a note she'd written previously, lifted the coverlet on Lara's bed and put the note where Lara would see it. Then she hurried to the side of the castle where the door to the turret was.

Will had left the door unlocked, as arranged. She made her way up the narrow spiral staircase, feeling her way, her heart beating. He'd left a candle and a flint at the bottom of the steps and this small flickering light was the only one she had to see her way.

She opened the door at the top and went onto the roof.

He was waiting for her, holding an oil lamp, hopping with nervous excitement.

'Dad might be back any minute!' he breathed, trying in a fumbling, grinning way to kiss and embrace her.

'No way!' she said angrily. 'Get the ladder!'

A disappointed look crossed his face but he handed her the

lamp and ran off straightaway to open the chest and haul the rope ladder out of the shed. It was very heavy; she helped him to drag it to the right position by a low wall at the edge of the roof. He fixed the ends of the ladder securely to some iron rings in the stonework and they heaved the ladder over the edge.

It dropped, slithering and clacking, into the darkness below.

'Are you sure it reaches the ground?' she asked him. Her legs and arms were shaking.

'Yes! You might have to jump a few feet but no more.'

He helped her onto the wall and then to find her first foot on a rung.

'Right!' she whispered, 'eleven tomorrow night, and if I don't come then, the following night – got it? Don't forget! Listen out for the clock chimes.'

'Okay!' he whispered back, wide-eyed. 'And you will suck me off then, okay?'

She ignored that. Glancing down, she found the next rung on the trembling rope ladder and started her descent.

At the bottom, she jumped onto the inner slope of a dry moat. There was no path, but some clouds cleared and there was a half-moon – enough to see her way through a dense, chest-high stand of bracken. She'd felt night insects biting her face and a soft, resilient cobweb stretching across her lips. Then she climbed up the other side, a steep bank covered in dry leaves. It took a few minutes in the dark to find a wide track he'd told her about, which led deeper into the pine forest.

The moon was still shining through the clouds but the track began to narrow and the trees closed in, so it was almost completely black. There was no wind that night, but all the same Star heard something crack, like the snapping of a twig or a branch some distance away.

She wanted to locate the Chester road, to see how far it was this way from the castle.

A large, moonlit clearing lay ahead.

Some primeval survival instinct told her that to run would be fatal. The hairs on the back of her neck bristled. She felt panic rising in her chest.

The tiger was facing her, weighing her up, its mouth slightly open. It was only a hundred feet away. Its eyes glinted in the moonlight. She willed the huge animal to pad back into the shadows, but it didn't.

Any sudden move and it would spring – she knew that. Stand stock still.

In the moonlight, the tiger's stripes of cream, black and orange-brown shimmered. He could have been an apparition. He stared at her, and she met his eyes.

Time passed – it could have been a minute or twenty minutes, she couldn't tell because she was in a kind of trance. Eventually the big cat looked away from her stare. He yawned, exposing huge yellow fangs. And then he sat back on his haunches, still regarding her with curiosity but seeming to relax.

She decided to risk stepping back. Slowly, slowly, slowly: keep your gaze fixed on the tiger's face.

In the years that followed, whenever Star was asked to recount the story of how she came face to face with a tiger in an English forest, she could recall every minute detail – except how she climbed the tree. That bit always remained a complete blank. One moment she'd been gingerly backing away – the moment of highest tension. The next she'd found herself looking down at the tiger from the top branches of a nearby spruce. She'd stared with amazement at the branchless lower trunk of the tree. Somehow she'd managed to shin up with hardly anything to hold on to.

The tiger padded slowly to the base of the tree and looked up at her. She could hear him purring – a sound like her motor bike engine, only muffled. Then he walked off to lie down a short distance away, curling his body like a domestic cat, and closed his eyes.

When Lara returned to the guest room corridor near midnight she wondered how Star was. She tapped on the door twice, waited, and then opened it. The room was empty. Her bed hadn't been slept in.

Lara had already guessed what Star had done before she found the note. Stupid girl, she whispered to herself, feeling angry.

She locked the bedroom door, feeling scared. Star's disappearance had unsettled her. Now all her escort had vanished – if only, she sincerely hoped, for another day or two. She got back into bed. Drowsy with too much wine and food, she drifted into a restless, uneasy sleep.

Star soon began to feel cold as well as tired. She'd found a fairly comfortable cleft in the tree branches to lean against, but sleep was out of the question as long as the tiger lay nearby on the forest floor.

Hours passed. Eventually the first grey light of dawn began to show. A trickle of birdsong started up. Within ten minutes it became a waterfall of sound, almost deafening. She let it fill her ears, strangely comforted by the way it completely enveloped her. She began to daydream, envisioning riding her motorbike on long, winding roads to the mountains of Wales, where Gwynfor was.

When she woke, the tiger had gone.

Stiffly, cautiously, she climbed down the spruce, trying not to slide or make a noise as she tested each branch with her foot. Pretty soon she was in the gloomy shadows below the canopy. The last bit – the smooth trunk with hardly any protruding knobbles – she had to jump. It was a long way. She bent her knees as she hit the springy carpet of brown pine needles, rolling over to soften her landing. Her left ankle hurt as she landed, but gradually the discomfort eased.

She had to decide what to do. First, she felt in her bag to make sure her journal was safe. Then she took out one of the bread rolls. As she ate, she wondered whether she'd done the right thing after all. How was she going to find her way to Chester? It was a mad idea to think she could have done it in the dark but equally mad to think she could get there in broad daylight without being seen and captured – or worse. Also, that tiger was roaming about somewhere.

Should I go back to the castle and face the consequences? They couldn't be that serious. After all, she wasn't a very important person. Lara would be angry, but it wasn't as if she'd done anything really wrong. And Lara would be relieved to see her in one piece. Star limped along narrow, shadowy forest paths for nearly an hour, not realising she was walking in circles until she glimpsed the main tower of Peckforton Castle through treetops.

Before that she came to a small stream. It contained clear, icy-cold spring water. Stooping down, feeling hot in the face, she dipped her cupped hands in and drank as much as she could. Afterwards she stepped on to the sandy bottom of the brook, keeping her worn shoes on, letting the cold water ripple around her sore ankle.

Then she retraced her steps, squelching along, and half a mile later took another choice at a fork in the path. She found herself gradually winding uphill to a clearing from which she could see the castle again. She was about to plunge on, resigning herself to facing the music, when she heard the dogs.

Her mind went back to the afternoon they'd arrived in the forest – Stettin and his band of hunters coming to the rescue, the muddy baying hounds bouncing into the forest clearing.

But this time a peculiar dread came into her heart. She was the one being hunted.

Okay, she told herself, stay where you are and wait to be discovered. Surely the dogs won't tear a human being apart as they would a fox? They'll frisk and bob around you until people come.

But fear took over. Star didn't stop to debate the point about the dogs. Hearing their baying and the shouts of men getting closer, she ran like hell. She made for the stream, back downhill, racing breathlessly through any brambles or bracken that barred her way. She remembered reading a story about how hunting dogs lose the scent of their prey if the hunted animal runs into water.

She made it to the stream, splashing along it recklessly, jumping over rotting logs and forcing her way through clutches of tall weeds, finding a stamina and ability to keep going that she didn't know she had in her slight frame.

Then, to her surprise, she found herself in a wide, sunlit clearing. Ahead of her was a group of six or so thatched cabins arranged in a semi-circle. She was looking at the rear of these cottages. Each cottage had a long garden surrounded by high wicker fences that were topped with bundles of thorns. Without pausing to think, Star prised open the gate to one of the gardens. She crouched low to avoid being seen – she could hear the voices of children playing some way off – and crept between seven-foot high rows of runner beans.

To her relief the baying of the hunting dogs got fainter. Perhaps they were hunting the tiger, not her. She lay flat on the ground and slowly pulled her slim body between two rows of canes, hiding in the deep shadow between the thick, green, angled walls of beans.

She lay on her side, feeling the soft earth beneath her right hip, watching a ladybird climbing laboriously around a leaf and onto her fingers. Heavy bees zoomed overhead to visit the scarlet bean flowers. Within minutes her thumping heart calmed down and her breathing eased. An hour or so later, a wedge of dappled sunlight found a gap in the bean leaves and fell on her face. Her eyeballs were filled with an orange glow, and she fell into a deep sleep.

27

That morning at about ten-thirty, Stettin sent a manservant to find Lara.

She'd gone down to the radio communications room, only to be told for a second time that Stettin had left strict instructions that no one was to be allowed inside to use the equipment; they were standing by to receive important messages.

She was walking back up to the ground floor, contemplating whether she herself should try to escape now, when the servant intercepted her.

'Mr Stettin's waiting!' the breathless servant said. 'Follow me please, Mrs Johnson.'

He led her to the main entrance and out into the courtyard. She could see Stettin, Sibila and a group of Stettin's more senior administrative staff standing in a group at the far end in front of a high wall. Other people – some of the house guests and a few servants – were also standing around the edge of the courtyard.

She could see the excitement in everyone's eyes and feel the tension, the air of expectation. This must be the VIP, Lara thought; the very important visitor Stettin was talking about. She walked over to Stettin's group, standing a little apart from them.

There was a cry from above: 'he's coming!' followed by a sudden hush. Lara looked up, squinting against the dazzling sun. A lookout on the battlements of the central keep was pointing and he shouted again: 'over there!'

But he wasn't pointing down to the plains and forest roads

below – he was pointing up into the sky, which was very odd.

There was a very gradually increasing sound she'd heard only once before when she was a child, and almost completely forgotten – a whispering chatter, gaining strength.

Suddenly a huge flying machine roared into view, directly overhead. It hovered over the castle like a giant insect. Now it was moving slowly sideways, filling their guts with noise and vibration as it came slowly down to settle in the centre of the courtyard. Clouds of dust surrounded it, blowing outwards.

The helicopter's engine was switched off; the rotors whispered to a standstill.

Silence returned for a few seconds.

Lara saw a servant rolling out a strip of red carpet. Stettin was forming his group into a reception party. 'Come, come, Lara!' he was saying, beckoning urgently. He wanted her to walk up to the helicopter with them. He led the way, Sibila by his side with her arm crooked into his. His leather trousers and loose-fitting white shirt had been exchanged for a dark Good Time-style business suit, complete with a traditional straight tie; Sibila was wearing a long dress, dark blue, with a matching dark blue straw hat.

The door of the helicopter slid open. By now some steps had been wheeled up alongside.

Lara stared up. Framed in the door of the helicopter was a slight figure of a young man in a white suit. He had a thin, pale face, eyes set close together, and he was looking down a pronounced, narrow nose at them. A cheer rose up from the servants standing around the edges of the courtyard.

Kieran Tyler and Ben had managed to cross the border the previous night, though not without incident. They lost their way several times: the track their informant had told them about did begin at the place he'd described, but after three miles it had simply disappeared into a thicket of brambles and young trees.

Tyler had cursed, reversing the jeep back up the narrow lane until he'd found another track that seemed to lead in vaguely the right direction. It was all the more difficult because Tyler was steering without lights most of the time – they didn't want to attract the attention of any border patrols or guards.

When the second track petered out, Tyler threw caution to the winds – he drove the jeep up a bank into a grassy field, switched on the headlights and surveyed the landscape ahead. In the distance was an area of scrubby heath land. He pressed the accelerator and the jeep plunged on, crashing through two fences and a low hedge, and then bumped across the heath that stretched in front of them.

A few miles on, as they reached more farmland, they were shot at – though luckily the two shots came from a considerable distance. 'Probably a farmer' Tyler said.

They decided to stop before sunrise; they'd found a decent road and were well into North Mercia, though exactly where wasn't clear. Both Tyler and Ben were utterly exhausted. Tyler edged the jeep into a dense hawthorn thicket, hiding it from view. He'd thought to bring blankets. He handed one to Ben, and they collapsed onto the ground under some nearby trees and fell asleep.

Mid-morning, they were on the road again. They were now in the grassy landscape of the Cheshire plain. As they bumped along the unmade country road, Ben marvelled at the neatness of the fields and hedges; the sleekness of the cattle; the fine stands of wheat and corn.

There were no passers-by on the road, however – no one to ask where they were. The whole countryside seemed to be unnaturally quiet – no one working in the fields, no one at the doors or in the gardens of the few log cabins they passed.

Before midday they reached their first road block. They'd just found a more major road – a fine road, smooth tarmac. A signpost told them they were only a few miles from the reclaimed city of Chester – New Deva.

Three soldiers in dark green uniforms and peaked caps surrounded the jeep, slouching with submachine guns in their hands, while a fourth questioned Tyler, asking him for ID and a travel permit.

Tyler smacked his forehead. 'Clean forgot! My mate here,' he said, pointing at Ben, 'his wife's having a baby. She's with her mother in Chester isn't she Ben?'

Ben nodded. He was feeling surreptitiously for the handgun, which lay at his feet under his bag.

'We're from Whitchurch, see,' Tyler lied. 'We got the news to come up this morning, quick as we could.'

'I've a mind to take you in, and this vehicle' the soldier said. 'But we've got better things to do. There's no way you're getting into Chester today mate, so fuck off back to Whitchurch.'

Lara had been told to wait in a small room next to Stettin's office on the ground floor. There was a tap at the door and a man in his early thirties with tightly curled brown hair and rather effeminate rosy-red lips came in. He was wearing a light grey Good Time-style suit and an open-necked pink shirt.

He shook Lara's hand and smiled. 'I'm Paul Severin, and I'm translating for His Royal Highness this afternoon. I'm very pleased to meet you, Mrs Johnson.'

He spoke very correctly and precisely, but with an accent Lara couldn't place.

'I want you to know,' Lara said, that I'm not prepared to address the prince as His Royal Highness.'

Severin smiled. 'There are no set conventions,' he said lightly. 'No need to curtsy or bow – you may shake hands – and 'sir' is a perfectly acceptable form of address, if that is all right with you?'

'Yes, fine,' Lara said, wondering what the archaic word 'curtsy' meant. Falling to your knees in front of him?

'Then let's go in' Severin said, leading her to Stettin's office door.

He opened it without knocking and Lara went in behind him.

The first thing she noticed was that Stettin had cleared the untidy piles of paper from his desk. A large crystal vase with twenty of more red roses stood in the centre of it.

As Lara entered, Stettin – who'd been sitting at one side of the desk – stood up and, with a broad smile on his face, introduced her.

Severin translated Stettin's words into French.

Prince Charles, still in the white suit, was sitting in a large leather armchair. He made no move to stand or to acknowledge her presence in any way. He regarded her impassively. To Lara, he looked even more willowy and insubstantial in the large armchair than he had while framed in the doorway of the helicopter. He had long, delicate-looking fingers; his right hand was playing with a gold cross which hung from a chain around his neck.

If he wasn't going to stand up, she decided, she wasn't going to proffer her hand.

There was an awkward silence until the prince asked something, looking at Severin.

'His Highness wants to know,' Severin said, 'where your

mother and father came from?'

Mind your own business, was the first thought that came into Lara's head. But she restrained herself and said 'my mother is English, sir, and I believe my father's family originated in North Africa, but I'm not sure because I never knew my father.'

The prince nodded, looking down his long, thin nose and studying Lara carefully. He spoke in a low tone to Severin.

Severin smiled. 'His Highness is sad to hear that you never knew a father's love. He too has experienced that loss. Also, he had guessed that you might be of North African descent, and he compliments you on your, er,' Severin stumbled, 'your appearance, your beauty.'

She gave the prince an amused look. 'Thank you very much. Tell him he looks extremely pretty too.'

Severin gave her a panicked look, but didn't say anything because the prince was speaking again.

'His Highness would be extremely pleased if you would accept an important position in the New Realm.'

Lara blinked. 'What? What does he mean?'

Stettin interrupted. 'Excuse me Your Highness,' he said, looking at Severin and then the prince. 'May I…?'

The prince nodded.

'Lara,' Stettin said, giving her an earnest look, 'the plan is to have an interim administration in each city state, just as there will be an interim administration for the whole country. We'll be appointing a governor for each city and . . . well, we'd very much like you to consider taking on this position for New Warwick.'

The room swam before Lara's eyes.

'What? No, definitely not,' she heard herself say.

'Just take some time to think about it,' said Stettin. 'Please, don't reject the idea out of hand. Even if you don't agree with all of our reasons or intentions, think about how much more you'd be able to achieve for New Warwick if you're with us rather than against us.'

Lara pressed both of her palms on the cool, polished table. She took a deep breath and then expelled all the air through her mouth.

'Don't say anything now. Just think about it,' Stettin repeated.

Star woke in the late afternoon to the sound of children's voices. She hadn't a clue where she was. Her limbs felt stretched and rested; her hip had snuggled comfortably into the warm, soft ground.

Then she snapped awake, alarmed, heart racing. Had the children spotted her? No, it was okay. They were gabbling excitedly in the next garden, the other side of the high wicker fence a good five yards away.

Turning over on to her back, she stared up at the bean foliage. She was ravenously hungry. Cautiously, checking no one was in the garden or looking out from the cottage, she reached up above her head and carefully picked, one by one, the long green beans that were dangling down. The tough ones with bulging sides she broke open, stuffing the smooth pink beans into her mouth. They were the most delicious thing she'd ever tasted, once she'd separated and spat out the translucent husk from each one. There were also the tender young beans, which she ate whole.

Then she opened her bag, eased out the remaining bread roll and ate that. As the hunger pangs lessened, Star looked down at her legs and feet. Her leather plimsolls were caked in mud and looked as if they were about to split at the seams. Her shins were streaked with mud and sand from running along the stream. The cut-off denims, which reached down to her knees, were similarly grimy and torn with bramble scratches, as was her shirt. She ran her fingers through her spiky hair and sighed. There was no way she could carry on hiding. She'd have to go back to the castle.

But by the time she stole quietly out of the garden, Star had changed her mind. It was early evening by then. Between five and six o'clock, she guessed from the angle of the sun. When it came to it, some instinct told her not to take the track back to the castle. Maybe going the other way would lead to the road to Chester, perhaps. Or maybe, she thought...maybe – a spasm of excitement crossed her stomach – maybe she'd find herself on the road that led to the Welsh border and to that town with the mysterious name; Gwynfor's home town. But no, she could never abandon Lara Johnson. It had to be Chester. She had to find Saleem and Anwar and their soldiers.

The track led her through an area of open cultivated land. Fields of cabbage and other green vegetables lay on one side, maize and tobacco on the other. At one point the track passed a fenced-off plot full of summer-fruiting raspberry canes, all neatly staked. Most of the fruit had already been picked. Star took a chance. Looking quickly each way, she pushed a rustic-looking barrier aside. Soon she was stuffing ripe raspberries into her mouth. No one shouted; no one seemed to be about. Star reflected on this as she trudged on. The countryside seemed unnaturally quiet in the still evening light.

After another mile or so she came to the edge of the forest again; she shuddered as she entered the cool shadows of the woods. But at least the road had widened. There might have been no traffic and a curious sense of expectancy in the air, but this road, she reassured herself, was definitely going somewhere.

By the time Star had walked another three miles her feet were beginning to blister. Under the tree cover it was already getting dark. She didn't want to spend another night alone in the forest. She remembered the tiger.

Sighing, she stopped to look down at her feet, grimacing at the splits in her shoes. The blisters were really stinging now. Through the thin worn-out soles she could feel every pebble and stone as she walked along. And, looking down like that, she didn't notice the pushbike coming the other way.

She looked up with surprise when she heard the bike skidding to a halt about twenty yards in front of her. The rider, a young boy, flung the bike down with a crash. He snatched a quick look at her and then turned tail, wailing, running back up the road for a few yards before jumping into the woods to the left.

'Hey, stop!' Star shouted after him. 'It's okay!' And then, after he had disappeared, she called again, 'Where does this road go?'

Her voice echoed around the silent tree trunks. Shaking her head, she wondered what had got into the boy. She picked up the small, dusty bike and set it back on the road.

It's me, she thought. An amused look crossed her face. I must've looked like a ghost standing there, or a wood spirit who took away young children. God knows what superstitions they've developed in these wild parts!

Chuckling to herself, she got on the bike and started to pedal along the forest road.

At the same time, in the castle courtyard, Lara Johnson was having an argument with Marek Stettin. Stettin had told her that tomorrow there'd be a crucial meeting. He wanted her to be there. He'd succeeded in bringing together most of the regional commissioners from the North and the Midlands, including Alexander Laczko. Representatives from Scotland would be there too, because the Scots were thinking of a union with the New Realm. They'd all be there to meet the prince.

Earlier that day when Lara had agreed to an audience with him, she'd done it more out of curiosity than anything. Now she felt compromised and angry.

'I can't agree with what you're doing, Stettin. It's terrible – it's profoundly undemocratic and it's going to take us back to the Dark Ages. And I don't want to be some kind of local despot over New Warwick. Do you think,' she said, 'that our grandparents, the people who died and struggled to put us back on the right track, wanted it all be to be dismantled in a few weeks and thrown aside, just like that?'

Stettin took a deep breath. 'I agree. They sweated blood, many of them. But they were trying to recreate a world that doesn't exist any more – a so-called democracy. But it's a fragmented shambles. England needs to be re-united! Drawn into one whole kingdom again and united with Wales and Scotland too–'

Lara snapped. '–It's you who's dragging everything back to the past!'

Before he could reply, she turned on her heel and walked away.

She couldn't bear the idea of going back inside the castle. She found the outside steps that led up to the perimeter wall and stood looking out over the countryside below, breathing in the warm late afternoon air.

Her anger gone, she tried to think things over objectively. What if they succeeded? What would happen to New Warwick then? Shouldn't she throw in her lot with them, if only for the sake of protecting at least some of New Warwick's hard-won freedoms?

But then, she thought, how could I convince myself, let alone them, that I was on the side of my fellow citizens rather than Stettin's? Shouldn't I distance myself as quickly as possible from the whole thing? If the coup failed – as it might – she'd face severe punishment as a rebel and a collaborator.

What about Arrow? Mental pictures of her young daughter's

face had been passing through Lara's mind all day. She ached to pick up her child, smell her skin and reassure herself that she was all right. How would she be able to protect her if she was caught up in a struggle for power?

Or was it the other way round? Will I be able to protect my mother and my daughter better, she wondered, if I work with the new powers? The idea that the country could become a monarchy again had initially struck her as wildly unreal – laughable, almost.

But now, when she ran the project through her mind she came to a more sober conclusion. The young prince from overseas would be presented as a charismatic hero, a saviour who had returned to unite England once again. He might just be a figurehead for a scheming band of provincial administrators, most of them descended from Polish and other East European immigrant families, but that wouldn't matter – the people wouldn't realise these things. There'd be no newspaper or radio station or group of political leaders to tell them otherwise.

Visions of cheering, excited crowds floated before her eyes. The young prince would be a direct descendant of Our Lady of Suffering, returning to bring justice and to redeem her name.

KEN BLAKEMORE

28

On the bike, pedalling hard along the forest road, Star made a lot more progress. A few miles further on, however, she had to stop, getting off the bike as soon as she saw lights ahead. In the twilight it was hard to make out exactly what was going on. A few hundred yards away, at the end of a long, straight stretch of road, there was a vehicle with its headlights on. It was facing her. She could also make out a barrier – a long pole that had been lowered in front of it. There were several figures – all men, probably soldiers she thought, standing next to a sentry box. Even at this distance she could hear their raised voices. Some kind of altercation was taking place.

She hid the bike carefully behind a tree in a clump of ferns and tiptoed carefully towards the barrier, keeping off the road. As she neared it she went deeper into the woods to avoid being seen. Then she turned about and, crouching down, crept back carefully towards the road, holding her breath. She listened to the voices of the arguing men.

Her heart flooded with relief, but also concern. She recognised one of the voices. It was Ben Frobisher – the farmer guy who'd been hanging around Lara Johnson! She was able to make out other figures: a man in shorts, standing next to Ben, and two soldiers – the barrier guards.

'I don't care who you fookin' are,' one of the guards was shouting. 'I'm tellin' yer for the last fookin' time we've got orders not to let any fookin' bastard past this fookin' post. Now for the last fookin' time will you fookin' well fook off or do I have to start usin' this fookin' thing?' He lifted up a submachine gun.

'Now hang on, mate, hang on.' The man in shorts was talking. He sounded calm and reasonable. Star had a strong feeling she'd met this man in New Warwick but because of the way he was standing she couldn't get a good look at his face.

'Come on, Kieran. We're not getting anywhere.' That was Ben.

Kieran? Star asked herself. It was the cop, Kieran Tyler!

'He's right, mate. Push off. Now.' The second barrier guard sounded calmer than his comrade.

Kieran tried one more time. 'Okay, okay. We'll go back. But all I'm asking, one more time, is for you to check. Like I said, we've got to pick up a VIP from Peckforton Castle – Justice Lara Johnson. If they tell you on the other end of the line she's not there, all well and good…'

Star gently pulled aside a small branch. The two barrier guards had their heads together. After some muttering the soldier holding up the gun stepped back a pace. He still looked angry and was shaking his head, but it looked as if he'd been persuaded at last.

'Okay?' the second one asked him.

'Go on,' the first one sneered. 'I'll watch these fokkers.'

Star realised the second guard was coming towards her. She ducked back behind the branch, almost tripping backwards over something – a heavy piece of wood.

She heard a flimsy wooden door opening. She parted the branches again and peered through the narrow gap. The guard was standing in a sentry box, his back to her. He was leaning over a shelf and turning a handle furiously. Star glanced up, noticing the thin telephone wire that led from the roof of the sentry box to a pole by the side of the road.

The guard had picked up a phone receiver, and was shaking his head and muttering. The receiver was slammed down. He turned the handle again.

Star knelt, feeling in the grass and ferns for the log. Her fingers closed around it. She parted the stiff fir branches in front of her as quietly as she could, stepped forward and lifted up the unwieldy piece of wood with both hands over her head. It was heavy; not light with rot. The man was saying 'Hullo, hullo?'

She swung the log down with all her strength. The sound was

like a carpet beater hitting a heavy rug.

Star let out a scream, not believing what she'd done, and dropped the log. The man had slumped sideways. As he fell, he slid down the side of the wooden sentry box.

Rooted to the spot, she heard confused shouts from the men. A second later she was staring into the angry, bewildered eyes of the second barrier guard, who was waving his submachine gun around. He suddenly rammed it into her chest, and she found herself sitting on the ground.

Another second, and Ben and Kieran were running up. Kieran threw himself at the guard. The two men were falling to the ground, wrestling with each other for the submachine gun. The soldier managed to get up, the submachine gun in one hand. Another gun went off.

Feeling refreshed and smelling of lavender from her bath, Lara made her way down the big central stairway to the great hall. Cheerful music – fiddles and flute – drifted up towards her, mingling with the enticing, spicy smells of cooking from the kitchens on the floor below.

An hour before, she'd been determined to snub Stettin and the royal party and stay in her room. But what's the point of that, she'd asked herself. I'm a prisoner whatever I do. The warrior inside her was stirring again – surely it was better to go down to dinner and find interesting ways of insulting the White Mouse (the name she'd given the prince) and embarrassing Stettin.

From her trunk of clothes, only one smart dress had been rescued from the Land-Rover, after the holdup. It was a silver-grey number made of shimmering fabric. It glittered in the light like the scales of a fish, bright shards of violet, blue and pink. The dress had a low neckline. She knew she looked good. This felt much better than languishing in her room with a headache.

And if there was still a trace of uncertainty about Stettin and his plans, any trace of indecision about what to do next was swept away when she reached the bottom of the stairway.

This was where two side corridors branched off to right and left. Going into the left-hand corridor was a tall man with a shaved head. He was wearing a sleeveless smock and a long, striped butcher's apron grimy with old bloodstains. He was whistling as he pushed a creaking wooden trolley – a high one with shelves laden with trays of meat.

He glanced at her only briefly, his eye caught for a moment by her shimmering dress and her cleavage. He didn't look her in the face but plunged on into the corridor, apparently without a moment's thought, still whistling.

She glimpsed it for only a second – but clearly enough to be absolutely sure. There, on the man's forearm, a dark blue tattoo in the shape of a hovering eagle. And there, on his left ear, that single gold earring.

As she walked into the great hall, proud and smiling, head erect, Lara's mind was racing. The implications of seeing the man with the tattoo were sinking in fast: it was Stettin who had laid the trap, diverted them off the main road and organised the holdup.

Perhaps it had been Laczko's idea, initially. Laczko was the one who wanted her to run New Warwick and Stettin had been only too happy to oblige by laying on a frightening theatrical holdup – all the better to show himself off as a rescuing knight, take her to the castle and keep her there until she decided to co-operate.

Well, Stettin, she said to herself as she took her seat at the dining table, perhaps it's time the White Mouse knew what you've been up to.

Star sat in the same spot in the grass behind the sentry box, shocked and speechless as Ben and Kieran dragged the guard's body a little way into the woods. She'd brought this about. She'd been the cause of this.

When they returned, she noticed Ben was trembling and white-faced. His hands were shaking.

'I can't believe I killed a man,' he said. 'I can't believe it.'

Kieran Tyler put a hand on his shoulder. 'And you saved a man – thank you.'

Star found she could stand. She too was trembling, and her voice quavered. 'What about the other one?'

Tyler gestured to Ben to follow him.

The other guard was still unconscious. Tyler ran to the jeep and came back with a pair of handcuffs, rolled the man onto his front and handcuffed his hands behind his back. Then, with Ben lifting the man's arms and shoulders and Kieran his legs, they hoisted him up.

They were carrying him towards the jeep when Star saw headlights – a vehicle approaching.

'Look out!' she shouted.

Tyler turned to look. In the gloaming light they could see the approaching vehicle.

'It's all right!' he shouted to Star. 'Stay there – it's okay!'

Why weren't they running away? Not wanting to take any chances, she walked into the shadows of the fir trees at the side of the road.

The vehicle drew up – and her heart skipped a beat. It was the Land-Rover!

However, the driver getting out now wasn't Saleem, but Anwar. And the soldier wasn't Private Roycroft, but Private Williams – the one who'd ridden with Anwar from New Warwick.

Tyler saw the confusion in her face. 'We were trying to get to Chester,' he said. 'But we got turned back. We stopped for something to eat, and who should we see...' He pointed to Anwar and Private Williams.

Anwar was talking animatedly to Ben and Kieran Tyler now. Where was Saleem? Where was the other Land-Rover?

Star felt faint for a moment. 'Wait!' she said.

They all turned to look at her.

'Does anyone know the time?'

The men shrugged their shoulders – none of them had a timepiece.

Tyler said, 'I don't know – the sun's set, so it's sometime between nine and ten I suppose. Why?'

'Come on!' she shouted, running to the jeep. 'Hurry up!'

29

Lara heard a tap at the bedroom door.

She put down the book she was reading. 'Yes?'

Another tap.

'Just a moment!' she called, and went to open the door.

She was still dressed. Half an hour before, she'd walked out of the banquet in honour of the prince.

Her plan to discomfit Stettin by telling the prince what he'd been up to hadn't worked, firstly because she'd been seated six places away from His Royal Highness. Sibila, who'd been seated next to the prince, had given her smug and disdainful looks all evening – absolutely infuriating.

Secondly, when she did manage to get closer to the prince after the dessert and before the entertainments, Severin, a smirk on his face, obviously twisted her words or didn't relay her meaning at all. She didn't know any French but from the look on the prince's face it was as if he was receiving a shower of compliments from her.

He'd smiled and proffered a ringed finger for her to kiss, and it was at that point she'd walked out.

Now, she flung open the door.

'Lara.' He looked very tense. 'I came to see how you are.'

'Go away.'

She started to push the door to, but he pushed against it and forced it wide open.

He was through – he was inside the room, right up against

her.

'I think I know what you need' he said. 'I think you need to be taught a lesson.' His voice sounded thick. He was speaking through clenched teeth. His pupils were dilated but otherwise his eyes were expressionless.

He closed the door. Lara's heart froze. This couldn't be happening. He wouldn't.

He was gripping her tight, pinning down her arms and pushing her backwards towards the bed. He was incredibly strong.

She wanted to scream but no sound came out.

'Yes,' she heard him say – but oddly it was as if he was a long way off. 'Yes,' he repeated, 'I know what you've needed all along!'

She spat in his face.

For a moment his eyes lost their expressionless look. Excitement and anger filled them. He laughed. He was forcing her back onto the bed. Now he had his left hand up her dress, reaching right up.

But in doing that he'd let go of her right arm. She used all her strength to twist her body out from under him and fling her arm up, digging long fingernails into his left eye.

He gave out a cry of pain and reared back, half-standing, putting one hand to his eye.

She kicked him as hard as she could in the crotch, and he gave out another cry of pain.

'Bitch!' he shouted. His anger now looked righteous.

She saw him raise his arm but she didn't see it coming, didn't feel any pain. All she knew was the ringing in her ears and the taste of blood on her lips. She was flat on her back, her dress right up. Her knickers had gone.

He was kneeling in front of her undoing his belt, staring down at her. He had a supercilious smile on his face which said one move and I will hit you again, much harder next time. He was easing his trousers down, exposing his erect penis, still staring; taking his time.

The door opened and all at once the room was full of shouting.

She heard a man's voice – 'No, Ben, no!'

It was Ben! He was standing in the middle of the room, pointing a gun at Stettin. His hand was shaking.

Stettin had gone as white as a sheet. He was at the foot of the bed with his hands in the air, his trousers around his ankles; his penis far from erect now.

'Cover yourself!' Ben hissed with utter disgust in his voice.

Lara burst out with uncontrollable sobbing; Star ran to her and put her arm around her.

'Star!' Lara cried, and sobbed again.

Tyler took charge. 'Right, you!' he said to Stettin. 'On the floor, face down!'

With Ben holding his handgun against the back of Stettin's head, Tyler used a knife to cut down the cord from the bell-pull. He cut that in half and used it to tie Stettin's hands and feet together. Then he took a pillowcase, folded it twice over lengthways and gagged him with it. Stettin started wriggling and roaring with anger but he was tightly bound and muffled.

Tyler and Ben pushed Stettin under the bed as if he was a rolled-up carpet. Then Tyler picked up the other half-length of cord. He tied one end firmly around a bed leg and used the other end to make a noose around Stettin's neck, tying it up with a slip-knot.

'If you wriggle or move more than a centimetre,' Tyler whispered, staring into Stettin's infuriated eyes, 'the slip knot will start to tighten and strangle you. Got that?'

Tyler got to his feet and pulled down the bed coverings so Stettin couldn't be seen.

While the two men had been tying up Stettin, Lara had rushed into the dressing room to change her glittering dress for loose trousers and a shirt. She felt unclean and defiled, but had no time to wash. She picked up a handkerchief to put to her bleeding lip.

When she came back into the bedroom she was carrying the slim black case crammed with German euros. She picked up her shoulder bag and gave it to Star to carry.

'I'm ready,' she said, although she still felt like bursting into tears. She managed a smile and said to Ben and Kieran 'thank you, both of you.'

'Right, let's go' Tyler said, moving to the door.

Star led the way. On her wanderings around the castle she'd found a route from one side to the other up and down back stairs and along the corridors used by servants. It was late now, almost midnight, and few were about. Once they heard the noisy, drunken voices of some house guests at the end of a corridor and had to push themselves into the shadows to avoid being seen.

In a few minutes they were almost at the gallery, where the door with the three ravens over it was, when they heard a sudden shriek.

Lara turned round to see Sibila at the far end of the long corridor. She was wearing a long red gown and was standing stock still, staring at them.

'Quick – get to the door – run!' Tyler shouted.

Sibila's screams filled their ears – she was raising the alarm.

Star got to the door first and wrenched it open. 'Get in, get in!'

Lara and Tyler rushed in, followed by Ben.

Sibila was running up, screaming at them to stop. As Ben went in, he tripped on the first step and fell. His gun clattered on the stone floor.

Star jumped through the doorway into the dark space and pushed the door to. But she found resistance. The door wouldn't close – light was still coming through the gap between the door and the door-post. Ben had got up now and was pushing too – but still there was resistance.

There was a howl of pain from Sibila on the other side of the door. Star could see her through the narrow gap – a strip of red dress; a sliver of her chalk-white face; an eye dark and wide with fury.

'No, no, no,' she was intoning again and again through clenched teeth.

They could hear men's voices now – shouts and footsteps getting closer.

Star looked down. Sibila had jammed her foot between the door and the door-frame.

No wonder she was moaning with pain – she was wearing soft shoes, embroidered and bejewelled – her foot was being crushed.

Without stopping to think, Star picked up the handgun, pointed it at Sibila's foot and pressed the trigger.

In the confined space, the explosion deafened her – but not so much that she didn't hear Sibila's piercing scream.

The door closed. Star frantically turned the key in the lock. As it grated they felt a sudden extra push on the other side, but the door held firm. Furious banging and shouting from the men outside echoed in their ears as they ran up the circling steps.

Will was at the top, white-faced and in utter panic. Private Williams was with him.

'You were seen?' the soldier asked.

Star nodded.

The boy walked around in a circle. 'Oh fuck, oh fuck, oh no, and Dad's here.'

Lara was panting. 'Stettin's sister saw us.'

Pascoe had come up and heard this. He stood for a moment, stooping slightly and resting one arm against a wall.

Will looked at his father. 'You'll have to come with us, Dad.'

The older man had untidy white-grey stubble on his cheeks. He was wearing only a grubby vest and baggy khaki shorts. A look of resignation crossed his face.

'That's it, then,' he said quietly. 'I'll lock the top door,' he said, nodding in the direction of the turret door that gave on to the castle roof. 'They'll have smashed the bottom one in, in no time.'

'You sure they don't know about the rope ladder?' Tyler asked.

Pascoe shook his head. 'They'll be thinking you're rats caught in a trap.'

They ran over to the parapet and lowered the rope ladder. Private Williams went first, followed by Lara, Star and Ben.

Will hesitated. He was giving his father an imploring look. 'Dad!'

'No!' Pascoe waved his hand – a firm negative gesture. 'You go – I can look after meself!'

Will shouted again, pleading: 'Dad, come on!'

'No!'

Tyler gave Will a gentle push. 'Come on, lad. Your father knows what he's doing.'

Will, tears in his eyes, climbed over the parapet. Then Tyler followed, gripping the ropes with his hands and reaching down with his feet to find the rungs.

Before his head went below the parapet he saw Pascoe running out of the aviary shed carrying a shotgun. Now there were loud thumps on the door and shouts from inside the turret. The pursuers had broken through the bottom door and had reached the top.

As Tyler descended, he heard a splintering noise. They'd be breaking through the top turret door with an axe and be on the roof any minute. He looked down. In the darkness he could just make out Will's head bobbing beneath him as he climbed down.

Luckily there was no sign of any guards on the ground rushing to head them off – but would their luck last?

He could feel the rope ladder moving and straining. Then it jerked and trembled as Will jumped off it at the bottom.

'Careful,' he heard Ben whisper to him in the darkness. 'It's quite a drop.'

They were all in a group now at the bottom of the castle wall. There was no moon but they could follow the trampled path they'd previously made through the bracken and brambles in the dry moat.

'It's this way!' Star whispered.

'What about Dad?' Will cried.

As if to answer him, they heard the bang of a shotgun and angry shouts.

Then, a moment later, the rope ladder came clattering down.

'Dad!' Will burst into tears.

'Shut up!' Ben whispered.

The shotgun banged again. Now two pistol shots: light cracking noises like fireworks.

They started to walk quickly along the trampled path, feeling their way.

Lara felt a searing pain in her right ankle. She'd fallen awkwardly on the slope when she jumped off the bottom rung of the ladder. She felt sick but she was determined to stand, pain or no pain.

Star was by her side. She took the money case off Lara, which Private Williams had carried down the ladder. 'Lean on me,' she said in a low voice. 'This way!'

A floodlight came on above them, illuminating the upper section of the wall and the turret. Fortunately, down on the ground they were still in the shadows. Private Williams, leading the way, had already reached the top of the slope on the other side of the moat.

Another bang – the shotgun again, so Pascoe was still alive – then shouts, some high and panicky, others angry.

Star turned to look up to the castle battlements. She saw what looked like black cloths swirling down, circling like ash flakes from a bonfire. Down, down they came – seven burnt pages silhouetted against the floodlight.

'He's let the ravens go!' Will choked.

One raven, unlike the others, was climbing into the night sky.

'That's Midnight!' Will said, pointing, his voice breaking. 'He can fly!'

'C'mon!' said Lara urgently to them.

'Didn't you see?' Star whispered to Lara.

She wasn't sure Will had seen – she hoped he hadn't. He was silent anyway, staring up. Surely he hadn't seen.

'What is it? Come on!' Lara hissed.

'Okay,' Star said, moving forward. 'Come on, Will.'

She'd tell Lara and the others later. Tell them about a figure falling from the battlements – a shadow on the floodlit wall, there and gone in an instant.

KEN BLAKEMORE

30

Once they'd got into the deeper woods a hundred metres from the castle, Ben and Tyler fell back and waited for Lara, Star and Will to catch up. Private Williams went on to tell Anwar they were coming and to check the coast was clear.

Ben saw that Lara was leaning on Star's shoulder, limping badly, and that Star was carrying the money case as well as Lara's shoulder bag.

'Kieran,' Ben said, 'why don't you take that case and I'll help Lara – okay?'

Tyler nodded and took the case. Lara hopped from Star to Ben, and leant on his broad shoulder.

When he felt her bodyweight pressing down on him, felt her warmth, he was overjoyed. Quite literally they weren't out of the woods yet. He still had to get Lara home through dangerous territory. But he'd done it – he'd rescued her; saved her from being raped and God knows what other dangers – so far so good. Oh how close he'd come to killing that bastard in the castle! He trembled inside, remembering the other killing only hours before – the smell, because in his dying moments the man had shat himself like an animal being slaughtered. Everything had a dreamlike quality. But now the dream was turning from bad to good, please God.

They walked on as quickly as Lara's limping would allow, treading carefully through undergrowth so as not to make too much noise. Soon they came to a fork in the path.

'This way,' whispered Tyler, taking the right fork.

'Anwar's waiting in the Land-Rover,' Ben told Lara.

'Anwar!' she said. 'Where's Saleem?'

Before Ben could answer, they heard Will's voice in the darkness behind them:

'I'm not coming with you.'

'What?' he heard Star say.

They all stopped.

'I'm not coming with you' Will repeated. 'I'm going home – it's Mum, she's got to know what's happened. We'll have to get Dad.'

'Come on, Star!' Ben hissed. 'Leave him! We've got to keep going!' He started to pull Lara forward a step.

'No wait,' Lara whispered. 'Without that lad's help we wouldn't be here now.' Then in a louder voice she said 'Will, you can come with us if you want – there is room. And you're in danger.'

'Yes,' Star said. 'Don't you want to come? You said you wanted to come to New Warwick.'

'For God's sake!' Ben said.

They could hear Will's plaintive voice. 'No – I have to get home. They don't know I was up there on the roof with Dad, do they? I'm going home. I've got to tell Mum.'

'Let's hope he doesn't tell anybody which way we've come' Ben muttered under his breath. 'Come on – we're almost there.'

Just as he said this, they heard the baying of hunting dogs in the distance.

Five minutes later they were at the clearing where the Land-Rover and Tyler's jeep had been left. The hunting pack sounded a little closer – they had to decide quickly on a plan. Star ran to the Land-Rover to get something.

'Going back past the castle and on to Chester's out of the question' Tyler said.

'Can't we just head south on the back roads?' Ben said. 'Travelling by night we'd get to South Mercia somehow, even if we have to hole up during the day tomorrow.'

Tyler looked sceptical. 'I don't know. There's all this military activity going on. Would we get through the border? Also, they're probably betting on us taking that route.'

Star waved a map in the air. 'Look, I took this from the castle. It's a local map – the Welsh border's the nearest – it's only ten miles away. We'd be safe in Wales.'

Ben shook his head. 'No, no! We've got to get back – Lara especially needs to get back–' '–Excuse me!' Lara said. There was perspiration on her brow. 'Let me think a minute – just wait!'

The dogs' howling and barking was getting much closer now.

'Misses…' Anwar said in a panicky voice.

'We're heading for Wales' Lara said decisively. 'All right? In my bones I know that's where David is. Let's get moving.'

Ben looked crestfallen.

'I think that's the best way for me too,' Tyler said. 'It'll be harder to get back to the Midlands – but like I say it's the less obvious route. You coming with me in the jeep, Ben?'

They careered along winding, narrow forest tracks that zigzagged along the northern edge of the Peckforton Hills. About five miles from the castle, Anwar brought the Land-Rover to a sudden halt. The jeep stopped a few yards behind them.

'OK, mate, time for you to leave us,' Private Williams said to the barrier guard.

It was the man Star had hit over the head with a log. He'd been left in the back, still handcuffed. She stole a glance at him. His hair was tousled and bloodied at the back of his head; his face was white with fear. He kept hiccupping – another sign of terror.

Star herself was fearful. 'What's going to happen to him?' she said.

Private Williams, bundling the man through the door, paused and gave her a grim smile.

Before Lara's restraining hand could stop her, Star got out of her seat and jumped out of the Land-Rover. Something more, something very bad was going to happen to this man. If it hadn't been for her actions, he wouldn't be in this predicament and his comrade, the other barrier guard, wouldn't be lying dead in the forest.

Private Williams was tying him to a tree. Kieran Tyler had got out of the jeep and was unlocking the handcuffs.

Tyler smiled at her, holding up the cuffs. 'Police property' he said.

Then he turned to the barrier guard, who was now thoroughly

bound to the tree with rope, and said 'we're leaving you, mate. You're a lucky man.'

The man still looked fearful, as if the barrel of a gun might yet be pointed at him.

'Now get back in the Land-Rover,' Tyler said to Star. 'We've got to get a wiggle on.'

They drove on. Following a track that led steeply downhill, they found the main carters' road west. As the Land-Rover picked up speed Star glanced back at the bumpy, sandy track behind them, a rising plume of brown dust lit by the dazzle of a single headlight from Tyler's jeep.

At any moment, she thought, we'll come upon a roadblock and a line of Stettin's men. But at each bend, the road ahead was clear and her heart resumed beating.

She felt a strange, peculiar lightness in her heart. She'd remembered the name of Gwynfor's town: Llangollen.

Lara, sitting next to her, seemed to pick up her thoughts. She said 'you know how Gwynfor's dad's convoy was set upon? I reckon Stettin organised it.'

Star nodded. 'Yeah, and it was probably him who sent those men to New Warwick – the ones who tried to get Gwynfor and me with a crossbow.'

'And he was definitely behind the hold-up we were caught in – another pantomime he organised.'

'What!'

Lara told Star about seeing the thug with the eagle tattoo.

Star thought for a moment. 'If Stettin did organise the attack on Sylvan's convoy, that means he was the one who had the motive.'

'The motive to stop David's messages getting through!'

'Yes, and to find out what was in those messages. My guess is, Stettin got a tip-off. Your husband had managed to put those messages on the memory stick and the tab. But someone else knew what he'd done and informed Stettin.'

You have to give the girl credit, Lara thought. 'Could well be,' she said.

'Are you definitely planning to carry on into Wales, Lara?'

Lara thought a moment. I've got the closest yet to finding my husband, she told herself. 'You definitely found out there was a connection between North Mercia and the nuclear power station in Anglesey?'

Star nodded. 'Wylfa – yes, they took it over.'

'That's my guess – that Stettin was keeping David a prisoner there.'

'So…'

'That's where we're heading.'

'I've got an idea,' Star said. 'We'll need a translator, won't we, and a guide? Can we go to Llangollen?'

'God, where's that…' Lara said, and then she gave Star a broad, knowing smile. 'Ah, I remember – Gwynfor!'

'It's not far away – only ten, twenty miles out of our way? I looked it up on this map.'

Before Lara could reply, Anwar interrupted. 'We're getting near the border!'

They sat in tense silence for another ten minutes as the Land-Rover sped along, the jeep still close behind. Then they came into a village with a lot of ancient half-timbered buildings, a village that had remained remarkably intact since Good Time – and throughout all the previous centuries.

A long queue of stationary carts and drays, interspersed with the occasional biodiesel truck, was waiting to pass through the English checkpoint to get over the bridge across the River Dee.

Ahead of them they could see a line of oil lamps glowing, one on each vehicle, each lamp surrounded by twirling moths. The line of lamps had the effect of creating a full set of street lights in this little border town.

Anwar stopped the Land-Rover and drummed his fingers on the steering wheel. The jeep came up behind them and also stopped, though Tyler kept the engine running and the single working headlight on.

Lara reached for the money case and opened it. She took out ten thick wads of German euro notes and held them up.

'I've thought of a way of persuading them to let us through,' she said. 'Let's hope it works.'

Private Williams, who was in the front seat sitting next to Anwar, turned round and said to her, 'trouble is, Mrs Johnson, they might take the money and us!'

But then he nodded in agreement. 'Yeah, we haven't got any choice, have we? Probably that is the only way we're going to get across. But let's try acting normal to start with – you're the VIP and we're your escort.'

'I'll distract them with the money; you improvise,' she told the soldier.

'Yes ma'am.'

Anwar got out and ran back to the jeep to explain to Tyler what the plan was. Then he got back in, restarted the engine and drove the Land-Rover slowly past the long line of carts. The few cart drivers who were awake groaned and booed them – they were jumping the queue.

When they reached the barrier, Anwar wound down his window and blew the horn. No one came. He blew the horn again. A minute later two young sleepy-looking soldiers came out of a small wooden building beside the barrier.

'Doesn't look like they've had any warning about us,' Lara whispered.

The face of one of the young soldiers' appeared in the driver's window. 'The border's sealed tonight. Go back please.'

To Lara he looked about seventeen; a cute seventeen, woken from his beauty sleep, rubbing his eyes and yawning.

She leant forward. 'Can we speak to the officer on duty? Is he or she in there?' she said, smiling her most gracious smile.

The boy soldier frowned. 'What? No. No, you can't speak to him.'

'He's not there?'

'No he is, but...'

'He's asleep.'

The boy soldier gave her a reluctant smile and nodded.

'I wonder,' Lara said, 'if you could wake him to see if this might be an acceptable fee for letting us cross out of hours?'

She waved one of the wads of banknotes under the border guard's nose.

His eyes widened. Then he shook his head. 'Oh no' he said firmly.

'What is it?' Star heard the other soldier say.

The two soldiers conferred. Inside the Land-Rover it wasn't possible to hear what they were saying.

The second soldier's face now appeared in the window. He was a little older than the first one. He's quite fit, Star thought. Dark curly hair, nice brown eyes, though his lips were a bit too thin and mean-looking.

'Look,' the second soldier said in an aggressive tone, 'who are you anyway? Show us your passports.' Turning to his comrade, he said 'Ash, check the other two in the jeep!'

As they were fumbling around for their passports, Lara took another wad of banknotes, a thousand euros, and passed it to Star.

'Put this inside your passport,' she whispered, putting the first wad inside her own passport.

As they were handing the passports over, the second border guard got suspicious about Private Williams. 'Where are you stationed then?'

'Chester' Private Williams said, improvising as instructed. 'I'm on escort duty for the Regional Commissioner,' he added, nodding at Lara.

The soldier looked even more suspicious but withdrew to look at the passports. The two border guards now stood together again, talking and looking up occasionally at the Land-Rover and the jeep.

Star looked out of the back window. Tyler had switched off the jeep's headlight and it was dark and quiet behind them, but she experienced a sudden wave of panic. Any minute now, she thought, they'll catch up with us. There'll be vehicles racing up and headlights and horns blaring and it'll be them. She thought about Sibila and how she'd probably crippled the witch for life, smashing every bone in her foot. She shuddered at what Sibila could do to her in revenge.

'It's not acceptable to offer bribes' the second soldier said. He'd appeared at Lara's window this time. 'You're in trouble but we'll let you off. Go back.'

Lara opened the door and got out. 'We're not going back,' she told them, 'because I'm on an extremely important mission on behalf of the Regional Commissioner. Haven't you had a message from him?'

The border guards shook their heads.

Phew, thought Lara, thank Diana in heaven for that.

'We'll be crossing back here tomorrow afternoon. Until then, I can leave you a more substantial sum as a guarantee that we're on official business.'

She held out eight wads of banknotes – eight thousand German euros.

The border guards stared at the money, their mouths dropping open. It was a fortune to them.

'Fuck me,' the dark curly-haired one breathed.

There was a panicky look in the younger-looking soldier's eye. He didn't bother to whisper any more. 'Let's do it,' he said.

'Any problems, lads?' Ben had got out of the jeep and had come to stand next to Lara.

She gave him a sharp look. For two seconds she thought Ben would put them off.

But the older-looking one nodded, said 'okay' and handed her their passports.

Lara handed them the money.

'Lara!' Ben said, appalled at how much money had been handed over.

'–Get back in the jeep, we're going' Lara said crisply.

As she got into the Land-Rover, the barrier was already going up. Anwar started the engine and she could hear the jeep's engine firing up too.

The barrier was vertical now. As they rolled forward, Lara glanced back. The younger-looking border guard had already taken off his military coat and had thrown his belt, holster and gun to the floor. The other one would soon be doing the same, and they'd both be running – like them – across the bridge, out of Stettin's net and into Wales.

31

Lara leant against the Land-Rover. Her sprained ankle was aching again. In Llangollen a local healer had treated it with a cold compress and then bound it firmly. He'd also given her a half-cupful of some birch-bark potion so bitter that it had almost made her throw up. A little later, though, the pain and swelling had eased.

Gwynfor's mother, a small, shy woman in her forties, had fussed over her. She'd insisted in a stream of Welsh that she rested her leg on a stool, bringing her oat cakes and goats' milk with honey, while Gwynfor and Star looked on, smiling.

After two days' enforced rest in Llangollen, Lara had been impatient to continue on to Anglesey. Ben had tried three times to dissuade her, arguing each time that she only had flimsy evidence David had actually been there, or was there now.

'It'd be worth carrying on, I can see that,' he'd said, 'if civil war wasn't about to start! Who knows what dangers your mother and little Arrow are in! We really ought to get back as soon as we can, Lara.'

Eventually her temper had flared and she'd given him a real tongue-lashing. She could see the way he was thinking: I'm the prince on a white horse who's rescued the helpless maiden and now I'm going to carry her home. She remembered his uncontrolled passion when he'd forced his kisses and his hands upon her; she knew what his agenda was.

At the same time, she'd felt conflicted – and bad for lashing out at him. She was profoundly grateful to him for what he'd done. After all, without Ben pushing Kieran Tyler into getting permission to bring the jeep up north, and without the courage of both men she might still be languishing inside Peckforton Castle. Even if she'd succeeded in getting out, what would have happened to her, and to Star?

She'd also noticed the conflict going on in Ben's mind. He'd been very close to David in the days and months after his wife's death. There was a big difference between them in their walks of life, their temperaments, their outlook – after all, David was the highly educated man who could see beyond the horizon, and Ben couldn't – but for all that they'd been good neighbours and mates.

After their row, Ben had retreated into moody silence.

'You don't have to come with me' she'd told him. 'Why don't you go back to New Warwick with Kieran?'

Kieran Tyler had also talked to her about the wisdom of pushing on to Anglesey – but he'd done it in a way that respected her right to choose.

'What about you?' she'd asked Kieran. 'Don't you need to get back now? I'll be safe enough.'

He'd shaken his head. 'The job isn't finished yet – I'll come with you, unless you tell me to turn round and go back. Mind you,' he said, breaking into a smile, 'I'll need a little bit of that money for fuel for the jeep – I'm down to the last can.'

On the afternoon before they left, Anwar guided Kieran to the Muslim garage in the centre of Llangollen where he was able to refuel the jeep with ethyl alcohol and fill up a dozen cans while Anwar filled up the Land-Rover with biodiesel.

As the refuelling was going on Anwar chatted to Ibrahim, the owner of Red Crescent Motors. He asked Ibrahim to put it about that he was looking for his brother Saleem.

Ibrahim, who had a chewing stick in his mouth, made a sympathetic clicking noise.

'That's a worrying business, brother,' he said. 'I will certainly do that.'

On the morning they left, Lara apologised to Ben. 'I'm sorry,' she said. 'I'm glad you're coming with us – and thank you for what you've done so far.'

He'd looked relieved and smiled at her, tears in his deep

brown eyes. He still had a hurt look about him, however – the look of the loyal dog that can't understand why it had been punished.

Now, three days later, all of them – Kieran Tyler, Ben, Gwynfor, Star, Private Williams and Lara Johnson were standing around the Land-Rover in a fine, grey drizzle on Anglesey wondering what to do next. The jeep, its hood up, had been parked behind the Land-Rover.

Anwar had his head in the engine. It had faltered a few times as they'd traversed the rough broken roads across the mountains of North Wales. Anwar had put it down to dirt in the fuel line, but clearly the problem had been something more serious. 'Probably fuel pump,' he said as he straightened up. He looked around at the flat wilderness around them, shrugged his shoulders and grinned. Anwar shared his brother Saleem's pessimism, but unlike Saleem he was usually able to laugh at what the fates brought.

Behind them, to the south, the impressive mountains of Snowdonia, clearly visible fifteen minutes before, had vanished in grey-white banks of cloud.

'Tsk, you'll have to tow me to the nearest town – if they got any towns round here?' Anwar said to Tyler.

'It's only a few miles back to Bangor, over the bridge' Gwynfor said, looking a little hurt. 'There are two motor workshops there.'

'Only joking,' Anwar grinned.

'And it's only another two miles or so for us to go, isn't it?' Lara said. 'I can manage to walk that far.'

Star shook her head. 'You shouldn't.'

'We could carry you?' Ben said, wiping the sheen of drizzle from his face with the back of his hand. 'Make a stretcher out of something?' he added, walking up and down the road. He wanted to see if he could spot some fencing or a disused gate.

'Don't step off the road, mate,' Tyler warned him. 'You know what the man said.' Then he turned to Lara. 'Seriously, Mrs Johnson, we could go on a recce, try to find a horse or something.'

Gwynfor shook his head. The young man's black curly locks were covered in tiny raindrops. 'All the farms on Ynys Mon have been closed. Because of the nuclear, see? Any horse you see will be running wild.'

'Probably on six legs,' Private Williams said.

Star grinned. She was beginning to notice Private Williams

265

was quite a comedian on the quiet. His face was always deadpan but there was a twinkle in his eye; his sense of humour was rather dark.

Lara recalled that phrase, 'the nuclear', hearing it again and again when they'd reached Bangor, two days ago. Yesterday, with Gwynfor's help as an interpreter, it hadn't taken her long to find out the person she needed to talk to: Huw Evans, the chief scientific officer for Gwynedd.

She and Ben had had an hour or so to wander before meeting him. The weather was different up here, the skies grey and cool and the air damp. In the narrow, crowded streets of the old town Lara had noticed how much poorer the people seemed than in North Mercia. Most of the adults were dressed in worn, patched clothes; thin children ran barefoot; mules carried loads of firewood and potatoes to a sparse market.

But she also noticed that despite the poverty they were cheerful and held their heads erect. It was a place where people looked you in the eye and smiled. There was none of that sullen, oppressed look she'd seen in the eyes of Pascoe, or of Stettin's other servants or of the farm workers she'd seen in the fields around the castle.

Lara had had to rest her ankle for a while, so they'd sat on rough wooden benches at a drinks stall that sold berry tea and milk drinks. From time to time, in the sea of Welsh around them, she'd spotted that dangerous English word bobbing like a conspicuous warning buoy. The locals pronounced it with a gap between the two syllables: 'new clear'.

Lara got up carefully from the wooden bench to avoid putting weight on her ankle. She took a deep breath. Her heart was thumping with anxiety and anticipation. Ben was also getting to his feet now, offering her his arm to lean on.

I want to go alone, Lara thought, but she couldn't bring herself to say so.

They walked together in the rain up a steep hill to the government offices.

Evans was a slim, wiry man in his late thirties wearing a Good-Time-style tweed sports jacket with leather elbow patches. He had short, tightly curled blond hair and intelligent blue-grey eyes.

Anxious to help, he stood quickly to shake hands with them as soon as they entered his office. He spoke quietly. His precise English was like an old-fashioned, good quality suit taken out for special occasions.

On his desk there was a neat block of writing paper; a blue china mug with 'Huw' inscribed on it; and two miniature flags on little stands – one for Wales, with its red dragon on green and white, the other for Gwynedd – a recently adopted flag with its harp, angel and fish on white and blue diagonals.

When the introductions were over and Lara had asked about David, a look of admiration and respect crept into Huw Evans's eyes.

'Duw, he saved our skins, that man,' Evans said, shaking his head. 'I can't tell you how much he did – a really heroic man.'

'So he was here!' Lara sounded emotional. Evans had used the past tense. David was dead.

Evans's eyes lit up. 'Is here,' he corrected. 'Here on Ynys Mon. He had to stay after Wylfa was closed down. He's not very far away, Mrs Johnson.'

This was all Lara had hoped for: David was alive!

Her eyes shone with tears and she couldn't speak. All the air had gone from her lungs. She heard Star saying to Huw Evans 'Ynys Mon, that's the place they called Anglesey, right?' and Evans saying something in reply. Then they'd both looked at her, waiting.

Lara swallowed. 'Sorry. I thought…it sounded like…'

'No, no, he is still with us' Evans replied gently. 'But afraid to say, I am…'

He paused to marshal his English words.

'Your husband, I am afraid to say, is very ill. We found him that way, when we took back Wylfa a few weeks ago. He is being cared for in a small place called Moelfre, which is on the east coast of Ynys Mon not many miles from Wylfa.'

Evans went on to explain more. The army and police from North Mercia had pulled out only a month ago. When he'd cautiously led the first team to the old nuclear power station at Wylfa he'd discovered David there.

He'd also found a hero, someone who had knowingly exposed himself to extremely dangerous levels of radiation. He'd directed a hazardous operation, two months before, to prevent another nuclear disaster. Unfamiliar words such as 'decontamination', 'magnox process' and 'silo' drifted in and out of Lara's consciousness as he talked.

There'd been several serious alarms at Wylfa over the years, Evans went on. At the end of Good Time the power station had closed itself down automatically.

There'd been no significant or detectable problems until it had started to become unsafe about ten years ago. North Mercia had stepped in, its panicky council fearing a meltdown and taking control of Ynys Mon from Gwynedd. It was North Mercia that had requested help from Oxford. Several top-level engineers and scientists were dispatched to Wylfa to see what could be done.

Evans, then in his twenties, had been a junior research scientist, but he had been allowed, along with more senior officials from Gwynedd – police and health people, mainly – to attend emergency meetings that discussed how the problems in the plant could be contained.

There had been a real prospect of nuclear catastrophe – but that time the danger was averted. In Bangor, Caernarfon and other places further away in the mountains Huw Evans and his fellow scientists checked radiation levels frequently. They remained stable, and then began to decline steadily from the worrying peak months before.

However, almost two years ago there had been another dramatic development on Ynys Mon. This time it wasn't dangerous radiation – at least not to begin with. The North Mercian authorities had suddenly refused entry to anyone from Gwynedd. Then the farmers on Ynys Mon were evicted from their land. All livestock was destroyed – you could see the palls of smoke rising. A stream of refugees with handcarts, suitcases and stricken faces trooped across to the mainland. The old Menai Bridge was closed off with barbed wire. Forbidding skull-and-crossbones signs were hammered on to posts. The local population was up in arms, demanding that Gwynedd fight back: didn't Ynys Mon belong to them, not to the English?

'But we didn't have the military force to do anything,' Evans explained. 'North Mercia virtually has a standing army, see? We've got very little by comparison. And the rest of Wales, well! They weren't ready to help. And nor were West Mercia or South Mercia willing to step in.'

He looked pointedly at Lara, then sighed and looked out of

the window for a moment. 'It was about then, I think, that they captured your husband.'

'Captured him?'

'That's what he told me. They took him to Wylfa – they captured him on his way to another nuclear station.'

'That's right, in Cumbria.'

Evans nodded. 'He was apprehended' – he liked these old-fashioned English words – 'apprehended in North Mercia, he told me. And taken across to Wylfa by sea, he said.'

'To help them fix the latest problems – the contamination?' Ben asked.

'No, that wasn't the reason – at that point,' said Evans. 'I'm sure he'd have willingly gone out of his way if it was to help with an emergency.'

'Of course!' Lara said with a laugh, unable to keep a trace of bitterness out of it. 'He would!'

'They captured him in order to do something else for them,' Evans said with a solemn expression.

Lara stared at him. 'Did he help them?'

Evans shook his head. 'No, I'm sure he didn't. He held out. That's the first reason he's a hero. They tried to force him – kept him prisoner, prevented him from communicating with you, with the outside world. They might even have put pressure on him in other ways. He didn't say.'

Lara and Ben were silent as they took this in. Huw Evans cleared his throat and shifted the block of writing paper on his desk a couple of inches.

'These things they wanted him to do,' said Lara eventually. 'We intercepted a message he'd managed to smuggle out.'

Evans nodded. 'You know, then.'

'They were trying to put nuclear material to some sort of military use?'

Evans nodded again. 'Yes. But then, some time after they took him to Wylfa, there was another emergency, see? About a year ago. We were very worried, very worried indeed. The radiation kept going up and up. We were a week away from having to evacuate all the people from the coast.'

'And that was when David...' Lara's voice trailed away.

'Yes. That's the second reason he's a hero. He worked at great risk to himself – along with some other very brave men and women, I must say. It would have been a real disaster. Not just for us in Gwynedd, Wales, but for the whole of England too – and maybe beyond. We knew about that because North Mercia suddenly started sending convoys of trucks through. God knows how they found that many. They wouldn't admit anything, though.' Evans sighed. 'Truck after truck after truck. Liquid concrete.'

The three fell silent again. Outside, seagulls shrieked and cackled – sounds Lara and Ben had never heard before.

Ben broke the silence. He asked the question Lara couldn't bring herself to ask. 'What I don't understand is why he's still there? Gwynedd's got control of Wylfa now, hasn't it? Why haven't you got him out? Couldn't you have got a message through to us about him?'

Evans leant back in his chair and looked at them, narrowing his eyes.

'We tried sending messages last week, but all communications between us and the rest of England have been blocked by North Mercia. 'I'm sorry,' he said, noticing Lara's eyes welling up again. 'I think it would be better if you speak to David yourself. He's very weak now, I'm told.'

Lara sobbed, putting a hand up to stem her tears. This gentle man, this Evans, was saying things that were too hard, too cruel.

'I'm very sorry,' he continued softly. 'Very sorry indeed. But there is time, I believe, if you go soon.'

32

'I wanted to look good for him,' said Lara, limping along. 'Look at me!'

Star surveyed Lara's torn, baggy trousers and country smock – clothes she'd bought from the market in Llangollen. Her boss's fine head of hair badly needed brushing. And it seemed she'd lost weight in the past few days – her cheekbones were more prominent. Her eyelids were red and swollen from crying, and there were dark shadows under them. It was certainly hard to believe that this was the Lara Johnson who'd left New Warwick little more than two weeks before.

But all Star did was smile. 'He'll think you look great.'

Soon after leaving the broken-down Land-Rover they'd stumbled through a small, deserted village. Broken roof slates and pieces of glass lay in the narrow road. It was still raining – a persistent misty drizzle that seemed to get under the skin. But as they passed between the empty houses and other buildings they noticed a salty tang in the air and a brighter grey in the sky.

'It looks different over there,' Star said.

'We're close to the sea, that's what it is', Ben said. 'Can you hear it?'

'The sea!' Star stopped for a moment to gaze at the lighter sky to the east, her eyes widening.

Gwynfor and Private Williams had walked on ahead to the village of Moelfre to find out where David Johnson was staying. The road turned inland now and straightened out. Moelfre lay only

271

a mile or so ahead of them. The three of them trudged on silently in the drizzle. Trees and overgrown fields were now giving way to a more open landscape of stones, scrubland and clumps of stiff, spiky grass. But despite its bleakness it looked entirely natural and untouched. There were seabirds in the air and rabbit warrens in the undulating ground. That sinister power station had released unseen, insidious dangers – maybe it still was doing so – but had anything really changed in the natural world?

'Just to be on the safe side, it's not advisable to stay too long on Ynys Mon,' Huw Evans had told them. At this, Lara's heart had sunk. She knew what that meant. Either it was a hint that David didn't have very much time left, or that she would be permitted to stay with him only a short while.

'Though we're allowing essential workers and guardians of the old nuclear plant back in – as long as they live in Moelfre,' Evans had added, as brightly as he could.

'What's radioactivity?' Star had asked. She'd never come across the word before.

'Nuclear radiation is something you can't see,' Evans had explained. 'But we can detect it with a special instrument called a Geiger counter. It varies in strength.'

Lara had known what it meant. 'Exposure to radiation can damage and distort the body's cells, the very fabric of your body,' she'd said.

Evans had gone on to advise them not to drink water from streams or rainwater supplies on Ynys Mon, nor to eat any food grown there or any fish caught from the surrounding coasts; and they weren't to wander on to soft ground where radioactivity could concentrate.

Star licked rain-moisture from her lips, enjoying the slightly salty taste. Did the sea taste like this? Then she remembered with a flicker of fear what Evans had told them. Did it matter, though? Wasn't it a bit stupid to worry about a raindrop? The whole place was probably radioactive, more than that Evans guy was letting on. They were probably all going to die next week.

She felt another flurry of excitement about the sea. What would it be like?

And then there it was, just like that. It took Star a moment or two to realise. They had suddenly, it seemed, come to the edge. This must be Moelfre. The drizzle was easing. She could make out a darker grey-blue beyond some houses.

Given the radioactivity danger, a surprising number of the old houses of Moelfre were still being used for human habitation. Some had fallen into disrepair and had been abandoned, their roofs holed by winter gales. But others had been freshly painted in white and cream. A few had blue curls of smoke coming from their chimney-stacks on this damp, still day.

Lara wanted to stop a moment to view the little settlement of weather-beaten cottages that lay ahead. Star rushed past her, whooping – she'd seen Private Williams tramping back up the hill towards them.

'The sea, the sea! Is that really it?!' she was screaming, running down to meet the soldier, bumping into him and nearly falling over.

Private Williams chuckled, steadying Star so that they could stand and wait for Lara and Ben to walk down to them. But Star wanted to joke around and play the kid. She hopped from one foot to the other, impatient to get down to the seashore. She broke away from the soldier and carried on down the hill, shouting 'Gwynfor; Gwyn!'

As she walked down, leaning on Ben, Lara could see that the road led past some larger houses on the left and then down to a small shingle beach. She could see Star running towards it, whooping. A few sailing dinghies and fishing boats had been drawn up on the pebbles. She could see Gwynfor now, too. Star had almost reached him, her excited shouts echoing back. She was pointing at the sea.

Gwynfor waved to Lara, Ben and Private Williams and started climbing off the little beach.

As he stepped on to the road Lara could see him pausing to talk to a woman standing next to a wheelchair. Somehow Lara hadn't noticed that woman until now, or the wheelchair. She was dressed in a white uniform: a nurse. Now she was grasping the handles of the wheelchair. She was turning it round; bending her head down to say something to the person in the wheelchair. The wheelchair man turned his bald head to look vaguely in Lara's direction. At this distance his face was a white disc, but she knew instantly who it was.

'You can come in now,' said the nurse, opening the door and

smiling at Lara and Ben. Her name was Bethan. She was a short, wide-bottomed woman in her late thirties with brown stringy hair. Luckily she was bilingual, like most of the people stationed at Moelfre. Her coal-black eyes were the most noticeable thing about her. Those eyes danced with laughter; wicked laughter at times. What was she doing out here on the edge of radioactive nowhere, battling along in her frayed white uniform? How could she be so cheerful?

They were entering a bare-floorboard front room of one of the larger houses above the beach. In Good Time it had been a small hotel; now it housed four men and a woman. All of these patients had been through the emergency at Wylfa. All of them were terminally ill and being looked after by Bethan and another nurse, and a Dr Hopkins.

Strong feelings swirled around in the pit of Lara's stomach: gratefulness to the nurses and the doctor for looking after David, but also guilt. I should have been the one doing this, she told herself. As she walked into the room, she also felt jealousy towards Bethan: she was the one straightening the pillows behind his back and she was gently sponging his face. I should have found him sooner. Her stomach clenched into a tight ball. I was too slow, too slow to work out where he was and come for him, she repeated to herself.

She looked down at him. His hairless head, yellow skin, sunken cheeks and prominent cheekbones made him almost unrecognisable to her; a skeletal body already corpse-like.

Ben was standing beside her, his arm loosely around her back. She could tell without looking at him that he was upset; he was making a sniffling noise and dabbing his eyes with a hankie. But she felt only numbness inside: no tears coming, just a cold numbness in the face of the finality of it all.

David was sleeping. He could barely breathe, it seemed, or lift a hand.

'It's the morphine,' Bethan whispered. 'It's settled him.'

'You can get morphine?' Lara whispered back, anxiously. 'I know it's very hard to find.'

The nurse nodded. 'There's a trading boat at Holyhead. From Ireland it comes, once a month or so. We never have quite enough.'

'I can pay for more,' Lara rushed to say. 'Whatever it takes,' she added, thinking of the crisp bundles of Euros left over after their escape from the castle. They were hidden in a strong-box in Anwar's Land-Rover. Bethan didn't respond. 'I mean,' Lara said falteringly, 'for everyone here, not just David.'

The nurse smiled. 'It would help. The Senedd in Caernarfon have promised extra for us, but so far nothing. We need canisters of oxygen too. There were plenty at Wylfa. Running out now, though, we are.'

Lara took David's left hand and stroked it. His fingers were bony, the flesh around them waxy. His fingernails were too long and had yellow dirt behind them. Lara longed for a nail file or something sharp and pointed to clean them with.

'He's been hanging on for you, you know?' Bethan said. 'That's why we didn't want to give him too much morphine. He needs it for the pain, but too much and they go too quick, you see.' After a few moments' silence she said 'A brave man. He knew you'd come.'

An hour later, David was still sleeping.

'You go and find something to eat,' Ben said to Lara. 'You look done in. I'll stay with him.'

Lara reluctantly let go of David's hand. 'I am exhausted,' she said. 'You sure?'

'I'm sure,' Ben said.

'Okay. I want to be with him later – stay here with him through the night.'

Ben frowned. 'Just see what you can manage – how you feel.'

She yawned and stood up. 'I'll be back in an hour or so – but come and tell me straightaway if he wakes and wants to talk to me.'

Ben pulled the chair closer to the bed and looked around the room. Early evening sunlight was coming in – the mist and drizzle must have cleared. A cool sea breeze was blowing in through the half-open windows, gently flapping the light cotton curtains.

His mind drifted on to the farm. Jack was supposed to bring a Hereford bull over from the Smiths' place yesterday to run with the cows in the bottom meadow. Would he have remembered? There were a hundred and one other things Jack was supposed to be seeing to. Would he remember everything or was the place going to rack and ruin already?

He shifted his gaze back to David. The top sheet had left his chest exposed: you can see their hearts beating when they're that thin and emaciated. His mind went back to when he was a boy going round the farm with his father and seeing the thin, wasted body of a calf; every rib showing. Winter coming on, it must have been. The calf had died in the field before they'd got to it to help it out. Bad old days.

Looking down on David, he thought if that was one of my animals the humane thing to do would be to put it out its misery.

Instantly he felt bad. Because when he'd first seen David there'd been a feeling he couldn't deny. He hated himself for feeling it. For feeling relief, yes relief, that David was so ill. That he wasn't going to make it. On his way here he'd pictured every possibility, and one of those possibilities had been David seriously ill but not dying. A David who'd have to be carried home, back to New Warwick, where he'd be an invalid cared for by Lara for who knows how long. Lara fussing over David and looking after her husband's every need; Lara having no time for him.

These bad thoughts were truly terrible because he also loved David, he now realised. This was the man who'd put his arms around him and hugged him when Tam had died in childbirth. This was the man he'd got drunk with afterwards; the man who'd been there for him. Ben had had no brother; no father; no mother to comfort him through that time.

Thinking of these things, guilt and self-pity took over. Ben felt tears streaming down his cheeks. He reached down and with a clumsy hand grasped David's hand.

'Come on, you old bastard!' he croaked.

There was no response – not even the fluttering of an eyelid. Just slow, laboured breathing.

Ben put his mouth closer to David's ear. 'I'm so, so sorry, old mate!' he whispered, stroking David's hand. 'But we are here now, Lara and me. Can you hear me? I got her here, okay? She was coming to find you...God, David, she's been trying so hard to find you! Anyway, she was coming to find you and she got held up – got into a fix. And I came up after her and found her and got her out. So that's why I'm here too...so it's all right, everything's going to be all right Dave...'

Ben felt David's fingers tighten around his for a second. It made his heart jump. He squeezed David's hand.

David had opened his eyes. They didn't seem to be able to focus at first, but then he smiled.

'Dave!' The tears in Ben's eyes were welling up again. 'Dave!'

David's fingers tightened around his once more.

'Dave, I'm so, so sorry but I love her! I love her so much – I can't help it!'

Ben couldn't continue – he bowed his head and sobbed.

When he looked up again, David's eyes had closed. He could still feel the blood pumping through his wrist, and the faint smile on his lips was still there.

33

'At eight o'clock that evening, Lara was back in the room with David. She sat on a simple wooden chair next to his bed.

There was a knock at the door. Star came in with two bowls of soup and some oat bread. She sat cross-legged on the floorboards next to Lara's chair, not saying much as they sipped the mutton, leek and carrot broth. The only sounds were their sipping and the clink of their spoons; David breathing; the tranquillising hush-swish of the sea as it came and went on the pebbles down by the shore.

When they'd finished their soup, another sound: a horn being played somewhere; a haunting, husky melody. As it washed through the still air it underlined the tranquillity of that little settlement of dying people.

'Sounds like a saxophone,' Lara said.

'Weird,' replied Star.

When it was getting dark Bethan came back with some candles, explaining they were cheaper than the oil lamp. Star had gone back to the lodging house they were all staying in. Bethan checked on David, lit one of the candles and said to Lara, 'Are you staying all night? Won't you lie down on that couch over there?'

Lara shook her head and smiled. She held up a battered copy of a hardback book she'd found on a bookcase in the corner of the room. On the spine of the faded red cover there was a single word, Donne.

'English, is it?' Bethan asked.

Lara nodded. 'A book of poems. It'll keep me going.'

'Here's another candle, then. We'll put it on this table here by the bed.' Bethan smiled. 'Just shout, won't you?'

Lara woke to find that she'd slumped forward over the bed, her head and arms resting on David's legs. The book had fallen to the floor and the bedside candle was out. Lara yawned and rubbed her eyes, disoriented. She decided to light the oil lamp. As she was doing so she saw a slight movement in David's body. He had opened his eyes and was looking at her. His eyes were glazed and unfocused.

Lara took his hand. 'I love you,' she said.

David's soul had come back. She could tell. She smiled at him.

He tried to smile back. His lips were dry and cracked. Lara moistened them with a damp cloth, and he rewarded her with more flickers of life. Those deep blue eyes. They still had traces of that spirit, that enthusiasm she remembered so well.

'I got here,' she whispered.

He breathed painfully, attempting another smile.

'About...bloody...time' he whispered.

Lara made a sound – something like sob and a giggle. 'I nearly didn't bother' she said, smiling through her tears.

'I love you too, Lara. I'm so sorry.'

'No. It was my fault!'

He was shaking his head. 'Bollocks,' he whispered, with the shade of a smile.

'There were more things I could have done.'

A look of panic suddenly came into David's eyes. He was trying to cough. He gestured at his chest and then pointed a hand upwards. Lara didn't know what to do.

'David! Should I call Bethan?'

Then she realised. He'd slumped down too far in the bed. Gently, as he strained to breathe, she slid her arms beneath him and behind his back. It needed a surprising amount of effort to haul him higher. His back was rigid and solid somehow, like a hard shell or carapace. But though it was hard to move him she was shocked by the amount of weight he'd lost – and by the fetid odour of his shrunken body.

A deep, slow cough came. David's face contorted with pain. He was negotiating with death for an extension, another breath.

This is what had happened down at the seafront when they arrived that afternoon. She'd run down, her weakened ankle forgotten completely, her loose smock billowing, hair everywhere, crying 'David!'

He'd been so excited, so overcome that he'd had to be rushed inside fighting for breath.

Thankfully, his face was clearing now. His cautious, shallow breathing resumed.

'It's all up, Lara,' he whispered. 'It's spread to my lungs.'

She nodded.

'But I'm the one. To say sorry,' he continued. 'I knew...' He paused. 'We knew. They were...going...to hijack me.'

'What are you saying? We?'

'Oxford. I never told you. I should have.'

'What? You were working for...'

'Inter-Region...' David tried and gave up.

'Inter-Regional Security,' Lara whispered.

David nodded. They both listened to the swishing of the sea for a moment.

'I came across one of them,' Lara said. 'A mean-looking character called File.'

David coughed again. 'File,' he breathed. He managed to shake his head slightly and to smile.

'So, you – they – knew something was going on in North Mercia?'

'I should have told you. About all this. Before I went. I'm so sorry, Lara. I was sworn to...'

'Secrecy, yes,' she finished for him. 'Shush now.'

He shook his head, determined to carry on. 'Still trying to compete. With Dad. Wasn't I? All that top-secret stuff! We knew Stettin. Would try. Get me. I had to...get inside. Find out. Oxford – we – thought they could. Get me out again.'

He laughed a short, bitter laugh.

Lara was replaying scenes in her mind: travelling the long, muddy roads to Cumbria, questioning blank-faced strangers, badgering police officers, returning home without any news. Trying to explain to Arrow where her daddy might be. Not to mention the many hours she'd lain awake going over tiny shreds of evidence and rumour. And all along there'd been a tiny secret service group in Oxford who'd known exactly where he was. She had to push all that to the back of her mind for the moment.

'I remembered to bring a photo of Arrow with me.'

His eyes moistened. 'My little tiger!'

'She's doing fine. She misses you so much…'

Lara's voice trailed off and she had to swallow. She looked away from him, noticing the grey-white light of dawn in the space by the window. 'Do you want to see the photo now? I'll go and get it.'

He smiled. 'Not yet.'

She nodded. Yes, he needed something for another day.

'There's something else.' His eyes were troubled.

'It's okay, it's okay, save it for tomorrow' she soothed, touching his forehead.

He nodded. 'Yes. It's okay. As long as. I do tell you. Tomorrow.' He ran a furry tongue across his lips. 'Make sure I do. Too tired now.'

'Bethan will be coming soon. And before she does…' Lara said quietly, slipping off her shoes, 'I'm getting into this bed with you.'

She limped to the couch, picked up two large cushions and took them to the bed. She laid them beside the bolster and pillows that were supporting David. The lamp wasn't necessary any more, so she blew it out; the dawn light was more evident now.

He'd already turned his head to gaze at her, his eyelids fluttering with fatigue, a faint smile on his face. His breaths were loud and shallow, but regular and easier.

Lara bent over him and kissed his forehead. In a single movement she slipped off her smock and put it on the chair beside the bed. Then, very carefully, she edged herself on to the wide bed, propping herself up to match the angle of David's body. Then, closing her eyes, she turned on her side, pressing her full, warm breasts against the thin arm that rested by his side. She felt his cool flesh, the wasted muscles beneath. She was pressing the whole of herself against him, imagining a life force passing from her to him like an electrical charge. The linen nightshirt he was wearing felt stiff and coarse. As the room lightened she fell asleep to the faint, rhythmic beating of his heart.

The following day the sea mist and drizzle cleared; the sun came out; David Johnson rallied. His breathing was more settled. He even managed to eat a little soup. Mid-morning, Dr Williams came in a two-wheeled trap. He'd brought two bottles of oxygen with him, one of which was for David.

'It's you cwtching up to him that done it,' Bethan said, her dark eyes twinkling sexily at Lara and Dr Williams. Then, in a louder voice, looking down at the bed, she said, 'Isn' it David, orright?'

Lara smiled. 'It's probably more the oxygen.'

'No, no, Bethan's right,' said Hopkins, a short, thick-set man in a sweaty dark green tunic. He looked more like an onion-seller than a doctor except for the stethoscope dangling on his broad chest. He had wavy black hair and skin that was, like hers, olive-toned. He grinned at her, exposing three gold-filled teeth.
This man exuded bustle and hurry. 'I'll look in a bit later,' he said to Lara. 'It's so good for him that you came—'

He broke off. Lara sensed that he was going to add 'before he died' but had thought better of it. He turned to go, talking in a stream of Welsh to Bethan as he left the room. The two women could hear him bounding up the stairs to another patient's room. Bethan rolled her eyes at Lara and grinned.

Later, after she'd eaten something about midday, Lara left David's bedside. They'd managed to talk some more and she'd shown him the photograph of Arrow.

It's amazing, she thought, how time has slowed right down. How I've adjusted to each new minute, new hour, new morning as a bonus. Last night I thought he would die; it's better now, he's just sleeping, and that's enough.

Outside the sun was shining. She walked to the window and looked out. She could see Star shrieking and laughing at the water's edge, being tugged in by Gwynfor. She could hear Gwynfor's deeper laugh. She thought about radiation in the sea; the air; the stones. Should they be doing that? Then she looked once more at David's inert body and went out, calling up to Bethan as she left, to let her know.

By the pebbly shore Star and Gwynfor were still larking around trying to push each other in. They were more or less hysterical now.

'You wouldn't credit it, Mrs Johnson,' Gwynfor panted, trying to straighten his face, 'but this girl here doesn't believe there are such things as mermaids.'

Lara shook her head. 'Watch out. I think it might shelve away steeply.'

'She really doesn't!' Gwynfor was grinning at Star. 'Tell her! Better still, I'll make her believe it!'

Star was a few feet from the shoreline, knee deep. 'Of course I don't! Stupid Welsh sheep-twat!' She burst into uncontrollable giggles.

He put on a pretend-angry face. 'Right, English tart!' He strode into the sea. Star shrieked with laughter, backing away.

'Careful! Don't swallow any!' Lara shouted.

She couldn't help smiling. Gwynfor was grappling with Star now. She was pulling away, screaming, little traces of fear in her laughter. She toppled backwards into the water and pulled Gwynfor in too. A wave splashed over their heads. They stood up, spluttering, still laughing, totally wet, and splashed back to the shore.

'You stupid things,' Lara said. They were wet dogs, shivering and shaking with cold. Lara noticed Star's nipples, hard and prominent under her clinging shirt.

'I didn't swallow any,' Star said.

'Yes you did' Gwynfor grinned meaningfully, and they both started giggling again.

Lara shook her head. 'And I don't suppose either of you can swim.'

It was a relief to act parental, be something other than David's comforter.

'I can,' said Gwynfor. His voice had gone hoarse after swallowing the seawater.

Lara noticed his beautiful strong limbs, textured now with gooseflesh, and thought about how David's wasted arms had looked in the grey dawn light.

'I'm going to teach her, I am!' Gwynfor looked with pretend-menace at Star. The young woman responded with another short scream and backed away. She picked up a towel she'd left on a rock and started rubbing her short hair.

Lara strolled over to her. Gwynfor, still shaking with cold, was now talking to a middle-aged bearded man in a blue woollen sweater. They were talking in Welsh by the water's edge.

'I think he's warning you not to go in the sea,' said Lara.

'Maybe,' said Star, her teeth chattering. She was wrapping the big towel around herself now. 'But I heard that man say piscodin. That means fish, I think. Or fishing. I think he's offering to take us out, for money. He came over before.'

Lara was impressed. 'You're picking up the language.'

Star smiled and shook her head. 'Before you nag me, I know what that Evans guy in Bangor said. Don't eat the fish from round here.'

'That's right.'

Star pulled the towel tighter around her and picked up her denim shorts. From one pocket she extracted her shades, which she put on, and then rummaged in the other. After a few seconds she brought out a small tin and some cigarette papers.

'I didn't know you used those,' Lara said.

Star had already opened the tin and was rolling a sizeable cigarette.

'I don't, not often anyway. It's his.' She nodded towards Gwynfor, who was still chatting to the fisherman.

Lara listened to the seagulls screaming as they circled overhead.

'You're rolling another one for him, now?'

'It's for you.'

Lara looked at Star blankly. 'But I don't.'

'Now you do,' said Star firmly, holding it out. 'Come on, Justice Johnson, come and sit down here with me, out of the wind.'

She took Lara's arm and led her to a sheltered sunny spot by the edge of the shingle beach.

They sat together. Lara could feel warm rock against her back. She closed her eyes and let the bright afternoon sun flood right into the back of her eyeballs.

Lara could hear Star turning the little milled wheel of the cigarette lighter and felt the lighted reefer being put into her hand. She took the heavy, pungent smoke into her lungs, coughing once or twice. The taste was earthy, like tomato plants in a hot greenhouse.

'There's more in this than tobacco,' gasped Lara. 'Isn't there?'

Star smiled behind her sunglasses and put a sea-cooled hand on Lara's arm. 'You're not very street-wise for a judge, are you?'

Lara inhaled again. A few minutes later she noticed that tears were coursing down her cheeks. So weird, she thought, the tears are coming out without any emotions to push them out.

She turned to say something to Star and realised she'd gone.

A shadow fell across her eyes. She looked up. It was Ben. He was bare-footed and wearing shorts and a T-shirt.

'Can I join you?'

'Yes. Where's Star?'

'Over there.' He sat down in the sand beside her and pointed to where Star was standing next to Gwynfor and the fisherman in the blue sweater.

To Lara, the sea seemed louder. The crashing of the waves filled her mind; the sea had taken her to another place.

'Help me finish this.' She handed Ben the still-lit reefer.

He took it without a word and inhaled, staring out at the horizon with her.

He offered her his hand, and she took it.

34

When Lara came to David's room she found the door closed; usually it was left open. She knocked gently. The door opened immediately – Bethan was on her way out. The nurse's usual mischievous smile was absent.

'Oh come in, Mrs Johnson, come in,' she said. 'He's all right now.'

'What happened?'

'Oh, it's all right now. The fluid in his lungs, it was.'

The nurse saw the shock in Lara's face.

'He'll be OK now. Had a bit of a fright, he did, that's all.' Bethan patted Lara's arm.

Lara noticed the nurse was holding a metal bowl covered by a towel. There were a few specks of fresh blood on the towel.

Dr Hopkins was there too. He was standing by the bed, putting some kind of metal instrument back into his bag. When Lara came across the doctor didn't say anything. He smiled briefly at Lara and motioned for her to sit by the bed. Lara looked at her husband.

David was lying propped up as before, his torso and head leaning to one side. His complexion was no longer ashen, more grey-green. His lips were red, too red, like a parody of makeup; not all the blood had been wiped from them. He was awake. She could see a residue of fear in his eyes.

Where there's fear there's a will to live, a quiet voice in Lara's head said.

Lara was surprised at how calm she felt. She sat down.

Dr Hopkins had finished packing up now. 'I've given him something to ease the breathing,' he said, as he washed his hands in a bowl of water that stood on a table near the window.

She nodded. 'Doesn't David need oxygen?'

Hopkins looked at her. 'Your husband got a little agitated.' He turned to look at the patient and smiled. 'Didn't you David, eh?'

David managed a weak smile. His lips were moving so Lara stood up, putting her ear next to his mouth.

'Last night...wanted to tell you,' he whispered.

'What is it?'

Hopkins had reached the door. 'Not too much talking with him now.'

Lara nodded.

The doctor left, leaving the door open.

David rolled his eyes in frustration. 'Woozy. Can't...'

'They've given you some more morphine, I think.'

'Got to tell you.'

'Yes, go on. Was it to do with Inter-Regional Security?'

David frowned and shifted his head slightly from side to side.

'The nuclear power station?'

She got the same response: another frown.

'North Mercia. Stettin. What's happening now?'

He nodded, his eyes lighting up.

'So it's the situation now – civil war? – what you said in your message?'

That's it, his eyes said.

She waited for him to gather his strength.

'Stettin thinks...they think...'

'They think what?'

'Think they have...radioactive...material.'

'Yes?'

'For putting in...a conven– ordinary...bomb. But...'

He was an Olympic runner dashing for the finishing line.

'I fooled them. They don't have it.' His eyes were alight, triumphant.

'So – have I got it right? They've taken something away, something they might want to use but it's harmless?'

'Harmless...yes...switched containers!'

Lara smiled down at him. 'You clever...'

'Mildly radio...' He couldn't quite finish.

'Only mildly radioactive,' she finished for him.

He nodded. 'Important to know...if they try...'

She patted the back of his hand firmly. 'Don't try to talk any more. I get it.'

He did try to say something else but she shook her head, putting her fingers gently on his lips.

'Later,' she said.

He smiled up at her, his face losing its tension, his eyes closing.

Next day – the final day, in the late afternoon – David's breathing slowed right down. Sometimes it seemed as if a whole minute passed between each long, sonorous, unearthly groan.

Lara was sitting by the bed, alone with him, when the peace was disturbed by the noisy roar of motors outside. Car doors slammed and she heard loud excited voices. For a moment her heart was clutched by fear. Had Stettin's men caught up with them? Had they somehow managed to break through the border and track them down?

A minute later Star came into the room. She tried hard to contain her excitement. 'Guess what,' she'd whispered. 'Anwar's here with the Land-Rover. They got it fixed. And Saleem! Him and Private Roycroft!'

'What! How?'

'They pinched one of those awesome black cars from the castle.'

When David Johnson stopped breathing thirty six hours later, Lara and Ben were with him. It happened when Star, who'd been sitting at the bedside with them, had gone outside for five minutes for a spliff with Bethan.

So that's it, Lara said to herself. That's it. She noticed her fingers gently tracing along the outlines of his stilled face, jaw and neck for the very last time. There was no urge to wail or sob. How strange, she thought to herself, not to have that urge.

She found she was propelling herself to the door. The sound of her shoes on the floorboards seemed unnaturally loud.

Ben, who was still sitting by the bed, looked up at her and

reached out a hand, beckoning her back. His eyes were glassy with tears. She didn't want to say anything to him. She needed to get out of that room.

Outside it was a still, cool, clear night. That slight breeze from the north was gently riffling the sea: hush, splash; hush, splash; hush, splash.

She looked up at the stars. There were too many of them; he was lost up there already. If only I'd found the old David, the David I remembered from before.

She felt the light touch of a hand on her elbow.

Ben and Star had come to fetch her inside.

Their voices sounded a long way off, even though both of them were standing right next to her.

The next day was the same. She could hear people's voices and the cries of the gulls, but it was like her ears had been stuffed with cotton wool.

And seeing things – she saw, but at the same time she didn't. Things were clear and sharp enough, not blurred, but that chair – those curtains – that face didn't register in her brain somehow.

Mysteriously, Saleem was here. At one point she was sitting and he came up to her, his eyes very mournful, and clasped her hands and said things.

Other people said things – as gently as they could, what shall we do with David, where would be best, but she couldn't tell them. Dimly, she was aware she'd been let off deciding until tomorrow. Yes Ben told her, leave it until tomorrow.

Yesterday was clearer – much clearer.

The stream of visitors to David's bedside – one last time, one last visit, may we…please.

Between visitors Star saying 'all in dark clothes, all black, they remind me of those ravens.'

Me saying but it does mean a lot to me – how many are coming, what they thought of him. But will they never stop coming?

The polite queue on the cobblestones outside the front door: hushed gentle solemn Welsh voices rising up, drifting in through the open window.

Huw Evans came from Bangor, his neat tweed jacket bejewelled with tiny raindrops. His face taut and controlled: I'm so very sorry.

Him choking, surprised by the depth of his emotion, me surprising myself, not thinking, putting my arms around him. His body stiff; like holding an ironing board.

After Huw Evans, all those ex-employees and survivors from Wylfa, some of them looking very ill themselves.

Solemn-faced, dark-suited bigwigs and local representatives remembering the hero who'd saved their land from perpetual irradiation.

An old-style Presbyterian chapel minister, an exotic historical throwback, I never knew such people existed. Silver-haired, late eighties, stilling her heart with his kind words: Does David need, Mrs Johnson, would you want Christian prayers and blessings...

I opened my hands, said nothing, but yes. Better than a Church of Diana priestess chanting and jingling little bells over him.

A hot, stuffy night: she woke from restless sleep and realised she could hear the sea quite clearly – no cotton wool.

She got out of bed, naked, wrapping a sheet around herself, and went to stand by the window. No stars. No moon. Only the darkness out there and the persistent, regular, hush-swish of the waves.

She couldn't get the dream out of her mind; the images of the men's bodies and what they were doing to her; what she was doing to them. Her body was tingling from head to foot; her nipples were stiff and hard. She reached down and touched herself, feeling the moistness and the desire.

But that wouldn't do, it wouldn't be enough, because a wave had hit her – not one of those gentle waves like the ones breaking now on the beach but a tremendous wave, an urge so strong it took her back to giving birth to Arrow.

That moment of final release, of pure pain and orgasm, and afterwards too, only twelve hours afterwards maybe, how she'd wanted David so badly, wanted him to climb into bed with her and feel his warmth and strength inside her.

I have to; I can't wait.

She pulled on her cotton trousers and loose country smock, opened the door and padded barefoot down the landing. Boards creaked. She could hear a gentle moaning from downstairs – one of the patients.

Ben was in the room at the end, sharing with Anwar and Private Roycroft.

Her heart was thudding as she edged the door open.

What if I touch the wrong man? Despite the tension, she smiled to herself: would it matter? Lara Johnson!

She could tell it was Ben from the shape of his hair – the mass of curls. And his smell: they'd been so close the last few days, him sitting beside her watching David, giving her hugs of comfort; she knew his smell.

When he woke, bewildered, she kissed him on the mouth to stop him from saying anything, tugged his arm and left the room.

They walked along the beach, away from the houses, to find a quiet spot. She could tell he wanted to say something, ask her why, but she knew he was too choked up.

She took his hand and led him into the sandy dunes. It was very dark. They stumbled through spiky marram but soon she found them a hollow where the sand gave way to low, sheep-grazed grass.

I'll make him wait a little, she was thinking, tease him and tease myself. He was easing her smock off, pulling it over her head and kissing her breasts, taking one full in his mouth now and sucking hard as if he was trying to swallow it.

She was unbuttoning his shirt, kissing his nipples and chest, finding she couldn't wait, couldn't bear that teasing after all.

'Fuck me,' she breathed into his ear; 'fuck me...please!'

He was making gasping noises, undoing the top buttons of his trousers. She reached down, clasping his buttocks – so firm and hard.

Through the pounding of blood in her ears, she heard him crying:

'I'm so sorry Lara, so sorry...'

He was naked now – he'd kicked off his trousers and they were standing up close together – and when she reached down, she felt the limpness.

He was crying now, gasping, 'I love you Lara, I want you so much! I'm so sorry!'

She knew what was holding him back but she wasn't going to acknowledge it.

'You've got to,' she told him. 'We've got to...' she added with a whisper, kneeling in front of him and taking him in her mouth.

It took longer than she expected. She was almost at the point of saying okay, let's lie together and wait and kiss and talk. But so great was her lust that she carried on, coaxing and teasing and sucking until he began to stiffen.

She felt him pushing her back onto the grass, his big, flat finger finding her, easing her, gentling her.

I'm so wet now, he's got both fingers inside me; he knows me – he knows.

She screamed – and thought straight afterwards God, I hope no one heard, they might think it was a seagull.

Then he himself was on top of her, he himself inside her, thrusting until she came again, and again, until a third time when he too cried out, and all was silent except the distant hush-swish of the waves.

KEN BLAKEMORE

35

Early next morning, as he gave himself a wash all over with two buckets of water, Ben caught himself singing. As he went downstairs for breakfast he was whistling cheerfully.

Private Roycroft, cracking open an egg, gave him a sour look.

'What have you found to be so cheerful about?'

'Oh nothing,' he said, struggling to put on a suitably sombre expression.

Ben didn't realise the other things that were all too obvious to everyone else: the spring in his step and the light in his eyes. His dreams had come true.

Lara and Star were on the seashore.

Hours earlier, at dawn, Lara had crept back to her room, spent and ashamed, hardly able to believe what had happened. She woke with a strong feeling that she wanted to avoid Ben as much as possible. She dreaded seeing his face. She knew what would be written all over it. Everyone would know. It was awful.

'What about a last walk along the beach?' she asked Star. 'Just the two of us.'

As she stepped onto the landing she heard Ben singing loudly in the bathroom. Oh no.

Star came out of her room.

Before Star noticed the singing or could make any comment on it, Lara asked her whether she could borrow her sunglasses.

'Sure,' she said, giving her a quizzical look. 'Not very sunny yet though, is it?'

It was a grey, warm, cloudy day: the sea, oily-smooth and obedient, lapped their feet as they strolled along.

The day before a fishing boat had come on these calm waters to Moelfre. It had brought blocks of ice to pack around David Johnson's body.

Star was content to walk along without conversation. When would she ever get this close to the sea again? She was enjoying the crunching sound their feet made on the pebbles; the salt-seaweed smell of the air; most of all, the big, open, endless sky. Today there was no horizon – the sea and the sky merged seamlessly – and she liked that.

Lara said 'I don't feel sad today. I feel relieved. Is there something wrong with me?'

'No. His suffering's over. Your quest's over. No wonder you feel relieved. I would.'

Lara stopped a moment to scrutinise Star's face. Young people can oversimplify, but maybe they're the wisest. She suddenly wanted to hug this spiky, unpredictable, one-off person.

'It's when I think of having to tell Arrow…' Lara said.

Star bent down to pick up a small, flat stone from the shingle. She skimmed it over the calm surface of the sea. Gwynfor had been teaching her how. The disc of stone kissed the water three times and disappeared.

'I know it'll be hard,' Star said, 'because it won't seem real to her. I never knew my parents – never saw a grave; never had anything to remember them with. That's why it's a good idea to take his body back.'

They walked back to the house where Star and Gwynfor were staying and they saw Saleem sitting on a bench at the front looking out to sea.

Lara sat beside him and he told her about his escape from Peckforton.

He was very worried about taking one of the SUVs from Stettin's fleet, he explained, because he was a good Muslim and stealing was wrong.

'But they'd impounded the bloody Land-Rover, right? And me and soldier Roycroft!'

'We couldn't find you – Stettin kept saying you'd gone away to get it fixed – and all the time you were just a few yards away, locked up! '

'That's right.'

'I'm so sorry, Saleem. It's all been beyond the call of duty.'

'They treated us okay, I s'pose – food an' that. No pork.'

'You're too reasonable.'

'The worst thing was not knowing when we'd get out o' that bloody place.'

'So how did you do it?'

'I tried to break the lock on the door or pick it, you know? Couldn't do it – only had a bloody fork to work with! But then, one day they changed the guard. They usually sent two in with food, but that day it was a different one, a soft-headed young guy. We heard a lot of noise and people runnin' about that day, you know? Anyway, Roycroft hit him over the head with a stool! When we got out we found they was all running round like blue-arsed flies. Like something was going on…'

'They didn't notice you?'

'We couldn't work out what was happening – so we peeked through a window and saw all these big cars pulling up to the main entrance, one after another. There was a line of them – looked like all these VIPs were arriving. Fat guys in suits, like.'

'Did you recognise any of them?'

'I recognised one. He's not fat – he's that chief from home, you know? The one that lives in that grand house – I've chauffeured people there a coupla times.'

'Laczko?'

'That's him.'

'So how did you manage to steal a car!'

Saleem looked pained. 'We didn't steal, Mrs Johnson. They got the Land-Rover, innit? We exchanged. Mind you,' he added with the hint of a smile, 'we got a good deal! It's not so much a car, like, as a bloody great wagon – an SUV. Immaculate, like it was made yesterday, kept mint since Good Time.'

'Come on Saleem, tell me how you did it.'

'There were so many people milling around; nobody noticed us. We got up close to an SUV that had already dropped off. The driver was sitting in it, just waiting. Soldier Roycroft crept up the side, opened the door and…'

'What?'

'Suggested he took a nap,' Saleem grinned. 'Then we just drove out, flag on bloody bonnet, through the gates and down bloody road.'

'What I can't work out is, how did you know where to find us?'

'We were in the hands of God. He steered us. We took a bush road to the west. Actually to be honest it was because we couldn't go the other way – road blocks and checkpoints. We crossed into Wales; got to a little town on the border…nobody spoke bloody English!'

'How did you get across the border – out of North Mercia?'

'When they saw us coming, that flag on the bonnet and the size of the bloody vehicle, the barrier shot up! They saluted us as we went through!' he laughed. 'Then, on the other side, I went to find one of our brothers – there's always one family, you know, in any little place? They'd heard about me going missing from another brother in Llan-whatsit…'

'Llangollen.'

'That's him. We went there, found that brother and he sent us on to where you were.'

She smiled at him. 'Brilliant!'

They looked at the sea.

'You know I want to take David home tomorrow. Do you think we can do it?'

'Of course we can, now we've got the SUV. It will be an honour to do that, Mrs Johnson.'

Gwynfor was holding her tight, one last time. They were trying to create, in this brief moment, a little make-believe universe that would never end.

Behind them in the muddy street in Llangollen under a grey sky, the huge black SUV, the Land-Rover and the jeep were waiting, their engines running. A crowd of giggling, barefoot children had gathered round the SUV. They were fascinated by its dark tinted windows.

'You will come one day? Soon?'

This wasn't how she thought it would be. So much had happened in the past week. She'd been carried along like a twig in a swirling river – the escape from the castle; finding Gwynfor in Llangollen; the journey to Anglesey; sitting with Lara as she watched over her dying husband.

Only now did she fully realise how close she'd got to Gwyn, through all this. If not right by her side, he'd always been near. When she'd taken breaks from the fetid room of the dying man, Gwynfor had been outside waiting to run along the beach with her, laugh and drag her into the sea. He'd shown her how to fly a kite and flip stones, things she'd never learned in the orphanage.

Every night he'd crept into her bed. His tongue had gently probed the inside of her ear, first the left ear, then the right, banishing all sounds, banishing all ogres and bad spirits. And each morning they'd found it hard to leave the bed. He'd taught her more Welsh words and let her talk about her journal and her plans for writing a book.

She nodded. 'I will...I'll try.'

'Try? You'd better!'

She laughed. 'I've got to go. They're waiting.'

'I could still come with you. I could–'

'–No, Gwyn, we said. It's too dangerous–'

'–That's why I should come.'

She shook her head and kissed him.

Anwar blew the Land-Rover horn.

'I love you, Gwynfor Roberts.'

He pressed a gold ring into her hand. 'I love you, Star; Seren.'

She stared at the ring, not able to speak.

It was a man's wedding ring, too big for her finger, wide-banded, worn and smooth. She held it up to give it back to him.

'Take it,' he said softly. 'Please take it. It was my father's.'

'But your mother should have this.'

'She didn't want it. She didn't want to wear it, have it made smaller, like. She wanted me to keep it. And now I'm lending it to you.'

'But I can't take your father's ring, Gwynfor...'

'I don't want you to wear it. Just keep it. I'm lending it, right? Trusting you with it. So you've got to bring it back to me. When you do,' he added with a smile, 'you might be able to exchange it for another.'

While Star was saying goodbye to Gwynfor, Lara said to Ben 'go and sit with Saleem in the front, will you?'

He frowned. 'Why? He's all right. I'd rather sit with you!' he added, whispering.

'Go on, Ben – I've got a feeling she'd like to be with just me.'

Ben said nothing.

Grim-faced, he got out and held the passenger door open for Star. She came up looking pale; swallowing back the tears. She turned to give Gwynfor a last wave and climbed in.

She expected Ben to get in after her, sit beside her in the back. She was surprised when Ben slammed the door, walked around the vehicle and got into the front to sit next to Saleem.

36

When they left Llangollen it was already late afternoon. The Land-Rover, driven by Anwar, led the way. Private Roycroft sat in the front with him, cradling his submachine gun.

The sleek black SUV followed. In the long, capacious rear of the vehicle was a lead-lined coffin draped with black cloth.

The open-topped jeep brought up the rear of this little convoy, with Kieran Tyler driving and Private Williams sitting beside him.

After they'd all eaten at a roadside snack bar they pushed on south-eastwards through the border country, keeping to the Welsh side and passing through small, reclaimed settlements. In one straggling village there was a fork in the rutted track. The better road, one used by traders' carts, led east.

Anwar found an old man who could speak English. He pointed with his stick and said that the better road came out somewhere near the southern edge of North Mercia, though he wasn't sure exactly where.

'We daren't risk it' Tyler advised, 'that way is a no man's land between Powys, West Mercia and North Mercia – and we'd still be too close to North Mercia, I think.'

There was nothing for it but to take the other fork, which was little better than a farm track used by cattle.

'Where does that one go?' Saleem asked. The old man had simply laughed and waved his stick in the air, walking away without saying anything.

The rutted, narrow track twisted and turned, so much so that sometimes Anwar, still leading the way, had to halt the Land-Rover simply to work out where it had gone. Sometimes it disappeared in a thicket of saplings. Elsewhere it meandered into old neglected fields of long grass. To make matters worse, recent floods had submerged it in places.

The old Welsh border country had suffered badly during the Great Plagues that brought an end to Good Time, but even in Good Time it had been thinly populated. Now it was virtually empty: the road was hardly needed by anyone, and often they had to stop, reverse or turn round to find the right way.

At nightfall they drove into the ruins of an abandoned city. Normally they would have pushed on. The old cities posed considerable risks, mainly from the danger of collapsing buildings, though there were other dangers too – toxic chemicals once used in industrial processes, for instance, or containers and canisters with unstable explosive materials in them.

Anwar brought the Land-Rover to a halt and the other two vehicles stopped behind it. He was tired and hungry, and suggested to Saleem and Tyler that they stayed overnight at this point if they could find somewhere safe and dry to shelter and prepare food.

As they stood around debating what to do, some nomads appeared. They were all, men and women alike, dressed in baggy clothes made of wool and goatskins. Some of the women wore colourful scarves and the men had long hair and beards.

It was hard to make out what these strange people were saying, so thick and foreign was their dialect – a mixture of English and Welsh – but it turned out that they were offering the tired travellers shelter and hospitality.

'Our great-grandparents lived in yurts and tepees in Good Time,' explained a white-haired matriarch, grinning and exposing blackened teeth. 'And we live in yurts and tepees.'

Star fell asleep that night in a tent made of whitened animal hides and decorated with symbolic animal designs – wolves, horses, deer, dogs and goats.

This was after they'd all been invited to sit round a large fire in the open, listening to the nomads singing their songs and playing their guitars, flutes and goatskin drums.

One of the nomad women – no older than Star, but with a baby and a three year-old child asleep on a mat beside her – told her they were making their way to a sacred place in England called Glastonbury, where they gathered every year with many other nomads for the Autumn Equinox festival. As well as the Thanking of the Great Spirit Ceremonies there'd be feasting, music-making and a horse, sheep and goat fair.

Star didn't know whether to tell her they might be walking across an area of disorder, upheaval, rape and theft. In the end she decided not to. There was something about the quiet resilience and peacefulness of these people that told her they'd survive. They'd step sideways out of danger; melt back into the landscape.

Were these nomads the future? She wrote down this thought in her journal, straining to see the page in guttering candlelight. Then she lay down, relaxing her aching back on an ancient, stained quilt. As she dropped off to sleep she could hear the keening howls of wolves in the distance.

Next morning, stumbling around among the weed-covered ruins, looking for somewhere to defecate she came across a statue surrounded by clumps of buddleia. Getting close, she could see it was the figure of an old man with a bald head and a massive beard. He was covered in moss and seated on a kind of throne overgrown with weeds.

Was it the statue of a king? A famous politician?

With a sharp stick it didn't take her long to rub off the weeds and moss covering the lettering beneath. She pulled out her notebook and stood back, squinting in order to make out the eroded lettering, and wrote down the name:

CHARLES DARWIN, 1809–1882

That morning the three vehicles continued their journey due south. They came across no marked frontier or boundary on their narrow, overgrown track. Perhaps they'd entered no man's land. At one point they passed a huge, elongated hill, smooth and treeless, which rose above the forest like a massive whale.

Eventually they came to another river crossing, an ancient stone bridge that led towards an old settlement on the other side.

It looked as if it was still inhabited; smoke was coming from the chimneys of some of the original Good Time houses. There was a white and red barrier pole at the bridge, and they could just make out the figures of two khaki-uniformed soldiers sitting beside it in the bright sunshine.

'Where's this?'

Anwar was leaning out of the window of the Land-Rover, shouting to a boy on the road who was wheeling a bike with a flat tyre.

'Ludlow,' the boy muttered.

'West Mercia?' Private Roycroft asked.

The boy shrugged his shoulders. 'Dunno.'

Saleem and Kieran Tyler had come up now to see what was happening.

'Let's go for it,' Tyler said. 'We've got to take our chance sooner or later, so let's do it now. We've come a long way south – surely this can't still be North Mercia.'

Anwar and Saleem nodded. The three drivers turned to get back into their vehicles.

'Just a minute,' Lara said. She'd got out of the SUV and had come up to them.

She looked at Saleem. 'Didn't you say something about the flag on the SUV we're riding in? The effect it has at border posts? Let's give it a try here – the SUV in front and the other two following.'

Saleem nodded. 'Definitely worked for me before.'

Two minutes later, the three vehicles sped towards the barrier. The SUV was in front, streaked and spattered with mud, headlights on, sporting the colourful flag from Stettin's castle. It had the crest of Chester on it – two golden lions, a shield and three wheatsheaves.

They held their breath as they approached the horizontal white and red pole. The two scruffy-looking soldiers jumped up when Saleem blew the horn.

One guard was picking up a rifle but the other was running to hoist the barrier and wave the vehicles through.

It was like that at every checkpoint and roadblock. Police gates were pulled back with alacrity. At military checkpoints the guards stood to attention as the big black official car passed, its colourful flag fluttering.

'It's strange,' Saleem said to Ben, 'there's nothing much on the road is there? No carts, transports, nothing.'

'No,' Ben said. 'But there are so many people out.'

It was true. In every settlement they came to it looked as if a public holiday was in full swing. Some places had colourful strings of flags and pennants across the road. In one town a march was going on, led by girl drummers and three old men playing fiddles.

'Look at them all! What's going on? It can't be because of us, can it?' said Star, pointing through the tinted windows.

The main street they were passing along was lined with people, many cheering and waving at them. Children danced, daring each other to dart across their path. Saleem blew the horn repeatedly as they slowed to push their way through. Many in the crowd were singing and chanting, holding up placards and boards upon which the figure of Our Lady Princess Diana had been crudely painted in white and blue. Some of the Diana's had angel wings and halos; some showed her in prayer, her hands held together and her head uplifted to heaven.

'And look at those flags!' said Lara. In the midst of the multicoloured bunting some larger red and white flags had been hung across.

'What are they? I've never seen them before,' Star said.

'It's the old England flag, the cross of St. George.'

Half an hour later they turned into a roadside workshop and bio-fuel depot. It was on a deserted stretch of road; there were no crowds here. Saleem steered the SUV in and switched off the engine. He explained that this was a place he and Anwar knew well: it was run by a cousin of theirs. They'd be welcome here, be able to take some food and refuel all three vehicles.

'And find out what's going on,' said Star, grabbing her journal.

The cousin, Saddam, had already emerged from the rusting corrugated-iron workshop. A big man with a big black beard, he was grinning and shouting Punjabi greetings to Anwar and Saleem. He was wearing loose, baggy trousers and a greasy, faded blue mechanic's smock. His large rectangular beard was like a mass of fine electrical wiring.

Once the greetings and back slapping were over, Tyler asked Saddam what was going on.

'To be honest mate,' said Saddam, switching to English and putting on a serious expression, 'I dunno really what's happening. Nothing on the road, see? Nothing coming this way or that,' he waved in the air, 'nothing really for the past two days, since all the army stuff went through, like.'

They were stunned. Surely Stettin's forces hadn't got this far south already?

'How many trucks?' asked Private Williams.

'Hard to say, mate. I wasn't counting, see?' Saddam paused to stroke his beard. 'Dozens, anyway. A lot. Soldiers all packed in; trailers with big guns. And horses, carts. Supplies, you know? And there were these massive transporters. Never seen anything like 'em! Eleven wheels on each side! So big you couldn't believe they'd fit on the road! They had these big bastard things on. Like each one had a gun sticking out of it!

'Tanks? No wheels on them, just tracks?' Private Roycroft motioned with his hands to illustrate.

'That's it.'

Private Williams let out a low whistle.

Saddam nodded. 'But no fighting, no trouble – not round here anyway. What we heard is, the West Mercia lot haven't bothered fighting much. Can't blame 'em – I know what I'd do – run like hell! Oh, sorry for the language madams,' he said, giving the two women an apologetic glance.

They looked around, scanning the horizon. There were no tell-tale smudges of black smoke on the horizon, no distant crump-crump of artillery.

'What are we going to do then?' Star asked Lara.

Lara looked at them all, thinking. Ben noticed how the sun was highlighting a few golden strands in her reddish-brown hair.

'I suggest we press on. We could stop here a while, try to get some more information about the military activity but you know, time is of the essence.'

She nodded towards the SUV.

They knew what she meant: the coffin and its contents.

'Yes,' Tyler said. 'We need to get nearer to the front line – see how far the attacking force has got.'

Private Williams had a gloomy face. 'If there is a front line – they could have reached Warwick.'

'Let's hope there is a front line between us and home, then,' Lara said, 'even if that means we've got to get through it.'

Everyone looked worried. How would they get through it?

Star broke the silence. 'Excuse me,' she asked Saddam, 'why are there all these crowds, everybody cheering, flags…?'

'Wait a minute,' Saddam said, 'I'll show you.'

He turned and strode towards his workshop, returning a few seconds later holding a small, greyish piece of paper. He held it out.

'They were chucking these off the trucks – handfuls of them. That's why everybody's going crazy.'

Lara took the wrinkled piece of paper. The others were too curious to wait and gathered round to look over her shoulder. Star peered at the crudely printed words, which seemed to dance in front of her eyes:

♦ ♦ ♦GOOD NEWS! ♦ ♦ ♦
PREPARE TO WELCOME YOUR KING!
HIS ROYAL HIGHNESS, CHARLES REX
GREAT GRANDSON OF OUR LADY,
THE PRINCESS DIANA
LONG LIVE THE KING!!
LONG LIVE A UNITED ENGLAND,
WALES AND SCOTLAND!
♦ ♦ ♦ ♦ ♦ ♦

37

Lara sat in a cold sweat in the back of the SUV. Star was sitting beside her; Ben was in the front passenger seat next to Saleem, as before.

It was pitch dark, almost midnight, and all three vehicles were bumping slowly along a little-known back road towards New Warwick. They were crawling along through the forest with lights switched off – the Land-Rover a hundred yards in front, followed by the SUV and Kieran Tyler's jeep.

Lara knew this was madness; madness to proceed without knowing what lay ahead. But she'd put on a calm face and told them there was no choice – they had to do it.

Saleem, Anwar, Kieran, the two soldiers, they'd all been great – just nodded and said okay, we'll do it tonight.

They were thinking yes she's desperate to get back to bury her husband and be with her family, just like we're desperate to get back to our families to see if they're safe. We're all in this together. But they didn't know even more was at stake. They didn't know Lara had vital information to get through – the information contained in David's dying words that could release New Warwick from terror and panic.

They were in the Forest of Arden now. New Warwick – or rather the ten-mile belt of territory surrounding the city – lay just ahead.

They'd had several false starts that evening. Frightened villagers had turned them back, warning them of encampments of soldiery

309

up ahead. The invading forces from the north seemed to have been welcomed all the way – until they'd reached this area closer to New Warwick and Stratford-upon-Avon.

Just before dark they'd driven slowly through the silent, smouldering ruins of a destroyed settlement. Lara saw what she hoped was just a bundle of clothes laying at the side of the road. In the fading light it was hard to tell.

Now Saleem was leaning over the steering wheel, peering ahead, trying to find the black shape of the Land-Rover, which he'd lost – it was some distance ahead of them, maybe more than two hundred yards.

A dazzling blink of light and whump! – a hollow thud like someone hitting a hollow log with a sledgehammer.

Saleem jumped on the brakes and they all jerked forward in their seats.

Silence for two seconds.

Ear-splitting bangs behind them – Lara felt tremors passing through the soles of her feet and up her legs. They ducked down, Lara and Star crouching together on the floor of the SUV.

The rattle of a machine gun. Three more loud bangs and more machine gunfire.

Lara felt sick. The worst had happened.

'Lara!' she heard Ben shout 'I'm getting out!'

'No!' she shouted. 'No!'

Saleem was muttering under his breath. In the blackness, she felt Star's hand grip hers.

Her heart leapt – someone was trying to open the door on her side.

Now a loud noise like someone had thrown a rock against one of the car windows: crack! She couldn't make out whether it had hit Ben's or Saleem's side.

A door was opening and Saleem was saying 'okay, okay' in a shaky voice.

Now Ben's door opening and Ben saying 'we have to get out, Lara.'

The five soldiers were all black. One – the tallest of the five – had his hair in long dreads; greased ropes that fell down from his loosely fitting helmet. In the forest gloom Lara could make out the glint of knife blades fixed to their belts. All of them had short, stubby sub-machine guns, one of which was pointing directly at Saleem's stomach. The others were pointing at them.

One man, who seemed to be in charge, had a grey wolf pelt tied diagonally across his chest; the wolf's head covered his shoulder like an epaulette. But otherwise their dark green uniforms looked new, neat and regular. Lara noticed that one of the soldiers had three small, child-size human skulls tied to his belt.

'Please will you tell me, sir,' Saleem was begging, 'what's happened to the vehicle in front?'

The soldiers looked at Saleem calmly and dispassionately. They said nothing. They seemed to be waiting for something.

Lara heard herself say 'open the back, Saleem, please,' she said as nonchalantly as she could manage.

Saleem hesitated, looking at the soldier who was pointing the gun at his belly. The man nodded briefly.

When the wide rear door of the SUV had been opened, the soldiers said a few words to each other in a rolling patois she couldn't understand. Lara leaned inside and drew off the cloth covering the coffin. She heard one of the soldiers whistle low with surprise.

'Inside that coffin is the body of my husband, David Johnson. I must cross into New Warwick.'

The tall soldier with dreadlocks stretched his arm inside the vehicle and tapped the coffin with a forefinger. He looked suspicious, making a clicking noise at the back of his throat.

'Open it!' He was staring at Saleem. He jerked his gun up and down. The other soldiers stood impassively.

Saleem hesitated again, his eyes black with fear, and he looked to Lara Johnson for guidance.

But before she could say anything the wolf pelt soldier said 'no leave 'im, we better fetch 'em to Colonel.'

Ten minutes later, Lara, Ben, Star and Saleem were pushed into a large tent lit inside by two oil lamps. Another black soldier, this time an officer, stood up from behind his desk.

The desk was, in truth, just a flimsy trestle table. It was covered with several maps. The officer was frowning at them. He was aged around forty, Lara guessed, judging by the grey in his closely cropped hair. Like his men he was dressed in a crisp, new uniform made of dark green material. But unlike them he had no flamboyant or fearful objects on display – no serrated blades, no little skulls, no wolf skins or black eye patches.

And unlike them he spoke south-east English like an official from the capital; an educated, Old London voice. Coming from the lips of a lean, muscular black man in army uniform, this seemed very incongruous.

He'd been wearing a pair of spectacles – neat, silver wire frames – which he'd now taken off to survey them, narrowing his eyes as he did so.

'What's this?' he asked Wolf Pelt.

The soldier replied in a low, respectful voice for over a minute, speaking in patois. Again, Lara could make out the occasional word but little of the meaning.

The colonel, still standing, listened and then waved the soldier away.

Wolf Pelt gave him a smart, energetic salute and marched out.

The officer sat down behind his table and gave them a disapproving look.

'I am Colonel Stanford Grant – Concordia Security. We have a contract to protect this section. Please explain who you are and why you are here,' he said, motioning for them to sit on flimsy collapsible chairs around his table.

'I'm Justice Lara Johnson, a citizen of New Warwick' Lara explained. Whose side are you on? she wanted to ask.

Colonel Grant ran his hand over his chin. He looked sceptically at her country smock and skirt and waited for her to continue.

Before Lara could speak, Star burst out saying 'what happened to the others – the Land-Rover and the jeep?'

The officer looked puzzled as if he wasn't sure where Star's voice had come from. Then he turned his eyes on her and took a while to decide whether to answer.

'The two men in the Land-Rover vehicle were injured,' he said. 'One badly. The driver. They hit one of our mines.'

Saleem groaned 'Anwar!' and began to sob quietly.

Lara froze when she heard him say 'yes and the other vehicle, the jeep...mm...I'm sorry to say that a combatant in the jeep was killed. That's what comes of being foolish enough to stray across a front line. Didn't you know the risks you were taking?'

Ben was muttering something but Lara ignored him and leapt on the officer's words.

'Did you say across the front line? Does that mean we're on the New Warwick side?'

Colonel Grant looked at her. 'You haven't yet explained who you are.'

Ben rose from his seat, his face flushing. 'Now listen here, this lady–'

'–Ben it's okay, sit down, she said, and began to explain.

Ben's head was spinning with tiredness and shock. He'd given up trying to anticipate what was going to happen next. The one thing that was fixed in his mind, the one thing he was determined to do, was to protect Lara. Unless he was forcibly dragged away he was going to stay by her side, whatever she herself said.

They'd been told by the officer that they couldn't go on to New Warwick. Not yet. He hadn't given them any explanation.

They were being led away by the tall soldier with dreadlocks. Star and Saleem had already been taken away by a black woman wearing the green military Concordia uniform, God knows where.

Dreadlocks led them along a silent woodland path to the SUV, which was being watched over by two other soldiers. Ben could make out the Land-Rover down the track. It was lying on its side. He looked the other way but in the dark he couldn't see the jeep. They still didn't know whether it was Kieran Tyler or Private Williams who'd been killed, or what had happened to Private Roycroft.

The soldier pointed to their bags and told Ben to pick them up and bring them.

'What about the case in the jeep?' Ben whispered to Lara. 'You know, the mon–'

'–Leave it,' Lara said quietly; 'maybe tomorrow.'

They were led back to the encampment. Dreadlocks did this wordlessly, just motioning to them which way to go. In a few minutes they came to a tent which the soldier pointed to. He pulled back the tent flap and pointed inside.

Ben could just about make out mounds of blankets piled up to make two beds. The soldier found an oil lamp, lit it and put it on the ground outside the tent. Then he indicated where the latrine was and made a cutting sign across his throat, pointing at the lamp. He understood: the lamp should be extinguished as soon as possible. The tall soldier nodded and loped away, his dreads swinging over his shoulders.

Ben waited while Lara went to the latrine, and then went himself.

When he got back to the tent, feeling his way inside, he found she'd curled up on the farther bed, her back to him. It was almost pitch black in the tent and he didn't know what to do – whether to speak to her, touch her, or what.

He was hurting so much inside. Why had she been so cold, so determined to push him away after what had happened only three nights before? She'd been angry and curt with him at times, surely drawing more attention to them than if she'd tried to behave normally.

And now, surely she knows I'm here? She can't be asleep, yet she's not saying a word to me.

He risked putting a hand on her shoulder, moving his body closer to her.

'Lara,' he whispered.

He heard a sniffle.

'Are you crying? Oh, Lara!'

He lay down fully and put his left arm around her.

'I'm sorry, Ben. I'm so sorry.'

'What for?'

She didn't say anything more, leaving him to puzzle.

But she wasn't pushing him away. He was happy enough with that.

She got up at dawn. Ben was fast asleep, his mouth open, snoring gently. She opened the flap of the tent and looked out at the grey, silent world of the forest clearing. Dew had settled on the grass. She felt very thirsty and wondered what dew would taste like if you sucked it off grass stalks.

As she stood outside, bleary and still in shock, she tried to stir cinders of hope. I've got through. I've survived. I'll see my daughter and my mother today, please God. Please say nothing has happened to them; please let them be there.

Today, if they would let her through, she'd be taking home terrible news and the body of a husband, a father and a son-in-law.

Suddenly dull agitated thuds some way off broke the silence. It wasn't from rifles or machine guns: she could tell that. They were heavier guns. The booming sounds reverberated around the surrounding woods.

Now it stopped. Off to her right, in a northerly direction, a cloud of black smoke was rising up. But it wasn't behaving like smoke. It was more active, whirling; a spiralling cloud.

Lara realised she was looking at a great flock of birds disturbed by the guns.

Twenty minutes later she'd washed herself and put on a change of clothes. The shock of washing with a bucket of cold water, splashing it all over her body and face, had brightened her eyes and toned up her skin. She'd even managed to find a hairbrush at the bottom of her bag. But she still felt hollow inside – not simply from hunger and thirst.

She went back to the tent and shook Ben's shoulder.

'I'm going to find something to drink,' she said.

The previous night she hadn't noticed there were dozens of tents in the trees surrounding the clearing. About six soldiers were standing in front of a mess tent, the front section of which had been lifted right up. Inside it an army cook was bent over a large charcoal grill. In the smoke he was flipping hefty steaks and talking to himself.

Seeing Lara, one of the soldiers came over and thrust a clean white enamel mug into her hand.

She recognised him as the Wolf Pelt corporal from the previous night. Now, without helmet and gun and wearing only a short-sleeved shirt and his dark green army trousers, he looked a lot less intimidating.

The cook had come out of the mess tent now, carrying a large blackened kettle. He looked Lara in the eye and tipped the spout of his kettle towards her mug. Black liquid poured into the mug.

Coffee! No expense spared, she thought. She wondered who'd signed the contract with Concordia. Whether it was the city council or the Oxford government, either way they'd be paying hand over fist for the coffee along with all the other costs of war.

As she sipped, feeling herself coming back to life, she heard two men talking inside Colonel Grant's tent. Their animated voices rose above the quiet hum of conversation among the huddle of soldiers standing nearby. One – not Colonel Grant's – sounded particularly excited, his voice rising to a fluting note.

Hang on, Lara thought. I know that voice. It can't be.

Just then the voices calmed, then stopped. A moment later Colonel Grant emerged from his tent. He looked across at Lara and lifted one hand smartly in greeting.

'Meet our war correspondent,' he said, inclining his head towards the tent entrance. Then the second man came out – a civilian, his wide girth accentuated by a bulky bulletproof vest.

She recognised the crumpled off-white cotton suit immediately.

'Lara! ' Blennerhassett grinned, 'You've saved the day!'

38

Three weeks later on a quiet, rainy Friday afternoon, Star Edkin was sitting in a reading room at the university library.

She leant back in her chair, sucking a pen. Two books and a few sheets of blank paper lay in front of her. She looked around, letting her thoughts wander.

The reading room was deserted. Normally by late September the students would be back. Several hundred fresh-faced youths up from the country and more savvy students from other towns and cities would be milling around, chattering and finding their way around campus. But everything had been put on hold because of the Emergency.

Her story was going to be an account of Lara Johnson's journey and what it told of the state of England and Wales at the time. At first she'd thought she could write it as a series of short, snappy articles for the Beacon. In fact Alex Blennerhassett had begged her to do that. His eyes had widened with interest when she'd waved her notebook under his nose. She'd given him a few titbits, teasing him with sensational highlights of her adventures.

Blennerhassett had already reinstated her as a full-time reporter on the paper – and she was delighted to get the motorbike back.

He was grumpy and disappointed when she insisted she wanted to write her story a different way. But he'll have to lump it, she decided. Anyway, edited highlights could always be serialised in the Beacon later, once she'd written it as a whole story with a beginning, middle and an end.

She smiled to herself at the prospect and hugged her knees. Writing a proper history – a book of two hundred pages or more that would be talked about and remembered!

It had been Lara's suggestion. The press at the Beacon would print and bind it.

Get on with it then, she told herself. She looked down at the books she'd chosen to make notes on. They'd caught her eye the previous week when she'd been browsing in a closed-off, extra-cobwebby section where most of the history books published in Good Time lay.

On top of the pile was The World Turned Upside Down: Radical Ideas during the English Revolution by Christopher Hill. She picked it up. You could tell by the coarse paper and the dull colours on the cover that it wasn't a Good Time publication. It had been reprinted recently by Cambridge University Press, which she'd learned had started functioning again after forty-plus years of silent presses.

The second book was a very old original hardback. It was falling apart. As she flipped through it several pages came loose. It was a specialist historical study written at the beginning of the 21st century — Lucca, 1369-1400: Politics and Society in an Early Renaissance Italian City-State, by Christine Meek.

She sighed. It was all very well for Lara to say 'write it with a bit of depth – you know, put what happened to us in some kind of historical context...' but words like that gave her a headache. Where was she going to start?

She'd picked out the first book because she'd remembered that there'd been civil wars in England once before, in the seventeenth century. The old groom at Boscobel House had told her about King Charles being on the run and having to hide in an oak tree. That was an exciting story but she didn't know anything else about those civil wars.

And the book about the city-state in Italy? She'd chosen that because New Warwick was a city-state. Were there any comparisons between then and now?

She picked up the book and gingerly opened it at a section in the middle. Densely worded detailed sentences trudged slowly down the page. This was going to be tough. It assumed a lot of prior knowledge in the reader. Like, what was the Renaissance?

Still, don't get yourself discouraged, Star told herself. You'll work it out – and find the right books as you need them. Just start writing. She took a deep breath, pulled her chair up to the table and reached for a piece of paper.

She decided to start at the end – the completion of Lara's quest. Yes, that would get the ball rolling. Then she could go back to the beginning – how and why they set off together on their journey.

'Lara Johnson's return to the city was dramatic.'

Well, maybe that wasn't quite right. It certainly didn't seem dramatic at the time. Star crossed it out. It acquired a dramatic interpretation a day or so later, though, once the Beacon and Radio New Warwick had done their work.

Lara Johnson became a tragic hero who'd saved the day, as Blennerhassett said.

He'd told them that in the two days before they'd reached New Warwick, rumours of a terrible destructive weapon had spread like wildfire through the community (rumours spread by agents of the northern uprising, he believed). Growing numbers of citizens had begun to flee New Warwick because of the threat.

Some believed a new plague was coming, unleashed by infected foodstuffs and clothing sent deliberately into the city by some sinister unknown group of terrorists. Others thought the city reservoir had been poisoned with a deadly virus, while yet other rumours circulated about a flying machine that would hover over the city, sowing it with anthrax spores.

It took a few days for Lara's news to sink in. The threat of a fearful weapon – an alien thing that could unleash horrible, invisible destruction – was an empty one after all.

Not everyone could believe these assurances, of course, but soon the majority had been persuaded. Radio New Warwick broadcast an interview with Lara over and over again. The Beacon made her return front page news – and followed up with an in-depth story (written by Star) about David Johnson, and how he'd foiled the enemy's plan to construct a 'dirty' radiation bomb.

The long lines of horses, carts and people leaving New Warwick were replaced by long lines returning. To Lara's great relief, she heard on the third day that Kieran Tyler had made it back unharmed. Star interviewed him for the Beacon. He told her he'd run for cover when the jeep came under fire. Thinking they'd been under attack by rebel soldiers, he'd run back through the forest in the direction they'd come from, hoping to lie low and make a second attempt to cross the front line. He'd been trapped behind the rebel lines for two days, subsisting on wild berries and drinking from a stream. After the second day he'd managed to creep back in dead of night through the rebels' and the Concordia Security forces' lines without being detected.

Star recalled that sunny August morning of their first day back in New Warwick; the journey into the city. It had been a sad, funereal journey. Not only were they bringing back David Johnson's body but also bearing the news of Private Williams's death.

At that point they didn't know what had happened to Kieran Tyler – he'd simply disappeared.

Saleem's brother Anwar had survived but would need to have his left leg amputated. Private Roycroft had been blown clear of the Land-Rover by the blast of the mine, but had lost the sight of one eye and had also sustained a dislocated shoulder, a broken collarbone and concussion.

Yet for Star, despite the air of sadness she'd been excited and on tenterhooks to find out what had been happening in New Warwick. When Lara had invited her back to Wellbrook for a few days she'd been in two minds. On one hand she'd wanted to head immediately for the city centre and meet up with friends and contacts, catch up with all the news. But she also knew it'd be an anticlimax later in the day, going back on her own to Mrs James and her little flat.

So on the first day she decided to go back with Lara to Wellbrook House. Blennerhassett persuaded them to let him take them in his car. The big, sleek SUV carrying David's body followed behind, driven by a Concordia sergeant.

Star stopped writing to dab her pen in the inkwell. She sucked the wooden end of the pen, distracted for a moment as she recalled the moment they arrived.

Shrieks and laughter of children playing in the swimming pool; Lara's cry of joy when Arrow appeared, dripping wet in her swimming costume, standing some way off by the pool fence.

The little girl had had a bemused look on her face and put her hand up to shield her eyes from the sun's glare, not yet ready to believe that the woman waving frantically to her from the driveway was really her mother.

Uttering a little scream and with tears in her eyes, Lara's mother had rushed out. She'd flung off her apron and thrown her arms around her daughter. Five minutes later, after a murmured conversation, the older woman was looking apprehensively at the black SUV. And then it was Lara, not her mother, who had tears in her eyes.

Star heard later that Lara's mother had been on the brink of taking Arrow with her to join the stream of people leaving the city. Lara's return was therefore a double relief: her daughter had returned and she and her granddaughter didn't have to become refugees.

After a month's military standoff it looked as if a hazy, temporary frontier between northern and southern England had emerged. North of a line that passed eleven miles north of New Warwick was a huge swathe of territory that included most of the Midland and Northern regions. It stretched across England to the border with Wales, and as far north as the Scottish border. This land, now known as the New Realm, was united under the banner of Prince Charles. The restoration of the monarchy and the coronation of Charles (as Charles III) had been announced: it was to be in York Minster in the city of Old York once renovation works to the Minster had been completed early the following year.

Star was fascinated to discover the number of Polish names among the Regional Commissioners in the Midlands and the North who had collaborated with Stettin to organise the rebellion.

She wasn't sure Stettin's was a Polish name and Laczko, she'd been told, was of Hungarian descent (though Laczko, of course, had so far been unsuccessful in bringing South Mercia into the rebel fold).

But most of the rest – Badowski in the North-West, Wozniak in the Pennine Region, Biernacki in Cumbria, Zajac in Yorkshire and Pietrowski in Northumberland were definitely from Polish families. Only Sharma in East Mercia and Barrett in North Norfolk and Lincoln had non-East European names.

How ironic, Star thought, that a French-speaking prince had been brought over by a secret alliance of powerful East Europeans to re-establish a kingdom in England! Clearly the shared East European origins of the Regional Commissioners were going to be the glue that held the alliance together, not any genuine loyalty to a monarch.

The king was for the people – the figurehead they'd kneel in front of, be dazzled by and be loyal to. Royalty would cloak the real power, the power of the Polish administrator-barons.

This will have to go in the book, Star realised. But what if the rebels were successful in taking over the rest of England – including New Warwick? Her book would land her in deep shit. She could be arrested and thrown into prison – possibly meet an even worse fate.

It was difficult to tell what the future held. There'd been little military action since she'd got back into New Warwick. Some of the regular soldiers from the north had been withdrawn. Several traders that Star had interviewed for the Beacon, in clandestine meetings on various forest tracks, had confirmed this. She was told that the soldiers from the far north – Yorkshire, Cumbria, Northumberland – were too far away from home; supply lines were stretched; they were often short of food and had received no pay. Excuses were being found to allow them to trickle away in small units of ten and twenty. Even some of the units from nearby East Mercia were packing up.

The army that Oxford and the southern regions had assembled was much smaller than their opponents'. But the shrinkage of the northerners' forces had evened things out. This mainly left the privatised companies on each side – companies such as Concordia Security – to engage in military action, as long as their employers could afford to pay their crippling daily fees.

To keep both human and financial costs down, the military commanders of these private units were instructed to minimise casualties. They'd been carrying out various feinting movements and manoeuvres to win tactical advantage without loss of human life or ammunition, each side hoping – as in Renaissance Italy, Star later found out – to be able to declare a victory as a result of brilliant strategy, as in a chess game.

So far, though, no such decisive victories had either been declared or acknowledged since the northerners had swept down to the borders of South Mercia. If there was going to be any big change, it looked increasingly unlikely that such change could be brought about by force.

This prompted a big question: what would the rebel regional

commissioners do now? It was the question on everyone's lips; the question discussed endlessly in the bars and cafés of New Warwick; the question that Star mused upon as she rode her motorbike into the city.

Later, Gwynfor was to laugh and tease her about how preoccupied she looked as she took off her helmet; put the bike up on its stand; rummaged in her bag. All this before she even bothered to look up and notice him.

She stared, transfixed. It took her a good five seconds to really believe it. He was just a few yards away, grinning, laughing at her absent-mindedness. Even then, with him right in front of her, she'd have thought it was a trick of her imagination but for his dog. There she was, Seren the collie, eyes bright, sitting obediently on the pavement to his left, head tilted to one side.

A second later he was holding Star in a tight embrace. As she nuzzled into the little depression above his collar bone, breathing in his smell, she remembered with some surprise how tall he was.

How weird is that, she thought. I'd already begun to forget the shape of him; the feel of his body against mine. In just a few short weeks. It can't – it won't – happen again.

'Your beard's grown' was all she could think of to say.

KEN BLAKEMORE

39

The sun was setting. She walked round the swimming pool, through the gate, up the hill and at the top turned to look down at the house and the grounds bathed in golden light. Above her head swifts darted through the air catching their last few insects before roosting for the night.

She remembered how three years ago these little birds had started to make mud-built nests on the side of the house under the eaves. As soon as they'd appeared she'd got Matt to go up a ladder and knock them down: all birds, even these curious things, were dangerous.

Lara wasn't sure she'd do that now. If they tried building nests on the house next year she'd leave them to it, whatever people said.

In a few weeks these birds would be gone. She'd noticed how every September they congregated in rows on the telephone lines that went into the city. David had once told her how he'd read in a Good Time book that swifts and swallows migrate incredible distances every year, thousands of miles from Europe to Africa and then back again the following spring.

She really missed him. It was worse now than it was when she was looking for him. People had tried to comfort her by telling her she'd brought him home and there'd been a funeral and so she'd find peace; find resolution. She'd be able to grieve 'properly', they said, and eventually 'move on'.

She couldn't tell them how angry and alone words like that made her feel.

At Ben's back door, she hesitated. There was a light on in the back room. She'd seen a shadow, the shape of someone move across the window and she wasn't sure it was Ben. She clanged the bell.

Ben answered the door, pulling it open abruptly.

He looked shocked for a moment. 'Ah, Lara!' he smiled.

'Can I come in?'

'Er yes, of course! Come in…'

Esther was in the back room. She was getting up from a chair. Two plates with the remains of food on them were sitting on the kitchen table.

'Hello, Esther. Don't get up!'

'–Mrs Johnson!' Esther's cheeks had reddened beneath her brown skin. 'I was just going.' She picked up an empty basket from the floor.

'No please – I'm not staying long.'

She smiled at Lara, lowering her eyes for a moment 'No really – I was about to go; thank you.'

Lara sat down. Ben had a whispered conversation with Esther outside the back door and then came back. He drew up a kitchen chair and sat facing her.

He gave her a big smile. 'It's great to see you. Can I get you something to drink?'

'No thanks Ben.'

'You sure? I've got some Kent cognac, like you've got at yours…'

'No really – it's all right.'

An awkward pause.

'Ben, I've come to say sorry.'

He frowned.

He's got a nice nose, she thought – the way it wrinkles when he frowns.

'Say sorry…?'

'Yes. For confusing you. That night in Wylfa when we…'

'You don't need to say sorry for that!'

'I do. My emotions were all over the place. I didn't know what I was doing. I'm…ashamed.'

'No! No, you mustn't be! It was beautiful – a bloody miracle!'

He came over and knelt on the kitchen floor in front of her, taking her hand.

She squeezed his broad clumsy fingers and looked into his eyes. 'Ben, I don't know what I feel at the moment.'

'Yes, yes, I understand!'

'And I'm sorry too about the way I behaved on the way back from Wales – I was snapping at you, I realise I was being aloof and cold and you must've wondered–'

'–I did, but it doesn't matter!' He'd taken both her hands now. 'I love you, Lara. Esther came to see me – she brought me some food but it doesn't mean–'

She pulled her hands out of his firm grip. '–No Ben, please! You're pushing me again too much...'

He looked downcast and got off his knees. Pulling his chair closer to her, he sat down and waited patiently for her to speak.

'I'm sorry Ben,' she said after a few moments. 'Right now I can't say I love you. Or anyone else for that matter. Not in the same way you think you love me–'

'–I don't *think* I love you. I do! I'll only ever love one person, and that's you!'

She noticed a note of anger.

'Oh Ben, I know. I'm sorry–'

'–Stop saying sorry!'

'Okay! Just...don't!' David has only been gone these past few weeks. I found him and lost him all in the space of a few days.' Her voice broke. 'You see...?' she managed to whisper without crying. She was crying.

Silence.

He sighed. 'Now it's my turn to say sorry.'

'Just give me time. I can't promise you anything but...'

It was good enough for him. He smiled and braved taking her hand again.

'And...' she said. 'I also came to ask you something.'

'What's that?'

'There's a big public rally tomorrow in the Vineyard.'

He groaned.

'The pro-Royalists will be there in force. The council want me to be there to make a speech against doing a deal. I know you've got so much to do – the farm...but would you come? Drive the carriage for me? I want you to be there.'

He made a show of looking reluctant. 'Of course I will!'

Mrs James had already left for the early Sunday service. Star had heard the front door slam; then silence, apart from the melodious song of a blackbird in the garden and the persistent dinging of the Diana church bell. And Gwynfor's gentle breathing.

He stirred. 'What did you say?' He'd opened one eye, his long black lashes struggling to come apart.

She ruffled his tousled hair. Glossy black spaniel curls.

'I said, you were joking?' She sat up, resting her naked back against the cool wall.

'About what?' he murmured. He was reluctant to wake. He reached out to put a warm hand on her thigh, gently stroking the smooth skin.

'About me learning Welsh.'

He sat up, rubbing his eyes, then yawned and smiled. 'Why shouldn't you?'

'What, with only a slow sheep like you to practise with?'

He removed his hand from her thigh and dug a forefinger into her ribs. She cried out, giggling, 'Ow! Stop it!'

Gwynfor gave her a quick, mischievous smile. Then his expression turned serious. 'Actually you're right. It's hard to learn a language unless you're with the people speaking it.'

She noticed a trace of sadness in his voice.

'Anyway,' she said, 'there's no point me learning Welsh yet – you're going to study to be an English teacher, aren't you?'

She was referring to the future he'd sketched out to her a few days before. His dream was to attend the university in New Warwick but it would remain a dream unless he could find enough money for the fees. Most of the money his father had left had had to go to his mother, for her to live. There wasn't much left over for the university course.

'Maybe Lara will be able to help,' Star had suggested. 'After all, think of what happened to your father – and to you – while you were here. The city might be willing to help.'

Gwynfor looked thoughtful. He'd already visited the stables in the traders' quarter to see if he could earn some money there.

She was determined to press the subject, but his fingers were slowly edging towards the inside of her thigh.

She put a restraining hand on his. 'We should go to see Lara Johnson,' she insisted. 'Really, I think she might help...' Her voice faltered, but she tried to carry on. 'But not today. It's Sunday,' she murmured.

His finger was on her – the lightest touch. 'Tomorrow,' he whispered. 'I'll make an appointment.'

'Anyway, you couldn't see her today,' she said, before giving up. She was pulling him towards her. 'There's that demonstration. In the Vineyard. We should...go and watch...later...'

'Yes,' he said, covering her body with his; easing himself into her.

'I don't think there'll be any trouble, honest.'

Star was trying to tempt Mrs James. 'It's, like, just a big public meeting – a debate. When Lara Johnson shows up it'll be fantastic.'

'Oh, I don't know,' said Mrs James, her big brown eyes full of concern.

'Oh go on, Mrs James!' Gwynfor said. 'There's smart you are today!' He liked overacting the Welshman sometimes.

The landlady was still in her Sunday best – a Good Time-style lilac suit with a short jacket. It was indeed smart, though it accentuated her height. Her cheeks coloured a little. She sat down on one of the dining room chairs and put one elbow on the table. 'Oh, Gwynfor,' she said, her excessively mascara'd eyelashes fluttering, 'you know it's not my cup of tea.'

'C'mon, Mrs James, be a devil,' Star said.

'Ooh, don't say that!'

'You're a Diana supporter, aren't you?' she said. 'There'll be lots of church people like you there. Lend them your support! Sing those hymns!'

'No, really. I don't agree with that sort of thing. Demonstrations, all that – what good does it do?'

'Ah, I know what it is!' Star said, looking at Gwynfor. 'She's embarrassed because we're on different sides!'

Gwynfor shook his head and gave Mrs James a sympathetic look. Star was too outspoken sometimes.

'It's not that, love,' Mrs James said with a weak smile. She'd picked up a table napkin and was folding and refolding it. 'I just don't like politics.'

Star had guessed why Mrs James had sensed trouble. The rally that afternoon was to demonstrate support for a peace treaty and for New Warwick joining the New Realm. While the moving force behind it was the Church of Diana, another organisation was also involved. It was a vociferous group who'd got together to form the pro-Royalist King's Party.

In the name of free speech and democracy, the rally had been permitted by the City Council only on condition that speakers against such a deal – including several city politicians and the biggest celebrity in town, Lara Johnson – would be permitted to address the crowds as well. The numbers turning up to support Lara and the city's independence were likely to outnumber the Dianists and royalists.

The King's Party worried Mrs James and many other Dianists. While the Church reflected a wide cross-section of society, including 'respectable' working and lower middle-class people like her, the King's Party was different. Most of its supporters were from the poorer, more disaffected sections of the city's community who'd migrated from the forests and backwoods in recent years – the street hawkers and vendors, night soil carriers, casual labourers, laundrywomen and servants.

What with the inflation and the money crisis and the lack of decent houses, life had been pretty mean to them in New Warwick so far; it could only get better under a king. They were convinced they'd be better looked after in the New Realm.

'Are you sure you'll be all right?' Mrs James said, following them into the hall when they were about to go. She was absent-mindedly twisting a table napkin in her hand.

On the front step, Star turned round and did something unexpected. She gave Mrs James a tight little hug and a kiss on the cheek.

Mrs James had a sudden, large tear in her eye. Her mascara would run, but she didn't care this time.

'I love you, sweetie,' she said hoarsely. 'Please take care, won't you?'

40

When Star and Gwynfor got to Vineyard Fields they found a bigger rally than they'd expected. It was nearly five o'clock. Such was the density of the crowd around the stage that they weren't able to get to the front, as they'd hoped. Star left Gwynfor on the edge of the crowd and pushed the bike into the garden of the Vineyard Bistro. She asked the waiter, who was standing outside with a bemused look on his face, if she could leave it there. He was an old man and a bit deaf. 'At your own risk' he said gruffly.

'D'you know if Lara Johnson has arrived yet?'

The old man shook his head. 'What?'

'Lara Johnson!' she shouted. The crowd was noisy. 'Has she come yet?' Star waved her arm in the direction of the big wooden stage at the far end of the Vineyard.

'Lara Johnson?' bellowed the waiter, an uncertain look in his eye. 'Bugger me if I know.' He turned his back on her to collect dirty cups and glasses from a table.

Star found Gwynfor and they decided to push their way through the crowd to get as near the front as they could. There was a chance that Lara might call Star up on to the stage.

They pushed past a large block of cheerful Dianists carrying placards and waving blue and white flags. The sound of one of their sentimental hymns filled the air. The singing was punctuated by the gentle sound of tambourines. More aggressive chanting was coming from a knot of King's Party supporters further away in the dense crowd. They were dragging out the word 'Charles' on a rising note, then very quickly adding 'our-king!': 'Chaaaarles...our king! Chaaaar...les . . . our king!' Each chant was followed by sharp rhythmic clapping.

The public mood was generally good humoured rather than nasty. As Star and Gwynfor pushed their way into the middle of the crowd she was reminded of the atmosphere at a soccer match, like the home game between New Warwick and Nottingham Forest she'd watched the previous winter. That's one fixture they couldn't have now Nottingham was in the New Realm, she reflected.

Now they were nearer the front they could hear people chanting support for Lara. Either it was just 'John-son, John-son!' followed by rhythmic clapping and 'John-son!' again, or a sung line: 'Lara John-son, Lara John-son; we'll keep our free-doms!'

Star remembered how, two weeks before, she'd been on the stage with Lara. A series of big rallies had been held in the Vineyard. The legislative council had called them to boost public morale and patriotic resistance to the idea of the city being taken over. Then, it really looked as though the enemy troops could break through at any moment. Lara, smiling, flushed, had come to the edge of the stage to insist that Star climbed up to join them. The heat from the crowd, the adulation, the roar of so many voices had been overwhelming. Star had seen how it could become addictive.

But was it like a drug for Lara? It was too early to tell. Certainly she seemed paradoxically to have found a release, a form of escape, in public appearance. She'd lost herself in the bright light of publicity and celebrity. There was definitely something deliberate – calculated would be too strong a word – in the way she'd hidden herself behind this public mask. The grieving widow had immaculate hair and no makeup; stylish sunglasses; black dress and headscarf.

She'd presented herself this way at the very start – at the state funeral for David.

It had taken place five days after their return. A massive public event hadn't been planned, but that's what it had turned into. Crowds of people lined the route to the centre of the city. Flowers were strewn in the path of a horse-drawn gun carriage carrying David's body. There was spontaneous clapping as Lara, accompanied by her mother on one side and her daughter on the other, passed by in a following carriage.

Lara had become the charismatic emblem of the city's solidarity and resistance. And she'd turned into an alternative heroine to Diana, Our Lady of Suffering.

Here (unlike Diana) was the faithful wife whose life hadn't ended in a car accident with her illicit lover. Lara had struggled against the odds to bring back David's body. Instead of being the victim and the subject of suffering and endless weeping, like Our Lady Diana, she'd become a symbol of plucky New Warwick – steadfastness and grit.

The crowds that gathered at this time of great crisis to listen to Lara Johnson's speeches had soaked up her every word. Here was their saviour. Here was the woman who had risked life and limb to bring them the news that they had nothing to fear. They cheered her until they were hoarse.

In return, she spoke up for New Warwick. She reminded them of what they stood for. She spoke about free speech and voting and schools and reading; she spoke about courts and justice – and why they should defend these things to the very last.

They noticed a sudden change in the crowd – a hush followed by applause. That meant that the first speakers were arriving. Star couldn't see very well so she dragged Gwynfor through the press of people, making for a slightly raised mound nearer the edge.

She stood on tiptoe. Yes, the Church of Diana speakers were already on stage – four middle-aged men, three in formal suits and the fourth in light blue robes – New Warwick's High Prelate. There were also two women, also in light blue vestments. One of the men introduced the prelate, who picked up a megaphone and, in a rasping, rather reedy voice, led a prayer.

Apart from the occasional shout and catcall, there was a respectful silence as the Dianist sections of the crowd intoned their responses.

Then, after the prelate's blessing, the first speaker began. Star grimaced at Gwynfor, preparing herself for the load of rubbish she was sure they were about to hear.

The Church of Diana, the speaker reminded them, stood for harmony. True happiness could only be found by giving up 'false independence' for the protection of a divine king. Individual rights were wrong and selfish. It was time to be saved by Diana's spirit and by her representative, her great-grandson prince who would be king. There was a burst of energetic clapping and cheering from the centre of the crowd, at this point. That meant a fresh start, a wiping clean. And if that entailed destroying books, compact discs and memory sticks – the sources of misguided, selfish, scientific knowledge from the past that had led to disaster decades before – then so be it.

Just as he was getting into his stride, however, there was a buzz of excitement through the crowd.

Lara Johnson had arrived!

Star and Gwynfor could see the open carriage drawn by two horses. She squeezed Gwynfor's arm and looked up at his face. He smiled at her, and then brushed the top of her nose lightly with his lips.

Lara refused to use the black limousine of the first minister, or any other official cars if she could help it. She preferred to arrive in a carriage or on horseback. Now Star could make out the black dress and headscarf. She was standing up in the carriage to acknowledge the crowd; there was a big cheer.

Three other dignitaries – two women and a man – were with her. They were waving too. The clapping and cheering spread to the edge of the crowd where Star and Gwynfor were standing. Was the man driving the carriage Ben? That's interesting, Star said to herself. Lara had kept him out of the public eye until now.

Lara and the VIPs were now making their way to the public stage. Star could see her nodding politely to the Church of Diana people as she approached. The man who'd been addressing the crowd had had to suspend his boring sermon. He stood, smiling awkwardly, holding a page of notes in his hand. Lara Johnson and the city representatives were going round the side of the stage to climb the steps at the back.

Star looked across the Vineyard field. The early evening sunlight seemed to bring out an extra depth and intensity of colour in everything as if the houses and trees around the park were shimmering under crystal-clear water.

Against the light blue sky, their white wings catching the golden brightness of the sun, dozens of grey and white doves were swooping and circling. They flew from behind a row of tall three-storey wooden houses on the far edge of the Vineyard.

'Whooh!' Cries of alarm came from various sections of the crowd. But there was also some laughter and extra clapping.

Star smiled to herself. Those birds were like carrier pigeons. She thought of Pascoe and his hunting hawks.

She felt a great surge of happiness. She was joined to Gwynfor. She didn't know what would come of it. She didn't know whether she'd go with him to the mountains of Wales or whether he might stay here. But no matter: today was today, and it was enough.

But now there was a different sound, hardly detectable at first above the chatter and excitement of the crowd – a persistent shushing chatter. She looked at Gwynfor, alarm in her eyes.

Everyone was looking up. A speck in the sky, now a quickly enlarging black blob, was moving rapidly towards them. Oh God, Star whispered to herself.

The flying machine had stopped moving now. It hovered noisily hundreds of feet above them. The crowd had fallen silent. Everyone's eyes were upon it. Very few had ever seen anything like this before.

Curiosity outweighed panic for twenty, thirty seconds. Then the balance teetered towards panic. Cries of fear and alarm: some at the edge of the field were starting to run. 'It's the bomb – the bomb!' they were shouting.

There was going to be a stampede. Star, still clutching Gwynfor's arm, not moving, saw the prelate pick up the megaphone and stride to the front of the stage.

'We should run!' Gwynfor said in a low voice.

'No – wait,' she said, holding his arm.

The prelate, raising his arm with a flourish to point at the helicopter, shouted into the megaphone:

'The prince is here to save us!'

His call was picked up. Several voices at first. Then twenty. Then a hundred. Then a thousand and more voices were shouting

'The prince; the king!'

And it wasn't just the royalists and the Church of Diana supporters. Others too were getting caught up in the excitement. Everyone began to cheer. A forest of arms waved back and forth at the flying machine hovering hundreds of feet above them.

Star wondered afterwards whether she'd been the only person, at that moment, to see what happened to Lara Johnson. Everyone else – including Lara herself, who'd climbed on to the stage by now – was looking up at the helicopter.

Star, though, had briefly taken her eyes away from the flying machine to see what Lara's reaction was.

She was staggering backwards, as if her foot had caught on a wire or something. But her arms had shot up to her chest! She was clutching something. She's been stung by a wasp or a bee?

The dignitaries were still staring up at the helicopters.

Star wanted to scream at them. But she couldn't. She just stood looking, going numb inside, disbelieving.

A second crossbow bolt had hit Lara now. Star could see the glint of metal. She was falling to her knees. The politicians by her side had turned to her at last. Star could see their arms reaching down. It was too late.

Star let out a desperate wail. It was the wail of a deeply wounded animal, louder even than the chattering helicopter blades above.

The people around her stared. Was this young woman having a fit? Star felt a hand on her arm: it was a bosomy, middle-aged lady wearing a Church of Diana sash. She looked concerned and was saying something.

Gwynfor was leading her to one side. He was making her sit down on the grass.

The words 'I can't believe it, I can't believe it' kept looping through Star's head. Then she realised she was actually saying it out loud.

Gwynfor was talking now but his voice was too gentle; a whooshing sound had filled her ears.

It was a strange dream – it must be. Everyone around her except Gwynfor was laughing and shouting as they lifted up their arms towards the helicopter – even the woman who'd been so kind a moment ago was distracted.

Some had fallen to their knees and were scrabbling on the ground. Were they laughing at her? Had everyone gone mad?

Star looked up at the chattering helicopter.

Leaves were falling from it, tiny golden leaves.

A shimmering cascade.

The leaves were pattering gently on the grass. The first heavy drops of a sudden storm.

Through the numbness, Star gradually took in what they were. They weren't leaves at all. They were golden coins.

Each sovereign, as it dropped, had momentarily caught the evening sun.

41

With his keen sense of hearing, the raven had been able to pick up the sound of human voices from more than a mile away. His pulse quickening, he clambered into the air. He sounded the Man's voice in his head again. He was thinking food; moist titbits of rabbit flesh thrown to him by a human hand.

Ever since he'd been cast out of the castle, feeling that bewildering rush of freedom as night was falling, he'd missed the Man deeply. The Man used to talk to him in a gentle, crooning voice. And He'd taught the raven how to reply.

The Man had fallen from the castle wall. He had become a carcass. The raven had stood by him, a black sentinel, until the morning light, as had three of his brothers.

When they'd come to carry the Man's body away they'd caught his brothers with a net. Then one human being had thrown a stone at him. He could fly, although his brothers could not and were caught.

He would not go back to the castle. The Man wasn't there.

The raven perched on the branch of an oak tree with his head on one side: watching; assessing. There was a silent sheepdog running ahead. And twenty yards behind the dog, a heavy open cart pulled by two great horses, pots and pans jingling and clanging at the back of it.

They'd left New Warwick seven days before: Star and Gwynfor; Arrow and Grandma Rae; Ben Frobisher and Esther.

Today, as they approached a great whale-back of a hill they felt cold November winds. Brown and yellow leaves lay in mounds ahead of them on the forest track. Few horses or people had passed this way to disturb them.

Gwynfor had explained that the great hill was called the Long Mynd. Once they'd passed it, they'd come to a little-used drover's road that would take them west into Powys, and from there northwards to Gwynedd.

'I remember that hill,' Star said to Arrow, thinking of the journey southwards in the sleek black SUV more than three months before.

'When you were with Mum,' the girl said. She was sitting between Star and Gwynfor on the front bench-seat of the cart. An hour before, when they'd set off from the previous night's camp, Grandma Rae had wrapped a quilt around the girl's shoulders to keep out the cold wind: Gwynfor's quilt.

Star looked at Arrow before replying. She hadn't really noticed before, but the colour of Lara's daughter's eyes was quite unlike those of her parents. Not green with flecks of gold, like Lara's, or bright blue like David Johnson's. Arrow had big, wide eyes, yes, but they were pools of light grey. They gave the girl a sober, detached appearance.

'With your mother, yes,' Star said. 'It was when we were bringing your father's body back.'

Arrow nodded, looking round. 'There's a bird,' she said, pointing.

Sure enough, as if he'd been waiting a long time just for them, a big black raven was perched in an oak tree on the right-hand side of the track.

At that moment Ben leaned forward, pointed to the reins in Gwynfor's hands and said 'want me to take over for a while?'

'All right,' Gwynfor said. 'How about when we're past the Long Mynd?'

This distraction meant that none of them except Arrow noticed the raven flapping towards the cart.

Arrow said nothing. She turned round in her seat to meet the raven's eye.

The bird perched on the rear of the bumping cart.

This coal-black raven could see into the human beings' hearts. It was well known, in those parts, in those days, that they could. He cocked his head to one side and looked into each heart in turn. He saw that

One had lost a heroine and a protector;

One had lost a father;

One had lost a father and a mother;

One a daughter;

One had lost the woman he'd loved the most, and a farm.

The raven could see other things, too:

Two tiny embryos, tinier than a baby's fingernail, one in the belly of Star and one in the belly of Esther;

Sheaves of notes in Star's bag stowed alongside the thirty eight books she'd rescued from the burning of the university;

A ring of Welsh gold in a tiny box;

Ben's vow to Esther that he would make another farm thrive;

Trepidation and excitement in the girl's heart;

Relief as well as sadness in her grandmother's.

Esther shrieked when she saw the raven, putting her hands up to the side of her face. The raven, startled, raised his wings. But he was brave enough to stay put.

The cart rumbled on. Ben, sitting opposite Esther, frowned and stood to shoo the bird away.

'No!' Star shook her head. She'd turned round and had lifted one arm. 'No, don't,' she said again.

She extended her forearm and called to the raven, remembering what Pascoe had done. 'Here! Here, old boy!'

The raven ran a scan of Star's face through his extensive memory of human features. 'Good morning,' the bird said in a clear voice.

Esther screamed. The terrifying bird was not just a bird; it was a witch.

Arrow looked at it with her big grey eyes, entranced.

'Come on my beauty,' Star said, coaxing the bird with Pascoe's words again.

'My name is Midnight,' the bird said. And then he flapped upwards.

'Come with me,' she said.

And the raven flew down again to settle on her arm.

WELL, DID YOU LIKE IT???

If you did, like it, please let everyone know and share the experience…Amazon is a good place to post your thoughts but any social media is a boon for getting great books into good hands. If you want to check out some more scintillating moonshine from the South Wales backwoods you can find us where we live at Jack Noir

www.iponymous.com

CPSIA information can be obtained at www.ICGtesting.com
Printed in the USA
LVOW11s2123030316

477651LV00005B/312/P